W9-CQE-530

Books by Herman Wouk

The Caine Mutiny
City Boy
Don't Stop the Carnival
Marjorie Morningstar
This Is My God
War and Remembrance
The Winds of War
Youngblood Hawke

Published by POCKET BOOKS

Most Pocket Books are available at special quantity discounts for bulk purchases for sales promotions, premiums or fund raising. Special books or book excerpts can also be created to fit specific needs.

For details write the office of the Vice President of Special Markets, Pocket Books, 1230 Avenue of the Americas, New York, New York 10020.

CITY BOY

THE ADVENTURES OF
HERBIE BOOKBINDER

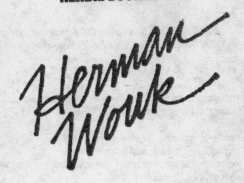

Herman Wouk

PUBLISHED BY POCKET BOOKS NEW YORK

POCKET BOOKS, a division of Simon & Schuster, Inc.
1230 Avenue of the Americas, New York, N.Y. 10020

ISBN: 0-671-46013-7

First Pocket Books printing May, 1974

10 9 8 7 6

POCKET and colophon are registered trademarks
of Simon & Schuster, Inc.

Printed in the U.S.A.

This story is dedicated to my mother

WHILE SERVING WITH the U.S. Navy in the Pacific during World War II, Lieutenant Herman Wouk succumbed to a literary temptation which may eventually ruin him in the eyes of serious critics who classify the trends of contemporary American and other literatures. Fortuitously Lieutenant Wouk happened upon a copy of *Don Quixote* and read it. He was impressed, as others have occasionally been before him, by the narrative skill of Cervantes and by his uncanny ability to delineate character. Owing to this encounter, Mr. Wouk decided to write a novel himself, and since then he has written three without ever entirely forgetting Cervantes. This means that Mr. Wouk is old-fashioned, according to present breast-beating standards. His works have a high content of entertainment value. He writes with ease and with humor. His scenes progress logically from one to another and are all designed to reach a definite conclusion. His characters are drawn with a writer's eye from the lexicon of Mr. Wouk's experience. He does not avail himself of Freudian symbolism. Though his style is easy and frequently distinguished, it never obtrudes itself upon his subject matter. He does not worry about tonal depths. He does not feel impelled to deliver an ideological message. In other words, Mr. Wouk is an author whose books I enjoy reading. In fact, for my money he is by way of becoming one of the ablest and certainly one of the most sympathetic of our younger writers.

City Boy, I think, possesses all the desirable elements

vii

listed in the preceding paragraph. It was written before *The Caine Mutiny* and does not compare with *Mutiny* either in scope or stature, but then Mr. Wouk never intended that it should. It does, however, furnish proof that Mr. Wouk is far from being a one-book writer. I have read *City Boy* twice with complete absorption and unabated amusement. The other day my daughter, aged twelve, picked up the book by mistake and could not put it down. This may indicate that I also have a twelve-year-old intellect, but I naturally prefer to think that *City Boy* possesses the same rare universal appeal that one finds in *Tom Sawyer*. Mark Twain, I am sure, would have liked it. Though Mr. Wouk's little Herbie is a mid-twentieth-century Jewish boy from the Bronx who never fished with a Huckleberry Finn in the troubled waters of the Mississippi, I believe he would have got on well with Tom Sawyer if these two could have met; and Becky Thatcher would have also understood Herbie. The truth is that both these authors had much the same idea in mind when they wrote these two vastly different books of childhood adventure. Plot to them both was an incidental problem. Their main preoccupation was to tell a tale of childhood in terms comprehensible to a reader of any age. Without attempting to carry the comparison further, any reader will discover that Mr. Wouk has accomplished this task admirably and with very considerable distinction.

JOHN P. MARQUAND

New York City
February 1952

Contents

CITY BOY:

The Adventures of Herbie Bookbinder

THIS TWENTIETH ANNIVERSARY edition of an early work gives me special pleasure. None of my novels ever had a less promising start than *City Boy* did. I had no reason to think then that it would survive two months, let alone two decades.

Just a year before, with a noisy splash, I had entered the American literary frogpond. My first novel, *Aurora Dawn*, a short facetious spoof of radio broadcasting, had caught a publisher's fancy. He launched it with a blast of ecstatic advertising. In quick obedience to Newton's third law, critics blasted back. All this dazed me. A naval reserve officer, I had written *Aurora Dawn* during the Pacific war, to while away boring hours at sea. I had never before published so much as a short story in a magazine. For my livelihood, before the war, I had been writing for the great radio comedian, Fred Allen. I did not know enough about the literary world to object to the overblown launching, nor to expect the counterattack. It was quite a debut. When the dust settled I had in hand a Book-of-the-Month selection of my first novel, a modest sale, and a literary reputation demolished before it was built. New authors, fuming over insufficient advertising of their masterpieces, might ponder this true tale.

But there I was, a professional novelist, if a somewhat black-and-blue one. I wrote *City Boy*, and found real delight in the task. If I have a favorite creation, to this day, it is the fat little hero, Herbie Bookbinder. My publisher, set back by the critics' onslaught, and perhaps convinced that no novel with Jewish characters could sell—this was a general opinion twenty years ago—launched the work as one buries a body at sea. *City Boy* slid off the plank, and with scarcely a ripple went bubbling down.

At the same time a novel appeared called *The Naked and the Dead;* the first big fiction work on the Second World War, written by a youngster of twenty-six, yet bitingly mature, and full of what people then considered shocking language. Soon afterward, my sister threw a party for me, featuring a cake baked like the *City Boy* volume. Not one guest had read, or even heard of, my book. Virtually all of them had read, or were reading, *The Naked and the Dead,* and wanted to discuss it with me. What an ordeal that party was! And when the book of the hour is that good, one cannot console oneself by sneering at the low taste of public and critics. Such transparent envy is a worse disgrace than silence.

So Herbie died, or seemed to. No club selected the book. Nobody bought it. Almost nobody reviewed it. The remainder shops were piled with this novel, while I was still reading scattered out-of-town notices. Amazingly, a film producer did stumble on a copy, and I salvaged from the wreck a small payment for movie rights. Hollywood proceeded to change the fat Jewish boy to a thin Irish girl, and the Bronx to a Midwestern town. *City Boy* in films became *The Romantic Age,* starring Margaret O'Brien. I did not see it. I have never met anybody who did.

Alas! Total disaster with a second book; a very usual thing. Still, I now had a family, and I had come to love the fiction art. I thought I had better have one more shot at the target. I wrote another novel. My habit was, and still is, to read my work chapter by chapter to a discerning, lovely, but taciturn wife. Once she suddenly remarked, when I was reading aloud an early scene in that story, "If they don't like this one, you had better try some other line of business." The book was *The Caine Mutiny*.

Meantime *Aurora Dawn* and *City Boy* had gone out

of print, and I had a new publisher. He liked Herbie Bookbinder, and decided to bring the book back to light. That was sixteen years ago. The publishing history of *City Boy* since then records several printings, translations into eleven languages, club selections, and usage in school textbooks and anthologies. But for many readers of my later works, *City Boy* remains unknown. This anniversary edition will, I hope, add to its discoverers.

I believe it is an honorable novel, funny without cheap jokes, and sad with the bottomless though transient sadness of boyhood. I am proud of it, and I am glad to see the hero's name restored to the title, where I originally had it. May the tale give its new readers, in this anniversary volume, a glint of the pleasure in the reading, that I had in bringing little Herbie Bookbinder to life, twenty years ago.

HERMAN WOUK

CITY BOY

1

The First Step
in the Mending of a Broken Heart

ON A GOLDEN May morning in the sixth year of Calvin Coolidge's presidency, a stout little dark-haired boy named Herbert Bookbinder, dressed in a white shirt, a blue tie and gray knee breeches, sat at a desk in Public School 50 in the Bronx, suffering the pain of a broken heart. On the blackboard before his eyes were words that told a disaster:

Mrs. Mortimer Gorkin

The teacher of Class 7B-1 had just informed her pupils that they must call her "Miss Vernon" no more. Turning to the board with a shy smile, she had written her new name in rounded chalk letters, and had blushed through a minute's tumult of squeals and giggles from the girls and good-natured jeers from the boys. Then Mrs. Gorkin stilled the noise with an uplifted hand. She pulled down into view a map of Africa rolled up at the top of the blackboard like a window shade, and the class, refreshed by the brief lawbreaking, listened eagerly to her tale of the resources of the Congo. But Herbert could not rouse himself to an interest in rubber, gold, apes, and ivory; not when the lost Diana Vernon was talking about them. The tones of her voice made him too unhappy.

The anodyne in this boy's life was food. No anguish was so sharp that eating could not allay it. Unfortunately lunch time was half an hour off. His hand groped softly

1

into his desk and rested on a brown paper bag. He felt the
familiar outlines of two rolls (today was Thursday—lettuce
and tomato sandwiches) and an apple. Then his hand
encountered something small and oval. With practiced,
noiseless fingers he opened the bag, unwrapped some
twisted wax paper, and drew out a peeled hardboiled egg.
This was a pretty dry morsel without salt and bread and
butter, but the boy popped the whole egg into his mouth
and chewed it moodily. Like an aspirin, it dulled the pain
without improving his spirits. He was aware that his
cheeks bulged, but he did not care. Let her catch him! He
was her favorite, first on the honor roll, and she could not
humiliate him without humiliating herself more. The boy's
calculation was correct. Mrs. Gorkin did see him eating,
but she ignored it.

In time a beautiful sound rang out—freedom, proclaimed by the clanging of the gong for lunch. At a nod
from Mrs. Gorkin, the children who had worrisome mothers ran to a shallow closet and returned to their seats
wearing coats, while those who had braved the changeable May weather without coats sat back and gloried in
their maturity. A second time the gong sounded. The
pupils stood and quietly began to form a double line at
the front of the room. Herbie, on his way to the head of
the line, passed the teacher's desk. She whispered, "Remain behind, Herbert." Pretending to have heard nothing,
Herbie strolled back to his desk and remained there fussing busily until the class marched out.

A classroom always seems three times larger when the
children leave it, and quite bleak. This gives a delicious
sense of comradeship to two people left in it together. For
months it had been Herbie Bookbinder's good luck to
share this sweetness with Miss Diana Vernon after
classes. She had detained him for such honorable offices
as putting away books, filling inkwells, closing windows
with a long hooked pole, and drawing the heavy brown
canvas shades; while she combed her long red hair before
her closet mirror in the late-afternoon sunlight and
chatted with him. It had been magical. Being alone in the
room now brought these memories vividly to the boy.

When the teacher re-entered the classroom she found her star pupil seated at his desk, his chin resting on his clenched fists, gazing downward at nothing.

The cause of his pain was a slim woman, possibly twenty-seven, with compressed lips, a thin little straight nose, and heavy red hair. She looked, and she was, strict. But she was a woman, and therefore susceptible to male charm, such as inhered in Herbie—and, unfortunately, in Mr. Mortimer Gorkin. The boy glanced at her and felt a pang of self-pity. He could tell by her soft look that she felt sorry for him and wanted to comfort him. Immediately he resolved not to be comforted at any cost.

"Herbie," she said, walking to her desk and drawing a metal lunch box out of a deep side drawer, "come here and talk to me while I eat."

The boy rose, walked to the front of the desk, and stood there with morose formality, his arms at his sides.

"Come," said the teacher, "where's your lunch? Or do you want some of mine?"

"I'm not hungry," said Herbert Bookbinder, looking away from her to the corner of the blackboard where his name headed a list of three in golden chalk—the honor roll for April. He decided vengefully that he would be last in the class in May.

"It seems to me," said Mrs. Gorkin, laughing a little, "that you were almost too hungry during the geography lesson—now, weren't you?"

Herbie stood on his constitutional rights and did not testify.

"What's the matter, Herbie, really?" asked the teacher.

"Nothing."

"Oh, yes, there is."

"Oh, no, there isn't—*Mrs. Gorkin.*"

The shot went home; the teacher colored a little. Perhaps pretty Diana Vernon was herself not quite happy about becoming Mrs. Gorkin. The name still rang strangely in the bride's ears.

"Herbie," said the teacher with an uncomfortable

smile, "even though I'm Mrs. Gorkin now, we're still friends, aren't we?"

(The injured male may be eleven or fifty; the approach of the injuring female does not vary.)

"Sure," said Herbie dolefully. He hitched up his sagging gray kneepants.

"Someday," said Mrs. Gorkin, "I hope you will meet Morti—that is, Mr. Gorkin. He's assistant principal at Public School Seventy-five. I know he'd like you. He admires clever young men."

Herbie saw through the compliment with contempt. "Sure," he said again.

The erstwhile Diana Vernon said, "Come closer, Herbie." The boy reluctantly obeyed, sidling along the edge of the desk, his hand resting on top. The teacher put her hand on his. He jerked it away.

"When you are as old as I am, Herbie," said Diana Gorkin softly, "you will be a handsomer man than my husband, and you will marry a finer woman than I am, and I hope you'll remember to bring her back here and let me meet her, but I doubt that you will."

This speech had no meaning at all for Herbie, who knew perfectly well that he would never be as old as a teacher. "Sure," he said once more. Mrs. Gorkin unwrapped a sandwich, and acknowledged defeat by a curt dismissal. The boy retreated to his desk, snatched his lunch bag, and scurried from the classroom.

Once outside, he stopped, assumed a dignified air, and pinned around his right arm a yellow strip of flannel decorated with three silver stars. He then sauntered along the deserted corridor to the boys' staircase. An ordinary lad at this hour was required by law to go without delay to the lunchroom or playground, under pain of receiving a purple slip for loitering. But Herbert could choose, in all the huge building, a private place for his noonday meal.

Herbert, you see, was one of those privileged beings of the school world, a head monitor. He was captain of the Social Service Squad. This was not at all the same thing as the dread Police Squad, of course, whose members stood at gates, doorways, and turns in corridors, shouting, "Double up! Hurry up! No talking!" The police could pounce on offenders with the fearsome green slips which meant wrath from on high, but Herbie's Social Service Squad had no power of arrest. Its members were assigned to various areas of the school, and their duties were simply to keep the building and yards clean. So the squad had irreverently been dubbed "the Garbage Gang" by the members of the police, who never tired of pointing the contrast between the might in their red armbands and the feeble symbolism of the yellow armbands of Herbie's squad.

Since the police were recruited from the tallest, huskiest students, Herbert had despaired of gaining the red band, and had therefore worked his way to the top of the Social Service Squad. He figured that if one was not destined for the proud life of a wolf, it was still better to be a dog than one of the helpless sheep. This proved perfectly sound. As captain of his squad he could rove everywhere on the pretense of inspection. He could come late and walk unchallenged through any gate he chose. All at once he had stopped accumulating the orange slips for tardiness which had plagued his days since kindergarten. His monthly conduct mark raised itself above B-minus for the first time in his career. Let the ignoramuses rave at him with their taunts of "Garbage King!" Herbie had found one of the great secrets of life, the immunity from public law that comes of being a public official, and he was fully enjoying the fruits of his discovery.

He skipped down the stairs, which echoed with metallic hollowness, to the third floor. Coming upon the brown leather-covered, brass-studded door of the auditorium, he decided that the big empty hall suited his melancholy mood. He pushed the door open, walked across the rear of the hall to one of the broad windows, curled up on a sill in the sunshine, and opened his bag of lunch with a sigh as nearly expressive of contentment as a broken heart would permit.

At this moment, through the small, high window of the

door leading to the girls' staircase, he caught a glimpse of red curly hair gleaming in the sunlight. Craning his neck, he saw that it belonged to a well-dressed, pretty girl about eleven years old.

2

Further Steps

IN THE PHILOSOPHY of Herbie Bookbinder there was a division in the concept, Girls.

As a species of the genus Mankind he regarded girls as low in the scale, a botched job. They played silly games; they had unpleasant shrill voices, they giggled; they pretended to be holy; they were in an everlasting conspiracy against normal human beings (boys of eleven); they wore queer clothes; and they were sly. He regarded most of these squeaky beings with plain scorn.

It was nevertheless part of the mystery of life that from time to time there came to Herbie's view a sublime creation which could only be classified as a girl, since she would have the outside features such as long hair, a dress, and a high voice. But she would be as different from girls as the sun is from a penny candle. One of these angels appeared every year or so. There had been Rosalind Sarnoff, of the black hair and bright smile, in the second grade. Sadie Benz, always dressed in billowy white, in the fourth. Blond Madeline Costigan, who could throw a ball like a boy, in the fifth. And two girls who had lived in his neighborhood, known only as Mildred and Frances respectively, who had reduced his life to ashes twice by moving to other parts of the Bronx.

The radiance of such a divinity could come to surround

an ordinary girl. Madeline Costigan had sat beside him in Miss O'Grady's class for two months, undistinguished from the rest of the chirruping females. Then one afternoon they had both been kept after school for tardiness. And while they were beating out erasers together, a grand chord had sounded in Herbert's breast, he had seen the glory envelop Madeline like the dawn, and lo, he was her slave. Equally strangely the spell could die away, as it had in the case of Sadie Benz, leaving a commonplace girl whom Herbie despised. But this was not the rule. Most of these super-beings had been removed from Herbie by the forces of time and change. Diana Vernon had succeeded Madeline Costigan, the first adult in the golden procession.

The little stranger on the other side of the auditorium door who sat on the stairs facing away from him, placidly munching a sandwich, had hair of the same hue as Mrs. Gorkin's, and this may have been the reason Herbert's heart bounded when he first saw her. But a prolonged look persuaded him that, on her own merits, she was a candidate for the vacant office. Her starched, ruffled blue frock, her new, shiny, patent-leather shoes, her red cloth coat with its gray furry collar, her very clean knees and hands, and the carefully arranged ringlets of her hair all suggested non-squeaky loveliness. At the moment of his so deciding, it chanced that she turned her head and met his look. Her large hazel eyes widened in surprise, and at once there was no further question of candidacy. She was elected.

It now became obligatory upon Herbert to pretend that she did not exist. He looked out of the window and began to make believe that an extremely exciting and unusual event was taking place in the girls' playground below— just what, he was not sure, but it called for him to slap his palm to the side of his face, shake his head from side to side, and exclaim very loudly, "Gee whiz! Gosh! Never saw anything like *that!*" (By this time the imaginary sight had started to take shape as a teacher lying in a pool of blood, her head split open, after a jump from the roof.) He was compelled to run, first down the side aisle of the auditorium to look out of the other windows, and then up the aisle again and through the leather door at the rear, feigning amazement at the discovery of the girl on the stairs. She was seated busily reading a geography book upside down, having snatched it after watching all his pantomime up to the point when she saw he intended to come through the door.

After enacting an intensity of surprise at the sight of the girl that would have sufficed had he come upon a unicorn, Herbert recovered himself and said sternly, "What are you doing here?"

"Who wants to know?" said the girl, putting aside the book.

"Me, that's who."

"Who's me?"

"Me is me," said Herbert, pointing to his three-starred yellow armband.

"Huh! Garbage gang," said the girl. Turning her back on him, she drew an apple out of a gleaming new tin lunch box and began to eat it with exaggerated nonchalance, her eyebrows raised and her gaze directed out at the smiling day.

"Maybe you'd like to come down to Mr. Gauss's office with me," said Herbie fiercely.

Mr. Julius Gauss was the principal, a heavy, round-headed gentleman seen by the children only at special assemblies, where he read psalms in a gloomy singsong and gave endless speeches which nobody understood, but which seemed in favor of George Washington, America, and certain disgusting behavior found only in molly-coddles. He was regarded by the children as the most frightful thing outside the storybooks, a view which the teachers encouraged and which several of them seemed to share.

"And stop eating," added Herbie, "when you're talking to a head monitor."

Red Locks quailed and put down the apple, but she tried to brave it out. "You can't make me go down there," she said. (It was always "down" to Mr. Gauss's office, possibly because of the general analogy to infernal regions.)

"Can't I?" said Herbert. "Can't I? It so happens that as *captain* of the Social Service Squad I have to see Mr. Gauss every Thursday, which is today, and make my report to him. And anyone who I tell to come with me has to come. But you can *try* not coming—oh, sure, you can *try*. I don't think you would try it more than *once*, but you can *try*."

The contents of this speech, excepting Herbert's rank, were a lie. But Herbert had not learned yet to draw the line between the facts devised by his powerful imagination and the less vivid facts existing in nature, and while he spoke he fully believed what he was saying.

"Anyway," said the girl, "he wouldn't do anything to me even if you did bring me down there, because I'm going to his camp this summer."

"His camp?" Herbie made the mistake of lapsing from his positive tone.

"Yes, his camp, smartie," sneered the girl. "I thought you knew everything. Camp Manitou, in the Berkshires. You just try bringing one of his campers down to him. He'll just demote you off your old garbage gang."

"He will not."

"He will so."

"He will not," said Herbie, "because I'm going to his old camp myself."

This was somewhat too newly minted a fact, even for the credulity of a small girl. "You're a liar," said she promptly.

"You mean you are," said Herbert, with no great logic, but with a natural grasp of the art of controversy.

"I'll bet you a dime I'm going to his camp," said the girl, falling into the trap and taking the defensive.

"I'll bet you a dollar I am," said Herbert.

"I'll bet you ten dollars you're not."

"I'll bet you a thousand dollars *you're* not."

"I'll bet you a million dollars."

"I'll bet you a *billion* dollars."

The girl, unable to think quickly of the next order of

magnitude, said with scorn, "Where are you gonna get a billion dollars?"

"Same place you'll get a million," retorted Herbie.

"I can get a million dollars from my father if I want to," said Red Locks, vexed at being continually on the defensive, though sensing she was in the right. "He's the biggest lawyer in Bronx County."

"That's nothing," said Herbert. "My father owns the biggest ice plant in America." (He was manager of a small ice plant in the Bronx.)

"My father is richer than your father."

"My father could buy your father like an ice-cream cone."

"He could not," said the girl hotly.

"My father even has a way bigger lawyer for his ice plant than your father." Herbie speedily searched his memory, reviewing conversations of his parents. "My father's lawyer is Louis Glass."

The girl uttered a triumphant little shriek. "Ha, ha, smartie!" she cried, jumping up and dancing a step or two. "My father *is* Louis Glass."

This astounding stroke left Herbie with no available fact, real or improvised, for a counterblow. He was reduced to a weak, "He is not, either."

"Is too!" shouted the girl, her eyes sparkling. "Here, if you're so clever, here's my name on my books—Lucille Glass."

Herbert deigned to inspect the notebook offered for his view, with the large childish inscription, "Lucille Marjorie Glass, 6B-3."

"You should of told me so right away," he said magnanimously. "You can stay here, as long as your father is Louis Glass. 6B-3, huh? I'm in 7B-1. First on the honor roll."

"I'm third on the honor roll," said Lucille, yielding at last the deference due an upperclassman, a head monitor, and a mental giant.

With this advance in their relationship they fell silent, and became aware of being alone together on the small landing. The gay voices of the girls playing in the yard came faintly to them through the closed window. Herbie and Lucille self-consciously turned and watched the darting, frisking little figures for a while.

"What were you doing up here, anyway?" said the boy at last, feeling that ease of speech was deserting him.

"I'm on the girls' Police Squad," said Lucille Glass, "and I'm supposed to watch this staircase during lunch."

She pulled a red band from her pocket and commenced pinning it around her arm. Encountering difficulty, she was gallantly aided by Herbie, who received the reward of a bashful smile. All this while Herbie was struggling with the question, whether it was not inconsistent for a Radiant One to be practically a member of his family, as Lucille's tie to his father's lawyer made her. His sister and his cousins were so empty of grace that he classed all family females in the low rank of girlhood. The aura of Red Locks seemed to waver and dim. However, as they grew silent once more, gazing out at the yard, Herbie felt himself quite tongue-tied, and the glory brightened and shone as strongly as at first, and he realized that charms sufficiently powerful could overcome even the handicap of belonging to the family.

"Well, gotta make my rounds," he said abruptly. "So long."

"Good-by," said the little girl, wrinkling her snub nose and red, firm cheeks at him in a friendly grin. As Herbie walked off the landing into the corridor, she called after him, "Are you really going to Camp Manitou this summer?"

The boy turned and looked down his nose at her in the crushing way teachers reacted to silly questions. He was no taller than the girl, so the effect was rather hard to get, but he managed a good approximation by tilting his head far back, and sighting along the edge of his nose.

"You'll find out," he enunciated after a dignified pause, and stalked off down the hall.

Mrs. Mortimer Gorkin had a weary afternoon of it with Herbie. Shortly after the children came back to class, she was summoned out of the room for a few minutes and returned to find her trusted monitor standing on top of her desk, reciting a parody of "The Village Blacksmith" with an idiotic preciseness that she recognized as a burlesque of herself. "The muss-uls on his ba-rawny arrrms," he was saying, "are sta-rrong as rrrrrubba bands-sah." She punished this malfeasance of office by ordering Herbie to sit in the last seat of the last girls' row and forbidding him to speak for the rest of the day. He broke the injunction twice by shouting spectacularly accurate answers to questions that had reduced the rest of the class to silence. This put the teacher in the bad predicament of having to reproach brilliance. The second time she tried sarcasm, saying heavily, "And pray, what makes you so very, very clever this afternoon, Master Bookbinder?"

It was a mistake. Herbert was inspired to jump to his feet and rejoin, "Just celebrating your wedding, Mrs. Gorkin," touching off a demonstration of screaming hilarity which the reddened, angry teacher could not control until she stood, pounded her desk and shrieked, "Silence! Silence!" She effectively snuffed out Herbert by offering to conduct him down to Mr. Gauss's office the next time he uttered a word. But this came too late. By his repartee, and by forcing her to a display of temper, he had clearly won the day.

When the class marched into the school yard at the end of the afternoon and broke ranks, he was at once surrounded, the girls giggling and shouting at him, the boys pounding his back, shaking his hand, and assuring him with various curses that "he was a regular guy, after all." It was admitted by everyone that he had been under the spell of a "crush," an ailment which all the children understood. The great Lennie Krieger himself condescended to lounge up to Herbert and say, "Nice work, Fatso," which set the seal on his acclaim. He was received back into society. He was even permitted to pitch the first inning of the softball game as a mark of his redemption, and no criticism was heard of his mediocre efforts.

An ugly little girl with a fat face and straight whitish hair, Shirley Schwartz, who secretly adored Herbie but had learned in lower grades, from other boys, the bitter necessity of hiding her hopeless loves, watched this triumph of her hero with joy. When he left the game after several innings, she decided to follow him home on the forlorn chance that he might speak to her. She hovered while he gathered up his books, and dogged him discreetly as he left the yard. But to her astonishment he did not take the direction to his house which she knew well, but turned and went into the teachers' entrance to the school. Love made her bold—she knew, anyway, that the entrance was not monitored after school hours—so she followed him in.

Five minutes later she returned to the yard, pallid and shaken, with a tale that set heads shaking and tongues clacking among the pupils of 7B-1. Shirley had seen Herbie's amazing new deed with her own eyes. Without being ordered to do so, and with no word to any pupil about his reasons for such suicidal folly, Herbie had walked up to the private door of the principal, Mr. Gauss, which even teachers never used, approaching the Presence only through the outer office; had knocked boldly; and, in response to a muffled surprised call from inside in the dreaded voice, had vanished within.

3

The Visitor

THE EVENING WAS purple, and the naked electric street lights cast a brightening glow from under their wrinkled reflectors along Homer Avenue in the Bronx, when Herbie Bookbinder wrested himself away from a discussion of religion around a fire in a vacant lot and wended homeward. The argument over the nature and powers of God had been raging for hours like the fire, and had been kindled, like the fire, by a piece of newspaper printed in Hebrew lettering.

It was known to Bronx boys of all faiths that to burn a Jewish newspaper on Friday was a piece of rashness that must bring disaster, and there was no youngster in Herbie's neighborhood who would have done it. A fine point of theology had arisen, however, when Herbie had recalled from a lecture at Sunday school that this day, Thursday, was a minor festival, the Thirty-third of the Omer. He suggested that it was perilous to light a fire with the sheets on this day, too, for, although it was not as dangerous a time as Friday, there seemed to remain an element of risk. The Christian boys had at once seen the point and agreed, but trouble ensued when Leonard Krieger saw a chance to cry Herbert down with jeers.

Lennie was a big, good-looking, black-haired lad, twelve and a half years old, a master of the education of the streets, a hater of school education, a lively athlete, and a natural leader of boys. His father and Herbie's were partners in the ice business, and the two boys had always known and disliked each other. The antipathy had deepened with the years as Herbie overtook the older boy in school, and it now flourished poisonously, with both of them in Mrs. Gorkin's class, Herbie as a sparkler and Lennie as one of the indifferent boys.

The athlete was verging on the age when the grosser superstitions break down. Expressing much fine sarcasm at the expense of "little fat 'fraidy-cats" and "superstitious yellow-bellies," he proceeded to crumple up the Jewish paper and light it. His bravado caused mutters of fear among the smaller boys. None of them would heap wood on the fire, and he was forced to tend it himself. Herbie darkly observed that he only hoped Leonard would not come home to find that his father and mother had dropped dead. Leonard at once offered to "show him whose mother and father would drop dead," advancing on him with raised fists, but the voice of the group, crying, "Pick on someone your own size," stopped the settlement of the problem by force.

A long general debate followed as to the chances of bad luck befalling Leonard Krieger, and the argument finally narrowed to these questions: whether God was watching Jewish newspapers all the time, or only on Fridays; whether He had eyes to watch and, if not, how He accomplished watching; and where God was and what He was like, anyway.

At last Lennie blew the discussion apart by exclaiming, "Aw, all this is a lotta bushwa. I don't believe in God."

None of the boys dared speak for a moment after this. Herbie glanced anxiously at the huge setting sun, as though afraid it would turn green or fall to bits. Frankie Callaghan, a red-headed little Catholic boy, cried, "I ain't gonna stay around here. Lightnin's gonna strike that guy," and galloped out of the lot. The others remained, but moved out of range. If such a spectacular end were to befall Lennie, they wanted to see it.

The Almighty, however, remained unperturbed, and no blue bolt fell on Lennie.

"What are you guys lookin' so scared about?" he sneered. "I said it an' I'll say it again. I don't believe in God."

"O.K., if you're so smart," said Herbie, cautiously moving closer to the atheist, "I suppose you're gonna say *you* made the world yourself."

"I didn't say I did. Who do you say made it?"

"Why, God, of course."

"All right, Fatso. Who made God?"

Two more boys, rendered uncomfortable by the discussion, departed.

"That's a dumb question," Herbie replied impatiently.

"Why is it dumb?"

"Well, *because.* If I could tell you who made God, then God wouldn't be God. The other guy who made him would be God."

"O.K., so nobody made God, is that right?"

"That's right."

"Then there ain't no God," said Lennie with a chortle of triumph.

A couple of boys snickered reluctantly. Herbie was not felled by the stroke.

"You mean to say God couldn't just *be,* without someone makin' him?"

" 'Course not."

"Why not?"

"Because nothin' just is. Somebody's gotta make it."

"O.K.," retorted Herbie, *"then who made the world?"*

There was a general laugh at Lennie's expense this time. Herbie had managed to twist the age-old circular argument so that he was now chasing his opponent. The athlete said angrily, "Well, if there's a God, let Him make a can of ice cream appear right here in front o' you 'n' me."

All the boys stared at the patch of grass between the debaters, half expecting a cylinder of Breyer's Special Chocolate to materialize. The Creator, however, seemed to be in no mood for showing off. He would produce neither lightning nor ice cream on Lennie's behalf.

"Well, what does that prove?" said Herbie after a pause.

"It proves," declared Lennie, with more passion than conviction, "that you're a dumb little fat slob, even though you're teacher's pet."

"Jer-reee!" A squawk from the little girl on the distant sidewalk. "Mom's hollerin' for you for supper."

"Holy cats, it's a quarter to seven," exclaimed the boy thus summoned, and ran.

The young theologians awoke to the workaday world again. One by one they left the circle around the fire, tramped away through the high green weeds of the lot, scrambled down a slope of rock to the sidewalk, and went away among the canyons of apartment houses. Herbie, who loved fires, arguments, and vacant lots more than anything in the world, except possibly movies, was among the last lingerers around the flames in the gloom. He bade a silent good-by to the cold roughness of rock on which he sat and the fresh smell of the weeds all around him, and dragged himself off to his home, his clothes reeking delightfully of wood smoke.

Not every neighborhood in the Bronx boasted vacant lots. Even those on Homer Avenue were being systematically blasted with dynamite, gutted by steam shovels, and plugged up with apartment houses. It was lucky for Herbert and his friends that the nearness of the avenue to the Bronx River (known to the boys as "the creek") and its situation along a ridge of tough rock had made building less profitable here than elsewhere, so that the tide of bricks had not yet swamped green earth along Homer Avenue. Of these matters the boys were ignorant. The parents settled on Homer Avenue because rents were cheap, and the children were happy in the choice because of the vacant lots. In Public School 50, teachers were always trying in vain to wake the love of nature in the boys by reading poetry to them. The compositions on the subject of nature were the dreariest and most banal of all the writing efforts wrung from the urchins, and the word "lots" never appeared in them. But the moment the lads were free of the prison of school they scampered to the lots, chased butterflies, dissected weeds and flowers, built fires, and watched the melting colors of the sunset. It goes without saying that parents and teachers were strongly opposed to the practice of playing in the lots, and were always issuing orders against it. This added the final sauce to the deed so grateful to the palate of boyhood.

Herbie went into 1075 Homer Avenue, a brick cliff very much like the other brick cliffs that stood wall to wall for many blocks along the less rocky side of the street. It was gray, square, five stories high, punctured with windows, and saved from bleakness only by the entrance, which tried on a little matter of plaster gargoyles overhead and dead shrubs in cracked plaster urns on either side of the iron-grilled glass doors. The stucco hallway had once been frescoed with highly colored fruits, but these, under the grime which gathers equally on walls and boys' necks in the city, had soon looked sickly. The wise landlord had repainted the hallway with a sad green tint that grew grayer and grayer each year without exciting protest. The boy skipped up two flights of the stair-case, his little shoes wearing the grooves in the stone slab steps infinitesimally deeper, and paused outside the door labeled "3A," which led into the brick pigeonhole sacred, while the lease ran, to the Bookbinder family and known to them as home.

He could hear his mother stirring about in the kitchen, just inside and to the left of the door. Chances seemed favorable for a tiptoe entrance and swift concealment of his wool sweater, which for some reason retained more smell of fire than all the rest of his clothing together. He tried the doorknob. It was unlatched. Softly he pushed open the door, counting on the clatter of dishes to cover the squeak of the hinges, and darted inside, past the steamy kitchen, down the hall to the bedrooms.

"Look, Ma. Here's Herbie." It was the voice of his sister, Felicia, full of the tone of righteousness.

"Herbie, you come here!" called his mother.

The boy arrested his flight and turned heavily back. The treachery of his sister caused no bitterness in his heart. It was one of the evil things of life, like school and bedtime, against which he had long ago worn out his indignation. He now bore it stoically, convinced that release would only come in the latter days of eternity when he reached the age of twenty-one.

Felicia's long, curly black hair hung about her face as she bent over a loaf of bread she was slicing when Herbie came into the kitchen. She was almost thirteen, short and slight for her age, and by some older lads she was judged very good-looking. Herbie regarded this judgment as lunacy, but he knew that as boys passed into their four-teenth year and beyond they underwent severe changes that seemed to lessen their common sense.

Felicia looked up from her work, shook the hair out of her eyes, inhaled with a loud sniff, said, "Ugh! Smoke!" and fell to cutting bread industriously again.

"I guess I'd smell better," replied her brother, "if I went up to Emily's house and tried on her mother's lip-stick."

"Oh, that old thing again," said Felicia scornfully.

Herbie knew that he had worked dry his discovery of his sister's dabbling in cosmetics a month ago, but any attack on another theme, however feeble, seemed better than staying on the topic of smoke. His mother put down her soup ladle, wiped her hands on her apron, turned away from the stove, and unexpectedly gave Herbie a hug and a kiss. "You do smell of smoke, but I forgive you this once," she said in a tired, good-natured tone. "Go, take off that sweater. Papa'll be home for supper in a minute." She held him at arm's length, surveying him fondly as though seeing him after a long absence, then let him go. Herbert fled, rejoicing in the unlooked-for mercy.

A half hour later, when the family was seated around the table in the dining room, Mrs. Bookbinder filled Herbert's plate almost to the brim with lamb stew, carefully fishing the choice morsels of meat out of the tureen for him. Felicia's outraged protests at this strange favoritism were cut short by her father, whose conversation she had interrupted.

The father was a thin, stern-looking man with scanty, graying hair, a long, fleshy nose, many deep, downward lines in his narrow face, and the abstracted look of one whose life passes in urgent business calculations. His talk at the table always consisted of narrations to his wife of the day's problems at the ice plant. He greeted the children pleasantly when he arrived home and forgot about them for the rest of the evening. Herbie and his sister were used to playing little games at the table while their father talked about "the Place," about his perpetual difficulties with his partner, Mr. Krieger, about something called a mortgage, and about someone called a mortgagee. It would have required an impossibly long lecture on the law of mortgages to make clear to the children some thousands of hours of conversation dinned into their small ears. Yet Herbie and Felicia had made many such transactions. Indeed, even now the boy's cousin, Cliff, held his roller skates pending Herbie's repayment of fifteen cents, which he had borrowed in order to see a crucial episode of a serial movie. Herbie would have been amazed to know that he had thereby been granted a "mortgage" and that Cliff was a "mortgagee."

"Papa," said the mother at last as her husband fell silent long enough to eat some stew, "I had an interesting phone call today."

"You had a phone call?" Mr. Bookbinder's surprise was genuine. He was not aware that anything resembling an event had taken place in his wife's life for fifteen years.

"Yes, from a very important gentleman. A gentleman who happens to think highly of your son."

The mystery of his mother's unusual kindness was suddenly explained for Herbie. His heart thudding, he began to plan speedily how to handle the coming crisis.

"In fact," went on the mother, her weary face lit with liveliness, momentarily suggesting beauty that had faded many years ago, "this very important gentleman thinks so highly of your son that he's coming here after supper to pay us a visit."

"Who is it?" asked the father, in whom the spirit of banter was not strong.

The mother uncovered the glowing gem of news with reluctance. "Mr. Gauss, the principal—the *principal*—of Herbie's school."

"That's very nice of him," said Jacob Bookbinder awkwardly, after a pause.

"Aw, I bet I know what that old Mr. Gauss wants," said Herbie.

"Ah, he wants something," said Mr. Bookbinder. This brought the situation nearer reality.

"Sure, I bet he wants me and Fleece to go to that old camp of his," said Herbie, adding quickly as he saw disapproval on the faces of both parents, "that camp that Lucille Glass and Lennie Krieger are going to."

"Krieger's boy going to camp? Since when?" said the father.

"How do you know Lucille Glass?" said the mother.

"I met her in school," answered Herbie, shrewdly ignoring his father's question. He went on, "I don't feel like going to no camp, an' I bet Fleece don't either."

"I hate camps," said Felicia, whose knowledge of the ways of a parental mind was not inferior to Herbie's.

"How do you know you hate camps when you've never been to one?" said Mrs. Bookbinder.

"What I'd like to know is, where does Krieger suddenly get money to send a boy to camp?" said the father irritably.

Herbie detected a drift toward a collision between the facts of his imagination and those of brute nature. "Well, Lennie *says* he's going anyway," he observed, "but he's an awful liar, you know."

"That's Krieger, isn't it?" said Mr. Bookbinder to his wife. "A man with a bank loan on his furniture and a Chevrolet car he has to borrow money from the business to pay the installments on, and the boy goes to camp. Glass, of course, can send a girl to camp."

"She's a sweet little thing," said Mrs. Bookbinder. "Help me clear, Felice."

"She has red hair," said Herbie, tingling all over at the mention of the girl. "I hate girls with red hair."

"I see her in gym. She's a baby," said Felicia as she scraped and stacked the dirty dishes.

The doorbell rang. Herbie jumped in his chair.

"That must be Mr. Gauss, but he's so early!" cried Mrs. Bookbinder, untying her apron with swift hands. "Pa, put on your jacket and go in the parlor. Herbie, answer the bell. Felice, shut the dining-room doors and finish cleaning up quietly."

These directives issued, she hurried to her bedroom, while the family moved to obey. The lines of authority were laid down in the Bookbinder household, and Mrs. Bookbinder was as clearly in command in matters of diet, furniture, clothing, and etiquette as she was subordinate in everything else.

Herbie's first feeling upon opening the door to the terrible visitor was disappointment at his size. In the assemblies, and behind his desk, Mr. Gauss gave the impression of skyscraping grandeur, but he managed to pass through the doorway without crouching. He was corpulent, and rather shiny of visage. His mouth, Herbie observed, was fixed in a peculiar smile, consisting of a straight, thin line of lips pushed upward at both ends and apparently held so by a pair of firm invisible fingers.

"Good evening, Master Bookbinder," said the principal

loudly, his mouth retaining the shape of the smile as it opened. "I trust your good dad and mother are expecting me?"

"Yes, sir," the boy mumbled, and led the way to the parlor. His good dad was standing by the upright piano (Felicia's chief sorrow in life) looking fully as wooden, upright, and hard to play upon as the instrument. Mr. Gauss, by way of compensating, unbent to the verge of slumping out of human shape as he exchanged greetings with the parent. The two men sat down on the red velours-covered sofa, driving a couple of feathers into the air through a seam Mrs. Bookbinder had planned to mend that very evening.

"Allow me to say, Mr. Bookbinder," began the principal, "that you have a wonderful daughter and a very wonderful son. Absolutely outstanding children, both of them."

"Their mother signs the report cards, so I wouldn't know," said Jacob Bookbinder, putting one hand in a jacket pocket and leaning back on the other in an awkward, self-conscious way.

"Absolutely outstanding. I keep my eye out for these outstanding children, you know. I want to remember in later years when they're grown up and famous that a very little bit of their success—just a very little bit—is due to the molding they received at my hands when they were still in the childhood state of impressionable clay."

"Education is a fine thing," answered the father, not being able to think of a more noncommittal remark.

"You have stated it in a nutshell," said Mr. Gauss. "My one sorrow is—"

Mrs. Bookbinder appeared, splendid in a red silk gown. Her face was newly powdered, her hair carefully arranged, and a long double string of amber beads clicked on her bosom. The men stood.

"And this is Mrs. Bookbinder, I'm sure," cried the principal, with an immensely happy smile. "No mistaking the resemblance to little Herbie."

"It is an honor and a privilege to welcome you to our home, Mr. Gauss," said the mother with a formal little bow.

"An honor and a privilege to be here, I assure you," said the principal, returning the bow with a nice mixture of grandeur and humbleness. As they all sat Mr. Gauss proceeded, "I have just been telling Mr. Bookbinder that you have a wonderful daughter and a very wonderful son. Absolutely outstanding children, both of them."

Herbie noticed the repetition of the extra adjective "very" applied to himself, and while it pleased him, he calculated that it might be due to the fact that he, not Felicia, had invited the principal to visit. He was already in an agony of fear that Mr. Gauss might reveal his rash deed, so the extra praise made him more uneasy than otherwise. But Mr. Gauss's motive was really much simpler. He knew that parents usually set more store by sons than daughters, and distributed his adjectives on that basis.

"And I was telling Mr. Bookbinder," he went on, "that I like to keep my eye on these outstanding children so that in after years when they are famous—as I'm quite sure Herbie will be—"

Mrs. Bookbinder turned to beam at her boy. Herbie was making a careful study of the wan roses and foilage in the carpet.

"—I will be able to remember that I contributed a tiny, just a tiny bit to their success by molding them while they were still in the childhood state of impressionable clay."

Herbie wondered vaguely what constituted molding at Mr. Gauss's hands, inasmuch as he had never spoken to the principal or even seen him at a distance of less than a hundred feet until today. But Mrs. Bookbinder had no such reservations.

"I'm sure the boy owes a great deal to you, Mr. Gauss," she said, "and I only hope when he grows up he'll appreciate it."

"Why, that's extremely gracious of you. I was just telling Mr. Bookbinder that my one sorrow in the case of these outstanding children is that I lose touch with them for two months each summer. Oh, for the common run of children it doesn't make much difference. But you know from your industrial experience, Mr. Bookbinder, that a fine, delicate piece of machinery, neglected for two months, can really be injured."

The father, who saw where the talk was leading, did not wish to assent to anything the principal proposed, but he was cornered. "That much is true," he said unwillingly.

"I'm glad we agree. And that is how I happened to hit on the idea of Camp Manitou."

The hour had struck. Herbie began to sidle from the scene.

"Must you go, Herbie?" said the principal at once, training his smile at the boy. "I should think you would be interested."

"Stay where you are," commanded the father.

Herbie stopped and leaned against the piano, looking unhappy.

But his fears were needless. Mr. Gauss launched into his "sales talk" without ever mentioning the boy's call at his office. Once or twice he nodded at Herbie with the cunning geniality of a fellow-plotter; that was all. He expanded on a double-barreled theme: the delights of Camp Manitou and the peculiar worthiness of the Bookbinder children. The boy was grateful to the schoolmaster for keeping mum, but he was also struck by his readiness to bypass the truth—a horrid sin, according to Mr. Gauss's own speeches in assembly. As the camp owner went on with his plea, passing booklets of photographs to the parents and to the boy, he fell into a manner of speech and conduct that seemed more and more familiar to Herbert. The boy had uncles and aunts who came periodically to wheedle favors from his father. So poor Mr. Gauss talked on and on, unaware that his shiny face and roly-poly form were sinking, in the lad's view, from his height of office to the depressed level inhabited by needy relatives.

"Herbie tells me," the mother put in after a while, "that Lucille Glass is enrolled in your camp."

"Ah, yes, Lucille. Lovely little child. Perfect example of a Manitou camper."

"And Lennie Krieger, too—is that right?" asked Jacob Bookbinder.

"Krieger?" said Mr. Gauss doubtfully. He reached for a notebook.

"Lives here on Homer Avenue, two blocks down. A tall boy, twelve or so. He's the son of my business partner."

"Of course. Lennie. I'm glad you mentioned that," said the principal, dropping his voice to a confidential tone. "I have a question to ask you. Do you feel—I must ask your honest opinion—that Lennie Krieger is the type I have described to you as a Manitou camper? The kind of boy you'd like to see side by side with a lad of Herbie's caliber?"

Mr. Bookbinder grumbled, "Nothing wrong with him that I know of."

The principal unscrewed his fountain pen and made a careful note in his book, saying, "Thank you. In that case perhaps—I say, perhaps—Lennie may be coming to Manitou after all." And he privately decided to call next evening upon the parents of the boy, of whose existence he had not been aware until a few minutes ago.

There were seven other children in the neighborhood deserving the honor of a summer at Camp Manitou, at the price of three hundred dollars per child, so Mr. Gauss did not tarry. His visit had clearly had some effect. Mr. and Mrs. Bookbinder were taken with the flattery of the principal's presence, the charm of the pictures of cabins by a mountain lake, and the descriptions in the booklet of the amazing mental, physical, and religious improvement of children in a summer at Manitou. When the principal left, he received their humble thanks for the honor he had offered them, and a promise that they would earnestly examine their resources to see whether they could afford to accept it.

Herbie went to bed that night in a fever, and dreamed, until Felicia shook him at seven the next morning, of lakes, cabins, shrubbery, Indians, campfires, roasting frankfurters, a lovely little redheaded girl darting among green trees, and religious improvement.

4

The "Place"

THREE DAYS LATER Herbert Bookbinder lay on a bank of new grass beside the Bronx River, explaining the astronomical reason for spring to his cousin, Clifford Block, who did not understand a word of it.

Both boys were dressed from head to foot in those articles of wardrobe which, being most recently purchased, had exclusive Sunday status. They wore the customary boys' costume of the time: black shoes, long stockings, "knickers," short jackets, white shirts with four-in-hand ties (askew five minutes after tying), and soft round felt hats, jeered at by boys too small to wear them as "cake-eaters." They carried their finery with mixed feelings, disgust at the constraint of it struggling with the bit of peacock that is not absent from a boy's heart. Their parents would not send them into the street on Sunday except in this gala state, especially so soon after Passover, when their new clothes were really so new.

The springtime will not be denied its annual entrance, even in Herbie's home town of stone. Beneath the buildings, beneath the streets, beneath the whole hard plating, there is quick earth yet, showing green at every chink, whether it be a little corner park, a vacant lot, or just a crack between cobblestones. Boys snuff the air and go wandering until they find a green place where they can inhale the pleasantness. The fit of nostalgia for the land under the stone does not last long, nor do the boys really understand what it is. Soon they resume their sports in the familiar paths of the angular canyons in which they live.

While it lasts, this springtime mood causes great waste of child hours, lowers school grades, and brings on scoldings and blows. For the boys it is little more than an inconvenient costly frenzy.

Herbie and Cliff found the vacant lots along Homer Avenue too commonplace to still the restlessness of the first warm Sunday in May. They had gone down the long hill of Westchester Avenue past Byron, past Shakespeare, past Tennyson Avenues, to the creek which they avoided all year round, partly in obedience to the sternest sort of orders from their parents, but more because of the legend that the river bank was the haunt of a pack of boyish cutthroats known as the "creek gang." Many bloody tales were told about this band. They all carried knives. The bigger boys carried guns. They captured boys and girls, robbed them, and performed nameless outrages upon them. And they killed each other, when there was nothing more profitable to do. Nobody of Herbie's acquaintance had ever seen a genuine gang member, but this did not prevent all the children on Homer Avenue from scurrying indoors and peeping out through windows whenever the cry "Creek gang! Creek gang!" startled the neighborhood. The cause of the alarm generally proved to be an exceptionally shabby, dirty boy from another avenue, ambling along the deserted sidewalks in puzzlement.

The thought that they might encounter these desperadoes lent an edge of pleasure to the excursion of Herbie and his cousin, for today they were in a mood for braving the unknown. To reach the bank of the stream they had to cross railroad tracks, another tremendous taboo. They slid carefully down a gravel embankment and picked their way across the cinder bed on which the tracks rested. Of course they avoided the rails, which were supposed to have a power of suction that could hold unwary treaders fast until the next train destroyed them, and they leaped anxiously over the death-dealing third rail, along which they both averred they could hear the hum of the fatal electric current. These hazards passed at last, the boys reached the side of the creek and lolled on the fresh grass and spiky weeds that covered the narrow strip of wasteland between the railroad bed and the river mud. The sun was high; the ground was warm; the smell of the mud and slime of the inlet at low tide was pungent and interesting. The boys were alone in a new place, lying on the ground in Sunday clothes, successfully defiant of their parents' orders and their own fears. Perhaps they could have been made happier at this moment by the arrival of the Messiah. More likely they would have regarded it as an unnecessary interruption.

Herbie's lecture on the mechanics of spring, delivered as both boys lay on their backs with hands clasped under their heads, had reached a point beyond which Cliff's earthbound imagination would not budge.

"Look," said Herbie in exasperation. "Let's start from the beginning again. What shape is the earth?"

"Round."

"Does the sun go around it?"

"No, it goes around the sun."

"O.K. You do know that much. Now you only gotta realize one thing more. The earth slants."

"That's what I don't understand."

Cliff's brows were knitted. He was a meek-appearing but sturdy boy, with light brown hair and exceptionally long arms and legs. He was two classes behind Herbie in school, though they were the same age, and he regarded his bright cousin with deference and affection.

"What's so hard about it? Watch." Herbie picked up a stick and held it vertically. "It slants." He tilted the stick. "Like that. It slants."

'Now, hold on, Herbie. The earth ain't no stick. It's a ball." Cliff pulled a rubber ball out of his pocket. "See this? I'm holdin' it straight up 'n' down."

"Yeah, I see it. So what?"

"Now I slant it." He tilted the ball. "Does it look any different? You know it don't. How the hell can you know when a round ball slants?"

Herbie was silenced for a moment. The question had never occurred to him during Mrs. Gorkin's glib explanation of spring. But after puzzling over it, he said, "Oh, now I get it. Look, there's a North Pole an' a South Pole, ain't there?"

"Yeah."

"All right. The North Pole points in toward the sun. That's how we know the earth slants."

Cliff nodded slowly. "Now you're talkin'. Well, but how does that make spring?"

"Easy. If the north part of the world is pointed toward the sun, that makes it warmer, don't it?"

"Sure."

"Well, there you are."

"Yeah. But that means it oughta be spring or summer all year round. Why ain't it?"

This question hadn't occurred to Herbie, either. But instead of admitting that his grasp of the subject was imperfect, he said, "What's so hard about that? After a while the earth just flips over 'n' slants the other way."

"Now, wait. Are you tryin' to tell me that the earth keeps goin' flip-flop, flip-flop around the sun every year?" Cliff turned the ball back and forth in his hand to illustrate.

"I ain't tryin' to tell it to you. That's what the books say."

"Well, those books are crazy, then. Herbie, you don't believe that, either. The earth wobblin' around the sun like a drunken bum. It don't make sense."

"You got it all wrong," mourned Herbie, standing up reluctantly. "This," he said, pointing to a rough gray rock imbedded in the mud, "is the sun. And this"—he placed near it a stone half as big—"is the earth." (Pedagogues always falsify proportions; it makes their job easier.) "Now the earth starts moving—" But the rest of the discourse was not to be spoken. "Cliff!" said Herbie with a violent change in tone. "The creek gang!"

Cliff jumped up, and looking in the direction of Herbie's terrified stare, he saw two small, swarthy, ragged boys with bottles in their hands, about fifty yards down the river, walking toward them.

"Let's run," said Herbie.

"What for?" said Cliff. He was a head taller than

Herbie, more agile of body and rather less inflammable of mind. "They're smaller than we are."

"Are you crazy?" said Herbert. "They've got knives. Come on!"

He turned toward the railroad tracks. At this moment, unluckily, a long freight train appeared, the engine chugging heavily as it dragged its chain of freight cars of different shapes and hues out of the mouth of the far-off river tunnel. To cross the path of an oncoming train was beyond the daring of both boys. To flee along the river bed was useless; a short way from them it was blocked by the concrete base of a bridge. Caught between sure destruction and probable destruction they stood at bay, their holiday mood quenched, and awaited their fate.

The two small terrorists came within a yard of them, stopped, and inspected them insolently with keen brown eyes. Then they exchanged guttural remarks in a strange tongue. They moved closer slowly until the unhappy cousins could have reached out and touched them. The bottles they carried were full of greenish water in which many tiny fishes were darting. The strangers' knee breeches were patched, their stockings were torn, their sweaters had huge irregular holes, and from the shoe of one of them a toe poked out. To boys brought up in the politeness of Homer Avenue and Public School 50 they were as picturesque as pirates—and more dreadful, because they obviously regarded boys as worthy antagonists.

Finally Herbert, unable to endure the tension of the scrutiny, said, "What you guys got in them there bottles?"—mutilating grammar as much as possible to suggest manliness, but making the mistake of swallowing loudly in the middle of the word "bottles." The quavering of his voice was full of information to the two strangers, who exchanged a swift glance.

"Never mind that," one of them snarled. "Gimme a nickel."

"Ain't got no nickel," faltered Herbie.

"All I find I keep?"

Herbie did not reply.

"All I find I keep?" repeated the enemy, with a gesture at Herbie's jacket pocket. The boy winced; it was the pocket containing the key to heaven, fifteen cents for the movies.

"I got a hundred dollars," said Cliff suddenly. "Let's see one o' you guys search me."

Herbert grew weak at this insane effrontery of his cousin. He looked for the glitter of long knives.

"Oh," sneered the talking one, turning on Cliff. "A fresh guy."

"That's right," said Cliff, and stepped up to him so that they were toe to toe. The well-dressed boy was several inches taller; even Herbert was almost as large as the bigger of the two strangers. Instinct, undistracted by a hot imagination, had risen to tell Cliff that the advantage was on his side so long as fear did not weigh in the balance. "How about searching me?"

"Yeah, or me?" said Herbert, plucking up heart the instant he saw the situation shifting. He faced the smaller foe.

There was a silent opposing of glares between the paired-off boys for several seconds.

The smaller bandit broke the spell, and informed Herbie, "I can fight you."

"You can not," said Herbie. He jerked his thumb toward Cliff. "Anyway, *he* can fight *him*."

"Who can fight who?" said the large opponent fiercely, turning on Herbie.

"My cousin can fight you—I bet," said Herbie, with slightly less assurance.

"I can fight you," barked back the big creek gang-man.

"Never said you couldn't."

"*He* can fight you." (Pointing to his small hench-man.)

"Well, *he* can fight *you*." (Pointing to his tall cousin.)

Cliff said nothing.

"I can fight both of you," said the leading enemy, "with both hands tied behind me."

"O.K.," said Herbie, "let us tie your hands, then."

"Pretty fresh, both of them, ain't they?" said the leader to his minion.

"I can fight him," said the small one doggedly, pointing at Herbie.

The fat boy, who was sure this was quite true, said, "You guys better not start anything. My cousin is the champion boxer of P.S. 45. He knows all the tricks."

"A regular Jack Dempsey, huh?" sneered bandit number one. But he sized up Cliff with a flicker of caution in his eyes.

"I'm getting tired of this blab," said Cliff. He poked the leader lightly on the shoulder with two fingers. "If you can fight me, start fighting."

The leader glared, and pouted, and breathed heavily, and dusted off the place that had been touched (not that it had been rendered any dirtier) with a clenched fist. But no knives flashed, and no blows ensued.

"I can fight him," said the smaller one again, indicating Herbie to the two big boys. "Please, I can fight him."

"And me, too?" said Cliff.

The small gangster looked at his chief questioningly. The leader spoke a few words in the strange tongue again. Then he glanced at Herbie with contempt and said, "Just let us catch *you* alone sometime. Come on," he added to his companion. "Let's let the sissies go."

"You still ain't told us what you got in the bottles," called Cliff to the retreating backs.

"If you weren't such a dumb mama's boy," shouted back the outlaw, "you'd know they were killies."

"Did you catch 'em out of the river?"

"Nah, we found 'em in a nest up a tree," came the jeering answer, and the two creek gangsters climbed up to the railroad track, where the freight train had finally gone by, and disappeared from view.

These menacing manikins were, in fact, children of one of the poor foreign families who lived then in wood shacks near the shore of the East River, kept goats, coaxed vegetables out of the neglected Bronx dirt, and maintained an obstinate separateness from the subway-

and-steamheat world during the first generation of their immigration. In time these lads were destined to be sucked into respectability, but meanwhile they lived in a free way rare among city boys. Inveterate truants, they knew a great deal about plants, fishes, and animals without benefit of Boy Scout training, and they haunted the river banks. Such was the basis of the "creek gang" legend, and it had this much truth in it, that several times a year unwary boys were deprived of their pocket money and pummeled if they fell in with these outcasts. But there was no gang, no knives, no guns, no horrid orgies, no killings. Romance had eked out fact, as it usually does in satisfactory and long-lived legends. However, none of this reassuring background being available to Herbie, he stood quaking in the aftermath of strain, hardly able to believe yet that he was safe.

The idyl by the river was gloomed. Aware of the gratitude he owed his cousin, but too shamed by his own show of fear to express it, Herbie passed the lead to him and said, "Where'll we go now, Cliff?" But the stalwart boy, his hour over, was content to follow the livelier ideas of Herbie, and said as much. So do generals, skilled in the art of violence, take the command of a nation in war and give it up when peace comes. Herbie looked up and down the river bank, and briefly considered an excursion toward the pebbly shore of the wide East River. But he decided it was too far. It then occurred to him that they might fish for killies, in the manner he had heard about but never tried, with a handkerchief. But they had no bottles, and the prospect of going home with a sopping handkerchief and a few dead little fish seemed less charming than it might have, an hour sooner. In short, he found the spring hunger waning.

"We'll go to the Place," he said, turning and running up to the railroad tracks.

Just on the border where grass met cinders he noticed the round, long, slender little stalks of a plant the boys called "wild onions," and he and Cliff pulled up and chewed several of the bitter little white root bulbs, vowing that they were delicious, and quickly spat them out and went their way. This was as close as they came to nature in the day's sortie.

On the other side of the stream there was a broad garbage dump, established when the growing city had been thirty years younger and the wise men had not imagined that the inhabitants could spread out so far. The flames from the dumps and the red sky-glow over them, contending with the sunset, the moon, and the stars for attention, had been a familiar sight in the Bronx for many years, but in Herbie's time the fires had ceased after bitter petitions from the new settlers in these remote stretches of the borough, and the dumps were being replaced by coal and sand piles. Jacob Bookbinder had built the Bronx River Ice Company plant on a tract of land close to the odorous heaps, and therefore as depressed in value, almost, as an acre of Sahara desert. The business had started with little money, most of it borrowed, and elegance of site had been a last consideration.

The "Place" was an oblong shell of concrete one story high, a city block long, and half as wide. Herbie had often heard his father speak of the plant as a "ninety tonner," and in his infancy had taken the phrase to mean "Ninety thunders," an apt nickname for the clanking, pounding inferno it had seemed to him. It was traditional in his family that, on first being brought into the Place at the age of four, to be shown the huge brine tank, the ice cans, the dynamo, and the rising and falling pistons of the compressors, Herbert had gone at once into a fit of screaming; and his father, who was not too far from his European boyhood to believe in omens, had always said sadly thereafter that his son would not inherit his managerial shoes. Herbert had since come to know that "ninety tonner" described the capacity of the plant for a single day's production of ice, also that his father's goal in the world was to build and own a two-hundred tonner. He had learned, too, to control his fear of the terrible machines, and even to find a sort of wild thrill in watching them.

"We'll have to climb through a window," he said, as the boys approached the long wall of the Place which faced the river. "There's nobody there on Sundays except the engineer."

Because of the menace of the poisonous ammonia gas used in refrigeration, one section of one of the broad windows of the Place was always left open, night and day. It was through this small vent, high on one side of the window, that Herbie painfully wriggled with a boost and a push from Cliff, who followed speedily, jumping up and sliding his slender waist through the hole like an acrobat. The boys found themselves in the large machinery-filled space known as the tank room. They could see the engineer manipulating the traveling crane over the brine tank in the far corner. Then, greatly to Herbie's surprise, the boys heard echoing through the large hollow building angry voices which came from the office at the other end of the plant. The loudest and angriest voice was that of Herbie's father.

"You have no right to sell!" he was shouting. "No right to sell!"

5

The Safe

JACOB BOOKBINDER WAS not, in the popular phrase, a man to be trifled with. A quick estimate showed Herbie that sneaking into the Place through a window came under the head of trifling. His first impulse was to climb out again with no delay, but curiosity was stronger. He crouched, motioned to Cliff to follow him, and stole along the concrete wall, behind the ammonia tanks, to the wooden partition which separated the office from the machinery space. The partition had a glassless window in it, with a sill about as high as Herbie's eyes.

"You have no right to sell!" The voice of Jacob Bookbinder was so harsh, strained, and stern that Herbie hardly knew it. "This is our place, mine and Krieger's. We built it and we've run it for fifteen years, and you, Mr. Powers, who have put your head into the building, if I may say so, a dozen times in your life, are not doing the right thing to discuss selling without our consent."

"Jake, why excited? I say this way, peaceable. Powers honest man. One way, another way. Maybe better off. Talk, decide. Friendly. Nobody rob us. Lot of cash. Reliable people. I say this way, cool off. Maybe—"

Herbie recognized the hasty high voice and the curious speech of his father's partner, Mr. Krieger. The partner was a timid, tall man with grizzled hair and tiny eyes surrounded by wrinkles. His most striking feature was his language, a scramble of words which might have graveled a military decoder. Mr. Krieger had astonishing lack of confidence in himself. He believed any one sentence he uttered might be enough to entrap him and ruin his life. He therefore took great care never to utter a sentence. Having framed a statement in his mind, he would dance tiptoe over it, so to speak, with his tongue, touching only about one word out of four. This ingenious principle enabled him to deny anything he said, on the grounds that he had been misunderstood, if it happened to sound wrong once out of his mouth.

Jacob Bookbinder, familiar with the code after years of unraveling, turned on Krieger with a fierce look that Herbie remembered well from a couple of historic lickings.

"Krieger, will you do me the favor to let me talk? Better off to give away our place for half of what it's worth and be left with a few dollars and our hands in our pockets?"

"Who means? Only peaceable. This opinion, that opinion. Not for two hundred thousand dollars. Only up to the majority. Thirty years in the ice business. I honest man, you honest man, Powers different opinion honest man. I say this way, peaceable—"

Mr. Krieger's flow of words was interrupted by a strange voice saying, "Pardon me for just a moment," in accents that indicated the speaker was an outlander, certainly not of the Bronx, possibly not even of New York. Herbie, peering cautiously over the sill, saw a burly, sandy-haired young man who gestured with a smoking pipe. He wore the kind of clothes that men affected in the "love movies" which the boy hated—well cut, new, and of soft materials not seen along Homer Avenue.

"I want to say you gentlemen are not being fair to me. I could have gone ahead and closed with Interborough on their offer, but I owed you the courtesy of this conference and I arranged it. We seem to be bogged in useless wrangling. It happens to be my wife's birthday today and I have to catch a train, and I'll really thank you to keep the discussion as short as possible."

"Please forgive us for taking a few minutes to talk over being thrown out on the street," said Herbie's father.

"Now, honestly, that kind of remark is untrue and hitting below the belt," said Mr. Powers. "Interborough intends to retain both of you in executive positions—"

"Fine," said Jacob Bookbinder bitterly. "We've still got jobs. I'm back where I was two months after I landed in this country, only twenty-five years older, but what's twenty-five years?"

Powers stood up and impatiently donned a wide gray and blue topcoat.

"Forgive me, gentlemen, trains don't wait and we're getting nowhere. A decision must be made, and I'm sincerely sorry and upset at our disagreement, but I must ask for a vote now—"

"A vote. Fifty-one to forty-nine, as usual," said Mr. Bookbinder. "We've had a lot of chances this year to be reminded of the figures."

"I regret you are being blunt and sarcastic, but it's your privilege, I suppose," said Powers, buttoning his coat. "Once again, if you please, I call for a vote."

Herbie and Cliff exchanged puzzled looks as they

squatted against the wooden panel and listened. They knew that big events were in motion, but the issues were beyond them.

"Gentlemen, I say this way." (Krieger again.) "Hard feeling nothing worth. How good? Look future. Everybody young. Unanimous all better. Changing times, a million businesses, could be not so bad. Maybe with Interborough bigger, better? I say this way. All good friends, above board, one, two, three, shake hands. Thirty years in the ice business, everybody knows honest man. If do it, do it—"

"Thanks, Krieger, for wanting to give our place away unanimously," broke in Bookbinder. "You, young Mr. Powers, be so kind as to sit down."

"I'm sorry, Mr. Bookbinder, but my train—"

"You're going to miss the train."

At a new desperate note in his father's voice, Herbie felt a peculiar thrill. He saw the beleaguered ice man walk to the heavy safe built into the wall of the office, and pause with his hand on the combination dial.

"The Bible says that for everything there is a time," he said to Powers. "This is the time for both of you to learn something." The two men stared at him as he spun the dial.

"You will be interested to know, Mr. Powers, the combination is my son Herbie's birthday, 1-14-17. I gave him that little honor because with his small hands he smeared the plaster for the cornerstone of this place when he was three years old."

Herbie wanted to whisper to Cliff, "Sure, I remember that," but he couldn't take his eyes off his father. Mr. Bookbinder swung open the safe door, slid from the back of a narrow shelf a green metal box marked "J.B." in rough letters of white paint, and began to unlock it. "Sit down, Krieger, and you, too, kindly, Mr. Powers," he repeated grimly. He set the open box on the desk before him, and faced the two men with a cornered air.

If Jacob Bookbinder had been hanging by his fingers to the edge of a cliff, or if he had been trapped in a pit with a cobra slithering toward him, his son would have recognized the state of things at once, and might have plunged to the rescue with a hurrah. He would even have recognized so abstract a catastrophe as the loss of a map to a gold mine. But his movie education went no further, and so he was unable to appreciate this scene. The disasters of parents usually happen inside a maze of arithmetic, hidden from the eyes of boys who are still struggling with improper fractions. The fact is, though, that Herbie's father was in peril.

Of one important fact Herbie was ignorant: namely, that his father and Mr. Krieger did not own the Place. They had started to build it with so little money that halfway through they had been forced to stop, and no bank had been willing to lend them funds to finish the construction. Faced with ruin, Bookbinder contrived an escape by selling a mortgage and fifty-one per cent of the stock of the Place to a rich, wise old Irishman named Powers, who had sold them the land on which the Place was being built, and saw in Bookbinder a man who would not fail to deliver dividends. With this help the ice company came to life again. The building was finished, the Place flourished, and Bookbinder did not greatly regret the cruel price he had paid—loss of ownership—because Powers was a kindly, silent master, content with the interest he reaped each year.

Seven years later, he died. His control of the Bronx River Ice Company passed, with the rest of his large property, to his son Robert, who soon showed himself a different kind of mortgagee. To be brief, Bob Powers was a gambler and a drinker. Sizable inheritances do often go to such young men; the effect is generally the same as placing a snowball for safekeeping on a hot stove. Some say that this is a good thing for society, as it brings about the redistribution of wealth without socialism. In any case, it was not a good thing for the ice company. When young Mr. Powers got into difficulties, he began hounding Jacob Bookbinder for more dividends and higher interest. He hoped for the day when he could find a buyer for the Place and convert his holding into a large lump of cash.

Now, there was a tremendous secret, known only to Mr. and Mrs. Bookbinder.

The mortgagee, a month before his death, had called Jacob Bookbinder to his bedside in a beautiful Catholic hospital overlooking Van Cortlandt Park. There the dying man and Herbie's father had talked heart to heart, and Jacob Bookbinder's eyes had filled with tears as the old rich man praised his faithful toil and honesty.

"You should really be the owner of the Place, Jake," he said at last, his gray face, sunk among white pillows, lit by a weak smile. "Even if you aren't, the best thing I can do to protect my son from himself is to make sure you are in control.—I wish you better luck with your boy than I had with mine, Jake." He took out of a folder on his bed a sheet of light blue paper, scribbled on it with a pencil, and gave it to Herbie's father. The puzzled ice man read the few lines written on the paper; then he walked to the window, stared out at the park that glowed with autumn colors, and began to sob. The paper contained these words:

For one dollar and other valuable consideration I hereby sell to Jacob Bookbinder two percent of the total voting stock of the Bronx River Ice Company. My purpose is to restore control of the company to Mr. Bookbinder and his partner.

It was shakily signed, "Robert Powers."

"Come, Jake," said the invalid feebly from the bed. "Pay me." He drew a thin hand out from between the sheets and extended it to Bookbinder. "You owe me a dollar."

So it was that Jacob Bookbinder came into possession of the memorandum, which Herbie and Felicia had heard their parents refer to once or twice, guardedly, as the "blue paper." And it was this memorandum which Herbie's father now drew out of the tin box and silently placed in the hand of the son of the dead man who had once written it.

Robert Powers glanced quickly at the paper, and exploded with, "Good God! Where and when did you get this?"

"Could look see, please? When through, please, of course, look?" said Krieger, sitting on the edge of his chair and stretching both hands forward. Powers passed the paper to him, and Bookbinder quickly told the story of it.

"Has Louis Glass seen this—this thing?" said Powers.

"Nobody has seen it until this minute," said Bookbinder, "except your father, may he rest in peace, and me."

The paper rustled in Krieger's trembling hand. "Perfect gentleman. Lovely old man. Justice, fair is fair. No more is right. Stand up a court of law? Maybe not regular. Wonderful family. Like father, like son. Honest man. I say this way thousand times, old man Powers do right thing. What afraid? Nothing—"

"May I ask," said Powers, damming Krieger with a wave of a hand, "why none of us have heard of it until now? I question your good faith, Mr. Bookbinder."

"Much obliged," said Bookbinder. "I knew your father when you were in public school, and till the day he passed away he didn't give me such a compliment."

"You don't answer my question."

"I'll be happy to. On the other hand, maybe we can take the vote and you can still catch your train."

"Gentlemen, I say this way, peaceable, all good friends," began Krieger, but Powers cut him off by walking to the door.

"All things considered," he said, "I think the vote had better be postponed, and I propose a meeting a week from today, with Louis Glass present."

The other men assented, and Powers walked out without another word, slamming the street door.

Krieger jumped at his partner and gave him an ungainly hug. "Jake, not for a million dollars. No sale. Why not show me before? Better this way, maybe. Powers first iron, not butter. Nothing doing. I say this way, hundred thousand dollars like dirt. Hooray! Who needs—"

Bookbinder disengaged himself, carefully took the

crumpled blue paper out of Krieger's fist, and, locking it in the tin box, prepared to close the safe.

"Don't shout hooray till Glass sees it. Whether it stands up legally, I don't know. I hated to use it. Either way we start a lot of trouble. I wish we could have let it lie." As he swung the heavy steel door Krieger arrested its motion.

"Jake, I say this way. You do anything. I behind hundred per cent." He dropped his voice and adopted a tone reminding Herbie of Mr. Gauss in the parlor. "Little short cash. Two hundred. Insurance, auto loan, Bessie sick, it happens. Take petty cash, deduct salary. Up to you. Positive last time—"

"Krieger, you're on the books for a thousand, two hundred now," protested Bookbinder. But when he saw Krieger take a deep breath and begin, "I say this way—" he said, "Never mind, never mind," and pulled another tin box out of the safe.

The boys watched with large eyes while Herbie's father counted out of the box and into Krieger's hand the immense treasure of two hundred dollars in cash. Bookbinder then locked the safe and the men began talking about machinery repairs in technical jargon that bewildered the lads. Herbie beckoned to Cliff, and the cousins tiptoed back to the window and climbed out of the Place into the sunshine.

The world looked yellow and green by the river, and the air was sweet and warm outside the gloomy tomb of business. "Come on, we'll go hunt for stuff in the dumps," said Herbie, and the boys set off to explore the rubbish heaps near the Place. "You know what, Cliff?"

"Yes, what?" said Cliff, in the idiom meaning "No, what?"

"Any time we wanted to, we could climb in the Place and get money out of that safe. All we want. We've got the combination."

"You wouldn't *do* it, would you?" said Cliff, stopping and straining his eyes at his cousin unbelievingly.

" 'Course not, fool, come on," said Herbie. "I'm only

saying that's a dangerous way to make a combination. Unless you have honest kids."

"How much could we get?" queried Cliff. "A thousand dollars?"

"A thousand?" said Herbie scornfully. "Fifty thousand! A hundred thousand, more likely. We could be rich like Monte Cristo—if we weren't honest."

The boys walked on in silence, each busy with his own picture of himself as Monte Cristo. In Cliff's mind the fabulous count was a young nobleman with an infinitely large array of new bicycles, ice skates, hockey sticks, footballs, and the like. Herbie saw him, on the other hand, as a stoutish grandee living on a constant diet of chocolate sundaes and frankfurters and possessed of a fawning female slave who much resembled Lucille Glass.

6

The Party

HERBIE STOOD BEFORE a mirror in his room the following Sunday, preening and preening and preening himself for a visit to Lucille Glass's home.

He had been at work on himself for an hour. It was not in the matter of washing that his new zeal had broken forth. No, Mrs. Bookbinder had compelled him to take off his tie after he had retied it ten times, and had gone over his neck and ears with a soapy washcloth. After submitting to this indignity, which he regarded as an adult superstition, Herbert went through all the tie trouble again, and then shifted his efforts to his thick curly black hair. He parted it once, twice, a half-dozen times, and each time rejected the result, because of a stray strand that crossed the white line, or because of a tiny jaggedness here or there, or because the part seemed too low or too high. On an ordinary school day, one swipe with a comb was the rule. Two made him feel noble. Three meant that he was in trouble with his teacher and was making a mighty effort to please.

The cause of all this care, an invitation engraved on thick white paper, was propped before him on the dresser:

Mr. and Mrs. Louis Glass
cordially invite you
to their
Housewarming
at 2645 Mosholu Parkway
The Bronx
1 p.m. Sunday, May 15th
R.S.V.P

At the bottom of the sheet these words were added by hand: "There will be a children's party in the playroom, and Lucille cordially invites Felicia and Herbie to attend."

This first visit to an actual Private House, a structure raised by man for only one family to inhabit, would in itself have been a marvel. But happening in this way, it was dwarfed by a vaster event. He was going to spend a whole real-life afternoon with his underground queen.

Herbie reigned each night before falling asleep in a splendid imaginary palace which he had discovered one night by falling through a trapdoor (in imagination) in the floor of the old "haunted house" on Tennyson Avenue—a device borrowed from *Alice in Wonderland* without acknowledgment. The girls with whom he was smitten succeeded one another as queen of his subterranean pleasure dome. Diana Vernon had been dethroned. Lucille's coronation, a spectacle of incredible magnificence, had already taken place, and she now held court nightly beside him.

But it was not only in such fantasies that he had seen her. There had been several meetings on the third-floor landing of the girls' staircase at P.S. 50 since the first one. In the entire maze of the school, that landing was the one space Captain Bookbinder never failed to inspect daily at lunch time, and of all possible posts along six flights of the girls' staircase, it was the one area that Policewoman Glass deemed most likely to be the scene of an outbreak of crime. These two guardians of the law therefore managed to greet each other daily. The conversations were brief and weak. Herbie was rendered speechless by romance—an unlucky foible, since nothing else had the same effect on him except acute tonsillitis.

The strange part was that he found no difficulty at all in having long, tender talks with Lucille when they sat on their golden double throne under the haunted house, eating chocolate frappés on silver salvers and carelessly viewing the gorgeous pageants staged in the great hall for their amusement (the pageants, except for the quantity of gold, diamonds, rubies, and silk in the costumes, were very much like the vaudeville shows at Loew's Boulevard). He not only managed brilliant chatter for himself but also invented the queen's affectionate answers. Something about the light of day, the matter-of-fact iron and concrete of the staircase, and the girl's appearance in street clothes instead of a robe of state, dried up his eloquence.

As he combed and recombed his hair, he pictured himself strolling with Lucille in the gardens of 2645 Mosholu Parkway, an edifice he had never seen. From the grand sound of the words "Mosholu Parkway," he imagined it to be something like an English castle in the movies. There, under arching old trees, amid the flower beds, deliciously alone, could Herbie and Lucille fail to come at last to the sweet mutual pledges of love?

It suddenly struck Herbert that he would look older if he combed his hair straight back without a part, as

Lennie Krieger did. He tried the experiment. The result appeared so strange to him that he hastily erased it with the comb. He next attempted, for the first time in his life, a part on the right side of his face instead of the left. This was hard to do, because the heavy hair, trained in one direction, sprang back from under the comb and stood up defiantly in the middle of his head. By soaking it with water he succeeded in bending it to his will, and surveyed the outcome with satisfaction. It seemed to give his face a new dignity which added years.

In his mother's bedroom he could hear the silk-stocking controversy raging. Since the hour of the arrival of the invitation, Felicia had been waging a campaign for her first pair of ladies' hosiery. The two-year advantage in age she had over Lucille Glass made her feel that she had been insulted by being asked to "a baby's party," and although she was perishing to go, she felt she could not appear at 2645 Mosholu Parkway without some token of her mature years. With silk stockings on, she reasoned, she could carelessly wander into the playroom and consume all the ice cream, cake, and candy that came to her hand, in the guise of a kindly visitor from the adult world.

Now, this was close logic, but Felicia knew that it was not likely to penetrate the opaque mind of a parent. Her lines of attack on her mother were three:

1. If I can't wear silk stockings, I *won't go* to the old party, and you can't *make* me.
2. Every girl in my class has at least *five* pairs of silk stockings, and even kids a year *below* me have them.
3. Herbie gets *everything* in this house, and I get *nothing*.

Mrs. Bookbinder had doggedly held out, because she resisted by instinct every move of the children toward maturity. She knew that in the end Felicia would go to the party, in rubber rompers if necessary. But with all her edge of experience, insight, and authority, she made a slip that cost her the victory.

Felicia howled, "Why, why, *why* can't I wear silk stockings?"

The mother answered, "Felicia, for the last time, it's too late now to argue. The stores are closed today, and I can't buy the stockings anyway."

Felicia pounced. "I can borrow a pair from Emily."

"They won't fit."

"Oh, won't they?"

The girl flashed open a lower drawer of the dresser, and from under a pile of her blouses pulled out a pair of the sheer hose. Before the astonished parent could protest, she kicked off her slippers and pulled the stockings on, saying rapidly, "I borrowed them Friday, just in case. I wasn't going to wear them without your permission. But do they fit or don't they? Look. Look!" She jumped up and pirouetted. They fitted.

"Well, anyway, Papa won't stand for it," said the trapped mother.

"I'll go ask him. Whatever he says goes. All right?" The girl was at the door of the bedroom, on her way to the parlor, where her father was poring over *Refrigerating Engineering*.

To have her veto overridden was a worse defeat for the mother than plain surrender, and she knew it. Dialogues between the children and the father always went so:

CHILD: Pa, can I do so-and-so?
FATHER: I'm busy. Ask your mother.
CHILD: She says it's up to you.
FATHER: Oh. (*Brief glance at the child, standing by him humbly with a winning smile.*) I guess so, yes.
CHILD: (*Top of lungs*) Ma! Pa says it's all right.

He had thus given consent even to things of which he later disapproved, growling, when the mother cited his permission, "Well, why do you send them to me?"

So Mrs. Bookbinder said, "Never mind. You can wear

them, just this once, and you'll return them in the morning."

The girl hugged her mother, agreeing with joyous hypocrisy. Her foot was inside the door of grownup life at last, and she knew she would not be driven out again by fire or bayonet. Nor was she. From that day forward she wore silk stockings.

Half past twelve, and the family assembled in the parlor for a final review before leaving.

"Herbert, there's something funny about the way you look." The mother examined him up and down, and her eyes finally came to rest on his hair. "What is it?"

The boy quickly put his cake-eater hat on. "Nothing, Mom. I'm just dressed up."

"Take your hat off in the house."

The boy reluctantly obeyed.

"Papa, can you tell what it is?"

The father inspected him. "He looks older, somehow. What's the difference? Let's go."

At the word "older," Herbert felt all warm inside, as though he had drunk wine.

"Ma, I see what it is," cried Felicia, and giggled. "He's parted his hair on the wrong side. Isn't that silly?"

"All right for you, Silk Stockings," snarled Herbert. In a red flash he considered informing his mother that Felicia had bought, not borrowed, the hose, with nickels and dimes fished out of her pig bank with a breadknife, but talebearing revolted him. "What's the difference which side I part it on, anyway?" he appealed to his parents.

"As long as it makes no difference, go back and comb it the right way," said the mother.

Mrs. Bookbinder was fertile in these argumentative dead ends. Herbert slunk off muttering, and combed away precious years of ripeness, but not before he had postured before the mirror for a couple of minutes, boiling at the injustice that forced him to mar the handsome world-weary effect he had stumbled on.

As soon as the secondhand Chevrolet that was the official car of the Bronx River Ice Company brought the family to 2645 Mosholu Parkway, Herbie began revising his plans of gallantry. The kiss in the garden was definitely not practical. The Glass castle was a two-story red brick house, flanked on either side by similar castles, with only narrow cement driveways separating them. The garden consisted of two squares of grass on either side of the entrance, each about as large as the carpet in the Bookbinder parlor. The little hedges surrounding these compressed meadows would not have provided enough privacy for a pair of romantically inclined cats.

"What a dump!" said Felicia, with ladylike tugs through her skirt at the tops of her stockings, which were tending to slide down her bony legs.

"Don't you dare say anything like that! It isn't polite," cried Mrs. Bookbinder. "And don't you dare fool with those stockings when anybody is looking."

Herbie, whose disappointment quickly melted in the anticipation of seeing Lucille, could hardly breathe as he ran up the white plaster steps and rang the bell. He managed to say thickly to Felicia, "Bet it's a rotten party."

"Oh, sure," sneered the sister, "you don't want to see that red-headed infant. Not much. I hope they have a team of horses to pull you through the door."

So when Lucille opened the door Herbie's face was red, but not nearly as red as the girl's instantly became under his intense, devouring look of admiration. And Felicia's face was reddest of all when, as the children entered the house, Herbie glanced back into Felicia's eyes, then at her legs, and burst out laughing.

Lucille Glass, eleven years old, her parents' spoiled darling, was also wearing silk stockings.

The children's party was at its full fury when the Bookbinders came. The basement of the Glass home, gaily decorated and finished as a game room, echoed with squeals, shouts, laughter, complaints, and clatter. Large piles of delicatessen sandwiches were vanishing under the onslaught of fifteen or twenty hungry children, and two temporary maids and a harrassed aunt of Lucille were trying to serve ice cream and cake on paper plates amid a tangle of clutching hands and glittering eyes. The parents were feeding upstairs in the placid manner of well-broken-in human beings, while their young cavorted below like pygmies around a kill. Fortunately, there was much too much ice cream for everyone, and it was not long before the clamor began to subside, the hands to cease clutching, and the glitter to fade slowly into a glaze.

Herbie emerged from the basement washroom in a happy fog, water seeping down the sides of his face from his hair, which he had plastered back again with the wrong side parted. He was in Lucille Glass's home. He had shaken her hand. He had sat beside her on a sofa for ten minutes, eating corned-beef sandwiches and no more aware of the taste than if he had been chewing straw. The girl, in her blue and white party dress, with a white bow in her hair, seemed not of this world, but a changeling fallen from a star. Time had slowed down as in dreams. He had been at the party sixty minutes but it was like a week of ordinary living. There stretched ahead the rich years and years before five o'clock, when he would have to go home.

Lucille emerged from the knot of children at the table and came to him with two plates of chocolate ice cream in her hands. "You almost missed this," she said. "Want some?"

He took the plate gratefully and was digging the paper spoon into the sweet brown mound when she laid her hand for a moment shyly on his arm. "Don't eat it here," she said. "Come where it's quiet." She slipped away, threading through the crowded basement, and he followed, wondering. They passed Felicia and Lennie near the table wolfing huge chunks of a white cake, and Herbie tried to avoid them, but the sharp-eyed sister called out, "When's the wedding, Herbie?" and Lennie graciously added, "Hooray for the sheik in short pants." (His own trousers were long.) Herbie said nothing, and hurried out through the little door at the back where Lucille had disappeared.

To his astonishment he was in a gloomy garage. Lucille climbed into the back seat of her father's new Chrysler and beckoned him to follow. Herbie had never been in any kind of automobile but a Chevrolet, and as he sat down on the soft gray upholstery he became dizzy with pleasure. Ice cream, cool dimness, solitude, a Chrysler, and Lucille! The world of fact was uncovering its treasures, and all his daydreams seemed tawdry. The underground palace crumbled in his mind.

The children ate their ice cream slowly.

"What are you going to be when you grow up?" said Lucille at last, putting her well-cleaned paper plate and spoon on the floor.

"An astronomer," said Herbie.

"You mean look at the stars through a telescope?"

"That's right. I can pick out first-magnitude stars right now. I'll show them to you some night."

"What are their names?"

"Well, there's lots. Orion, Sirius, Betelgeuse, Andromeda, Gemini . . ." He paused. Herbie did much reading about stars, but very little looking at them. The figures of their sizes and distances fascinated him, but they all looked pretty nearly alike in the sky, and anyway, they were none too visible beyond the street lights of Homer Avenue. He was not sure of the difference between a star and a constellation and was fairly confident that his listener wasn't either, so he reeled off any names out of the jumble he remembered. It worked.

"Gee, those names are beautiful."

"I know lots more."

"Can you make money that way?" asked the girl. "Just looking at stars?"

"Sure. Plenty."

"Enough to get married and have a family?"

"Easy."

The girl pondered for a moment, then said doubtfully, "How?"

Herbie hadn't the least idea. But he was not the first male to be challenged by a woman's common sense, nor the first to override it. "By discovering new stars, of course," he said promptly.

"Then what happens?" inquired the girl.

"Why, you win a prize," said Herbie.

"How much?"

"I forget. A million dollars—maybe ten million. Something like that."

"For *one* star?"

"I'll show it to you in the encyclopedia if you don't believe me," said Herbie. "What can a guy do that's more important than finding a new star?"

Lucille was convinced, and silenced. There was a pause.

"This is a swell car," said Herbie. The remark fell into the silence like a stone into a pond and vanished, leaving ripples of self-consciousness in the air. The boy and girl happened to look into each other's eyes. Both blushed.

"Are you—are you going to get married?" said Lucille.

"Not till I'm old," said Herbie.

"How old?"

"Real old."

"How old is that?"

"I don't know."

"Twenty-five?"

"Older than that."

"Thirty?"

"Fifty-five, more likely," said Herbie. The tendency to go higher was irresistible. Lucille seemed properly awed at being in the presence of a man who was not going to marry until he was fifty-five. She was still for a moment, then said, "Have you got a girl?"

"No," said Herbie. "Have you got a fellow?"

"No. What kind of girl are you going to marry?"

"I don't know," said Herbie. Then, with a burst of audacious gallantry, "But she's gonna have to have red hair!"

There, it was done. The ardent look which went with these words made them a plain declaration of love. Lucille rewarded him by timidly putting her little hand into his and returning his look with tenderness. What were golden thrones or underground palaces now, compared to the rosy glory of this moment? Here in an attached garage was a corner of heaven, upholstered in gray. Herbert had not known there was room for such swelling bliss in his heart.

But the tenderness was fading from Lucille's glance. She was no longer gazing into his eyes, but above them.

"Gosh! Lookit your hair," she said.

Herbert put his hand to his head and felt his hair, still damp, standing away from his scalp, straight up. Ten minutes of drying and it was full of fight again, thrusting back toward its old place. Herbie pressed it down. It sprang back erect, like good turf. Twice he did this, and an awful thing happened. Lucille Glass giggled.

"That's funny, the way it jumps up," she said.

"Aw, it's nothing. I can fix it," stammered Herbie, and began thrusting the locks downward, palm over palm. Drops of water ran down his forehead from under his fingers. In effect he was pressing his hair dry. When he stopped at last and took his hands away, the hair rose, and stood straight out in all directions. He looked some-what like a boy being electrocuted. Lucille fell back in the seat, exploding with laughter, her hands over her mouth. Herbie wiped his oozing palms on his breeches, and mut-tering, "Dunno what's wrong with this crazy old mop," he began to comb his hair furiously with his fingers. This frantic clawing at his head looked extremely strange.

An unwelcome voice spoke through the car window: "What's the matter, Fatso? Got cooties?"

Lennie Krieger and Felicia were grinning through the glass.

"My clever brother," said Felicia. "Combs his hair on the wrong side 'cause he thinks it makes him look older. How you doing, Grandpa?"

Herbie's cheeks were on fire. He turned with a feeble smile to Lucille, but he saw only her back as she clam-bered out of the car. "Auntie must be screaming for me," she said and was gone.

Back before a mirror in the bathroom once more, Her-bie fumed and agonized as he put his treacherous hair to rights. He blamed Felicia for the blasted afternoon, blamed Lennie, blamed his mother, blamed everyone and everything except himself. He murmured aloud, "I'll show 'em! I'll get even! Try to make a fool out of *me*, will they?" and lashed himself into such a state of indignation at a plotting world that he soon felt much better.

Not for long, though. When he stepped out into the party room, he was surprised and sickened. In the middle of a circle of children, Lennie Krieger was dancing with Lucille to music from a radio. The little girl's movements were stiff, and her face intently serious, as she followed the adept boy's steps. Herbie joined the circle and heard the low comments—envious and jeering from the boys, admiring from the girls—and tasted the gall of jealousy. He tried to catch Lucille's eye. Once she looked at him with unseeing gravity as though he were a piece of furniture, and spun away. Felicia came to his side and said, "Hello, sheik," but the heart was not in her spite, for she was suffering, too. Lennie was her admirer, and snubbing him was the food of her feminine nature, but for once he had snubbed her when the music started, to ask the "baby" to dance.

A game of pin-the-tail-on-the-donkey was next played. Herbie, blindfolded, fell over a chair on his face, and caused roars of merriment. When Lennie's turn came he worked loose the bandage on his eyes, pretended to grope to the donkey, and pinned the tail squarely where it belonged, to great applause. Herbie detected the cheat, but felt powerless to do anything about it. They played a number of kissing games under the watchful eye of the aunt. Somehow it happened that Lennie kissed Lucille three times and she kissed him twice. Herbie only had once chance to do any kissing, and then it fell to his lot to kiss Felicia. It was a thoroughly ghastly afternoon. And when, at a quarter to five, Herbie managed to corner the red-headed girl, and whispered, "Come on back out in the garage a minute," she froze him with, "I can't. I promised to show Lennie my camp pictures," and dashed away.

From the demeanor of the four members of the Bookbinder family when they rode home, 2645 Mosholu Parkway might have been the address of Woodlawn Cemetery. Jacob Bookbinder broke the bleak silence once to say, "If you ask me, Louis Glass is being paid by Powers to say the blue paper is no good—" but his wife said, "Please. Even in front of the children do we need to discuss it?" No further sound was heard, except the rattling song of the Chevrolet, until it drew to a stop on Homer Avenue.

As she opened the door, Mrs. Bookbinder said to the children in the back seat, "Why so quiet? Did you enjoy the party?"

"Party!" sniffed Felicia. "Please, Mom, don't drag me to any more nurseries."

Herbie said nothing. He was already out of the car, on his way to the highest rock in the vacant lot, where he often sought solitude. There in the sunset he undertook some emergency repair work. For an hour he tried to rebuild the ruins of the underground palace, but it was wrecked forever. Nothing was left but its queen, and she no longer wore crown and robe, but a white bow and a party frock. And he could not even compel her to sit by his side. Her faithless Majesty went on and on dancing with Lennie.

7

The Romance of Art and Natural History

"MA, CAN I go to the museum with Cliff today?"

It was Saturday morning. Herbie and Felicia were eating breakfast at the luxuriously late hour of eight-thirty in the Bookbinder kitchen. The narrow white room was bright with a shaft of sunlight that illuminated it for about forty minutes each morning, when the sun appeared in a cleft between two apartment houses across the street. It shone not into the kitchen but upon the windows of the

Feigelson living room across the court, which cordially bounced the glittering beam over to the Bookbinders.

"I suppose so," said the mother, busy with onions at the sink. "What's at the museum?"

"Aw, you know, it's just a museum. Mrs. Gorkin said we should all go."

"Where is it?"

"Downtown in Central Park."

"How much is it?"

"It's free, Mom."

"You can go."

"How come," said Felicia, spooning lumps out of her oatmeal with a wry face, "that you're not going to the movies today?"

"A museum is more important than an old movie," said Herbie haughtily.

"More important than episode fourteen of *The Green Archer?*"

How was it, wondered Herbie, that his sister had such skill in prodding his weak points? His heart yearned to know what had happened when the Archer's mask had been shot off by a bullet from the hero's gun. By the worst luck Archer had had his back to the camera when his face was bared, and the episode ended. Who would he turn out to be? After following the serial through snow, rain, bankruptcy (solved by mortgaging his skates), and illness (he had seen episode eight with a temperature of 103½), he found it hard not to be in at the kill. But greater matters were afoot.

"Aw, the heck with that old serial," said Herbie. "What's the sense of payin' money 'n' sittin' through a rotten movie every week, just to see an episode that lasts five minutes?"

Mrs. Bookbinder jumped with surprise and dropped an onion. She had been using this line of reasoning on Herbert for three years with no effect. To hear it now from his mouth gave her as joyful a thrill as a missionary might feel over his first converted cannibal. She stopped peeling onions long enough to pat her son's head and say, "You're growing up, Herbie. Bless you."

Herbie basked in the approval, and tried to look like a profound man of affairs.

"Which museum are you going to?" pursued Felicia. She sensed intrigue strong in the air.

"Which one do you think?" parried Herbie.

"There are two, you know," said his sister.

"Well, whaddya know! Two museums! Imagine that! Guess you hafta be in 8B to know that," said Herbie, and, drinking his milk, he rose and walked out of the kitchen.

He put a rubber ball in his pocket and sauntered forth to kill the morning. Saturday morning was the laziest, therefore the best, time of the week. The release from school was fresh and sweet, and the boredom of aimlessness had not yet set in. Boys from more religious families went to Sabbath services at the synagogues, where cake, candy, and cream soda rewarded their devotion after the last hymn was sung. But Herbie had tried worship and found the sugar coating too thin for the struggle with Hebrew. He knew that on his thirteenth birthday he would have to chant a chapter from the prophets before the congregation, and he rather looked forward to the brief chance at being the center of all eyes, but thirteen, to a boy of eleven, seems like seventy to a man of thirty-five. Meantime, since the weekly visit of old Mr. Taussig, the Hebrew teacher, for one hour's wrestle with the strange backward-printed language satisfied his parents, it more than satisfied Herbie.

Bouncing the ball with relish as he walked into the street—it was a new red solid-sponge rubber ball, not one of your pumped-up gray shells that go all flabby when they have a pinhole—Herbie spied Harold Sorensen, and smiled. Harold was a blond boy with white eyebrows, even fatter than Herbie, dogged and bad-tempered. He was not quite a match for Herbie at the constricted little sidewalk games that have evolved in the Bronx; a perfect opponent, in short. Harold promptly took up a challenge to a duel at boxball, and was beaten. Next they played double boxball, each boy guarding two squares in the pavement as they slapped the ball back and forth, and

Harold lost again. Then they played "points," tossing the ball against the line of plaster molding along the ground floor of the apartment house. Herbie won. Next they clashed in something they called baseball, using the same molding. The number of times the ball bounced in the gutter before being caught was hedged with a scoring system that produced the illusion of a game played by eighteen men in a ball park. Herbie won this, too. An encounter at handball followed, and another at Chinese handball; the blond boy sweated out both victories. But Herbie came back to conquer him at hit-the-coin and dodgeball. They tried punchball, but that really required at least two men on a side, and they abandoned it. They cooled off with a game of pickups, which Herbie also won easily, and were in the midst of stickball when the noon whistle of the nearby power plant blew. Thereupon they reluctantly parted and went home to lunch, regretting that they had lacked time to play at least two or three more games, such as stoopball, slugball, and salujee.

These were just a few of the games that city boys have created out of two elements: a world of hard, flat surfaces and a bouncing ball. Herbie knew the rules and tricks of more than twenty games. The effort of memory by which he had acquired these, applied to school work, would have made him the wonder of the New York school system. But that was impossible, of course. Street games were the business of life and required devotion. School work was the penalty for the crime of being a boy.

Back in the Bookbinder kitchen, Herbie bolted his lunch and then said, "Mom, how about carfare for the museum?"

"Can you wait until I finish my tea, or is the museum going to run away?"

"Sorry, Mom."

"Say," said Felicia, "how about me going with you? I haven't been to the museum in a long time."

Herbert was appalled, but kept a cheerful face. "Why, sure, Fleece, come on. If you want to spend the day walkin' around with me and Cliff, that's fine. Mrs. Gorkin says the museum is real educational. You'll have lots of fun."

"That's nice, Felice," said the mother. "I'm glad you want to be with your own brother one day instead of that rotten Emily with her lipstick and rouge. You can take carfare for both—"

"No, no, Mom, wait," said Felicia hurriedly. "I'm going to the movies. I just wanted to see what he'd say." She looked at Herbie, baffled. "You really are going to the museum, aren't you?"

"Yes, and you *will* go with him," said the mother. "What's playing at the movies that's better than the museum?"

"Mom, please," cried Felicia, panicky at finding her foot caught in her own trap. "I promised Emily I'd go with her last week. I can go to those stuffy museums any old time."

"Aw, be a sport, come with me, Fleece," exulted Herbie. "Is a girl friend more important than a brother? Please, Mom, make her go with me."

Felicia rose from the table, declaring that she would *die* rather than be seen anywhere with a slovenly little thing like him who didn't even wash below his chin. Mrs. Bookbinder was diverted to an examination of the boy's neck, and his sister escaped from the room under cover of this thin smoke screen.

All this played into Herbie's hands. Loudly declaring that he would show Fleece who was slovenly, he proceeded to beautify himself. When he left the house with a quarter clutched in a hand reeking honestly of soap, he looked as strangely clean and gentlemanly as he had a week before en route to the Mosholu Parkway disaster, but neither mother nor sister became suspicious.

Cliff was waiting for him under the clock at the Simpson Street subway station. As Herbie walked up the cousin inspected him from head to foot, and slowly, softly whistled.

"There ain't any girl I could like that much," he said.

"Wait till you see her," answered Herbie.

A Lexington Avenue express thumped and shrieked its way into the station, and stopped with a jerk that shook the platform and every other platform along the track for a mile either way. The boys ignored the terrifying shudder under their feet and boarded the train. They had been permitted to travel by themselves on the subway since their ninth year, and were calm about it. The rickety railway, which ran on steel stilts over their heads in the Bronx and dived into a narrow black hole to go to Manhattan, was part of the world, like the stars and the wind. The subway might fall down, and so might the stars, but Herbie and Cliff were not worrying about either possibility.

They walked to the front of the train, rolling with each sway and bump like sailors, and posted themselves at the front windows where they could enjoy the hurtling. Tracks flew under them; apartment houses careened drunkenly by. Intervale, Prospect, Jackson Avenue stations went past; the waited-for lovely moment came, and with the squeals and howls of a lost soul plunging to hell, the express rushed crazily downhill into the darkness. This crashing change from sunlight to night in an instant was one of the most agreeable experiences in the boys' ken. They looked at each other and sighed with pleasure. Herbie glanced back at the people in the car, and saw them staring vacantly, or reading newspapers, or dozing, all oblivious to the poetry of the event.

"Cliff," he said, "whaddya suppose is the matter with them?" He jerked his thumb back over his shoulder. Cliff took his eyes from the window to look at the passengers briefly.

"They're old," he said. And the cousins returned to the enjoyment of the blinking red and green lights, the jeweled brilliance of stations far down the dark tube, the sensation of terrible speed imparted by the close tunnel walls, and all the other subterranean delights that a small boy gets so cheaply in New York.

They climbed out of the subway at Eighty-sixth Street into the sparkle and roar of Manhattan traffic.

"Now the question is," said Herbie, "which museum?"

"Didn't she tell you?"

"No. All she said was her mother was takin' her to the museum Saturday. She don't even know I'm comin'."

"Say, I thought you said you were gonna meet her."

"I am gonna meet her, if it takes all day. Look, if you were Mrs. Glass, would you take your daughter to the Museum of Art or Natural History?"

"Depends on whether I wanted to show her statues or skeletons."

"You're a big help."

"Anyway, how do you know it's one of them two museums?"

"That's all there are."

"A lot you know. There's the Museum of the American Indian. They took our class to it in a bus last week."

"How was it?"

"Awful. Baskets, blankets, and feathers till you wanna throw up."

"Well, I never heard of it and I bet Lucille's mother didn't neither. Anyway, you know Natural History is way better. They got that big whale hangin' from the ceiling an' everything. Ten to one she's there."

"O.K. Let's go."

The boys climbed into a crosstown bus. Cliff paid a dime for the two fares. "I better stick close to you now," he said as they clung to swaying straps, "Mom only gimme fifteen cents today. I'm busted."

"How come? You usually get a quarter on Saturday."

"Mom caught me hitchin' onto a truck yesterday."

Herbie, who was not agile enough to hitch, said, "Serves you right. Thousands of guys get killed hitchin' every day."

"Aw, I never saw one."

"I did. He fell off a truck in front of a trolley car on Westchester Avenue. His head 'n' feet got cut off. His head was rollin' around in the gutter like a ball. You couldn't get me to hitch."

"Must of been some fat slob who didn't know how to hitch."

Herbie became silent, not knowing whether this was a personal thrust, while Cliff, who had said it in innocence, mused pleasantly over the vivid picture of a beheaded and footless fat boy bleeding in a gutter. He wished he had been there. It was his luck to miss all these marvels which Herbie saw and described so well. When the bus stopped at the west side of the park and the boys got off, he suddenly said to Herbie, "Where on Westchester Avenue?"

Herbie, who had completely forgotten his fiction after it fulfilled its use in the argument, said, "Where what?"

"Where did this fat guy get his head cut off? I figure there still oughta be some blood there I can go look at."

"No, the fire department came and hosed the whole street down," said Herbie.

"My tough luck," said Cliff.

The boys walked rapidly to the gloomy red pile of the Natural History museum, and roamed the halls. When they halted before the skeleton of the mastodon, Cliff surveyed the towering fossil and wistfully wished there were a live mastodon in the Zoo; Herbie looked at the strolling crowd through the dry ribs and sought a little figure with red hair. For an hour and a half they quested through corridors of bones, horns, skins, rocks, and stuffed beasts and fish. When they halted at last at a water fountain, Herbie said despondently, "She ain't here."

"Who cares? This is fun," said Cliff. He narrowed the fountain aperture with his thumb, and the water jumped to the ceiling. "We oughta come here every week."

"We mighta known an old lady would want to look at pictures 'stead of a lotta bones," said Herbie. "This is a terrible museum. Let's go across the park to the other one."

"How much money you got?"

"Twenty cents. We better walk if we want ice cream after."

Paintings, statues, tapestries, and mummies there were in plenty in the art museum, and several little live girls

with red hair too for that matter, but Herbie was seeking
the priceless original, and these were imitations. Nature,
like a lazy artist, had turned out one good thing and then
cheated the market with a lot of bad repetitions. The boys
worked their way listlessly to the top floor, pausing to
gawk only at the fat red nudes of Rubens.

"Looks like you ain't gonna find her," said Cliff, as the
boys sat on a marble bench surrounded by the gilded
saints and martyrs of Italian old masters.

"Aw, who cares? We had our fun," said Herbie glumly,
waving his legs to and fro to cool the hot soles of his
feet.

"Too bad you got dressed up for nothing."

"Who dressed up on account of her? I'm just tired of
walkin' around like a bum. You oughta be, too."

Cliff surveyed his scuffed shoes, wrinkled stockings,
sagging breeches, soiled shirt, and limp, threadbare tie,
and said, "This ain't Sunday. If I dressed any different,
I'd look funny."

They raced down the flights of broad stone stairs with
a clatter that brought angry guards to the landings after
they had gone by. Before leaving they detoured through
the Egyptian collection to have one more look at the
partially unwrapped mummy of a princess. As they
passed the great sandstone statues of the Pharaohs, Herbie's heart banged hard against his ribs, for there she was.
This time it was she, no mistake, her hand in her mother's, peering into a glass case full of scarabs. He squeezed
Cliff's arm once and walked straight toward them, scarlet
faced and wondering what to do with his hands. He thrust
them into his breeches at the last and said with unnatural
loudness, "Hello, Mrs. Glass. Hi, Lucille." His reward
came instantly in a blush and a look of pleasure on the
girl's face.

"Why, hello, Herbie," said Mrs. Glass. "It's nice to see
you interested in culture. Is your mother with you?"

"Naw, I go everywhere by myself," said Herbie. "This
here is my cousin, Cliff."

"Very nice," said Mrs. Glass. "Most boys would rather

go to the movies than to the museum. Come, walk along with us."

Herbie found himself on the other side of Mrs. Glass, who luckily was a very thin woman, so that it was easy for him to exchange several ardent peeks with Lucille as they strolled among the cases. The chances of prying her away from her mother for a little whispering seemed remote. Mrs. Glass kept explaining the objects they passed, and made them seem amazingly uninteresting.

"Now, children," she said, "here is one of the wonders of the city. A whole Egyptian tomb dug out of Egypt and set up here just as it looked when the explorers first found it. We can all go inside—"

"Gosh, you know all about this stuff, don't you, Mrs. Glass?" said Cliff.

"Not quite all," Mrs. Glass smiled. "I did teach fine arts in high school, many, many years ago."

"Mrs. Glass, I sure would appreciate," said Cliff, "if you would explain a picture I saw on the fourth floor. It's all full of angels, and devils, and naked ladies, and I think maybe God, but I couldn't make head nor tail of it."

Flattered, the mother said, "It's a pleasure to see a boy take such interest. Come, let's all go up there—"

"Oh, Mother, I want to see this tomb, and anyway I'm tired," spoke up Lucille, for the first time since Herbert's arrival.

"Well—suppose you stay with Lucille, Herbie, and visit the tomb while I go upstairs with Cliff. Do you mind?"

"No, ma'am," said Herbie. Behind Mrs. Glass's back Cliff threw his cousin a colossal wink, and walked off.

Hand in hand, Lucille Glass and Herbie Bookbinder walked into the tomb of Pharaoh. A narrow passage meandered between stone walls more than a foot thick, decorated with processions of people with strangely twisted shoulders, the colors of their costumes faint but still visible after several thousand years of slow fading in darkness.

"How did you happen to find me?" whispered Lucille, partly in awe of the surroundings, partly because what she said seemed to call for whispering.

"I looked," said Herbie.

"You didn't even know which museum," Lucille said archly.

"I been at Natural History already. Just like you not to tell me. If it was Lennie Krieger, I bet you'd have told him."

"I don't like Lennie," said Lucille.

"No, but at the party you wouldn't look at anyone else. An' you hardly spoke to me at school, the one time I found you on the landing. Luckily I got you to mention the museum."

"I'm glad I did, now."

"Lennie's goin' to Camp Manitou, too. He told me."

"I know."

"Lucille," said Herbie desperately, "at camp will you be *my* girl?"

She considered the question gravely under lowered lashes, then looked frankly at him. "Yes, Herbie," she said. "I like you."

Herbie knew joy once more. The ground lost by the hair episode was recovered, and he had even made an important advance. The Green Archer had been well sacrificed.

Fingers interlaced, the children leaned against the cool glass covering the stones in the last crypt of the tomb, and swung their hands idly back and forth in pleasant silent intimacy. They found the tomb a romantic, wonderful place, not because it was artistic but because it was private. A big packing case would have done as well. Had the Egyptian artist who painted the walls known that he was decorating a love retreat for two Hebrew children who would ignore his decorations four thousand years later, he might not have worked so hard and so successfully to make his colors permanent.

They heard Cliff's voice, loud enough to reverberate, "I bet they're back in here, Mrs. Glass," and quickly disengaged their hands. The mother came upon them studying a line of hieroglyphics intently. Herbie said, "I wonder if anybody can read these, anyway. Your mother would know. Oh, hello, Mrs. Glass. Hi, Cliff." He repeated the

question to the mother, who explained all about hieroglyphics as they emerged into the sunny main hall.

"Now," said Mrs. Glass, "what do we all say to some
ice-cream cones?"

A gleeful chorus answered. As they walked out of the
museum, Herbie said, "Did you figure out that picture for
Cliff, ma'am?"

"Strangely enough, we couldn't find it," said Mrs.
Glass.

"They musta moved it," said Cliff.

"I remember a coupla guards comin' in the room with
stepladders when we went out," Herbie assisted.

"Strange, they don't usually change the exhibits Saturday afternoon," said the mother. "However, I did point
out a few examples of what I imagine was the same type
of baroque. Cliff asked very intelligent questions."

An ice-cream vender stood in the center of a little plaza
in the park. Mrs. Glass ordered three strawberry-flavored
cones. Lucille said, "Come on, Mother, you have one,
too," whereupon the lady laughed and asked for chocolate, "just this once." Lucille ate off her ice cream in a
few bites and threw the cone of cake away, while the boys
licked the cream, forcing it down into the cone, so that
they nibbled cake and ate ice cream until all vanished in
a last mouthful. Mrs. Glass offered a ten-dollar bill to the
vender, who indignantly refused to make change.

"This is awkward," said the mother. "I have no smaller
change with me, and I don't see—"

"*I'll* pay, Mrs. Glass," said Herbie grandly. He held out
two dimes to the vender.

"Now, Herbie, really, I can't let you treat us," said
Mrs. Glass.

"I got lots more. Don't worry, ma'am," said Herbie,
feeling six feet tall.

"Your mother is very good to you."

"Yes, ma'am."

They walked toward the subway. Cliff pulled Herbie
behind a few paces and hissed, "Are you nuts? We're
broke now."

"She'll pay our fares home, don't worry," whispered Herbie.

But he had miscalculated. At the corner of Lexington Avenue and Seventy-seventh Street Mrs. Glass turned to the boys and said affably, "Sorry we can't take you downtown with us. Good-by." She vanished into the subway entrance with her daughter before the astounded boys could say a word.

The cousins were stranded, ten miles from home.

"Of all the dumb stunts," said Cliff. "Now what do we do?"

"Aw, how should I know she'd go downtown? They live uptown," said Herbie feebly. The intoxication of playing host to an adult before the eyes of his girl faded into the headache of being penniless.

"How far is it home?" said Cliff.

"I dunno. A hundred miles, I figure."

"More, I bet. We'll never walk it."

The subway was a magic carpet. Its stations were oases in a desert of immeasurable distances. With a handful of nickels the boys could go anywhere in the city, unerringly; without the little metal disks that made them lords of the magic, they were helpless. They did not even know in which direction to turn their steps.

"Aw, we'll meet somebody, or something," said Herbie.

But they did not meet anybody, or anything. An hour and a half passed by in pointless wandering up and down Lexington Avenue. The sun went down; the street lamps flared all at once in every direction; a cool wind blew. Herbie and his cousin, exhausted and hungry, leaned against the window of a cafeteria and looked in at the steam tables piled high with hot food.

"I could eat a horse," said Cliff.

"I could eat an elephant," said Herbie.

"I could eat two elephants."

"I could eat a sandwich—an elephant between two mastodons," said Herbie, but the exaggeration game gave neither boy pleasure this time, and they abandoned it.

After a pause Herbie said, "Cliff, I'm sorry I pulled such a stupid trick."

"Aw, heck, Herbie, that's O.K. Only I bet our mothers are gonna start worryin'."

Steeling himself, Herbie walked up to a stout, red-faced man who was striding by, and said, "Mister, my cousin 'n' I ain't got carfare. Could you lend me ten cents and gimme your address—"

"Get away from me, you little beggar," said the man, without seeming to look at Herbie, and hurried on. The fat boy dropped to the curb in his clean new suit and sat, his cake-eater hat pushed back on his head, a picture of dejection. Cliff squatted beside him.

"Cliff, we gotta get home. Let's give ourselves up to a cop."

"Listen, Herb, I don't wanna have nothin' to do with no cops."

"Aw, maybe he'll just give us a dime."

"No, sir. No cops. Not me."

Cliff's misfortune was that his mother had, since his earliest childhood, threatened to call a policeman to come and fetch him away whenever the boy was mischievous, or refused to eat. As a result, cops stood for devils in the boy's mythology.

"Well, that's my idea," persisted Herbie. "Now you say something better."

"Come on down in the subway," said Cliff.

They tripped down the stairs into the hole in the ground, and a few moments later stood by the turnstiles. People hurried past, in and out, with the crashing metallic *brope!* that is the song of New York as the murmur of trees in the wind is the music of a forest. The boys loitered there for a while, as far from the change booth as they could get, obscured from the eye of the station master by the crowd. Each knew what was in the other's mind. Neither would speak first. *Brope!* A little gray-haired man dropped his nickel and pushed through the turnstile. *Brope! Brope! Brope!* Three laughing girls followed each other out. A train rattled into the station, disgorged a crowd through its many doors, sucked in another crowd, and went squealing away—homeward bound, without the boys. They were still barred from home, marooned, exiled, for the want of two small disks. The absurdity and injustice of it smote Herbie.

"Just 'cause we ain't got a couple of lousy nickels, why can't we go home?" he demanded. "We got a right to go home."

"Well, if everybody got on free how could they run the old subway?" countered Cliff.

"Well, all I know is they oughta run it so everybody could get home whether they had a lousy nickel or not," said Herbie. He was laying a foundation of moral theory for the next suggestion, which came after a short silence.

"If you ask me, we oughta duck under them turnstiles. We got a *right* to," he said with a great show of indignation.

"I guess we better, if we wanna get home," said Cliff.

"Don't you think we got a right?"

"No, but who cares? We gotta get home."

But Herbie was one of those people who will not act unless the whole moral order of the universe is on their side—according to their own view, at least.

"*Why* ain't we got as much right as anybody else to ride the subway?"

" 'Cause it costs a nickel, an' we ain't got no nickel," said Cliff patiently.

"I just explained to you—"

"Listen, Herb, what's the sense of arguin'? I'm game to sneak under the turnstile if you are."

"It *ain't* sneakin'."

"O.K., it ain't. Just don't do it while the guy is watchin', that's all."

"Tell you what," said Herbie. "After we get home we mail a nickel apiece to the subway company. How's that?"

"Sure, sure. Let's get under the turnstile first."

"Cinch," said Herbie, and darted under the bar, followed by his cousin. The fat boy would have done well, however, to examine facts as closely as theory. "The guy" had a clear view of the boys as they took the plunge. A moment later he was thundering down on them. He was a tall, fat colored man with a badge.

"Whah you boys think you goin'?" he bellowed. They turned to flee. Cliff got away through the turnstile, but the man collared the clumsy Herbie and shook him, repeating his pointless question. The boy, weak with terror and short-winded due to the insertion of a big brown hand in a collar just large enough for his throat, gulped and stared. Seeing him trapped, his cousin came back.

"We're stuck, mister, that's all, an' we wanna go home," Cliff cried. "We ain't crooks. We were gonna mail the company a coupla nickels as soon as we got home."

"Yeah, that's right," Herbie wheezed. The man released his grip on the collar, and the boy babbled the entire tale of their misadventure. The station master inspected the well-dressed lad curiously, and before the story was over he was hiding a cavernous smile behind his hand.

"So you gonna mail the company the nickels you owe us, hey?"

"So help me, mister, both of us."

"You sure, now?"

Herbie kissed the little finger of his right hand and swept it skyward. He was actually swearing to the under side of Lexington Avenue rather than to heaven, but the colored man seemed satisfied. A train was sliding to a stop beside the platform.

"G'wan home, then," he said, giving Herbie a friendly little push, "an' don't go treatin' gals with the subway's money no more."

Next day Cliff duly mailed his nickel to "The Subway Company, New York." Herbie begged five cents from his mother for a frankfurter and started out to mail it, but passed a delicatessen store and fell. As he devoured a steaming wienie with mustard and sauerkraut, he promised his uneasy conscience that he would pay the subway tomorrow. Walking home, he noticed black clouds gathering overhead. Just as he came to the entrance of his house an electric storm, the first of the year, broke with a thunderclap and a single sheet of lightning that seemed to split the sky. It appeared to Herbie that the heavens had opened and that God on his great white throne was peering down to earth, looking for Herbie Bookbinder. He scrambled up the stairs, shivering, and burst in upon Felicia, who was doing homework in her room.

"Fleece, gimme a nickel, please, please. You got money."

"I should say not. What for?"

"I gotta have it. Pay you back a dime Saturday."

"No."

"Fifteen cents!"

"Tell me what it's for and you can have it for a dime."

Crash! A great fork of lightning sundered the sky. Rain pelted the window.

"*Please* give it to me!"

Felicia regarded the white-faced boy for a moment. She raised her eyebrows.

"All right."

The sister went to the kitchen and returned with a breadknife. She inserted the knife into the slot of her pig bank and tilted it carefully over her bed. Several coins slid out along the knife and fell noiselessly to the spread. Felicia picked up a nickel.

"You can pay it back whenever you want. Never mind telling me what it's for. Just pay me a nickel."

"Thanks, Fleece."

A few minutes later Herbie was stumbling through a gale to the mailbox. He deposited the letter and returned home drenched, but wonderfully relieved in spirit.

It never occurred to Herbie that the Almighty was going to unusual trouble to collect a nickel.

8

The Dubbing of General Garbage

CONCRETE PRESSED ROUGHLY against one's nose is not enjoyable at best, and when the concrete is part of a schoolyard and has been baking in a May sun, it is hot and dirty enough to be positively unpleasant. So Herbie decided, as Lennie Krieger sat on his back twisting his left arm up behind him with one hand, thrusting his head against the ground with the other, and requesting the utterance of the word "uncle" before changing this state of things. With Lucille Glass standing a foot away looking on, this was not easy to do. "Uncle" is a code word understood by all children to mean "You're a better man than I am." However, Lennie was much heavier and stronger; the lunch period had twenty minutes to go; and the concrete was very hard, hot, and dusty. So Herbie said, "Uncle," adding under his breath, "in a pig's eye," and the two boys rose, brushing themselves.

Lucille bent a lively glance at Lennie and said, "I think you're awful, picking on someone smaller than you."

"Let him not be so smart, then," said Lennie, carelessly tucking his flapping shirt back into his trousers.

It was the Thursday after the museum meeting. Herbie, not finding Lucille at the accustomed landing, had wandered around the school and finally come upon her eating lunch with Lennie in a shady corner of the boys' yard. He had cheerfully joined the conversation, hiding his jealous pangs. The topic had been Lennie's boastful plans for playing football in high school.

72

"What'll *you* do in high school?" he said to Herbie derisively. "Try out for the tiddlywinks team?"

Herbie looked foolish and was silent. Lennie went on, "I bet I play halfback in my first year. Maybe even fullback."

"Maybe even left back," chirped Herbie.

It was a good shot. Lennie had been left back twice in his school career. Lucille choked over a bit of her sandwich, coughed it out, and shrieked with merriment. A short scuffle between the boys followed, ending in the nose-to-concrete situation described above.

"Look out, Lucille," said Herbie as he got up, ruefully rubbing the dirt off his nose and forehead. "He'll beat you up next. He's real brave."

Instantly Lennie had him by his shirt front and tie, grasped in an upthrusting fist. "What's the matter, you want more?" he said, and when Herbie answered nothing he beat the fat boy's chest lightly with his other fist, in time to this chant:

> *"Three, six, nine,*
> *A bottle of wine,*
> *I can fight you any old time."*

This was a challenge which a Bronx boy was supposed to take up even if it meant getting all his bones broken. But Herbie had had enough pounding of his ribs and concrete in his face for one day, so he let it pass. A code that required him to take two successive lickings from the same bigger boy seemed to have a flaw in it somewhere. He did not miss the flicker of disappointment in Lucille's eyes as Lennie released him with a contemptuous little push.

"O.K., Herbie darling," he said. "You can play jacks with Lucille now. So long." He strode off.

A vender of water ices pushed his wooden cart past them on the other side of the steel webbing of the school fence. "How about ices, Lucille? I got four cents," said Herbie humbly.

"No, thanks." Then impulsively, "I'll be glad when I'm

transferred to the Mosholu Parkway public school next term. I hate Lennie and I hate you!" She stamped her foot at him and ran to the girls' yard.

It is a sad thing to be beaten and humiliated in the presence of one's lady fair. Herbie moped around the yard without aim, and was so poor in spirits that it actually made him happy to hear the gong summoning him back to class. He pinned on his yellow armband, and took his privileged way up the stairs ahead of the other pupils, lonely and chopfallen. Even his imagination was chilled by Lucille's frostiness. It refused to produce the usual comforting pictures of Lennie in beggars' rags at the age of twenty-one, pleading with a prosperous, glittering Herbie for a small loan. The fat boy was indeed brought low.

The depression lessened when he came back to Mrs. Gorkin's classroom. There, lying on his desk, was his costume for the assembly play: an Army general's cap, a long overcoat with brass buttons, and, most wonderful of all, an honest-to-goodness cigar. In honor of Decoration Day he was to play General Ulysses S. Grant in *The Surrender at Appomattox.*

Mrs. Gorkin had spent a year at dramatic school before abandoning her dreams and becoming a school teacher. She was therefore the official theatrical manager of Public School 50. Her class benefited by the excitement of rehearsals, irregular hours, release from homework, and other privileges of a troupe of actors. She rarely troubled to go outside her own classroom for talent; it made control more difficult. Herbie, quick-witted and something of a showoff, was the natural choice for the long part of Grant. The casting of Robert E. Lee was harder. In the end Mrs. Gorkin had reluctantly given the role to Lennie Krieger, despite his low marks and truculent manner, because he was taller than any other boy and had the handsome figure required for General Lee—whom Mrs. Gorkin, with many historians, regarded as the hero of the scene.

When it was too late she regretted the choice a dozen times. Lennie's entrances, exits, and warlike gestures were things of spread-eagle beauty, but he couldn't remember lines, and those he did recall he mumbled jerkily out of the side of his mouth. He obviously believed that clear speech would compromise his manliness. Coaching, threats, and pleas by Mrs. Gorkin induced him to say a few speeches correctly at a rehearsal; next day, Robert E. Lee once more sounded like a bad boy reciting, "I must not throw erasers, I must not throw erasers." But the mistake was past remedy. Mrs. Gorkin instructed Herbie to memorize Lee's lines as well as Grant's, and to prompt Lennie whenever necessary.

Class 7B-1 lined up in front of the room and marched gaily to assembly hall for dress rehearsal. Eight of the boys carried costumes and props hired by Mrs. Gorkin from a downtown shop. Only Grant and Lee had complete outfits. The minor military figures were represented by a cap here, a jacket there, a pistol elsewhere. In the interest of economy two uniforms were furnishing out two chiefs of staff, four orderlies, and several miscellaneous generals. The rest of the class was coming along to watch the fun, freed from the drone of study by Mrs. Gorkin's theatrical duties.

In a tiny dressing room on one side of the assembly-hall platform the boys put on their costumes. Lennie soon became a dignified, glittering man of war, with a noble white beard that looped over his ears with elastic threads. By contrast, Herbie made a shabby Grant. The brass-buttoned overcoat slumped and lost its military aspect on his narrow shoulders and chubby body. The braided cap flopped down over his ears. He looked like the son of a doorman wearing his father's castoffs. Worst of all, the item of whiskers had apparently been overlooked in his case. Out of all his ludicrously oversized attire there peeped a round, clean pink face with a cigar in it. When Mrs. Gorkin came into the dressing room, she was greeted by a wail from the victor of Richmond. "Gosh, Mrs. Gorkin, where's my beard?"

"You have a beard."

"I have not."

"It's in your overcoat pocket."

"Oh." Herbie reached into the pockets and brought out a square piece of greasy black felt. *"This?"* he said in horror.

"Yes, *that,*" said Mrs. Gorkin. She took it out of his hand and affixed it to the bottom of his hat with two snap fasteners. "There, you look fine," she said heartily.

Herbie hurried to a mirror, took one look, and almost burst into tears. The black felt looked exactly like what it was: a piece of black felt. It no more resembled a beard than it did an American flag. He tried putting the cigar in his mouth. That gorgeous effect was also ruined. He had to raise the beard like a curtain, and it hung over the cigar on either side, leaving his mouth and chin bare. It was a fraud, a monstrosity.

"What the heck is that thing on your face?" The voice of Lennie Krieger spoke out of a resplendent form fairly resembling the Robert E. Lee of history books.

"A beard," Herbie faltered.

"A beard!" Lennie emitted a hoot and called, "Hey, guys, look what Herbie calls a beard!"

The wolves descended, baying with laughter.

"Haw! It looks like a shoeshine rag."

"It looks like a Mohammedan veil."

"It looks like something out of a garbage can."

"It is."

"He looks like he's playin' cops an' robbers."

"Is that a hat or a soup pot?"

"Is that an overcoat or a laundry sack?"

"Hooray for General Garbage!"

The last was Lennie's contribution. The boys took it up with whoops. "General Garbage! General Garbage!" They danced in front of Herbie with mock bows and salutes. Mrs. Gorkin came charging to the rescue, and silenced the din with a yell of "What's going on here?"

The teacher was wild of eye and mussed of hair. Calm, controlled at all other times, she became a jumpy artist when staging an assembly-hall show. She had once thrown a memorable fit of hysterics just before curtain time at the Gorkin production of *Pinafore*. Glaring at the cowed boys, she snapped, "Another whisper out of any of you, and there'll be no show," and went out. Lennie drew his sword and brandished it at her retreating back in a highly impolite gesture. The other actors covered their mouths and snickered.

Dress rehearsal had just started when one of the rear doors of the hall opened and Mr. Gauss walked down the center aisle in lone majesty. Mrs. Gorkin was seen to shudder. She rose, stopped the rehearsal with a wave of her hand, and said, "Class, stand." The children came to attention at their seats while the actors froze in their attitudes. Mr. Gauss strolled alongside the teacher and sat placidly in the front row beside her. "Class, sit," said Mrs. Gorkin.

"Boys, go right on with your play as though I weren't here," said Mr. Gauss.

The actors resumed their roles. Lennie, scared by the principal's presence, barked out his lines so that the hall echoed, to the teacher's great surprise and pleasure. Herbie, however, could not be understood no matter how hard he shouted. The black felt over his mouth worked as well as a Maxim silencer. His roars were reduced to murmurs.

"I remember you well from the Mexican War, General Lee," he howled.

"A rumble you bell your Max can whoa," was what reached the front row.

"What on earth is that thing over Grant's mouth?" whispered the principal.

"That," said Mrs. Gorkin, clenching and unclenching her fists, "is a beard."

"It looks like a flap of black felt," said the principal.

"Herbert, speak louder!" cried the teacher.

Herbert screamed so that his ears rang. "I regret we meet again in such melancholy circumstances."

"Rugger meegin smellnek shirtshtan," Mr. Gauss dimly heard.

"Really," he said to the teacher, "the boy must take that thing off."

"And have Grant look like a fat boy of eleven?"

"Yes, rather than have him sound gagged."

So Herbert's beard came off, to his relief. But Mrs. Gorkin steamed. Things went smoothly after that, however, and she was beginning to simmer down, when Lee drew his sword to hand it over in surrender.

"One moment," called the principal. Action was suspended.

"Wherever did you get this playlet, Mrs. Gorkin?" said Mr. Gauss.

"I wrote it myself."

"Surely you are aware, my dear, that the legend of Lee's surrender of his sword is spurious?"

"Yes," said the teacher. "But it's a famous legend and has a good moral."

"Nothing that is false has a good moral. I think we will cut out this part."

Mrs. Gorkin gasped and trembled. "There's no point to the play without it. The curtain line is what General Grant says as he returns the sword: 'General Lee, I have not defeated an enemy; I have found a lost brother.'"

"A very nice line, my dear. But we can't go on planting these silly stories in children's minds."

"There's no drama, no entertainment whatever without the sword," shrilled the red-haired teacher.

The invisible fingers pushed the ends of Mr. Gauss's mouth up in his well-known smile.

"We are not here to entertain, but to instruct," he said with satisfaction.

Mrs. Gorkin threw her head back and screamed into her handkerchief.

The children were aghast and delighted. Mr. Gauss was stupefied. The silence of the huge hall was rent by a second muffled shriek. The principal rose, patted Mrs. Gorkin's arm, and said, "Please, please, collect yourself, my dear. (*Shriek*) I had no idea you felt so strongly. (*Shriek*) Please, we'll *leave* the scene as it is."

Two or three short sobs, and Mrs. Gorkin emerged from the handkerchief, bright-eyed and happy. "Thank you, Mr. Gauss," she said. "On with the rehearsal, boys. All right, Lennie. 'Sir, in yielding this sword—'"

Lennie, who had been staring open mouthed at her, quickly drew the sword once more and held it high.

"Sir, in yielding this weapon I give you the sword of the South, but not its soul," he said.

"One moment," said Mr. Gauss.

Mrs. Gorkin jumped as though a spider had walked on her.

"May I merely suggest," said the principal, "that etiquette would require him to unbuckle his belt and hand over sword, scabbard, and all?"

"Mr. Gauss," said the teacher, her voice like the plucking of an overtightened banjo string, "it is more dramatic to see the sword drawn." She took her handkerchief from her cuff again.

"Merely a suggestion," said Mr. Gauss hurriedly. "I withdraw it."

But at this moment the gong rang, summoning the school to assembly, and the dress rehearsal had to be adjourned. Children lugging violins, cellos, trumpets, and trombones began straggling in through the rear doors. Mr. Meng, the slight, dark teacher who played the piano and led the school orchestra, appeared with three boys staggering under piles of folding chairs which they dropped at the piano and began setting up with much scraping and banging. Mrs. Gorkin left her acting troupe in the dressing room with a terrifying final warning, spoken with hands shaking and eyeballs showing white all around the pupils, and then led her class out of the hall.

Mr. Gauss took his place in the large ornate armchair at the center of the platform. The assistant principal, Mrs. Corn, large, yellow-haired, and ferocious, sat on one side of him; on the other was a stout lady from the Board of Education. The school gong clanged once more. Mr. Meng, at the piano, lifted one hand in the air and looked at Mr. Gauss. The principal nodded. Down came the hand, yowl went the wind instruments, and an obscure, muddy fog of sound arose, through which the piano could vaguely be heard, pounding out "The Stars and Stripes Forever," double fortissimo. A line of boys began marching in from one side, a line of girls from the other. Mrs.

Gorkin, whatever her trials as a theatrical manager, had this unique blessing: her productions never failed to play to a full house.

Soon the hall was full. Heads, eyes, and arms of the standing children were motionless. Mrs. Corn stepped forward and shouted like a drill sergeant, "Color guard, forward—MARCH!" Three well-combed and -washed honor boys from the eighth grade came down the center aisle, the middle one carrying a flag on a staff. The drum and cymbal speeded them on their way, dying off uncertainly as the flag reached the platform. Mrs. Corn snapped her right arm to her forehead; all the children did likewise. From a thousand young throats came a chant: "I pledge allegiance to the flag . . ."

The eye of Mrs. Corn swept the hall, looking for a wavering hand, a straying eye, a dirty shirt, or a neckerchief of the wrong color. At the end of the pledge two piano chords sounded, and all the heads sank at once as the children sat. Mrs. Corn came down the steps of the platform and silently glared a girl (who had yawned during the pledge) out of her seat, up the aisle, and into her office to await doom. As she returned to her armchair Mr. Gauss rose and read from a Bible on a stand the Psalm beginning, *"Lord, how numerous are my persecutors,"* but if the children caught the appropriateness, there were no grins to show it.

Meantime, the actors stranded in the dressing room were very gay. Few things are so sweet in this world as seeing your fellows go through a foolish rigmarole while you are free from it yourself (this is the secret of the popularity of all parades and military reviews). A hot game of "tickets" was going on, organized and dominated by Lennie. It was a sort of poker, evolved in the gutters of New York like scores of other games, played with small villainously colored pictures of baseball players which sold in strips of ten for a cent. Herbie, having no tickets, was out of the game, and was curiously examining General Lee's sword, which lay in a corner. Finally he buckled it on, and drew and brandished it a few times, yearning over it.

"Take off that sword, General Garbage, or I'll push your face in," growled Lennie, looking up from the game. The other boys laughed.

Herbie, his face burning, obeyed. As he was putting the sword back in the corner he noticed a little black button on the hilt. He pressed it. With some difficulty it yielded, and the sword settled another inch into the scabbard. He tried to pull the sword out again, but it remained locked in place until he pressed the catch, whereupon it slid out easily. This was a feature of the weapon which Lennie had clearly overlooked. In his boastful flourishing he had pointed out every detail he had noticed to the envious boys. Herbie glanced over his shoulder at General Lee, intent on heavy betting of tickets, his beard pushed up on his forehead. The small stout boy reviewed several incidents of the day in his mind: concrete against his nose, jeers at his black felt beard, "General Garbage," and the recent threat to render his face concave. Then he softly pressed the catch, locked the sword in its scabbard, leaned it against the wall, and strolled away to watch the assembly through the crack of the dressing-room door.

A tall girl with lank black hair and heavily rimmed glasses was standing in the center of the platform, reciting "In Flanders fields the poppies blow." The rows of rigid children sat listening with eyes dulled by an overdose of poppies, for this was the third rendition of the poem in ten minutes. The fifth, sixth, and eighth grades had each been asked to furnish one recitation, and had each sent its best English student to the stage primed with the same Decoration Day warhorse. Nothing could stop the repetitions. An assembly, once started, ticked itself off like an infernal machine. For the third time the children heard the performer make the daring turn around the elocutionary corner in the last verse:

Take up our quarrel with the foe:
To you from failing hands we throw THE TORCH;
Be yours to hold it high.

instead of the usual:

Take up our quarrel with the foe:
To you from failing hands we throw
The torch; be yours to hold it high.

This was considered original and very fine by each of the three teachers who had coached the reciters. It was sad to find that the others had all had the same inspiration. The unlucky girl reached the last line and sneaked off the platform to feeble applause.

Now Mr. Gauss introduced the stout lady from the Board of Education, Mrs. Moonvess. He stated that a great musical treat was in store for the children, as she was going to teach them a song of her own composition. Mrs. Moonvess stood, adjusted her pince-nez, produced a conductor's baton, and came forward, coughing nervously.

"Boys and girls of P.S. 50, I have set to music a piece which is very appropriate to this holiday. I shall now sing for you with the aid of my good friend, Mr. Meng, the first stanza of my song—a musical setting of 'In Flanders Fields.'"

By the laws of nature there should not be any such thing as a silent groan, but a sound describable in no other terms swelled through the hall. Mrs. Corn glared around, but all the children were sitting with faces of stone. The silent groan went unpunished and Mrs. Moonvess caroled the first stanza of "In Flanders Fields." During the next fifteen minutes she tried to browbeat the children into learning it. They had no trouble with the words, which by now they knew almost from memory, but Mrs. Moonvess's bizarre tune was beyond them. At the last, when she drove them through it mercilessly with her baton from beginning to end, the effect was strange and dismal, like a hymn chanted by Chinese monks. Mr. Gauss jumped up as she seemed to be rallying herself for another try, and thanked her for her beautiful contribution to the holiday. Loud applause ensued as she backed unwillingly into her seat.

Mrs. Gorkin now sidled up the platform steps. Herbie whispered, "Chickie!" The card game broke up and the tickets all disappeared in a twinkling. The actors were standing around virtuously when the teacher came in. Lennie had just finished buckling on the sword, but in his haste he forgot to pull the white beard down from his forehead, incurring a tongue lashing. Mrs. Gorkin faithfully promised to put him back to 7A if he spoiled her show in any way. Lennie was hangdog and mute.

Introducing the playlet, Mr. Gauss reviewed the whole Civil War from Fort Sumter to Richmond. He paused at Gettysburg long enough to quote Lincoln's address verbatim. He painstakingly explained that the surrender of Lee's sword, which they were about to see, never really happened, so they need not pay attention to that part of the play. At this, Mrs. Gorkin, who had been wringing a handkerchief between her perspiring hands, ripped it in half.

"And now," said Mr. Gauss to the drooping audience, "Mrs. Gorkin's play, *The Surrender at Appomattox.*"

The principal sat. Mrs. Gorkin gave Herbie a push, and he walked out on the stage, followed by a general and an orderly. As instructed, he strode to the center, faced the audience, and was about to bellow his first line when lo, he beheld in the second girls' row the face of Lucille Glass, turned up to him with eager eyes. The speech vanished from his memory. He became aware of a thousand faces staring at him in a dead silence. His knees shook. His mouth hung open. Panic gripped him.

A hoarse whisper from Mrs. Gorkin floated to him. "What can be keeping General Lee? *What can be keeping General Lee?*"

"What can be keeping General Lee?" he declaimed. The sound of his own voice filling the hall gave him new life, and he ranted on with zest, "True, as my senior by sixteen years he is entitled to keep me waiting. Ha, ha." He thrust the cigar vigorously into his mouth, causing shocked chuckles in the audience. From then onward his performance was in the best tradition of that approach of the stage art known as "chewing the scenery." The absence of a black beard went quite unnoticed in the fireworks of his style.

General Robert E. Lee looked so dashing when he came on the stage that he received an ovation.

"I trust I am not unduly tardy, General Grant," he said, in a murmur that barely reached Mr. Gauss, sitting five feet from him. Lennie was not frightened. He simply balked at speaking clear, correct English before all the boys he knew, and casting an everlasting shadow on his virility. No vengeance Mrs. Gorkin could take was worse than that. He loved the uniform and the sword, and was happy of the chance to be showing them off before the school. That was enough for him, and it would have to do for Mrs. Gorkin.

The scene proceeded, General Grant shaking the windows with his lines and General Lee confiding his answers to the orderly at his right (away from the audience) because it was his practice to speak out of the right side of his mouth. To the audience, the effect was to make Robert E. Lee out as bashful and deaf, an unexpected characterization. Mrs. Gorkin had revised the lines so that the audience could follow the scene merely from what Grant said, but the alternation of shouts and murmurs was decidedly queer. Mr. Gauss finally intervened.

"Speak up, General Lee, nobody can hear you," he said, and a wave of giggles went through the girls.

Stung, Lennie blared out, "Sir, in yielding this weapon I give you the sword of the South, but not its soul." He clapped his hand to the hilt, gave a vicious tug, and spun himself clear around. The sword remained fast in the scabbard.

He was astounded. Once more he wrenched at the weapon; it would not budge. The audience was tittering. He took a deep breath. "Sir, in yielding you this weapon," he yelled, "I give you the sword of the South, but not its soul." With both hands on the hilt he heaved at it and pulled the belt halfway up his chest, hauling up his jacket and shirt so that his naked chest showed. But the sword did not come out.

"Never mind your soul," said Herbie in a flash of inspiration. "I'll settle for the sword."

There was a deluge of laughter. Mrs. Gorkin was almost shouting from the dressing room: "Unbuckle the belt! Unbuckle the belt!" Lennie lost his head, tugged and tugged at the sword, and began to swear. Mr. Gauss rose to take action. Herbie, emboldened by success, suddenly held up his hand and bawled, "One moment, General."

The laughter stopped and Lennie looked at him wonderingly. Herbie reached over to General Lee's side, seized the hilt, and drew out the sword as easily as if it had been greased. The audience gasped in astonishment. Herbie turned to his orderly and blandly said, "Give General Lee a cup of coffee. He seems to be weak from hunger."

Amid the roars and handclapping which followed this coup, Mr. Gauss stepped forward and shook his hand. The play was over, and was acknowledged a great hit.

Lennie lay in ambush near 1075 Homer Avenue from four until seven-thirty that evening, waiting for Herbie to come home. The only result was that he missed his dinner. Herbie came home at six, via the basement of 1042 Tennyson Avenue and a connecting passageway to his own cellar. General Garbage outmaneuvered General Lee to the end.

9

Promotion Day

THE ENMITY BETWEEN the two boys was now established forever, apparently. Yet at the hot noontide of a sweet-smelling day in June, only a week later, Lennie and Herbie were sitting together on the granite steps of a stoop on the shady side of the street opposite P.S. 50, eating ice cream turn and turn about out of one paper cup. Lennie was on a lower step, looking up humbly at Herbie. It was he who had paid for the ice cream, and each time he passed the cup up to Herbie it was like a peace offering.

Every phenomenon, however remarkable, has an explanation. This was the first day of promotion tests. Lennie was trying, in one hour, to suck the honey of six months of wisdom accumulated by Herbie on the subject of English grammar.

"Tell me again," he said, "what the difference is between a phrase an' a clause."

"Well, a clause is like a sentence inside a sentence, see," said Herbie patiently, "an' a phrase only has a preposition an' a noun."

"What the blazes is a preposition again?"

"Well, like 'on,' 'in,' 'to,' 'of'—you know."

" 'If'?"

"Heck, no, 'if' is a conjunction."

"Well, how do you tell 'em apart? Don't a preposition always have two letters?"

"Lennie, for cryin' out loud, don't you ever do homework? Two letters! Holy smoke, there's 'from,' 'toward,' 'into,' 'under'—"

Lennie crushed the empty paper cup in a callused hand and slung it angrily into the gutter. "I'm skunked for sure."

"Look, Lennie, it's a cinch. A clause always has a verb in it. A phrase never has."

"A verb. You mean like 'run,' 'jump,' 'fly'?"

"Right."

"Well, O.K. Gimme an example."

"Sure. 'He threw me the ball an' I caught it on the run.' Pick out a clause."

" 'On the run,' " said Lennie promptly.

"No, no, that's a phrase."

"You're crazy. It's got a verb in it—'run.' "

"That ain't a verb."

"Look, you little punk, make up your mind. You said a minute ago it was a verb."

"Well, see, sometimes it is, sometimes it ain't. English is funny."

Lennie's eyes became slits. "You wouldn't be tryin' to mix me up an hour before the test, would you, General Garbage?" he said, grasping Herbie by the shirt.

"Look, Lennie, I could be studyin' by myself if I wanted, couldn't I? That was a bad example, that's all. Here's an easy one. "I walk while he runs.' Which is the clause?"

Lennie paused, looked at his tutor suspiciously, and said, 'While he runs.' "

"Right! Lennie, you got it now."

The bigger boy brightened. "Well, if that's all there is to it I'll be O.K. Say, will we get any of them dumb poetry questions?"

"Sure as you're alive."

"She's got a nerve. None of the other 7B classes got that stuff."

"I know, but she's bugs on poetry. Anyway, it's easy, Lennie. All you got to know is the difference between dactyl, trochee, and iambic."

"That's all, huh? What the hell *is* the difference?"

"Well, it's all rhythm, see? Dactyl is one long and two shorts. Trochee is one long and one short. Iambic is one short and one long. There's a thing called anapest, too, but she said we ain't gonna get that on the test."

Lennie yanked a baseball covered with black tape out of his pocket and smacked it from hand to hand, his head hanging. "I couldn't remember that stuff if I spent the whole lunch hour on it. I guess I flunk that question."

"Listen, you gotta know it." Herbie pondered a moment, his eyes following the movements of the baseball. He snapped his fingers and said, "Hey, here's an idea. See if you can remember it this way. 'Outfielder' is a dactyl. 'Shortstop' is a trochee. 'Yer out!' is a iambic."

"That's more like it!" Lennie slapped the ball sharply into his right fist and put it away. " 'Outfielder' dactyl, 'shortstop' trochee, 'yer out!' iambic. Got that. But how'm I gonna—"

"Wait a second. She'll give us a line o' poetry on the

blackboard, see? Read it to yourself. If it sounds like 'outfielder, outfielder, outfielder,' put down dactyl. If it goes 'yer out, yer out, yer out'—iambic. An' so on. That's all there is to poetry."

Lennie mumbled the magic formula to himself several times. "Boy, I got that cold. I hope the whole lousy test is poetry."

"Now, y'oughta know somethin' about participles—"

"Aw, can it a minute, Herbie. I'll get some more ice cream."

The athlete sprinted to the ice-cream wagon at the corner and returned in a matter of seconds, breathing easily, with another paper cup. For a second time that day the foes ate ice cream together. This was the closest they had come to truce in all the lifelong war between them. Herbie, forgetful of years of bullying, felt almost an affection for the enemy he was helping. Lennie, for his part, was ready to forgive Herbie his quick wits, now that they were useful to him.

"Say, Herb," said the bigger boy, as the cup shuttled, "how come you know that stuff? You sure don't study much. You're always foolin' around down by the candy store at night, same as me."

"Shucks, Len, how come you run so fast and can chin fifteen times? It comes natural, don't it? Same with me."

Lennie smelled sophistry. "Now, hold on. I *like* athletics, that's how come I'm good. You ain't sayin' you like grammar?"

"Are you nuts? I hate it," said Herbie stoutly. To confess his guilty pleasure in the machinery of language would have been as bad as admitting a taste for opium; in fact, Lennie would have been much readier to forgive the opium. "It just comes easy somehow."

Lennie considered the matter. "Well," he said at last, "I sure as anything would rather be like me and play good ball than be a teacher's pet like you an' know about clauses an' participles."

"Anybody would," said Herbie humbly, "but I can't help it. What should I do—answer a lot of questions wrong on every test? That still wouldn't make me run fast."

This put things in a new light. It occurred to Lennie that his enemy might not be depraved, after all, but simply constituted badly. "Look, Herb," he said, "sometimes you're almost a regular guy. You're not so bad at stickball, f'rinstance. Only why ain't you interested in the same things all the guys are? Baseball teams, now. I bet you don't even know who's leadin' the National League."

Herbie did not answer.

"I bet—no, this is impossible—you *do* know the Yankee lineup, don't you?"

"Sure. Babe Ruth plays right field 'n' bats fourth, Lou Gehrig plays first base 'n' bats third, and—and—" The stout boy broke off lamely.

"Boy, you even got that wrong. Gehrig's fourth and Ruth's third. Herb," said Lennie kindly, "that's awful."

Herbie nodded, his face red with shame. It was his turn at the ice cream, but his appetite was gone and he declined it.

"Why, Herb, even Bunny Lipman, that stoop, knows the leadin' ten battin' averages in both leagues. See, there *is* somethin' wrong with you."

"I wish I knew what it was, Len, honest," said Herbie, out of the depths of humiliation. It was true, he had always had this mysterious blind spot toward baseball. Boys who were fools in the classroom could juggle names and figures by the hour: "Rabbit Maranville batted .235 in '26, Wilcey Moore pitched one shutout in '27," and so forth forevermore, it seemed, while he knew nothing. He had tried in vain to study the sports pages of the newspapers. The figures evaporated from his brain like sprinklings on a hot pavement in July.

"It ain't too serious," said Lennie. "With your brains, if you really wanted, you could get to be a regular guy in no time."

"So help me, Lennie, I'm gonna try," Herbie said, and made a mental note to spend the summer studying the baseball scriptures, Spalding's Handbook. He forgot about it five minutes later, but at the moment it was an iron resolution, and he felt thankful to Lennie for showing him the straight path. He resumed his coaching with a will, and with such good effect that Lennie came to Mrs. Gorkin's classroom muttering all the necessary secrets of English sentence structure.

The sternness of promotion time was marked by the legal-length yellow sheets lying on each desk. The majestic, oversize sheets seemed instruments of judgment. To add to the frightfulness of the tests as well as to make prearranged cheating harder, the seating order of the children was scrambled. Herbie found himself in the last seat but one in a former girls' row, and Lennie, by dextrously putting himself before the teacher at the right moment, managed to be placed directly behind him.

Mrs. Gorkin read the articles of war. She described to the grim-faced children the horrid penalties for talking, signaling, or looking anywhere but at blackboard or desk. No more than the class did she regard a promotion test as a simple examination. It was battle. On the children's side, a half year of life was at stake; on the teacher's, revenge for stupidity and indifference. She would show no mercy; they would have no scruples. Detection in crime meant being left back. All this was clear.

"Now," said Mrs. Gorkin, "I shall raise these maps that cover the blackboard. Do *not* start writing until I give you permission."

Africa and Asia rolled up at her touch, revealing the naked face of Fate. Ten questions were hand-printed on the board in blood-red chalk. White chalk was good enough for every other day of the year—in fact, it was much more readable than the colored—but the scarlet queries added a nice touch of terror.

"Begin!" barked the teacher. Thirty small hands dipped thirty new steel pens in thirty freshly filled inkwells, and on the yellow sheets the answer to the first question took form in thirty different scrawls.

Herbie Bookbinder danced through the examination in half the allotted time. His frivolous mind, barren of the useful facts of batting averages and league standings, was a weed patch of foolishness like infinitive clauses and subjunctive moods. He settled back to enjoy the luxury of doing nothing while others sweated. Suddenly from behind him came a hardly audible "Pss-s-st!" With the caution of a cat preparing for a steep jump, he very slightly leaned back his head to acknowledge the signal.

"Herbie," came a desperate whisper, "what the hell is a dactyl, again?"

Now, Herbie was not used to cheating. Most school children develop a callus over that area of their souls, as a horse will where the harness galls him, but Herbie had always done well without it, and his conscience was still tender. When he had entered the first grade, his father had taken him aside to say, "Son, whatever you have to do, do it as good as you can. Don't cheat. Fail. But don't cheat." He had never forgotten.

"Herbie, for Pete's sake, can't you hear me? What's a dactyl?"

The whisper was louder now—dangerously loud. Mrs. Gorkin looked straight at Herbie, and he felt his face flush. Then she turned her glance elsewhere.

"Herbie, are you a regular guy or ain't you? *What's a dactyl?*"

Since Cain and Abel were young, what boy has been able to resist the challenge, "Are you a regular guy?" Whatever the crime involved—cheating, stealing, lying to parents, cruelty to the weak, or worse—what boy has the courage to refuse to be "regular"? Herbie pretended to resume writing his test. Carefully he extracted a scrap of paper from a trouser pocket and wrote the word "outfielder" on it. He leaned back and dangled his arm at his side. Lennie's hot, perspiring hand came groping for the paper, and seized it.

The voice of Mrs. Gorkin came through the air like an arrow of ice.

"Herbert Bookbinder and Leonard Krieger, stand!"

A thrill of horror ran down Herbie's spine. He and Lennie leaped to stiff attention in the aisle, arms hugged to sides.

The red-headed teacher strode to the vacant desk, and after a short search pounced on the crumpled bit of paper lying under Herbie's seat. The rest of the class watched with saucer eyes as she smoothed it out and read it. Upon seeing the single baseball term she looked so comically astounded and foiled that several children laughed aloud. A burning glance around the room withered them.

"Go back to your work, everyone who doesn't want to join these two!"

Twenty-eight heads bent low over desks.

Mrs. Gorkin looked long and hard at "outfielder." Then she stared at the boys, who stood dumb and rigid. Then she turned the paper over. Then she turned it back and surveyed it upside down. Then she held it up against the light. But there was only one piece of intelligence to be gleaned from it: "outfielder." She turned and walked to her desk, muttering, "Outfielder—outfielder—outfielder?" Snatching paper and pencil, she scrawled half a column of gibberish like fielderout, outerfield, fielddouter, outrefield, and so forth, studied her work for a moment, crumpled it, and dashed it into the wastebasket.

"Outside with you!" she snapped at the standing boys. "Faces to the wall and not a word, not a sound, do you hear?"

Herbie led Lennie out of the room, with the sense that his young life was coming to an unnatural end.

For fifteen torturing minutes the boys stood in the silent hall, their faces to the plaster. At last the school gong rang the end of the hour. A shuffle of feet and rustle of paper could be heard inside the classroom.

Lennie broke silence with a whisper, "She can't do nothin' to us."

Herbie said nothing.

"Betcher scared."

No answer.

"I ain't. That's a lotta bull about gettin' left back."

No answer.

"What's the difference if we do get left back? We'll skip right back up in a month."

Silence.

"Whatsamatter, Herb?"

"Sh-sh," spoke up Herbie at last. "Ain't we in enough trouble?"

"I thought so," snarled Lennie. "You're yellow. Just plain yellow, that's all you are. Yellow."

Herbie was enraged. "You're as scared as me, Lennie Krieger. I can hear your voice shakin'. You're just showin' off like you always do. Shut your big trap."

"O.K., General Garbage. I'll remember that. Gettin' all ready to snitch on me, ain'tcha?"

The classroom door opened.

"About face!"

Herbie and Lennie wheeled. Mrs. Gorkin confronted them with the scowl of a destroying angel.

"Now, then, Master Bookbinder, just what is the meaning of 'outfielder'?"

"Why, ma'am, it's a guy on a baseball team who lays back of the bases—"

"Don't you play the fool with me! I want an explanation of *this!*" She thrust the paper scrap toward him.

Lennie interjected, "I never seen that paper."

"Silence, you! Herbert Bookbinder, why did you pass the word 'outfielder' to Lennie?"

"That's—that's what I want to play on his softball team—outfielder, ma'am. We were talkin' about it at lunch."

Mrs. Gorkin seized him by the ear. "Are you trying to tell me that in the middle of a promotion test you (yank) the fattest of all the little fat boys I have ever seen (yank) were thinking about athletics?"

"Ow! I finished my test, ma'am. I guess it was bad for me to pass a paper, but I sure don't have to cheat, ma'am, an' what good could 'outfielder' do Lennie?"

Mrs. Gorkin stared at him. He returned his best cherubic look. She shrugged her shoulders hopelessly. "I would give a week's salary for the answer to that question," she said. "Your papers are both forfeited. Return to your seats."

After school Lennie whispered to Herbie, as they left the play yard, "She won't do nothin' to us, Herb. You'll see. Thanks for bein' a regular guy."

Herbie often read in Sunday supplements about the end of the world. The fright which seized him at the thought that a comet might strike the earth, or the moon fall into the ocean, or the sun grow cold was not unlike the fear with which he now waited for promotion day. Each morning he woke to a sinking of the heart as he knew himself one day closer to being left back. But the ignorance that makes boys easy to terrorize also gives them hope of miracles. Herbie awaited his doom, nursed a secret faith in a last-minute pardon from the Governor or the President, and said nothing to his parents about his misery.

The day came. In Mrs. Gorkin's classroom thirty scrubbed children, dressed much too elaborately for a weekday, trembled for their good names as the teacher deliberately removed the rubber bands from the pack of report cards which were to be handed out for the last time. Nobody shook worse than Herbie and Lennie, but Herbie's obvious anguish invited pity, while Lennie made a point of looking around with lifted eyebrows and a mocking smile.

"Larry Ravets, promoted to 8A-1," called the teacher.

Ravets, a sallow little boy with black-rimmed glasses, who had steadily held second place on the honor roll, leaped forward with glee, took his card, and stood against the wall. One after another the bright pupils, all promoted to the next grade, were summoned, received their cards, and lined up beside Ravets. Next the mediocre children, also promoted, joined the procession. The number remaining in their seats dwindled to ten, to six, to four. Herbie and Lennie were two of those four. The teacher paused. She had given out all the cards in her hand.

And now she stood and calmly walked out of the room.

A buzz arose.

"Tough luck, Herbie."

"Don't worry, Lennie, she's just scarin' you."

"She's a mean one."

"See you in 7B, fellows!"

Shirley Schwartz, Herbie's ugly little silent worshiper, shed tears in her inconspicuous place near the tail of the line. Although the two criminals had been mum to all questions by their classmates, she knew with the others that if cheating had occurred, it could only have been for Lennie's sake. The sympathies of the class were divided. Some were sorrier for the trapped athlete, and some for the fat boy who had tried to help him. But all felt much pleasure in contemplating the disaster from the safety of the promotion line.

The door opened, and Mrs. Gorkin returned to her desk amid graveyard silence. She carried four cards, each copiously marked with red ink.

"Tomaso Gusi, 8A-2—on probation."

The bad boy of the class, swarthy, wiry, a dead-eye marksman of the rubber band and paper clip, darted forward, clutched his card to his breast, and fell into line.

"Mary Kerr, 8A-2—on probation."

A large, slovenly girl, truant and stupid, rose, blubbering loudly, said, "Thank you, teacher," amid sobs, and received her passport to happiness.

"Leonard Krieger."

A long pause.

"7B-3."

A gasp and a groan from the class. One head had fallen. Lennie swaggered up to the teacher. He plucked the card from her hand with an insolent jerk that would have brought severe punishment—except that one doesn't punish the dead—and took his place, grinning defiantly.

"Herbert Bookbinder."

The teacher spoke the name and no more. Uncertainly, Herbie got to his feet. The teacher allowed a minute to pass while he stood thus in suspense, alone among the rows of empty desks, before the eyes of the whole fascinated class. Then she spoke.

"My opinion is that you are a disgrace to your parents and to me. I believe you cheated on the English grammar test. Leonard Krieger's part in the act is not clear, and he has not been punished for it. His average was low enough to fail him. But a note was passed in your handwriting. A cheat with perfect marks is worse than the stupidest pupil in class.

"I give you one last chance to make a clean breast. You won't be sorry if you do.

"What does 'outfielder' mean?"

The room seemed to be rotating around Herbie. He tried to sort out the dizzy jumble of his thoughts. But there seemed no way to tell the truth without accusing Lennie. It was the same painful choice: whether to be honest or "regular." Pity the boy torn between the children's code and the schoolteacher's code.

"Ma'am, I told you," he said in a thick voice.

"Step up here."

Herbie falteringly obeyed.

"Children," said Mrs. Gorkin, "always remember that in a free country a man is innocent until he is proven guilty. I have no proof that this boy cheated. As it happens, his promotion average was ninety-seven."

She handed Herbie's card to him.

"Herbert Bookbinder, 8B-3."

Herbie had won the ultimate prize of promotion day. He had "skipped."

In the yard, after assembly, a knot of children were congratulating Herbie when Leonard Krieger walked up to him. The talk died.

"Well, General Garbage," said Lennie, "I see you got away with it and I didn't. I guess it pays to be a teacher's pet. But I'm satisfied. I'd rather get left back a hundred times than be a fat sissy like you an' get skipped."

The attack flabbergasted Herbie. "Lennie, I done my best—"

"Who asked you to pass me any notes, you fat barrel? If I'd of finished that grammar test, I might of passed. Just you stay out of my way, Fatso. The next time you cross me up, I'll knock your block off. . . . Come on, who wants to play softball?" he said to the silent group, and walked off without waiting for answers.

Herbie strolled home to bring his mother the glad

news, but he was not happy. He tried to understand Lennie's blaming him, and reviewed the whole sorry affair without finding light. He thought he was a victim of injustice; but he had only had an encounter with ordinary human nature.

As he rounded the corner of Thackeray Street and Homer Avenue he heard "Herbie!" called in sweet tones. Outside Hesse's ice-cream parlor Lucille Glass stood, licking a strawberry ice-cream cone.

"Want some?" she said demurely as he came toward her. "I had one already. I'm waiting for Mama to pick me up in the car."

Herbie accepted the cone, took two polite licks, and returned it.

"I hear you skipped, and Lennie got left back."

The boy nodded.

"C'mere, closer." She beckoned to him, although he was only a foot away. Wondering, he moved beside her. "Closer. I wanna whisper in your ear."

What new delight was this? Herbie bent his head to the girl's little red mouth. He felt her warm breath in his ear, a delirious pleasure. She barely murmured. "What does 'outfielder' mean?"

Herbie shook his head obstinately.

"If you told, Lennie might of got put back to 7A, huh?"

The boy was human. He shrugged, and nodded. Next moment his cheeks were surprisingly rosy, and the girl was running down the street. She had kissed him, halfway between his ear and his eyebrow.

Herbie Bookbinder's escape from being left back was narrower than he knew. After the grammar test, Mrs. Gorkin spent an entire evening discussing and analyzing the "outfielder" mystery with her husband, assistant principal Mortimer Gorkin of P.S. 75. The next day she took it up at a meeting of the seventh-grade teachers during lunch hour without any luck, and finally submitted it to the wisdom of Mr. Gauss himself, who hummed and grunted and finally threw up his hands. It has gone down among the teachers of P.S. 50 as one of the great unsolved crimes of pupil cunning. Strange! Teachers set themselves up to be so wondrous wise—yet to this day it has not occurred to one of them that "outfielder" is a dactyl.

10

A Man Among Men

"A CHOCOLATE FRAP, please, with chocolate sauce."

Old Mr. Borowsky, the sad, thin, gray candy-store man, looked at Herbie with the ghost of an expression of surprise. Mr. Borowsky was the perfect candy-store man; the yearnings of the flesh and the emotions of the soul were dead in him. He could trust himself never to go on a rampage and eat up all his wondrous wares. He had not consumed a gumdrop or drunk an ice-cream soda or laughed out loud in the memory of all the youngsters of Homer Avenue. What moved him was the instinct to stay alive, which needed only a knowledge of the relative values of coins and sweets, and wisdom about the shallow devices of hungry and thirsty children. Such wisdom he had in plenty, and it caused the phantom of suspicion— all his emotions were ghosts, not living things—to show on him when Herbie Bookbinder, a known penny customer, ordered a ten-cent item on a weekday.

"That costs a dime," he said.

Herbie laid a thin bright coin on the wet marble counter with the air of a lord.

"I got skipped," he said.

Mr. Borowsky received this great news as he would have received the news of the sinking of the continent of

Europe into the sea, with a blank face, and made up a chocolate frappé.

Herbie carried the tin dish with care to the dusty little table with two wire-backed chairs that stood in a corner by the magazine shelves, and sat down to feast like a mighty man. He had bought the privilege with the frappé. (Nobody ever sat at the table except a rare "big guy" who, too lazy to walk his sweetheart around the corner to Hesse's, would regale her amid Borowsky's dinginess.) All that was needed now to fill the boy's cup of joy was some other boy to come into the store and envy him. But it was a quiet time; he waited until the treat was half melted, and was forced at last to eat it alone and unadmired. Every pleasure in life seems to come equipped with such a shadow.

Still, it was an event to be treasured. Come what might, he had eaten a frappé on a weekday. Herbie was ignorant of the French origin and pronunciation of the word, but the dish was not the less lovely for that. Some adults, who have nothing better to do, like to argue about what the most beautiful word in the English language is. The leading contenders are usually dawn, violet, starlight, golden, moonbeam, and the like—which proves nothing except what kind of people the arguers are. For the boys on Homer Avenue there would hardly have been a rival for that glorious sound, Frap.

Licking his lips, and wondering why life was not an eternal eating of chocolate frappés, Herbie left the candy store and went home. He came upon his parents sitting together on the red sofa in the parlor, and from their silence and smiles he guessed that they had been talking about his feat at school. Modestly he walked toward his room, but his father called, "Come here, my son."

Herbie had not been addressed as "my son" by Mr. Bookbinder since his last birthday. It was a signal for something pleasant. He returned to the parlor, pretending that he suspected nothing unusual. His mother rose at the same time, patted his head, and left, saying, "I suppose you gentlemen have plenty to talk about."

"Sit down, my son," said Mr. Bookbinder. The formal

invitation was another novelty, as unnecessary as inviting a cat to sit down. But Herbie was equal to the event, and took an armchair with aplomb, sitting back with his legs crossed as he had seen grownups do. Not having much slack in his legs, he lost contact with the floor, but he liked the effect nevertheless.

"So, I hear you skipped again," said Jacob Bookbinder, with a smile that softened and warmed his stern face.

"Yes, Pa."

"And you go into the last grade of public school next term."

"Uh-huh."

"You know, my boy, that was the last class I ever attended. After that I went out and made a living. Of course, that was in Poland. You, thank God, will be able to go to high school and college. Still, you're growing up to be a man faster than you think."

Herbie would have felt a little more like a man if he had not sunk backward into the armchair so that his crossed knees were as high as his head. He wriggled forward and grasped the arms of the chair to hold himself upright.

"You're not comfortable. Come here on the sofa."

Herbie obeyed.

"My boy, I'm taking you out to dinner with me tonight in a restaurant. That is, if you want to come."

A restaurant! This was a glory of even higher magnitude than a frap. Herbie was nearly speechless, but he managed to say, "Sure, Pa. Gosh, that's great."

"Yes, I'm having dinner with some business associates, and this is a good time for you to start going like a man among men. You've earned the right."

"Thanks, Pa. I'll go get dressed right away."

Herbie would have bounced up and down on the sofa, but he knew that a man among men didn't bounce. His father put a hand on his arm.

"Wait. I hear Krieger's boy got left back?"

"Uh-huh."

"Too bad, too bad. How could such a terrible thing

happen?" said Mr. Bookbinder, his smile broadening into pure pleasure.

"Aw, I guess Lennie is just dumb. Anyway, all he thinks about is girls."

"Foolish. A boy shouldn't bother his head about girls until he's twenty-one."

"I don't, that's for sure," said Herbie, and believed it. A frap and prospective dinner with his father in a restaurant had brought a new, mature Herbie Bookbinder into being. The Herbie who had been childishly smitten with Lucille Glass belonged to history.

"Well, Krieger will be at dinner with us. We won't make him feel bad by mentioning it."

"No, Pa."

"Of course, there's nothing wrong in mentioning you've been skipped," said the father, and dismissed his son with a pat on the shoulder.

Herbie trotted gaily to his room, put on a clean shirt, a new tie, and his "other" suit—the new suit bought at Passover was always known as the "other" suit, until the next Passover came. Felicia, returning from an afternoon of loitering along Southern Boulevard, sniffed at him and said, "Hm, the other suit, hey?"

"Yes, the other suit," said Herbie. He savored the enjoyment of saying no more, and Felicia would not give him the satisfaction of asking questions, so he finished dressing in glee while the girl ate herself alive with curiosity. Just as Herbie was leaving with his father, he heard an outraged howl from Felicia, who had finally pried the answer from her mother: "Why can't I go to the restaurant, too?"

"Hush up, you didn't skip," he heard the mother answer, and he closed the door behind him with a sigh of perfect happiness.

The two men strolled up Westchester Avenue in the humid evening. Trolley cars banged by, women embracing great brown paper bags of food jostled past them, trucks blasted clouds of poison gas at them, children darted under their feet after marbles and rubber balls, and every little while a questing mother a few inches from them would affright their eardrums with a shriek like "Bernice! Come home to supper!" All this plebian bustle was delightful. It sharpened Herbie's anticipation of the noble act of eating in a restaurant.

"Herbie," said his father, "what do you want to be someday?"

"You mean when I grow up?"

"That's right."

"An astronomer," came the usual prompt reply. But it did not have the usual effect. In discussions with boys the announcement of Herbie's ambition always caused awe among the future firemen, policemen, big-league ball players and candy-store keepers, but it fell very flat with his father. Mr. Bookbinder made a face as though he had bitten into a green apple, then smiled.

"That's fine. That's a very fine profession. You'll never make a good dollar, but if you're interested in stars, you should by all means be an astronomer. A great astronomer."

"Astronomers make lots of money," said Herbie, a little less positively than was his habit.

"How?"

"When they find new stars—er—they win big prizes."

Mr. Bookbinder laughed. Then he said gravely, "Whoever says so, my boy, is a terrible liar. It ought to be so, but it isn't. People only pay for things they want— clothes, laundry, meat, movies, and ice. Who cares about new stars up in the sky? Discovering stars is a great, wonderful thing, but nobody gets fat doing it. Still, you should by all means be an astronomer, the finest astronomer in the world, if that's what you want."

They crossed the gutter of Austen Avenue at a run to dodge a black coal truck howling toward them, and walked on in silence. Jacob Bookbinder and his son had taken the tone of companions on a walk, and the change from the father-son relationship made them both feel clumsy. The father longed for his usual evening monologue on the problems of the Place, but his boy's ear seemed somehow a less fitting receptacle for it than his wife's. As for Herbie, none of the things that came into his mind seemed worth saying to a fearfully wise man like his father, after the puncturing of his astronomic fiction. The result was that they arrived at Golden's Restaurant on Southern Boulevard without exchanging another word.

Herbie's heart glowed within him at the sight of the steaks, fruits, layer cakes, and thickly creamed pastries in the glittering show window of Golden's, while Mr. Bookbinder, seeing Powers, Louis Glass, and Krieger seated at a table near the window, suddenly wondered whether bringing Herbie had not been a foolish deed. An impulse to honor the boy, a vague sense that he was in the habit of neglecting him, and an equally cloudy notion that the time had come to give his son the baptism of fire of a real business discussion had combined to cause his act. Now he sensed an urge to send him home. But Jacob Bookbinder was not in the habit of altering his resolutions. In fact, it was his way to quell his own hesitancy with grim pleasure. "Do it and see," was his favorite word to himself. He had invited Herbie to dinner at Golden's, and dinner at Golden's Herbie would have.

"Come, my boy, I see we're late," he said, and led his son inside.

Introducing Herbie was as awkward as his father expected, but he met the astonished glances of the others squarely and explained that he was rewarding his boy with a treat because he had skipped. Louis Glass, a fat, rubicund man with a black mustache, shook Herbie's hand and congratulated him. He had seen many youngsters ripen into clients yielding fees. Powers, already out of sorts at being dragged up to the Bronx after dark, permitted himself to look annoyed as he rapped the ash out of his pipe and thrust it into a pocket.

Krieger delivered his views as follows: "Same father, same son. Haybie big future. Maybe not go too fast better. Little fat boy in college better maybe not. Slow and steady turtle beat rabbit. Haybie different naturally. Smart is very fine——"

The table had places only for four. As Mr. Krieger

rattled on, the waiter moved a narrow serving table along-side, projecting into the aisle. Here Herbie sat, looking like an extremely unnecessary appendage to the group. Menus were placed in the hands of the diners, and the men ordered their meals carelessly and quickly.

Not so Herbie.

"What should I have, Pa?" he said nervously, bewildered by the menu.

"You're old enough to order for yourself. Have whatever you want."

Herbie ran his eye up and down the page and got a confused impression of a meal composed of sponge cake, pastry, smoked salmon, goulash, vegetables in sour cream, roast chicken, chopped herring, prunes, and ice cream.

"I—I'm not very hungry," he faltered.

"Then skip down to the main course. That's all we're having," said the father, and indicated a section of the bill of fare with his finger.

This was a help. But having to choose among lamb chops, broiled chicken, roast duck, steak, and so forth was still torture—not less for the youngster than for the waiter, a squat, bitter-faced bald man in greasy black trousers and spotted gray cotton jacket. This functionary shifted from foot to foot while Herbie puzzled; he yawned, he rapped his pencil against the order pad, he went "ha-hem" several times, and he stared malevolently at the boy, obviously wishing him far away and in bad health.

"Come, Herbie, the man can't stand there forever," said the father.

Powers said, "The kid evidently doesn't know what he wants. Order for him."

"I'll have boiled haddock," Herbie burst out all at once, picking the item under his eye at that instant.

Everybody, even the waiter, looked amazed.

"Don't be silly, boy," said Jacob Bookbinder. "Boiled haddock, with all those delicious meat dishes to pick from? Come, take a steak."

But Herbie felt that his self-respect, his whole grip on

manhood, depended on his sticking to the haddock now, although he loathed it. "Can't a guy order what he wants?" he complained. "I ordered boiled haddock, and that's what I'd like."

"Give him boiled haddock," said his father with a shrug. The waiter pried the bill of fare out of Herbie's spasmodically clutching fingers and walked off. Herbie gloomily watched the stooped back disappear through the swinging kitchen doors, and cursed his own folly.

The consequences were worse than he imagined. Golden's was mainly a meat restaurant. The fish was a desultory item placed on the menu for the rare customer who insisted on fish. Soon the waiter reappeared with four sizzling steaks that smelled heavenly, and a plate containing a pair of round blobs, white and green. The white was the haddock, buried under a thick flour sauce; the green was an unexpected horror, creamed spinach, which came with the fish. As the waiter put Herbie's plate down he winked, and all the men laughed. Herbie felt a blush rise to his face.

"That fish looks disgusting," said his father. "Waiter, take that mess away and bring the boy some lamb chops."

"Pa, please, this is just what I want," cried Herbie angrily. He placed his hand protectingly against the plate, and the gluey white mass trembled a little. The boy's throat crawled at the prospect of eating it. But he was going to eat it or die.

"After all, Bookbinder, he's grown up," said Powers with a grin. "Didn't he just skip to the eighth grade?"

Herbie's father glanced at the young man from Manhattan with narrowed eyes.

"All right, my boy," he said to Herbie. "But as long as you ordered it, eat it."

And Herbie, who understood his father's appeal not to disgrace him, ate it, with all the men watching him. Not a morsel of spinach or haddock remained. Heroes in other books do more noble and colorful deeds, but Herbie Bookbinder stands or falls as a hero for swallowing down every trace of those two ghastly mounds, green and white, and smacking his lips over them.

"Well, Bookbinder," said Powers when the steaks were eaten, leaning back and packing his pipe from an alligator-skin pouch, "do we talk business or do you send the boy home first?"

"The boy's doing no harm," retorted Bookbinder, "unless you other gentlemen object to him."

There was a difficult pause.

"Why, I think," said Louis Glass heartily, "that it'll do Herbie good to hear a business talk. Hear a business talk. Nothing like starting early in life, early in life, eh, Herbie?" He slapped the boy lightly on the back, and lit a cigar.

The waiter brought dessert. It was a house custom at Golden's to serve French pastry on a little flat stand, which was placed on the table when coffee was served, and left there. The stand accommodated eight pieces. The waiter simply counted the number missing at the close of the meal, and charged for them on the bill. None of the men accepted a piece when the waiter offered it to them, so he set the little stand down before Herbie and departed. The boy felt his shattered appetite pull itself together as he surveyed the eight creamy pastries, all of different shapes and colors.

Louis Glass polished the pince-nez that hung on a black ribbon around his neck. "Well, gentlemen, I see no reason why we can't settle our business between the time we start our coffee and finish it. Start our coffee and finish it," he said.

"That'll suit me beautifully," remarked Powers. "I'm late for a theater party now."

Bookbinder and Krieger said nothing.

Herbie tentatively selected a chocolate-covered cylinder filled with whipped cream, and sank his teeth into it. He seemed to hear chimes of Paradise. By comparison with this, the frap itself sank out of sight.

"There's only one thing to be discussed," went on Louis Glass. "I've described to you, Bookbinder, the advantages that will accrue to both you and Krieger from a merger of

Bronx River with Interborough. I've made it as clear as I can that Interborough, which is now the largest ice company in New York, will guarantee to give both of you top executive positions. As I happen to be their attorney, I am speaking with some authority, with some authority. I have also given you my opinion that the so-called blue paper is a totally irregular document, no more than a scratch-pad memorandum, in effect, which does not transfer in due and proper form any stocks to you, and have advised you that if you choose to stand on it your stand will be overthrown in court. Overthrown in court."

During this speech, Herbie finished the whipped-cream roll in three rapturous bites. He now chose a charming oval piece entirely covered with green and chocolate cream, and bit into it.

"Your decision, then, as I see it," proceeded the lawyer, waving away clouds of blue smoke from Powers' fast-puffing pipe, "must be the sensible one of accepting this great increase in your good fortunes—I refer to the merger—or the highly dubious one of a court fight as to whether you or Mr. Powers has control of the Place, which I have stated you will lose. Stated you will lose."

Herbie heard these words dimly through the fog of ecstasy conjured up by French pastry, and wondered why Mr. Glass had the habit of acting as his own echo. But he forgot the perplexity as the last bite of mint and chocolate vanished, leaving him with the urgent question, which cake to eat next. The boy was not aware that these things would have to be paid for. They had been set before him like a bowl of fruit at home, and so he regarded them. After the haddock horror, it seemed to him that the only way to retrieve the glory of a restaurant meal was to consume as many pastries as he could hold. So he selected a chocolate éclair, and went to work on it.

When the lawyer finished talking, Bookbinder and Krieger looked at each other. Herbie's father started to speak, but Krieger hastily and loudly broke in, "I say this way. Blue paper maybe yes, maybe no, who say for sure? I say peaceable. Executive position ten thousand a year very fine, maybe three thousand not so fine. But peaceable black and white on paper how much guaranteed? All gentlemen, word good as gold, but black and white on paper not yet. Thirty years in the ice business always black and white more peaceable. Mr. Glass very fine explain, everybody good friends all stick together. I say this way—"

(The éclair gone, Herbie commenced a rapid demolition of a round brown pastry that looked rather like a potato but was filled with exquisite orange-flavored cream.)

"If I understand you correctly, Mr. Krieger," interrupted Louis Glass, "I believe you need say no more. Interborough is prepared to guarantee in writing, as a condition of the merger, both of your salaries at"—he glanced at Powers, who continued puffing at his pipe and gave a tiny nod—"five thousand a year, merely as a beginning. Merely as a beginning."

"You understand him wrong, and what he said meant nothing," exclaimed Jacob Bookbinder, his expression so drawn and belligerent that he hardly resembled the man who had been smiling at his son a little while before. Herbie had seen this expression, which he thought of as his father's "business face," more than once, and it terrified him. He paid more attention to the talk now, as he absently began to eat a flaky yellow Napoleon.

"Jake, I say this way, peaceable," began Krieger, but Herbie's father said coldly to the lawyer, ignoring his partner, "Krieger is repeating what he said to me when he and I talked this out, but I guess what you want is our conclusion. In short, it's no sale. I think the blue paper is good."

Powers said, "Mr. Krieger, is that your opinion, too?"

Sardonically, Bookbinder put in, "I'll save you a half hour of talk. Krieger and I and our wives have a voting trust binding all our stock. Krieger must go along with me."

The lawyer and Powers looked at Krieger. The partner nodded half-heartedly.

Herbie could not follow the duel and lost interest. For

some reason the Napoleon did not taste as good to him as the first four pastries had. He finished it quickly and began on a cherry tart. And now he became aware of a new, disturbing fact: the waiter was standing near by, staring at him with a mixture of horror and fascination. With each bite he took of the tart the waiter's eyes seemed to open wider. Herbie could not imagine what the man was looking at. He glanced uneasily at his suit to see if a blotch of food had fallen on it, and looked behind him, but evidently there was no marvel in sight but himself, a perfectly ordinary boy. The waiter's eyes made him self-conscious. He gobbled down the tart, not enjoying it very much, and reached for something he had been saving, a morsel consisting of four walls of solid chocolate brimful of coffee-colored cream. As he bit into it he saw with some discomfort that the waiter's jaw dropped open and he actually grew pale. He concluded the man must be sick—probably from the food in this miserable restaurant. Herbie was feeling none too well himself. The beautiful chocolate cake somehow tasted not much better than the boiled haddock had, and was just as gluey.

The conversation had jumped ahead several notches during Herbie's preoccupation with the waiter. He tried to pick up the thread, nibbling at the pastry more and more slowly. Powers was saying, "—certainly don't see why I had to come uptown at night to hear this same foolish story. I thought you men had come to your senses."

"I cannot help calling it most ill-advised, most ill-advised," the lawyer said, crushing out his half-smoked cigar. "I assure you the blue paper as it stands is worthless. In my opinion, Mr. Powers would be justified in proceeding to sell Bronx River Ice, but we must recognize that as the attorney for Interborough I cannot advise them to purchase a property, title to which is in any way doubtful. Any way doubtful."

"I'll talk to Burlingame in the morning," said Powers angrily, "and if he wants to buy I'll sell, with no provision at all for Messrs. Bookbinder and Krieger. Businessmen don't act the way they have done, and they have forfeited any claim to consideration. That's all I have to say."

"Yes, I'm a crazy businessman," Bookbinder shot back. "I want to remain a businessman, instead of becoming Burlingame's assistant."

"Pa."

The word came faintly from Herbie's direction. His father turned and looked at him.

"Pa, I don't feel good."

Herbie was slumped in his chair, looking straight ahead with dull eyes. In one listless hand hanging at his side was a fragment of chocolate cake. The color of the boy's face was not unlike that of the creamed spinach he had eaten.

"Lord in heaven! He's sick. Why did you have to eat that rotten fish, boy?" said the father in great distress.

"Mister, don't you blame our food!" shouted the waiter. He advanced to the table and raised his right hand high. "I hope I drop dead if that boy didn't eat seven pieces of French pastry. Seven pieces, mister! I saw him with my own eyes. From that even an elephant would get sick. I personally don't feel good from watching him."

Herbie stood up unsteadily.

"I guess I'll go home, Pa," he said. His stomach seemed to him to be rippling like a lake in a breeze; he could see mistily before his eyes the colored images of all the pastries he had eaten, swimming slowly around; and the word "frap" kept repeating itself in his brain—frap, frap, frap—and was somehow the most loathsome sound that man had ever uttered.

"Come, my boy, I'll take you." Bookbinder jumped up and grasped the boy's arm. "Gentlemen, our business was finished anyway, so excuse me for leaving like this. Mr. Powers, believe me you'll live to thank me for keeping our business in our own hands. Krieger, pay my check. Good night."

He rushed the boy outside and stood with him at the curb, signaling for a taxi. But none came at once, and Herbert, teetering on the curb, endured all the agonies of a rough sea voyage and then suddenly enjoyed the sovereign relief that comes of leaning over the rail. His father sympathetically gave him aid, and then walked the pale, shaky boy home. Fresh air was better for him, now, than

a taxi. The walk gradually revived Herbie, and through
the darkness of his discomfort the drift of the business
talk began to come back to him.

"Pa," he said timidly, "can Mr. Powers really sell the
Place and throw you an' Mr. Krieger out?"

"Don't you worry about that," said Bookbinder. But his
face was tense and sad. "Forget everything you heard,
Herbie. For you it's castor oil and bed."

And thus, with castor oil, bed, and a chilly awareness
that he had failed to distinguish himself, ended Herbie
Bookbinder's first evening as a man among men.

11

On to Manitou

THE FOLLOWING MONDAY, the first of July, the emigration
of children from the city began.

For the first time, Herbie Bookbinder gave up the
well-known city pleasures of summertime—baths under
fire hydrants, cold watermelons from horse-drawn wagons, picnics at city beaches or parks, and infinite lazy
loitering in sun and shade wherever he pleased—and set
out to taste the unknown delights of a country camp. The
Bookbinder family loaded baggage and selves into the
Chevrolet in front of 1075 Homer Avenue for the trip to
Grand Central Station. An ancient watermelon wagon
went by, pulled by the same old white horse, with the
same old ragged, dirty-faced driver chanting his call:
"Waw-dee-MAY-lun! Waw-dee-MAY-lun!" The wagon
was piled high with fat green melons and chunks of ice;
Herbie felt a pang of yearning for a chilly slice, and a
wisp of regret at leaving home. But these sentiments faded

as the car grunted and started on the journey. What was
"Waw-dee-MAY-lun," after all, compared to the coming
feasts and splendors in far-off Manitou?

A beam of dusty sunlight slanted down across the
empty dome of Grand Central Terminal and struck a
large square yellow banner hanging on the wall in one
corner of the huge concourse. Sewn on the banner in
letters of red were the words:

CAMP MANITOU
IN THE BERKSHIRES

Mr. Gauss was proud of the Old English lettering, so
full of dignity and distinction. Unfortunately for Herbie,
Felicia, and their parents, who were frantically searching
for the banner ten minutes before train time, MANITOU
is rather hard to read at a distance of more than ten feet.
On all sides they could see banners: Camp Hiawatha, red
and blue; Camp Algonquin, green and white; Camp
Penobscot, green and gray; Camp Iroquois, blue and
gold; Camp Pueblo, Camp Wigwam, Camp Totem, Camp
Tomahawk, Camp Nokomis, Camp Tepee, and so on in
fifty shapes and a hundred colors. If these flags suggested
a renascence of the race of the American Indian at a
tremendous war council, the huddles under them did not.
In fact, nothing less resembling the noble naked redskin
could have been imagined than these boiling knots of
perspiring, peevish city children dressed in their "other"
suits and frocks, submitting sullenly to last-minute kisses
of red-eyed mothers or quarreling with each other or
balking loudly at orders from the camp leaders.

Here and there the solid Indian array was pierced by a
"Camp Williams" or "Camp Happiness." Herbie was very
glad he was not going to one of those dull places, but to
one with a magic name like MANITOU.

"There it is! I see Mr. Gauss!" cried Felicia at last, and
the Bookbinders hurried to present themselves to the fat
Pied Piper who was leading a line of children to his own
private land of wonder.

To their disappointment, the manner of Mr. Gauss was far less cordial than it had been. He seemed, indeed, quite short with them. This was not really so; Mr. Gauss simply had a limited supply of the butter of good nature. Spread on one family at a time it was rich, but thinned over eighty at once it left a dry taste.

Herbie cast his eye around the mob under the yellow banner and quickly noticed Lennie Krieger at the center of an admiring cluster of smaller boys, loudly making predictions about the baseball pennant races. Separate herds of boys and girls seemed to be forming. The fat boy peered here and there, and spied Lucille in the girls' group. He smiled and waved at her, but she turned modestly away.

"Looks like fun, huh, Fleece?" said Herbie, but there was no answer, and he perceived with surprise that his sister was no longer beside him, but was being led away by a tall, bulbous woman whose face was a field of freckles. He later learned that this was Aunt Tillie, "head counselor" of the girls. Now in his turn he felt his hand grasped in a large, dank, leathery grip. He looked up at his captor, an immense fair-haired, square-faced man with tiny eyes and thick, rimless glasses.

"I'm Uncle Sandy, your head counselor," said the man, "and you're little Herbie Bookbinder, aren't you? Come along."

Herbie came along, not liking it particularly, and was brought to a harried-looking, thin young man with a deep tan, standing amid a batch of small boys. "This is Uncle Nig, your counselor," said Uncle Sandy. "Bunk Eight, highest bunk of the Juniors. Isn't that swell?"

"Sandy, I've got six already," protested Uncle Nig, but Uncle Sandy hurried off, saying over his shoulder, "We'll straighten everything out on the train. He looks about Bunk Eight size."

Herbie glanced askance at the six short boys among whom he had been thrust, and they surveyed him with equally obvious distaste. They all looked disagreeable and very young.

"And what's your name, pal?" inquired Uncle Nig.

"Herbie Bookbinder," said the boy. He turned to the lad nearest him. "Say, what class are you in public school?"

"5A, and what's it to you, Fat?" replied the boy.

"5A?" cried Herbie in horror. "I'm in 8B!"

Uncle Nig raised his eyebrows and said soothingly, "Don't start off telling lies, Herb. Be a regular guy."

"But I *am* in 8B. I can prove it!"

The boys laughed at him. One said, "That's nothing, I go to high school."

"Me, I go to Harvard," added another, and raised more giggles.

Herbie was assailed with an extremely positive feeling that he was not going to like Camp Manitou.

"All aboard!" shouted Uncle Sandy through a megaphone. Aunt Tillie began pulling down the banner. "Say good-by, folks, we leave in three minutes."

Herbie's waist was encircled by clutching arms. His mother had dropped to a squatting position beside him, her eyes streaming, her faded cheeks flushed with emotion.

"Good-by, my boy, my boy, my darling," she sobbed. "I know you're going to be happy, so I'm happy, too. We'll come to see you."

While she hugged and kissed him his father managed to free Herbie's right hand and shake it. "Be a man, Herbie," he shouted over the tumult of the departure.

"Where's Cliff? I ain't even seen Cliff," said Herbie petulantly, not knowing what else to say in the bewilderment of the moment. "Ain't he comin' to camp?"

"Is that all you can think about—Cliff—when you're going away from home? At least kiss me good-by," complained the mother. Herbie considered kissing in public a mean business for a boy in 8B, but everybody else seemed to be doing it, so he obliged his mother with a brief smack on the nose.

"We'll take swell care of him, don't you worry, Mrs. Bookbinder," said Uncle Nig. "All right, pals, let's get going."

Driven, coaxed, shoved, and barked at by the young men and women known as counselors, the two flocks of children straggled to the train. The more emotional parents bleated at the flanks of the procession right up to the last gate. Jacob Bookbinder and his wife stood where the banner had hung, and waved at their retreating son and daughter whenever they glanced back. Just at the gate, Herbie took a last look at his mother and father. Standing amid the hurrying crowds of well-dressed tourists, wearing their everyday Bronx clothes, smiling and waving, they seemed like two tired, shabby little people to the boy; and, curiously enough, he saw something at that distance that he had never noticed when he had been much closer to them. He saw that his father's hair was almost all gray.

"Good-by, Ma! Good-by, Pa!" he suddenly shouted at the top of his lungs, when it was no longer possible for them to hear him.

"Keep in line, Herbie," said Uncle Nig.

It was not possible for the boy to start crying amid other lads, and his face remained calm, but his eyes filled, his throat swelled, and he hardly saw where he was going, or knew what he was doing, or came to himself again, until the starting jar of the train told him he was really leaving New York City.

Some take it soon, some late—but it is a long step along the path of life when a child first pities his mother and father.

However, the feelings of boyhood, like the skies of spring, change quickly. A few minutes later he was absorbed in the unfamiliar view of the back parts of the city along the railroad track. Within five minutes he was bored by this novelty, and in its place the injustice of being classed with fifth-graders awoke in his mind as a great outrage. He rose and started to edge his way out of his seat, past the strange boy beside him.

"Where are you going, pal?" came the voice of Uncle Nig. The dark-faced counselor was in the seat behind him.

"Just to find my cousin Cliff."

"Well, ask my permission first. I can't have you wandering off in all directions."

"O.K.," said Herbie, and stepped out into the aisle.

"Well?" said Uncle Nig.

"Well, what?"

"I'm still waiting for you to ask my permission to leave your seat."

"I've already left it."

"Well, then, get back into it."

"But that's silly. I'll only have to get out of it again."

"I decide what's silly and what isn't. Get back into your seat."

Herbie hesitated, and briefly weighed the advisability of declaring his independence with a formal statement, such as "Horse feathers." The right of this young man to order him about was not at all clear. He was putting the saddle on Herbie for the first time, when the tamest beast tends to balk; besides, he seemed to be himself in a twilight state, not quite boy, not quite man. But children of eleven are so used to the despotism of the adult race that they can hardly tell usurped authority from the real thing. Herbie added up the elements, took the sum, and climbed back into his seat.

"Fine, pal. Now go ahead and find your cousin."

But to obey this would have savored of jumping through hoops. "Naw," said Herbie gloomily, "I changed my mind."

Uncle Sandy bulked huge at the head of the aisle.

"All right, gang," he bawled through his megaphone, "here we go for another summer of rip-roaring fun at good old Camp Manitou. What say, you old-timers, let's show the new gang the Manitou spirit. Uncle Irish is back with us as swimming counselor, and he's going to lead you in the good old camp cheer. Now, give it a lot of spirit."

A young man with the broadest shoulders Herbie had ever seen, and a shock of bright red hair, leaped into the aisle, shouted, "O.K., fellows. Let's give 'em 'Oink-oink, bow-wow.' All together now. Hip, hip," and began waving his arms in strange jerky motions. A ragged chant came forth from some of the boys, consisting of imitations of animal noises, railroad noises, and what sounded like fire-cracker noises, with no English words that Herbie could understand except a repeated exhortation to "get a rat trap bigger than a cat trap."

When it was over, Uncle Irish cried, "O.K., now, you new fellows got it? Let's give it to 'em again, everybody, twice as loud."

The thing was repeated. It was not twice as loud, however, but approximately half as loud. This time Herbie thought he heard, amid the squeals, hisses, croaks, and choo-choos, certain references to shanty towns, Chevrolets, chiggers, and cannibals, but he imagined he must be mistaken.

Uncle Sandy was on his feet again.

"That was pretty good, gang, pretty good. 'Course it'll sound a lot better when you new fellows really catch on. Now Uncle Irish is going to lead you in 'Bulldog, Bulldog,' our camp song. And I want plenty of spirit this time, particularly from you Seniors. You fellows know this song well enough. Now, come on, put some spirit into it."

He pointed at a group of boys across the aisle from Herbie, about fourteen or fifteen years of age. They lolled in seats they had reversed so that four of them could face each other, and seemed very grand and old in their long trousers and fedora hats. When they were thus publicly rebuked, Herbie saw them grin evilly at each other and whisper.

"Bulldog, Bulldog" was duly sung in draggy discords. The older boys sat with locked lips. The voices of the head counselor and Uncle Irish boomed out through the car. As soon as the song ended, the silent long-trousered clique burst forth with the following chant, rendered in a sneering singsong, with much more spirit and precision than either the song or the cheer:

> *Here comes boloney,*
> *Riding on a pony—*
> *Hooray, Uncle Sandy!*

The head counselor strode up the aisle, smiling a joyless smile. He stopped and towered beside Herbie's seat.

"All right, Bunk Sixteen, I can take a joke," he said for

all the car to hear. "But there are a lot of new boys here who don't know what's right and what's wrong. If you fellows want to spend the first two weeks without senior privileges I'm perfectly agreeable. Just remember, once you're on this train you aren't behind your mama's skirts any more. You're in Camp Manitou. If you can't show real camp spirit, then keep your faces shut."

As Uncle Sandy walked back to the front of the car in a heavy silence, Herbie scanned the group of older boys. Smiles and whispers there were none—just shamed, resentful faces. The long trousers appeared to hang less jauntily on their gangling legs.

"Now, gang," said the head counselor in a pleasanter tone through the megaphone, "a few simple train rules. No leaving your seat, no changing of seats without your counselor's permission. No opening windows. Absolutely no visiting in the girls' car up ahead. If I catch anyone in the girls' car, it will be just too bad. It's a three-hour ride, so make yourselves comfortable, get acquainted, and get all set for the swellest summer you've ever had. That's all."

He sat down. Like a counterweight on a rope, Uncle Irish jumped up.

"Come on, fellows. Let's give an 'Oink-oink, bow-wow' for the good old head counselor, Uncle Sandy."

And so a third time the chant was repeated, in such a dreary, tattered way that it all but died between the Chevrolets and the cannibals.

The train was bowling through suburbs, now, and green was beginning to show here and there through gray and brick red. Herbie's spirits, dampened by the recent shows of force, began to revive. He watched the fleeing landscape with pleasure as the city grimness dwindled and the world in its pristine colors came more and more to view. After a while a cow flashed by—a living cow, an animal the boy had never seen except in picture books and milk-company advertisements. His heart leaped up. Perhaps camp would be fun, after all.

Two counselors came along the aisle with baskets, and Herbie was handed a cardboard container of milk and a wrapped sandwich. He undid the paper; it was lettuce and canned salmon on rye bread, one of his favorite foods. He sank back into the seat, and munched and sipped and gazed out of the window at trees, brooks, and meadows. There was no longer any doubt about it: he was en route to the Promised Land.

"Hey, Herbie, where you been?"

His cousin, Cliff, was standing by the seat, a red and yellow felt cap, with the monogram "CM" on it, pulled down rakishly over one eye.

"Hi, Cliff, where *you* been? Whereja get the cap?"

"One of the guys in my bunk give it to me. They're a swell gang."

"What bunk is that?"

"Twelve. Come on over. I been tellin' them about you."

Herbie got up and started to edge out; then he remembered.

"Uncle Nig, permission to leave my seat?"

The counselor, his nose in a heavy blue book entitled *Comparative Literature, Third Year,* grunted consent. Herbie joined his cousin in the aisle.

"What're you doin' with these kids?" said Cliff in a low tone. "They don't even look like Intermediates."

"What's Intermediates?"

"I'm an Intermediate. So's my whole bunk. It goes Midgets, Juniors, Intermediates, Seniors, and Superseniors."

"Jumpin' cats, I remember now. Cliff, you know what? These kids are Juniors. Juniors! One of them is in 5A. They've stuck me in with *Juniors!*"

Herbie pronounced the word "Juniors" as a minister says "pagans," as a Southerner says "Yankees," as a millionaire says "bolsheviks."

"Aw, it's a mistake," said Cliff. "Come on an' talk to my counselor. Bet he gets you in with us."

Tilting the cap back, for the slant seriously cut down his vision, Cliff led his cousin to the group of boys surrounding the red-headed swimming counselor near the front of the car. "I'm in Uncle Irish's bunk," he said proudly. Herbie observed lads his own age (and therefore somewhat larger than himself) laughing and joking with the cheer leader. He hoped mightily that he would be taken into this happy circle.

"Hey, Uncle Irish," said Cliff, "here's my cousin Herb I been tellin' you about."

"Oh, hello, boy wonder," said Uncle Irish genially. (The name of Uncle Irish, by the way, was Abraham Potovsky.) "So you're the kid who's eleven years old and in 8B."

"Eleven and a half," said Herbie, bashfully.

"According to your cousin Cliff, you're about the smartest guy alive."

"Heck, I'm too fat to run a lot, so I read a lot," said Herbie.

This answer was a success both with the counselor and the boys, who had been staring at him rather critically. Uncle Irish laughed. A stocky boy with black hair that stood straight up said, "Well, he admits he's fat, anyway," and smiled, and shifted so that Herbie could sit opposite the counselor.

"What bunk are you in, Herb?" said another boy.

Herbie felt ashamed, but he said, "They got me in Bunk Eight."

The cheer leader was amazed. "Bunk Eight for a boy in 8B? Why, that's impossible. They're Juniors."

"I guess it's a mistake. I hope so, anyway," said Herbie.

"It certainly is," said Uncle Irish. "Come along right now. We'll talk to Uncle Sandy."

"See, I told you, Herb," whispered Cliff.

"Get 'im in with us, Uncle Irish," said the boy with the standing hair.

The counselor led Herbie by the hand to a front seat of the car which Uncle Sandy occupied in lone state, surrounded by charts, diagrams, and papers. He was preparing schedules of athletic activities, plotting them on sheets clipped to a writing board which he held in his lap. The one he was making at the moment bore the cryptic heading, "Basketball—Toothpaste." It would bear fruit in due time, in desperate games between the Pepsodents and the Listerines, the Forhans and the Colgates. Boys who were Pebecos would vow everlasting hatred for boys who were Ipanas. Boys unfortunate enough to find themselves on the feeble Odonto team would tearfully ask their parents in mid-season to take them home. Uncle Sandy knew the simple truth that boys, and not only boys, will fight ten times more bitterly in a contest between labels, however inappropriate and silly, than in a vague and casual tussle. So at Camp Manitou when baseball was played it was Fords against Cadillacs; volleyball, Greta Garbos against Joan Crawfords; track meets, Buffaloes against Polecats; and so forth, and so forth, the thin trick repeated and repeated, and never failing to goad the children into showing "camp spirit." It ended at last in a so-called color war between the Reds and the Yellows. The whole camp, including counselors, was divided, and boys lost weight, made lifelong enemies, fought with fists, nearly drowned, and sometimes broke legs and arms defending the glorious name of Yellow or Red.

"Sandy," said Uncle Irish, "may I talk to you for a minute?"

"Hmph," said the head counselor, not taking his eye off the line he was drawing alongside the word Squibbs.

"There seems to have been a mistake in placing one of the kids in Bunk Eight."

"Bunk Eight? That isn't your bunk, Irish," said Uncle Sandy, rousing himself and peering at the speaker through thick lenses.

"I know. I just happened to find out about it. This boy here, Herbie Bookbinder, is in the eighth grade, and you've got him among the Juniors."

Uncle Sandy transferred his squinting gaze to Herbie. His eyes had been nearly ruined in medical studies, of which he was now in the last year.

"Oh, yes, Herbie Bookbinder." He meditated a moment, while Herbie fidgeted.

"I'll be glad to take him into my bunk," said the swimming counselor. "That's about where you should have put him, anyhow."

Unluckily for Herbie, Uncle Irish said the wrong thing. Sandy was a good-hearted sort of drudge; he had little humor in him and less warmth, but he was anxious to do his work well. Above all things, however, he disliked being forced to admit a mistake. The cheer leader's innocent phrase "you should have put him" was absorbed into the thick fluid of Uncle Sandy's mind as a criticism, and therefore set up irritation.

"I'm not so sure of that," he answered slowly. "The basis of camp subdivision is physique, not academic standing. The boy's the size of a Junior, isn't he?"

"I suppose so," said Uncle Irish, astonished that Sandy was even arguing the point, "but surely the kid's an exception. Why, he'll be miserable among boys he can't talk to. He simply won't stay the season."

Herbie listened to the debate with a pounding pulse, and thought that angels in heaven must have bright red hair and wide shoulders.

Said Uncle Sandy grudgingly, "Why are you so anxious to have him in your bunk? Think his parents will be good tippers or something?"

"Gosh, Sandy, I don't care where he goes. I just thought you'd be glad if I mentioned it."

Uncle Sandy was glad to correct the blunder, which he would have had to do in any case, but it was necessary for him to make the correction his own instead of Uncle Irish's. He picked up the chart of bunks and checked it over crossly.

"Anyway, it's impossible to put him in your bunk. You seem to forget that with the space cut out for the water tank you have room for five, not six."

"But I only have four now, Sandy. You know, Arnold Osterman didn't show up at the station on account of mumps."

Sandy hauled his large mass erect. "Never mind, Irish, I'll take care of this. Your bunk stays as it is. Just go back to your boys. I'll place Herbie Bookbinder myself."

Herbie felt his hand once more enclosed by Uncle Sandy's moist, tough paw. He was cut off from Uncle Irish's bunk now, as surely as if it were in another camp.

What small things determine happiness and disaster sometimes! Had the cheer leader spoken differently—a change of two or three words would have been enough—Herbie would have attained his desire, instead of being separated from it beyond recall. The head counselor hauled the boy back along the aisle and stopped beside the seat of a dumpy, middle-aged man, whose pale face was blue where it had been shaved. Herbie observed uneasily that Lennie Krieger was sitting in the seat opposite.

"Uncle Sid," said the head counselor, "here's one more boy for Bunk Thirteen. He's a little too smart for the bunk we assigned him to originally, so you get him."

At this auspicious introduction, Herbie became the target of five glares from five boys seated around the counselor.

"Don't tell me we're stuck with General Garbage!" cried Lennie. "My summer is ruined."

"That's enough out of you," said the counselor in a flat voice, but he regarded Herbie with no enthusiasm himself.

"Uncle Sid is our dramatic and music counselor," said Uncle Sandy, "so a smart boy who isn't very athletic should fit right in. Make room here, Ted." He addressed a hawk-faced boy with pale blond hair and a wide mouth that seemed to split the face into two parts. The boy threw a mutinous look at the head counselor and hitched himself across the seat which he had been occupying alone. Herbie sat. The head counselor walked off—and there the fat boy was. Like a sailor embarked in a hell ship, like a policeman assigned to a tunnel, like a priest sent to a squalid settlement in the fever belt of India, Herbie Bookbinder was committed beyond hope of release to a summer in Bunk Thirteen.

"What's your name?" inquired Uncle Sid.

Herbie told him, but he had hardly done so when Lennie chirruped, "General Garbage. His name's General Garbage."

"Hi, General," sneered a sallow boy in a red and yellow sweater with the CM emblem in front. Cruel nicknames catch on among boys like sparks in dry straw. Complimentary ones are almost unknown.

"What bunk were you in before they moved you here?" said the counselor.

"Bunk Eight. It was a Junior bunk," Herbie answered defensively, with a weak show of indignation.

"Guess maybe you belonged there. You're too small for this bunk, that's for sure," said the hawk-faced boy, looking out of the window.

"Now, let's be fair to him, fellows," said the counselor. "He has a right to have a good time."

"Not if it spoils ours," said Lennie. "Look, Uncle Sid, I know this kid from way back, from school an' everything. He can't run, he can't play ball, he can't fight, he can't do nothin'. He's just a fat sissy, and a teacher's pet, what's more, and none of us don't want him in Bunk Thirteen."

It seemed to Herbie that every word Lennie spoke was true, and that he himself was an abhorrent little thing, unworthy to stay alive.

"Uncle Sid," he said, "I sure don't wanna stay in the bunk if the fellows don't want me. Heck, I'd rather go back to Bunk Eight. Come on, let's go to Uncle Sandy."

Ted, the hawk-face, looked around at him. "Never mind, General Garbage," he said. "They stuck you in with us. I been goin' to this camp five years and I never saw no short punk like you in Bunk Thirteen. But now you're here, stay here."

"Now, that's the spirit," said Uncle Sid. "We'll get to know each other and all have a dandy time."

This effort brought on a thick cloud of silence. The dramatic counselor, by profession a teacher of music in a girls' high school, lacked the touch for his summer job.

Herbie ventured at last to say to his neighbor, "Are you guys Seniors?"

"I sure shoulda been a Senior after five years in Gauss's Gruesome Gulch," said Ted. "But catch 'em doin' anything right in this chain gang. We're the highest bunk of Intermediates."

Uncle Sid felt it behooved him to uphold the camp's

fair name, little as he knew about it. "Why do you keep coming back to camp if you think it's a chain gang?"

" 'Cause my folks gotta park me somewhere while they play golf all summer, and ol' man Gauss has my mom hypnotized, that's why!" Ted burst out bitterly. "If he hanged me it would be O.K. with her." He pulled a piece of chalk out of his pocket, drew a horrible skeleton on the side of the car, and labeled it, "Uncle Sid after two months at Manitou." Herbie laughed. Uncle Sid noticed the art work and made the hawk-face rub it out.

A long, dismal quiet ensued in Bunk Thirteen, while around them the rest of the camp chattered vivaciously.

Herbie thought about the day's events and concluded that no more mischances could befall him. He seemed to have had more concentrated bad luck in the past hour than in the previous eleven years of his term in the world. But he was mistaken in thinking it was over; he was about to bring on himself the worst trouble yet.

"Uncle Sid, can I go get a drink of water?"

The counselor said, "Yes, and don't bother me with such questions. You're with the big boys now." Herbie sneaked off, still more crestfallen—nothing he did seemed right today—while Lennie jeered after him, "Unkie Siddie, pwetty pwease may I get a dwinkie water?"

The cooler with its rack of paper cups was at the forward end of the car. Herbie drew himself a tepid cupful and stepped out on the platform, being uncomfortably close to Uncle Sandy at the cooler. As he raised the cup to his lips he saw Lucille looking at him through the glass of the door in the next car. She smiled, and beckoned.

Now, Herbie had almost forgotten Lucille. He did not at all remember that his wild impulse after their first meeting had set in motion the chain of cause and effect that had deposited Lennie, Cliff, and himself on this train speeding to the Berkshire Mountains. A long-headed politician would have congratulated himself, at this point, on the success of his scheme, but the importance of the moment was lost on Herbie. Lucille was only an immediate temptation, sweet, but dangerous. Uncle Sandy's warning rang in his ears.

He beckoned in return, but Lucille shook her head and waved at him, somewhat imperiously, to come to her. There are times when a man has no choice. He glanced over his shoulder to make sure he was unobserved, and slipped quietly through to the other car, to Lucille's side. They shrank into a corner of the platform.

"I ain't supposed to be here," Herbie whispered.

"Well, I ain't supposed to be talking to you, either," retorted Lucille. "Go on back if you wanna."

They leaned against the wall and silently savored the delight of being together in violation of the law.

"What bunk are you in?" said the boy after a while.

"Eleven. Intermediates. How about you?"

"Thirteen. That's the highest Intermediate bunk there is."

"What bunk is Lennie in?"

This question vexed Herbie very much. To spend time talking about Lennie, practically at the risk of his head, seemed ridiculous.

"What difference does that make?" he growled.

"Oh, you!" The girl gave him a sly look. "I'm just curious."

"Well, he's in my bunk, if you wanna know, an' I wish he was down in you-know-where instead."

"Herbie, why do you hate Lennie so much? He's a nice boy."

Herbie was trying to think of a devastating answer when the train door opened—and Uncle Sandy entered the girls' car!

He did not notice the two culprits, but stood on the platform with his back to them, so close that the boy could have touched him. "Aunt Tillie," he called, "may I speak to you for a moment?"

Frozen with fright, the boy and girl heard the voice of Aunt Tillie, drawing nearer as she spoke. "Certainly, Uncle Sandy. What is it?"

"About the busses at the station, Tillie. Mr. Gauss only hired four," said Uncle Sandy, and proceeded with an involved conversation about unloading the campers from the train. He did not move, and placed where he was he blocked Herbie's escape. The children stood silent and rigid as lizards.

Many moments passed. It began to seem more and more likely that the weak-eyed Sandy might actually finish his business and go away without catching them in sin. Herbie, at first terror stricken, found the danger slightly enjoyable as time went by. He turned to Lucille at last, and winked. This was a fearsome blunder, for the little girl's self-control, already at the breaking point, blew completely apart. She burst out in a loud, raucous giggle. Uncle Sandy jumped several inches in the air at this startling sound directly behind him; then he whirled, and confronted Herbie.

But the feelings of the small fat boy at this juncture are not to be described. Suffice it to say that he was marched back into the boys' car, publicly held up as an example of an undersize Romeo who wouldn't obey rules, and compelled to sit beside Uncle Sandy, with a large sign, reading "Camp Goop Number One," hung around his neck. And it was in this unenviable condition that Herbie, now universally known as General Garbage, rode into the Promised Land.

12

Mr. Gauss's Camp Manitou

THE LEGEND THAT there is a pot of gold at the end of every rainbow must have been started by city people to entertain their children, who never see more than a broken section of the glorious arch between the roofs and so

can easily believe that where the bow touches earth there
are places of glamour and marvels. But anybody who has
lived in open spaces has seen that the end of the rainbow
rests on plain old ground no different from the rest of the
world and that there's no pot of gold at the foot, either,
just a mud puddle after the rain.

Herbie's vision of Camp Manitou had been woven of
rainbows. He had dreamed of smooth, grassy playing
fields freshly marked in white, luxurious cottages, a wide,
gleaming lake with a sandy beach, and sundry other
charms compiled from books of English school life and
movies laid in summer resorts. The reality was a mud
puddle after the rain.

Camp Manitou was a huddle of weather-beaten wood-
en bungalows half walled with rusty screens, situated on
the shore of an anonymous body of water too small to be
called a lake but too large to be dismissed as a pond, of a
pretty blue color, and rather swampy than otherwise. The
"bunks" stood in two rows, with a gravel path known as
Company Street between them, and it was down this
thoroughfare that Herbie marched with the rest of the
camp, taking his first look at the rainbow territory. Company Street began at the dining hall, a large, crude wood-
en building midway on a hill, sloped down to the bunks,
and branched off to a swimming dock at the water's edge.
Coming down the hill, Herbie had a good view of the
playing fields. There were two baseball diamonds knee
high in daisies and less attractive weeds; a clump of tennis
courts with nets sagging, net posts askew, and ragged
dandelion patches flourishing in the red clay; a basketball
court with one basket erect and the other flat on its back;
handball walls with the sun shining through loose boards;
and a rickety swimming dock hauled up on a rock-strewn
shore, with one end lying in the shallow water beside a
half-sunk rowboat.

When Uncle Sid and his seven charges entered the
bungalow labeled "13," what met Herbie's eyes reminded
him even less of a crock of gold. Bare iron cots were
scattered about, seven new mattresses were dumped in the
middle of the floor, and rust-streaked canvas flaps, evi-

dently designed for protection against rain, were dangling along the walls and slapping against the screens when the wind blew. The roof was decorated with various names of boys carved, chalked, or painted in barbarous letters; outstanding among them was an inscription two feet long in thick red paint, reading "WILLIE 'STUPID' SCHNEI- DERMAN." Herbie's trunk, which had been sent on to camp a week earlier, was lying in a pile of luggage, upside down.

As may be imagined, the boys did not observe this decay and neglect without loud grumbling. Lennie de- clared that Mr. Gauss was a "crook" and that he wanted to take the next train home. Uncle Sid was so surprised and disheartened that he could not silence the rebellious comments on all sides of him. When he came into the bunk and saw the chaos, his self-command gave way, and he slumped forlornly on the bare springs of a cot, saying, "Oh, dear. I never bargained for this." The boys, baffled by having the representative of authority come over to their side, stood or sat around in silent dejection.

But a leader always arises in time of trouble.

"Look, guys, this ain't half as bad as it was in '25," spoke up Ted, the hawk-faced boy. "Some of the bunks didn't even have screens on 'em then. I guarantee you in a week you won't know the joint. Come on, let's divvy up the cots and mattresses and get this mess cleaned up. We gotta live in here."

Heartened by having something to do besides com- plain, his bunkmates went to work. They put the cots and mattresses in place, changed from city clothes into the brief camping costume, made up beds with the new linen and blankets each boy had brought, swept the floor, brushed the festooned cobwebs from the corners, rolled up the rain flaps, and by degrees began to be gayer and gayer.

The same process went on throughout the camp. Even- ing came on swiftly. When the double line of about eighty boys trooped up to the dining hall, there was more sing- ing, cheering, and gay banter than one would have thought possible after seeing the glum and angry faces that had come down the hill that afternoon. Mr. Gauss, whatever his faults, had a working knowledge of the minds of boys. The dinner was a spectacular feast of chopped liver, chicken soup, steak, fried potatoes, fruit salad, and ice cream. A letter-writing period was announced immediately after dinner, and free camp stationery was distributed. Shining, happy epistles went forth in dozens from the gorged boys. Had the correspondence period been announced when the young population first arrived at camp, the tenor of the letters might have been much different, but, as has been said, Mr. Gauss knew his boys. Herbie, like the others, had resolved to write a scorcher, but the text of his communication ran:

> Dear Ma and Pa,
>   It sure is swell here. We had steak and ice cream for supper just now. The place is real beautiful, with grass and trees and a lake. I'm in a swell bunk and the counselor is great. Everything is swell. This is a great camp. Well, have to quit writing now and finish unpacking. Will write more soon.
>
>   Your loving son,
>   Herbie.

This may seem a rather intoxicated screed, and so it is. Boys can get just as drunk on steak and ice cream as their elders do on cocktails.

Next morning howls of rage and protest rang through the camp again as it developed that the campers were going to be used to repair the fields. It was the new campers who did the howling. Veterans like Ted shrugged, and shouldered their spades and hoes. The objections grew so loud that Uncle Sandy called an assembly on the "parade ground," a clearing between the bunks and the lake front.

"I can hardly believe it," he shouted, squinting around at the array of frowning boys whose garden tools glittered in the strong sunlight, "but I'm told that there are one or two lazy, shiftless slackers in our midst who don't know what camp spirit means.

"Who's going to play on these fields, anyway? We are! Then who should fix them up so they can be played on? We should! If anybody will work harder today on those fields than I do, let him come to me, and I'll give him Super-senior privileges for the whole summer. And if there's anyone who doesn't want to work today, let him step right out now and say so."

Nobody stepped out, of course.

"Well, I guess I've been told wrong, and I'm glad of it!" cried Uncle Sandy. "Every one of you guys has got the real Camp Manitou spirit after all. On to the fields, men!" He brandished a pitchfork with a great display of heartiness and marched off, the campers following with laggard steps, confused but not convinced by his argument.

It was a diddle, of course. Uncle Sandy was being paid, and if Mr. Gauss imposed gardening on him as part of his job, that was his bad luck. The parents of the campers, however, had paid three hundred dollars per boy for a summer of games and pleasure, not for the privilege of digging weeds. Mr. Gauss was certainly cutting the corners of honest policy.

But again, he knew his boys. A day's toil in the fields was as healthful for them as sports, and once they warmed to it they enjoyed it, especially when the counselors joined them in jokes about "Uncle Gussie's" greed. He saved a lot of money by this procedure and the fields were swiftly made usable, and another excellent dinner, followed by a new Western movie, plugged the possible leaks in his scheme via angry letters. He had pursued this method for several years, and a few campers had actually been withdrawn by indignant parents who learned of it, but, balancing the loss against the gain, Mr. Gauss had decided it was sound practice, and he stolidly persisted in it.

For a few days Herbie alternated between liking camp life and hating it—liking it when the sun was warm on him, or when he was diving into the sweet waters of the lake, or when he was eating, or when he sat with Cliff watching the sunset in the honeysuckle-scented evening breeze; hating it when the bugle coarsely called him out of bed, when he had to stand rigid for inspections, when he was marched out to play games he didn't enjoy, and when anyone called him General Garbage, which was often. He gradually came to the view that camp was like the rest of life, with good and bad in it, most of the bad being traceable to adults or to Lennie Krieger. So faded this particular rainbow, once for all.

But there was another bow that glowed brightly as ever in the changeable sky—Lucille Glass. Herbie's first exploration of the grounds in his free time was in the direction of the girls' camp, and soon brought him up against a tall, thick hedge reinforced by a barbed-wire fence. He patiently examined its entire length, and found that it ran to the water's edge at one end and buried itself in brambles at the other end, near the top of the hill. There was one break in it about thirty yards from the water, wide enough for a pair of good-sized boys to walk through side by side, but this was closed with a heavily padlocked gate. Evidently Mr. Gauss was no encourager of romance.

"Uncle Sid," Herbie said diffidently that night in the bunk, "do we ever get to see the girls?"

A couple of the boys looked at him quizzically; Ted Kahn's grin was so wide that the upper half of his head seemed to be floating in free air. Quickly he added, "I got a sister over there."

"Why, yes, we'll see them at sundown services Friday night," said Uncle Sid.

Herbie became more anxious for religious improvement than ever.

13

The Green Pastures

ON THE SECOND day of camp Ted Kahn was elected captain of Bunk Thirteen. It galled Lennie to play the follower, but the other boy was so wise in camp ways that for the present he was not to be rivaled. The captain's post was a good one; he assigned the cleaning chores and did nothing himself but inspect, supervise, and make formal salutes and reports. It was Lennie's natural role in life; he felt it, and he knew Herbie felt it. There was something degrading for the athlete in sweeping the floor side by side with General Garbage. He made up for it as well as he could by heaping indignities on the fat boy, at which the others all laughed, but his heart was unsatisfied. He awaited his chance to challenge the captain.

Wednesday night after the bugle had rendered a cracked "Taps" and the camp lay under a misted half-moon, the boys of Bunk Thirteen heard Ted whisper loudly and hoarsely, "Psst! Fellers! Who wants to go with me for a moonlight swim?"

After a pause the voice of Eddie Bromberg, the sallow boy, was heard in an undertone: "Won't we get caught?"

"Naw. I done it a million times."

Lennie spoke aloud. "Sure, I'll go. Come on."

Ted answered softly, "O.K., but don't be so doggone brave. Keep your lousy voice down."

"I'll talk as loud as I please, and come over here and stop my lousy voice if you don't like it."

"O.K., O.K. Take it easy," whispered Ted. "Who else is coming?"

No answer.

The captain waited, then said to the small round form in the cot beside his, "How 'boutcha, General Garbage?"

Herbie answered, "How 'bout Uncle Sid? He's apt to come in any second and find we ain't here, then what?"

"He won't. They always have counselors' meeting Wednesday. The first week it never finishes up till midnight. It's O.K., I tell you. Whaddya say?"

Lennie put in, "Don't waste yer breath. That little sissy don't break no rules."

"Who says I don't?" whispered Herbie indignantly. Lennie's tone left no doubt that an inclination to break rules was the sign of manhood. "I'm game. Let's go."

"Who else?" said Ted.

"I guess I'm a sissy. I ain't breakin' no rules the first week," said Eddie Bromberg.

Now that one boy had had the courage to say it, the others whispered a chorus of "Me, too, same here, not me thank you," and such sentiments. Had Eddie but spoken up sooner, Herbie gladly would have joined the majority opinion, which sounded sensible to him. Flouting the law was very well for Ted, who seemed to be serving a sort of life sentence in Camp Manitou, so that nothing mattered any more; also for a bravo like Lennie. For Herbie it was a foolhardy, unappetizing venture. But his word was passed, and he had to make good. He crept out of bed and followed the dim forms of Ted and Lennie out of the bunk and down the hill to the waterfront.

A clammy fog was rising from the water and curling around the dock, so thick and white that the lake was invisible. Herbie stood at the edge of the dock with the other two law-breakers, nerving himself for a plunge into the whiteness.

"Hey, General, gonna swim in yer pajamas?" jeered Ted.

Herbie was embarrassed to realize he had forgotten to take them off. Lennie was stripped. Ted had a towel around his middle, which he dropped to the dock as he spoke. Two quick splashes, and Herbie was alone in a milky world with the half-closed eye of the moon peering down at him. He took off his pajamas, wondered sleepily what had brought him into these awkward, eerie circumstances, shivered at the dankness of the air, and threw himself off the dock. The water was shockingly warm. He essayed a few splashing strokes and began to feel gay and heroic. Really he should try harder to be like Lennie, he thought. What fun such guys had! He floated on his back, arms clasped under his head, and winked at the moon.

"Boy, this is the life!" he shouted.

Suddenly Herbie's head bashed hollowly against wood, the moon vanished, and all was eternal blackness.

"Hey, General, you drowned?" came a voice from directly overhead.

Herbie floundered and grabbed in panic, and found himself clutching a mossy, slimy post. He had drifted under the dock. His head ached and he could see nothing. But he got a grip on himself, shouted "I'm O.K.," and carefully felt his way under the dock to the ladder that hung deep into the water. He pulled himself into the light again and climbed out of the water, his legs trembling on each slippery rung.

Ted was drying himself with sharp, fast motions. Lennie was dancing around the dock, hugging and slapping himself.

"Didn't you bring no towel neither, General?" said the bunk captain.

"Naw, I'll use my pajamas."

The thin cotton cloth, hard buttons and all, felt delightful on his skin as it soaked away the moisture. After the swim the air was brutally damp and cold.

"How 'bout it, Lennie?" he said. "Want a lend o' half my pajamas?"

"Aw, who needs to dry off? Come on, let's get back."

Herbie would have sworn he heard Lennie's teeth chatter, had he not known that such a sign of weakness in the athlete was impossible.

But as they made their way up the hill, the impossible

became not only possible but obviously true. Lennie's teeth rattled so loud that Ted became worried at the noise, and made Lennie cover his mouth with the towel. When they came to the bunk, Lennie seized a dry towel, rubbed himself furiously, then dived into bed and lay hugging himself. His teeth were no longer chattering, but while Herbie and Ted boasted to the other boys in low tones of how marvelous the swim had been, Lennie said not a word. Herbie suspected that he was lying with rigidly clamped jaws to protect his reputation.

The next morning Lennie had a temperature of 102, and was transferred to the infirmary with a diagnosis of chill and incipient grippe. His plan for dethroning Ted was postponed.

It was the Fourth of July, and rumors were splendid about the fireworks display to come in the evening. Even Ted grudgingly admitted that "Uncle Gussie" was prodigal with fireworks. He shot them off himself from the girls' swimming dock while the boys and girls sat on the sloping lawn of the girls' camp in the gloom and watched. The truth is, this fireworks spree was one of Mr. Gauss's few really happy moments in a summer of spying, nagging, penny squeezing, and groveling to parents. And because it did the harassed man's heart so much good, he always indulged in an immensely spectacular display. It was his Frap, in a word. It was perhaps the only moment in camp life which he and the campers equally enjoyed. The rest of the time they glared at each other, so to speak, over the sack of money which the parents had provided, and in which lay the possibilities of happiness for both; and every time one side drew a benefit from the bag the other side suffered.

Bunk Thirteen, like the rest of the camp, was in a state of joyful eagerness at sundown, when lightning struck. An insolent small boy poked a shaved head into the bungalow and announced a message from the camp doctor to the effect that he and the nurse intended to go to the fireworks, so Bunk Thirteen would have to provide someone to stay with Lennie in the infirmary during the display. A bombardment of resentment, rage, rebellion, and exasperation was duly shot off by the boys, all aimed at Uncle Sid's innocent head. Vows to heaven not to submit to this new iniquity were made. Ingenious curses were heaped on the absent doctor. When the noise subsided the question still remained—who was going to stay with Lennie? Uncle Sid wisely ordered the boys to choose among themselves, gave Ted five minutes to report the name of the victim, and slipped out of the bunk.

Ted, looking more like a hawk than ever, surveyed his followers one after the other.

"Volunteers?" he said at last, with a lopsided grin.

The boys stirred and fidgeted, but none spoke.

"We oughta pull straws," said Eddie Bromberg.

"Aw, forget it," said Ted. "I seen them fireworks five years already. I'm sick o' watchin' old Uncle Gussie have a good time for himself while we sit around swattin' fireflies and mosquitoes. I'll stay in the infirmary."

He spoke bravely, but his face was grief stricken. All day he had been saying that the fireworks were the only fun in a whole summer at Manitou. He was like a poorhouse inmate cheated of Christmas dinner. Herbie felt such a strong impulse of sympathy that to his surprise he heard his own mouth utter, "I'll do it, Ted."

The captain stared. "You? Why should you of all guys stay with Lennie? He rides you silly."

"Aw, I just don't care about fireworks, that's all."

"Look, General Garbage, it's my fault he's in the infirmary. I got him to go swimming. I'll take the knifing."

"O.K., then there'll be two of us with him," said Herbie. "I ain't gonna see no crummy fireworks and sit around with no bunch o' gigglin' girls."

The other boys, amazed and delighted, kept stone still. Ted looked around at them and at Herbie. The wrestle going on inside him showed itself in a popping of his eyes and strange contortions of his big mouth. He loved the fireworks. Herbie had not seen them, and he had; Herbie did not know what a brilliant contrast they were to the rest of the camp routine, and he did.

"You're crazy to do it, Herbie," he said at last, putting out his hand, "but I'll sure say thank you. I know it oughta be me. Thanks, Herbie." He pumped the other boy's arm happily.

Nobody, least of all Herbie, overlooked the significance of his given name twice repeated by the captain. It fell sweetly on the fat boy's ears. The speaking of a name can be the conferring of an award above gold medals.

Herbie missed the fireworks, but he never regretted them. From that day he was "Herbie" to all the boys in his bunk except Lennie. Outside the bunk, however, Herbie's designation was fixed. First impressions are hard to change. He had been publicly pilloried on the train as General Garbage, and General Garbage he remained all summer. And if at the age of seventy he should run into a seventy-one-year-old gaffer formerly of Bunk Thirteen, he would be remembered, if at all, as General Garbage.

Despite the delight of a restored name, Herbie's stay in the infirmary was painful. His strong imagination kept contriving images of himself and Lucille, sitting hand in hand on the lawn under the stars, watching the colored fireballs of the Roman candles and the golden showers of the rockets. Actually, his sighs were wasted. The boys and girls, away in the happy ground beyond the hedge, sat on two separate sets of hard benches twenty feet apart, with the corridor between them constantly patrolled by counselors. No word was exchanged between campers of opposite sex that evening. But not knowing this, Herbie suffered for the dream, not for the paltry reality. More and more he yearned for tomorrow's religious services. He was reasonably sure that the doctor and nurse would not insist on attending them, too.

So it turned out. Next evening after dinner, Bunk Thirteen joined the march to the girls' camp, complete except for Lennie. Evidently the doctor and nurse had felt compelled to attend the fireworks in the line of duty, in case Mr. Gauss set fire to himself, but they would not for a moment deprive a single lad of religious improvement.

In planning services for Camp Manitou, "Uncle Gussie" had a tangled problem which he solved with his usual neatness. Although he was not Jewish, most of his campers were, having been recruited from those areas of the

Bronx adjacent to Public School Fifty. Mr. Gauss himself
was of German descent, and his grandparents had been
stout Protestants. In a life of trivial preoccupation and
struggle he had lost interest in church and Book. This is
not to say that he was behindhand in praising church or
quoting Book when necessary, but his doing so was merely a compliment to popular feelings which he knew about
but didn't share. In his visits to parents he raised no
religious questions. He had observed that strict Jewish
parents brought up the topic at once, and their children
were lost to him in any case, since the Manitou kitchens
did not at all follow the Mosaic food laws. The others,
from whom he drew most of his campers, were satisfied
with a few words in the booklets about "beautifully inspir-
ing services each Friday evening under the shining Berkshire stars." The timing of worship on Friday night instead of Sunday morning was adequately Hebraic for his
purpose.

On the other hand the Christian children who drifted
into the Gauss fold were not ill at ease. The services were
carefully designed. They included only those Psalms of
David which have found place in both Jewish and Christian prayerbooks, and a few hymns praising the Almighty
in very general terms. The sermons were five-minute
speeches by various counselors on nature, camp spirit, or
Indian lore. It all went swimmingly.

Two by two, the campers of Manitou marched through
the gate in the hedge. They made a colorful procession,
these boys all in white shirts and trousers, winding across
the green lawn in the sunset. Herbie felt a pulse of
excitement as his turn came to walk through the narrow
passage to the forbidden ground, and the thrill increased
as he saw the girls in another double line of white, far on
the other side of the lawn. The girls' grounds were prettier
than the precinct of his own sex, he perceived. On the
brow of the hill the bunks stood in a semicircle amid a
grove of pine trees, and the slope to the water's edge was
all well-tended grass, with here and there a shade tree
and rustic benches. It happened that the guest house
where the parents stayed on weekends was at the top of

this same hill, separated from the girls' bunks by an avenue of pine trees. Why not? It was only just, after all, that the parents who were paying for Camp Manitou should have the best possible view of it.

For religious services the banks of benches were moved close to each other. Uncle Sandy and Aunt Tillie may have thought there was less chance of flirting in such a solemn time, or that the counselors, undistracted by rockets, would be able to stem romance. In any case, the aisle between the boys and girls was three feet wide, instead of twenty.

Uncle Sid, perched at a battered brown upright piano on a small wheeled platform, struck up Handel's "Largo." The lines of girls began to file into their places. Herbie watched for Lucille, and at last saw his light of love on the point of entering the benches. The line was broken and directed into a new row with Lucille in the lead, so that she found herself on the aisle near the boys' rows. Now the boys began filling the benches in the same manner. Herbie feverishly counted heads, calculated the number of boys necessary to fill all the places up to the precious spot opposite Lucille, and compared it to his position in line. Worse luck! He was six too far forward. Four of his bunkmates were behind him. Without explanation he shifted to the place back of them.

"Psst, Ted."

"Yeah, Herbie."

"See that red-headed girl on the aisle there?"

"Yeah. Some pot."

"Never mind that. I wanna sit next to her. When you go into the row in front spread out, huh? Spread out!"

Ted looked at him sideways, nodded, and whispered to the others. When the turn of Bunk Thirteen came to take places, they spread so effectively that the line was broken at Ted. The bunk captain threw Herbie a birdlike wink and marched triumphantly toward Lucille, who permitted herself a peep at the oncoming boy. Just short of the aisle Ted stopped, and Herbie slipped past him into the coveted seat. He had gained great riches. For a whole hour he would be sitting three feet from his girl.

"Hello, Lucille," he whispered.

"Hi, Herbie," came a soft reply.

"Hey, ain't this lucky?" said the boy, and was rewarded with a sweet, knowing smile that threw him into a transport.

The sunset was in full glory. Banks of reddened clouds suffused the air with a rosy hue, all the more visible because of a faint ground mist that caught the color. The moon and the evening star shone through the haze and cast parallel silver paths, one broad, one pencil-thin, on the quiet lake. The scents of pine and honeysuckle came and went with each stirring of the wind. For a while the two camps sat in silence while Uncle Sid played a melancholy, simple religious melody. Such was the setting that each note, even from the cheap, toneless piano and the heavy hand, seemed to gleam out like a new star.

Mr. Gauss rose, book in hand, and began reading while the music played.

"The Lord is my shepherd; I shall not want. He maketh me to lie down in green pastures. He leadeth me beside the still waters—"

Herbie was suddenly overpowered by a terrible, wonderful new sensation—a tingling all over his body, a feeling of a mighty presence filling the sky and earth about him, and a hot gush of tears to his eyes. A hundred times he had heard these words read in this same voice in school assemblies: dry, meaningless sounds. All at once they seemed tremendous truths. He was in green pastures, beside still waters, with Lucille Glass three feet away, and it all seemed the doing of the Lord God himself, Who was so close that He might reach down and pet Herbie's head if He wished.

"He restoreth my soul—"

The words of the Psalm penetrated to the boy's heart and vibrated there. He looked around him, wondering if anybody else was caught in this miraculous feeling. Ted and Eddie were whispering together and grinning. Lucille, as soon as he glanced at her, turned her eyes to him with a slightly mischievous smile, then looked down at her fingers in her lap again. Nobody in all the rows seemed rapt. He was alone, evidently, in his exaltation.

"Yea, though I walk through the valley of the shadow of death, I shall fear no evil—"

Herbie closed his eyes. He saw, as clearly as he had been seeing the sunset, the Valley of the Shadow of Death. It was a gaunt, narrow plain covered with bones and broken stones, with straight black cliffs rising on either side as high as the sky, and only a faint greenish light everywhere. He was walking along the plain, which sloped steeply downward into increasing darkness, but he was not afraid. . . .

"Thy rod and thy staff, they comfort me—"

A slender rod that came straight down into the valley from the sky was in his hand, pulling him gently forward, guiding his steps. . . .

Herbie opened his eyes and was actually startled to see the lake, the rows of children, and Mr. Gauss. It was like waking from a dream. The music stopped, and the camp owner hurried through the last lines of the Psalm, though Herbie could have begged him to go more slowly, perhaps for the first time since he had become familiar with Mr. Gauss's oratorical manner. Reluctantly he felt the magic fade. He tried to renew, to cling to the strange trance, but the world was looking more and more like itself again.

"Boys and girls," said Mr. Gauss, "here we are again at dear old Camp Manitou. How nice it is to get away from the hot, dirty city and commune in the bosom of nature once more, by the side of our beautiful lake nestled amid the Berkshire Mountains."

"At only three hundred bucks apiece," whispered Ted, "payable in advance."

Herbie covered his mouth and laughed. He glanced across at Lucille and boldly winked. For a moment she looked arch, then she winked back and chuckled quietly. Things were thoroughly normal again, and Herbie found himself glad of it.

The effect of the passing seizure was no more than a slight exhilaration that lasted the evening. Thinking back on the peculiar brief ecstasy, he decided that if it had gone on any longer it might have become painful, and certainly would have made him behave like a halfwit. With this conclusion he forgot about it. Nothing like it ever happened to him again that summer, for the services became a matter of routine like everything else, incapable of surprising or stirring him.

But Mr. Gauss, though he undoubtedly hadn't the least idea of what he was doing, had fulfilled one of his promises in the booklet. With a little help from David, King of Israel, he had effected in Herbie Bookbinder a tiny, temporary, but unmistakable religious improvement.

14

The Coming of Clever Sam

THE SUMMER WORE on. It quickly became established that Lennie Krieger was one of the leading lights of the camp, and that Herbie Bookbinder was a negligible fellow. Every team that included Lennie was a mighty engine; the Ipanas, the Oldsmobiles, the John Barrymores, and the Palmolives each led their leagues. The Intermediates actually beat the Seniors at basketball, an event unheard of in Manitou records, and Lennie scored thirty of his team's thirty-six points. Within two weeks a new election was held in Bunk Thirteen, and Lennie added this captaincy to his other honors. It was soon agreed that as a citizen of Manitou, Lennie stood second in distinction only to the massive Super-senior Yishy Gabelson.

Herbie, on the other hand, was known as a dead loss. Among the Juniors he might have passed as a mediocre player, but as an Intermediate he was undersize, overweight, and slow as a snail. When he ran from one base to another, he appeared to his raging teammates to be wading through mud. When a basketball was thrown to him it often as not knocked him down. In track meets his efforts to run and jump were not only comical but dangerous. His first try at the high jump brought down the bar and both its supporting poles in a heap, one of the poles hitting Uncle Sid on the head and stretching him on the ground. After a couple of weeks of such performances, he found himself a universal substitute on all teams. He seldom appeared on the field, but presumably was ready to relieve any boy who was injured or who dropped dead. The rate of accidents and fatalities being low, he took to wandering away from the fields as soon as games started, picking up a book somewhere, and spending the athletic period reading under a tree. He would have preferred not to bother with the hot hike out to the field, which was simply a waste of a good half hour, but the conscience of the counselor in charge usually balked at this. No, Herbie had to go through the rite of marching out to the baseball diamond or handball court. Once there, he would take the first exciting moment of the game as his cue to disappear quietly, and the Uncle in charge either didn't see him go or pretended that he didn't. This arrangement soon became a settled thing, and suited Herbie well enough. He would rather, of course, have been a hero like Lennie, but it was obvious to him that he was marked for obscurity.

His cousin Cliff was considered an ordinary boy, neither very very bad nor very good. A single shot-put in the first track meet was his main distinction. He had thrust the iron shot so far that the judges had measured the distance three times before announcing the result with wonder. But the excitement that sprang up around Cliff died quickly when it turned out that he was unable to do it again. Cliff was powerful but awkward, and only by chance could he co-ordinate his movements to put forth strength. Once in a baseball game a week later he astounded both teams by throwing the ball from deep left field to home plate. But again, he was unable to do it a second time. Casually, in the heat of a moment, Cliff could perform these incredible stunts, as Herbie knew. On the whole, he was regarded as a good-natured, quiet, second-rate camper.

He was so regarded, that is, until the coming of Clever Sam.

Horseback riding was one of the delights promised in the booklets. Although Herbie had never ridden a horse, the paragraph of Mr. Gauss's fine prose describing this kingly sport at Manitou had set him dreaming of gallops through forest and meadow, up mountainsides and across shallow streams, in company with other dashing horsemen resembling the extras in an English hunting movie. This vision had been deflated in an early talk with Ted. It had developed that the Gauss stables consisted of one ancient beast named Baby, who was so old and stiff that a ride on her resembled (so Ted said) walking on four stilts. The disillusionment went further when the boys arrived at camp and found the stable empty. Baby, it appeared, had died and been buried by the caretaker in May.

Once dead, Baby took on a new aspect in the memories of old campers like Ted. She had been, so they now maintained, a "swell" horse, a swift, gentle, yet fiery steed, the only good thing in the whole camp, and so forth. Dark rumors went around that Mr. Gauss had sold her. Three old campers swore that they had seen her, alive and full of fire, pulling a farmer's wagon in a nearby village. Now, this was a malicious untruth, for Baby was as dead as Julius Caesar, but the boys were ready to believe anything evil of Mr. Gauss. The murmuring reached Uncle Sandy's ears. At a parade-ground speech he first denounced the slanderers of "the Skipper" (nobody else ever referred to Mr. Gauss by any sobriquet but "Uncle Gussie," but his official nickname, selected after an essay contest in the first year, was "the Skipper," and Uncle Sandy was compelled to use it). Next, he proudly proclaimed that, disregarding expense, the Skipper had advertised for a horse in the local papers, so that the noble saddle sport would be restored to Camp Manitou in a day or two. He concluded by advising all slanderers and skeptics to consult the bulletin board of the camp, nailed to a pole at the foot of Company Street. With unconscious humor the entire camp crowded around the board as soon as the speech was over. There they saw this newspaper clipping from the Panksville *Observer:*

WANTED—to purchase—one horse for riding purposes in children's camp. Must be gentle and inexpensive. Call 913-R, Mr. Gauss.

Thus the murmurers were mostly silenced, though one or two held to the theory that the advertisement was a Gauss trick to cover his tracks in the crime of selling the magnificent Baby. These diehards—Ted was one of them —offered to bet "a million dollars" that no horse would ever be bought. But nobody appeared sufficiently interested in winning a million dollars and the controversy languished.

The very next morning, the injustice of such prejudices was proved, when Mr. Gauss bought a horse—under circumstances which are worth describing.

The camp owner was sitting in an easy chair on the veranda of the guest house, going over the kitchen accounts with the chef and wondering how much money he could save by eliminating the children's desserts at lunch time, when the handy man, a slow-talking, slow-moving young rustic named Elmer Bean shambled up the steps of the porch and announced, "Feller with a hoss at the gate, Mist' Gauss."

"Ah, yes." Mr. Gauss closed the account book. "Does it look like a good horse?"

"Nope."

At this reply Mr. Gauss might have been expected to dismiss the matter. He didn't, though. He nodded with satisfaction, and pushed himself out of the easy chair.

"Why? What's wrong with it?"

"Dunno. But it don't look good," said Elmer, and went away.

Mr. Gauss walked to the camp gate behind the guest house. He made a picturesque figure: flapping straw sandals, bare thin legs burned pink by the sun, khaki-colored shorts stretched over his wide, round stomach and wider, rounder stern, green sun glasses, and peeling bald head. Mr. Gauss never became tan and never looked in the least countrified, no matter how he varied his costume. Had he been found unconscious and naked in a forest, he would have been identified at once as a New York City school principal who owned a summer camp.

A Negro was standing at the gate, holding a rope which was affixed to the bridle of a horse. The horse, a rusty black creature, was cropping grass.

"I'm Mr. Gauss," said the camp owner. "Is that the animal for sale?"

"Yas, suh."

"Hmm. Is he a good horse?"

"No, suh."

Mr. Gauss, somewhat taken aback at such frankness, regarded the animal critically. He certainly did not look like a good horse. He had a swollen belly, spindly legs, a queerly stretched neck, and a long, sad, gnarled face.

"Why do you come to me with a horse that isn't good?"

"He cheap, suh."

"How cheap?"

"Five dollars, suh."

Even Mr. Gauss, bargain hunter that he was, was staggered.

"Five dollars for a *horse?*"

"Yas, suh."

Mr. Gauss looked again at the beast. It was obviously alive, and, even dead, could hardly be worth less than five dollars.

"Where did you get him?"

"He ain't mine, suh. He b'long Camp Arcadia. Ah wuk in de stable dah."

Camp Arcadia was a summer place for adults near by, and Mr. Gauss was slightly acquainted with the proprietor.

"I see. How old is this horse?"

"Dunno."

"What's his name?"

"Clevuh Sam, suh."

The camp owner glanced askance at the animal that
bore this strange, slightly ominous name. The horse, having eaten bare the ground around the Negro, began devouring a clump of poison ivy near the gate. Mr. Gauss
was troubled, but he noticed that the Negro saw the act
and made no move to stop it.

"He's eating poison ivy."

"Yas, suh. He hungry."

"When was he fed last?"

"Don' matter none, suh. Clevuh Sam he just hungry."

"Wait here, please."

Mr. Gauss flapped his way back to the guest house and
telephoned the proprietor of Camp Arcadia, a Mr.
Zasi.

"Oh yes," said Mr. Zasi to his inquiry, "how are you,
Gauss? Do you want the horse?"

"I'd like to ask you a question or two about him, if you
don't mind."

"I'm rather busy, but go ahead."

"Is he broke to the saddle?"

"Of course. That's what you advertised for."

"Gentle?"

"I guarantee he won't hurt anybody."

"Sick?"

"Don't make me laugh. That horse'll outlive you and
me."

"How old is he?"

"I don't know. Old."

"Why is he called Clever Sam?"

There was a slight hesitation before Mr. Zasi answered.
"Well, I think you'll find he *is* pretty clever."

Somehow this answer did not reassure Mr. Gauss.

"In what way is he clever?"

"Look, Gauss, this whole deal means very little to me,"
said the other camp owner irritably. "I'm not going to
spend the day on the telephone discussing a five-dollar
transaction. If you don't want the horse, send him back.
His carcass would be worth more than the price."

"Yes, yes, I know. Just routine inquiries, you understand."

"I understand. Good-by."

On the way back to the gate, Mr. Gauss puzzled and puzzled over a possible catch in the bargain, and could detect none. So, with an indefinable misgiving, he counted out five single bills to the Negro and was handed the rope that symbolized possession of Clever Sam. The Negro heaved a happy sigh.

"Thank you, suh. Good-by, you rusty ol'——," he said, slapping the horse on the rump and using an extremely unprintable word. And he ambled off down the road, alternately whistling and laughing.

In view of these suspicious proceedings, Mr. Gauss was prepared for anything on the part of Clever Sam. Very cautiously he tugged at the rope. "Come on, Clever Sam, into the stable with you," he said.

To his amazement, the horse raised his head and followed him like a lamb to the barn.

This book is in no sense a mystery story, so it should be said now that the reason for the absurd price of the horse was simply the tender-heartedness of Mr. Zasi's wife. The owner of Camp Arcadia wanted to be rid of the beast for reasons which will soon be evident, but his lady, who formed warm attachments for all four-footed creatures, would accept no solution which involved the slaying or ill treatment of Clever Sam. He had therefore boarded in Mr. Zasi's stable, an unwanted guest, for a year. Mr. Gauss's advertisement was a lucky opportunity.

The campers had their first inkling of the arrival of a horse when Uncle Sandy strode into Bunk Thirteen in the evening during letter-writing period.

"Say, Uncle Sid," he said, sitting on Ted's cot to a screech of protesting metal, "what do you know about horses?"

"Horses?" said Uncle Sid mildly. He looked up from the score of *The Mikado,* which he had been cutting down for performance in twenty minutes.

"Yes, horses. Ever done any riding?"

"As a matter of fact," Uncle Sid answered with a

modest smile, "quite a bit. I seldom miss my Sunday morning canter in Central Park in the spring and fall. Of course I don't do jumps—"

"Well, that won't be necessary. Will you take Uncle Irish's bunk and your own in a riding class tomorrow? We've just gotten a horse."

The boys jumped and cheered.

"Hey, Uncle Sandy, is it a good horse?" said Ted.

Uncle Sandy gave him a genial wink that meant exactly nothing.

"Why, I'll be happy to," said Uncle Sid, and so it was decided.

Quickly the word of the renewal of riding spread through the camp, and it was the general opinion that somebody should sneak up to the stable at once and inspect the new steed. However, a marshmallow roast was to take place after letter writing, and the marshmallow supply was known to be limited. Some boys claimed they had found the fingerprints of Mr. Gauss on marshmallows at previous roasts, proving that he counted every one. Nobody would risk missing his marshmallows, and so Clever Sam was not seen that night.

Next morning at the parade ground Uncle Sandy announced, "Bunks Twelve and Thirteen"—dramatic pause—"horseback riding!" This brought forth a cheer, partly derisive and partly genuine, from the campers. When the boys of the two bunks wended up the hill a few minutes later, led by Uncle Sid in a handsomely tailored riding habit, there was no denying that they were envied.

They came upon Clever Sam tethered in the middle of a weedy clearing that bore obscure traces of having once been a riding ring. A sad ruin of gray boards in one corner suggested a jumping hurdle in the way that a small skeleton on the road suggests a cat; there is no resemblance, yet only the dissolution of the one could produce the other. There was also a belt of weeds around the edge of the clearing slightly different in size and color from the rest—the remains of the trotting path.

Clever Sam had eaten away the greenery close to the tether and was moving slowly in a widening circle, crop-

ping as he went. A saddle and bridle were on him. Elmer
Bean sat on a fence at the far side of the clearing,
chewing a wooden match and watching the horse absently.

"Hey, Elmer!" shouted Ted as the riding party approached the ring. "Is he a good horse?"

The handy man looked at Ted, but said nothing. He
eased himself off the fence, strolled to the animal, and
untethered him. Clever Sam kept munching.

"All ready for you, mister," said the handy man to
Uncle Sid.

The music counselor looked Clever Sam over with a
wry face. He had not seen such a decrepit, queerly
shaped horse before. His experience in horseflesh, to tell
the truth, was not wide, being limited to polite Sunday
trots along city bridle paths in the company of a lady
music teacher toward whom he was lovingly inclined, but
who thought Uncle Sid too fat for romance. She had
persuaded him to take up riding, and he had grown rather
proud of his horsemanship. The stables near Central
Park, however, housed glossy, pretty beasts; a camel
would have resembled them as much as Clever Sam did.
He was a long-faced quadruped, and equipped to be
ridden on; that was the extent of the similarity.

"Have you—have you been on him?" he inquired of
the handy man.

"That ain't my job, mister, that's yours," said Elmer
Bean. "You got him now. His name's Clever Sam." He
passed the reins into Uncle Sid's hands, walked off, and
hoisted himself up on the fence again to watch what
would follow.

The music counselor took a deep breath and vaulted
ponderously but neatly onto the horse's back. Clever Sam
took no notice whatever of the circumstance, and continued to feed, his neck stretching here and there for tasty
purple thistles.

"Ride 'im, Uncle Sid," came a voice from a group of
breathless boys—a voice sounding very much like Lennie's.

"All right, Clever Sam, let's go!" cried Uncle Sid heartily. He gave the animal the sort of light kick in the ribs to which the well-trained, well-fed young horses in Central Park responded. Clever Sam was of a different school. He ignored Uncle Sid with majestic indifference, and grazed on. Not knowing quite what to do about a horse whose neck seemed to slant permanently downward, Uncle Sid braced himself against the stirrups, gave a tremendous heave on the reins, and pulled the horse's head up into a normal position.

"Tha-a-at's better," he said. "Now, giddyap!" And he relaxed his hold upon the reins. The horse's head dropped to the ground again like a dead weight, and the yellow teeth resumed a methodical massacre of weeds.

"Say, haven't you fed this horse?" called the counselor angrily to Elmer Bean.

"Mister, that horse been eatin' grass since dawn. I ain't seen his head above his knees but just that once when you hauled it up."

"Give me a stick, someone!" called Uncle Sid to the boys. Much scrambling ensued, and Herbie came up with a broken broom handle. He handed it to the counselor at arm's length and scuttled out of range. Uncle Sid flailed away at Clever Sam's flanks, making dry, thudding sounds as though he were beating a carpet.

The horse ate placidly.

Thoroughly enraged, Uncle Sid reached forward and hit his mount over the head with the broom handle.

For the first time, Clever Sam showed an awareness of his rider's existence. He raised his head and looked around inquiringly at Uncle Sid. Then he fell over on his left side and gave vent to a series of horrible groans, kicking his long skinny shanks back and forth. In great alarm the counselor disentangled himself from the stirrups, wriggled his leg out from under the horse, and sprang free. As soon as he was gone Clever Sam stopped groaning, rose, shook himself, and resumed eating.

"That horse," fumed Uncle Sid to the world at large, "is unfit to be ridden."

Lennie came forward. "Please, can I try to ride 'm, Uncle Sid? I can do it. Please, can I try?"

"Go ahead, but don't get killed," said the counselor peevishly.

Lennie picked up the broom handle, which Uncle Sid had flung aside in fright when the horse toppled over, and leaped boldly into the saddle. He commenced a series of actions and sounds derived from Western and racing movies. With one hand he whipped the reins from side to side on the horse's neck, and with the broom handle in the other he beat the animal's rump, all the while bouncing up and down and shouting, "Gee-yap! Hi-yi! Come on, pal! Go it, boy!" Since the animal stood stock still during this transaction, the effect was a curious one—not unlike what small children achieve by pretending a fence rail is a galloping charger.

Lennie, being an eminent citizen, was fair game for jeers, and they were not long in coming.

"Oh, you Tom Mix!"

"Lookit the Bronx cowboy!"

"Don't go so fast. The horse'll get tired!"

And finally, inevitably:

> *"Here comes boloney,*
> *Riding on a pony,*
> *Hooray, Lennie!"*

—which perhaps had never been chanted under more appropriate conditions.

Elmer Bean had been watching the futile scene calmly. Now he plucked the match out of his mouth and called, "Saw the reins, feller, saw the reins."

Lennie sawed the reins back and forth, tugging first at one side of the horse's mouth, then the other, with all his strength. Clever Sam shook his head with displeasure and tried to keep on grazing, but the annoyance was evidently too great. He lifted his head slowly, looked once at his rider, and broke into a gentle trot, straight ahead.

Immediately the sneerers became cheerers once more.

"Good old Lennie!"

"Boy, he can do anything!"

"That's ridin' him, Lennie!"

Said Uncle Sid, to nobody in particular, "Of course I knew sawing the reins would do it, but I just can't stand being cruel to an animal."

Clever Sam was headed for the open camp gate.

"Turn him back, Lennie!" called the counselor.

Lennie pulled on the left rein. Clever Sam's head obediently twisted on his elastic neck completely around to the left, but his body continued straight on as though it and the head had no connection at all. It was a ghostly sight to see a horse's body trotting calmly in one direction while his head was looking the other way. Out through the gate went horse and rider in this uncanny fashion. Lennie threw a helpless glance backward, and then he and Clever Sam disappeared around a slight bend *to the right*. How the horse negotiated that turn, which was entirely invisible to him, is not known, but that is what happened.

Uncle Sid stood with his mouth hanging open for a moment. Then he said, "You boys wait right here," and started to run to the gate. He had not taken more than a few steps when Elmer Bean sang out, "Hold on, mister. That won't do no good," and came toward him.

"That boy is my responsibility," fretted Uncle Sid, but he stopped running.

"Yeah, an' the hoss is mine. Won't neither of 'em get hurt. They'll both be back soon."

"What makes you so sure?" said the music counselor. The boys gathered around the two men as they talked. An oddly assorted pair they were, too—Uncle Sid forlorn, flabby, and uncomfortable in his fashionable riding clothes, towered over by the lanky, fair-haired Elmer, who, in his dirty shapeless overalls and green cotton shirt, looked as easy and natural in the field as a milkweed.

"Heck, I know that hoss. I knew him years ago when they called him Blackie. He been bounced around from one half-baked camp stable to another out here ever since I kin remember. He done four years with a egg farm, too. Ain't no harm in him."

"He's obviously useless for camp purposes now," said

Uncle Sid. "You should have warned Mr. Gauss not to buy him."

"Mister, either you got hosses at a camp or you ain't. Mr. Gauss ain't takin' on no more hands than me, an' no more hosses than that one. If they's gonna be one hoss just to have a hoss, it might as well be Clever Sam. He ain't no trouble to me an' he'll eat anything. He'll eat bark offa young trees. He'll eat old clothes, if they got a hay smell. A billy goat ain't in it with Clever Sam. He ain't never lived good, see?"

At this moment the subject of the talk plodded into sight, greeted with yells by the boys. He was minus Lennie.

"If anything has happened to that boy," cried Uncle Sid, staring at the riderless animal, "I'll hold you responsible, Elmer."

"Keep yer ridin' britches on, mister," said the handy man. "Ain't nuthin' happened to the boy 'cept he ain't ridin' hossback no more."

Clever Sam trotted to the spot where his grazing had been interrupted, dropped his head, and resumed his favorite activity. He had only taken a bite or two when Lennie came walking through the gate. Uncle Sid and the boys dashed to him. He was unhurt, as Elmer had predicted, but from head to foot he was covered with mud and dead leaves. And he was very angry. To the questions from all sides he responded with unintelligible growls. At last the music counselor said loudly, "Lennie, I demand to know what happened."

"O.K., he rubbed me off against a tree, that's what happened!" exclaimed the boy furiously. "And he didn't pick any old tree, neither. He kept lookin' around an' lookin' around until he found a tree with a puddle under it. Nothin' I done made any difference. I pretty near pulled his head off to one side an' another. His head comes around like it's on a swivel, but it don't do nothin' to his feet. I swear to God he was lookin' right in my eye half the time he was goin'. That horse is crazy! My father can sue Mr. Gauss, an' I bet he will." He dabbed at the mud and leaves, but only smeared them from one place to another.

"I certainly wouldn't blame him," said Uncle Sid.

"Look, feller," said Elmer Bean, who had sauntered up in time to hear most of Lennie's tirade, "that hoss ain't crazy. He's old, see? And he's never had it good, see? And he's had so many city boobs on his back that he hadda develop a rubber neck an' a thick skin er drop dead. He ain't stupid. Every other hoss in the world that lets people git up on their back an' shove 'em around is stupid. Clever Sam's been livin' a hoss's life for maybe twenty years and fin'ly figgered out how to git around it. And he ain't takin' no more of it than he can help, that's all."

"Which all adds up to the fact," said Uncle Sid, "that he's totally useless as a riding horse, and I shall so report to Mr. Gauss."

"Hey, Uncle Sid," interrupted Herbie. "Lookit Cliff."

He pointed in the direction of the horse. Herbie's cousin was standing beside the animal with his hand on the scraggly black mane, talking to him.

"Cliff, come away from that dangerous beast!" shouted the counselor.

"It's O.K., Uncle Sid," Cliff called back. "He ain't gonna hurt me." He resumed his murmuring. To everyone's surprise, Clever Sam stopped eating for a moment and raised his head a little way from the ground.

"Feller looks like he been around a hoss before," said the handy man.

Herbie, feeling an access of family pride, said importantly, "Cliff is my cousin. His father used to keep a stable for delivery wagons an' horses."

This was the first time in Herbie's life that the stable-keeping background of his uncle seemed an ornament to the family name. Usually it was not mentioned. He could not help observing a new deference among the other boys toward him as soon as he told of it.

All at once Cliff swung himself easily onto Clever Sam's back, patted the horse's neck, and spoke in a coaxing tone. Clever Sam picked up his head and began to trot.

"Wait till they get to a tree," said Lennie bitterly.

But they never got to a tree. Clever Sam trotted once around the ring, then, at a snap of the reins, he broke into a dignified, creaky, but quite genuine gallop. The onlookers were confounded.

"Boy, what a cousin you got, Herbie," said Ted respectfully. Herbie, fat and grounded as ever, beamed in reflected glory.

Horse and rider swept past the group to a volley of cheers. Twice more Clever Sam pounded around the ring, seeming to enjoy himself more as he warmed to it, like an old gentleman who has been persuaded to waltz. At last he turned sharply off the ring, and, as the boys gasped and Uncle Sid uttered a warning cry, headed straight for the pile of boards that had once been a hurdle. Everyone could see that for the first time Cliff was frightened. He stiffened and pulled back on the reins. Clever Sam galloped straight on and jumped clumsily over the barrier, barely missing the top board with his hind legs. As he landed Cliff toppled forward and almost tumbled down over the horse's neck, but he clung and managed to straighten up. He turned Clever Sam toward the spectators, cantered within a yard of them, and pulled up short. Clever Sam huffed and puffed, shook himself, and pawed the ground a few times. Then his head sank once more, and chomp! chomp! went the great teeth again.

Cliff dismounted and received the plaudits of a hero. Amid the noise of congratulation and excited questions, the sallow boy, Eddie Bromberg, said, "Bet I can ride him now, too." He approached the horse with kind words, but when he was about to put his hand on the long neck, Clever Sam bared his terrible teeth at him. Eddie leaped backward, with a vivid picture of his arm being bitten in two like a daisy.

Elmer Bean said, "Clever Sam he had his day's exercise. Ain't gonna be no more ridin', boys."

Nobody else wanted to try. The group went down the

hill, still clustering around the modest Cliff, who found little to say. Herbie, his arm linked in his cousin's, did a very satisfactory job as spokesman, and reveled in it.

"Say, Cliff, how'd you stop him so short?" asked Ted.

"Well, you know, just stopped him," said Cliff.

"Gosh, ain't you got eyes, Ted?" said Herbie. "Clever Sam don't like no rough treatment, see? Cliff rides with the reins real loose, see, then at the last minute just a good tug, an' whoa, boy!—there you are. Right, Cliff?"

"Um," said Cliff.

In this way all questions were answered, and Herbie's replies were listened to with eagerness and received as the final word. It was the fat boy's happiest time since his arrival in camp, and it lasted all day, for the fame of Cliff's feat spread, and more and more boys kept coming to Herbie, asking him to repeat the story and explain his cousin's secrets of horsemanship.

Lennie and Uncle Sid retired to the showers together, and cleaned themselves. It was noticed thereafter that they maintained a heavy reserve on the subject of Clever Sam. Whenever the horse was mentioned, in fact, and Herbie began to expound, Lennie was observed to snort loudly and take himself off.

That night, at a meeting of the Royal Order of Gooferdusters, the secret honor society of the camp, Cliff was proposed for election. He was blackballed by two Superseniors who maintained scornfully that his achievement was nothing, because they could ride Clever Sam themselves. In time they tried, and learned they were mistaken. Clever Sam, in his old age, had simply come to dislike horseback riding as a sport, and his cleverness lay in the fact that, without resorting to the violence of a bronco, he could get any member of the human race off his back if he so chose.

Despite the Gooferduster injustice, Cliff's stock jumped twenty points on the Manitou market. And even Herbie's, hitherto practically a bankrupt issue, sluggishly went up about five.

15

The Envelope Mystery

MEANTIME, Mr. and Mrs. Jacob Bookbinder, like all New Yorkers in the summer, were steaming unhappily. In July and August the delusion that a city apartment is a home disappears, and the dwellers know it for what it is—a shelf; a small, complicated shelf of iron and brick, lined with plaster. The Bookbinders stayed out of their apartment as much as possible, supposedly to be in the fresh air. But there was no fresh air; only the blanket of steam, smoke, and a little oxygen that drops over New York after the Fourth of July fireworks and is not lifted until September.

The absence of the children made matters worse. True, the Bookbinders were not very demonstrative parents, yet once Herbie and Felicia were gone a shadow fell on their days. The father caught himself in his office in midday leaning back in the swivel chair, staring out of the window, and wondering why he was overworking himself and hurrying to the grave. The mother spent hours over old photographs. Their talk in the evenings was no longer all about the Place, but about the children, and about the forgotten times of courtship in their first years in America. The shaking up of their lives awoke memories, with an effect more often bitter than sweet. At the halfway mark of life it is not always pleasant to think of old times.

The consolation of the parents was letters. Twice a week Felicia wrote long accounts of her doings, sprinkled with adoring references to her counselor, Aunt Dora, in whom she had found the sum of human perfection. Herbie wrote every day. He had begun magnificently with four-page letters in his best English-composition manner. This burst of literary force lasted a week, and then the letters dwindled to dry one-page notes. These were soon followed by a series of penny postcards containing one or two sentences. Unsatisfying as the terse cards were, they did, at least, come each day without fail, and the mother and father commented happily on the devotion of their boy.

One evening Jacob Bookbinder came walking wearily home along Homer Avenue after a vexing day. For perhaps the twentieth time he had refought with his partner the question of selling the Place. Krieger, compelled by his voting agreement to side with his partner, was still trying to change Bookbinder's mind by nagging, a form of persuasion for which he was well equipped. The flood of disjointed language had all but carried away Bookbinder's resolve to stand by his claim based on the blue paper. Powers was offering the ice company for sale on the assumption that the memorandum was worthless; and Krieger was cowed, and wanted to give in and get the best possible terms. But there was a core of revulsion in Bookbinder's spirit against disposing of the fruit of his lifetime while he was in health. It kept him from agreeing to sell, but it did not save him from a heavy dose of Krieger's eloquence.

With the phrases "peaceable—I say this way—thirty years in the ice business" ringing in his ears, Herbie's father opened the door of his apartment to be faced with fresh woe. Mrs. Bookbinder was weeping in the kitchen, mumbling incoherently about a letter from Herbie. She pointed to an envelope on the table, the ink of which was blurred with fresh tears. Bookbinder seized the envelope and pulled out the letter with a shaking hand.

It was a blank page.

"I just came home from the market," wailed the mother, "and found it in the letter box. My boy is sick; he can't even write. Oh, Jake, let's get in the car and go up there right now."

The father puzzled over the empty sheet in silence for a

minute. Then he said, "If he was so sick, how could he address the envelope? You see it's his handwriting."

Mrs. Bookbinder snatched the envelope and examined it. Her husband was obviously right.

"I'll tell you what," said Bookbinder. "The boy wrote a letter and then foolishly mailed a blank sheet instead."

"You think so?" The mother looked a little more cheerful.

"What else could it be? Let's wait till tomorrow. He writes every day, that's one sure thing. We'll know tomorrow."

Mrs. Bookbinder slept restlessly that night. Next morning she sat at the kitchen window, watching for the postman. In time he came, with a letter from Felicia and a penny postcard from Herbie with the usual two sentences. It read: "I'm feeling fine and hope to hear the same from you. Can you send me a jar of lemon sourballs? Your loving son, Herbie." She was so relieved that she immediately telephoned the father, who gruffly said he had known all along there was no reason to worry. He was glad to hear the news, all the same.

The next day and the next brought more penny postcards. The following day, Saturday, an envelope came from Herbie. Mrs. Bookbinder tore it open eagerly and with a little foreboding.

It was another blank page.

That evening she debated the mystery again with her husband, who explained it as absent-mindedness once more, but with less assurance. He prevailed on her at last not to telegraph or telephone, but to wait for one more mail. The next day was Sunday. The mother fumed and fretted all day and wanted to know what was wrong with a government that couldn't arrange to have mail delivered on Sunday. This was the one political criticism that Mrs. Bookbinder was heard to utter in her lifetime.

Monday morning the mail brought two more blank letters from Herbie.

Frantic, Mrs. Bookbinder rushed into the street and took a taxi to the ice plant. In her husband's office she indulged in mild hysterics, and was finally calmed by

Bookbinder's decision to call the camp at once by long-distance telephone. He picked up the receiver on his desk and put through the call.

It was impossible for the parents to have acted otherwise, unless they had been monsters of coldness. Yet Herbie was in excellent health, and there was a simple explanation of the mystery of the blank letters.

The mother and father had erred, in the first place, to praise the boy's devotion. The fact was that Mr. Gauss, after much trouble in previous years over the failure of boys to write home, had issued an edict requiring a daily communication from each boy. No rule was made as to length or content, but Mr. Gauss insisted that a piece of mail of some nature leave Camp Manitou every twenty-four hours, bound for each set of parents. The girls were exempt, experience having shown that they were less neglectful than the boys. This order of Uncle Gussie's was, of course, mightily resented, the more so when the discrimination between the sexes became known. But Mr. Gauss was not a man to be swayed by the mutterings of boys, or he would not have been either a school principal or a camp owner. This was the third year the law had been in effect, and it was enforced by "dockings." A boy who failed to hand in a letter was docked from the next day's swimming. A second offender was docked from the movies. There were few second offenders. Movies were too precious a release from camp routine.

At first Herbie had greatly enjoyed the novelty of letter writing. Perhaps his first rapture would have tapered away in time, but it shriveled very swiftly when he learned that he was writing under compulsion. It changed the nature of the deed. He was fond enough of his parents, and missed them enough, to have written fairly full letters once or twice a week, but Mr. Gauss's law erased the natural motive of love, and substituted the more reliable but less pleasant one of fear. Herbie quickly followed the lead of the old campers like Ted in supplying himself with a stack of penny postcards. His way was by no means the worst. A senior in Bunk Fifteen actually used a rubber stamp with the words "I am feeling fine and hope to hear the same from you." This was one of the most durable jokes at Manitou.

Herbie's blank letters were inexcusable, but they came about in a natural way. A dance for Intermediates and Seniors was impending, and Uncle Sandy had scheduled a dancing class during the letter-writing period. A letter collected at the door was the price of admission to the class. Now and then Herbie was crowded for time, and it took a few seconds less to address an envelope than to write a postcard. He had sent off the first blank letter in desperation when a few more seconds would have meant being locked out of the class. He expected a surprised reaction either by mail or telephone. When nothing of the sort developed he congratulated himself on his luck. Next time he was pressed he used the trick with a smaller twinge of conscience; and thereafter he did it with no misgiving at all.

The last thing Herbie wanted to do was to torture his parents, but the mind of a normal boy is like a criminal mind in a way. He does things that he knows are wrong, and, because of an incomplete awareness of how the world goes, he blithely hopes that somehow he will escape the evil consequences. The iron working of cause and effect is a reality which all of us only reluctantly accept. In time it impresses itself on the criminal, and he goes to jail; and on the boy, and he grows up. In both cases there is a sad, if necessary, loss of freedom.

Herbie was lying on the grass under a white birch that overlooked the lake, having the most peacefully pleasant time of his life, when the law of cause and effect caught up with him in a shattering instant. One moment he was a delighted spectator of the bloody fight between Tarzan and Caraftap in the underground wonder world of the Ant Men; the next moment he was a miserable culprit in this dry old world of ours, slowly being dragged to his feet by one ear which was in the grip of Uncle Sandy.

"Bookbinder, why aren't you out on the handball court where you belong?" grated the head counselor, with a terrifying squint at his prey.

Herbie babbled something meaningless.

"Do you know that there's a long-distance telephone call for you, and that I've been searching the grounds for you this past half hour?"

The news struck Herbie dumb, and took so much starch out of his knees that he would have sat down again if not for Uncle Sandy's helpful support of his ear. He knew at once that the crime of the blank letters had come to light, and he felt the horrid sickness of heart that comes only to the guilty when they are found out. The lake suddenly was bluer than it had ever been, the air sweeter, the grass more inviting; and he would gladly have bribed the head counselor with a hundred thousand dollars, if he had had a hundred thousand dollars, to set him free, explain everything satisfactorily, and erase the bad thing he had done. Guilty grownups who are rich enough sometimes do exactly that by means of a lawyer. But Herbie was a guilty little boy, without the means to conjure away punishment. The past, the hidden past which fools say is gone forever and of no concern to us, had reached forth its dead hand into the present, pointed a blue finger at Herbie, and spoken hollowly, "There is the man."

Marching up the hill with Uncle Sandy, the boy stammered a full confession of what he had done. To his amazement, the head counselor seemed to grow less stern with every step they took toward the telephone. When Herbie finished the tale of his mischief, they stood outside the camp office, and Uncle Sandy was actually smiling.

"Well, Herb," he said, "you've been pretty foolish, but boys will be boys. The main thing now is to let your folks know that you're in good health and happy. Isn't that right?"

"Sure, Uncle Sandy," said Herbie, ready to grovel with gratitude.

"Well, then, let's tell them that, shall we? I've already explained about the letters, and all you've got to do is make them feel you're O.K. and having a swell time. Come on."

He led the boy up the steps of the guest house to the camp office. This was a hot, small room, pervaded by a smell of mimeographing ink, and full of papers, charts, and files. A wall telephone hung beside the scarred wooden desk. Uncle Sandy rang the operator by cranking a little handle.

"Ready now with our party," he said, and handed the receiver to Herbie. Just as the boy put it to his ear, Mr. Gauss mysteriously appeared through the open doorway, wearing his best pushed-up smile and nodding his head genially and regularly like a mechanical Buddha.

Herbie heard various buzzes and a click that almost broke his eardrum, and then the voice of his father.

"Hello, Herbie?"

"Hello, Pa. Gee, it's swell to hear your voice."

"Mama was worried about you. You're all right, aren't you?"

"Oh, sure, I'm swell, Pa. I'm havin' a wonderful time. Gosh, this is a swell camp. We're havin' all kinds of fun."

The mechanical Buddha went into high gear and nodded faster.

"That's fine," said his father's voice. "You shouldn't have sent us those blank letters, boy. Uncle Sandy explained all about it. But if you're in that much of a hurry next time, just don't bother writing."

Herbie, mystified by this, looked at the two men, then said, "Sure, Pa. I'll remember."

Uncle Sandy hadn't quite explained all. He had told Mr. Bookbinder that boys who were in a hurry to catch the mail often did the same thing just to let their parents know they were thinking of them. He had omitted the detail of compulsory writing. Herbie surmised as much, but he had no intention of arguing.

"All right, Herbie. How's Felicia?"

"Fine, Pa."

"Good-by, boy. We'll come up to visit you when I'm not so busy. Here, talk to your mother."

"HELLO, darling." His mother's voice was charged with emotion. "Are you really all right?"

The query irritated Herbie. Being treated as a criminal was not pleasant, but it was part of a man's lot when he had done wrong; being fussed over like a baby was unendurable.

"Heck, Ma, if I wasn't all right I wouldn't be talkin' to you, would I?"

At the change in his tone the Buddha head stopped nodding with a jerk, and wagged reprovingly from side to side.

Herbie heard his mother laugh a little wildly. "It's so wonderful to hear you sound healthy and happy, darling. Don't send me any more blank letters. They give me sleepless nights."

"O.K., I won't, Ma," said Herbie impatiently. "I promise."

"Are you having a good time, darling?"

Herbie looked at the head-wagging Mr. Gauss and the yawning Uncle Sandy. Everything he did not like about Camp Manitou flashed before his mind's eye in an instant —repairing the fields, sweeping floors, marching out to games he hated, writing postcards under duress, submitting to Uncle Sid's stolid rule, living under one roof with Lennie, being cut off from Lucille, eating, sleeping, and waking to the calls of a bugle: in a word, the cage of rules which was the price of the joys of the country. A loud "No!" rose from the depths of his heart to his tongue, and he had to clamp teeth and lips shut to keep from uttering it. Flanked by Gauss and Sandy, who held peace or misery for him in their hands, how could he risk frankness?

"Herbie, I asked you something," said his mother anxiously.

"Ma, I'm having a great time. Best fun I ever had in my life."

The head-shaking stopped at once and reverted to such a fast nod that Mr. Gauss's face seemed to become a pink blur.

"God bless you, my boy. Kiss Felicia for me. We'll see you soon. This call is costing a lot of money. Good-by."

"Good-by, Ma," said Herbie, and hung up the receiver.

Let parents who ask such questions of children confined

in institutions, be the institution camp, a school, or anything else that relieves them of their parental duties, make very sure of two things: first, that the child has privacy; second, and this is more important, that the child can trust the parent's secrecy. Many of these institutions are excellent and necessary. Children who can spend a summer at camp are generally considered lucky. But none of these places can be run wholly without that cheap universal lubricant—fear.

As soon as the telephone talk was over, Herbie saw a change for the worse in the aspects of the owner and the head counselor. Uncle Sandy's face hardened, and Mr. Gauss shook his head sorrowfully.

"I am very disappointed in you, Herbert," he said. "Incredibly disappointed." He did not pause to inquire whether the boy was disappointed in him and his camp. "Is there no honor in you boys? No decency? I have been scrupulous," he went on in an injured tone, "I have been scrupulous, I say, to forbid any form of censorship or reading of campers' mail, and is this the thanks I get?"

Herbie hung his head. He was too innocent to answer that Mr. Gauss was not entitled to much thanks, since censoring the letters might have landed him in prison for tampering with the mails.

"And I have always regarded you, Herbert, as one of the finer boys in school and at camp. I repeat, I am incredibly disappointed. Aren't you, Uncle Sandy?"

"Can't say he shows much camp spirit," said the head counselor.

"Incidents such as this," pursued the camp owner, "make me wonder whether the uncertainty and toil of running a camp are worth while. Or perhaps you believe there is no uncertainty, no toil in it? Answer me, Herbert."

"I—I'm sorry, Mr. Gauss," mumbled the boy. "I promise I won't do it no more."

"Any more."

"Any more."

Herbie saw a hand appear under his downcast eyes. He looked up. Mr. Gauss was beaming once more, and offering a handshake.

"Then I'll say no more about it, and I think I can promise you in turn that Uncle Sandy will not be too harsh this time," he said.

Herbie shook the hand dutifully. "Thanks, Mr. Gauss."

"Don't mention it, Herbert. And don't call me Mr. Gauss. I'm Skipper here in the great outdoors."

"Thanks, er—Skipper," said Herbie, choking a little over the name as he did over cold oatmeal.

Mr. Gauss walked out of the office. When Herbie realized he was being left alone with Uncle Sandy, he almost wished the Skipper would stay, but the broad back vanished. He looked up at the head counselor timidly.

"Well, Herbie," said Uncle Sandy in a dry tone, "what do you think the punishment ought to be?"

This bland assumption that there would be a punishment put Herbie in an awkward case. He would have liked to point out that the main object, the soothing of his parents, had been attained, largely through his help; therefore, the whole episode might be forgotten. But Uncle Sandy was obviously wedded to the law of cause and effect.

"I get docked a coupla movies?" the boy suggested faintly.

Uncle Sandy considered the proposal with pursed lips.

"Well, no," he said at last. "That's pretty severe, and the Skipper wants me to be easy. Tell you what, Herb. The dancing class seems to have caused all the trouble. I think we'll just have you forget about dancing class."

"If it's all the same to you," pleaded Herbie, "I'd rather miss the movies."

The head counselor laughed. "Go on. I know you guys don't even like dancing class. No, that's what I said, and that's how we leave it. Run down the hill, now, and report to your activity."

"Yes, Uncle Sandy," said the dejected boy, and turned to go.

"And don't *ever* let me catch you reading during an

athletic period again," called Uncle Sandy after him as he walked out.

"No, sir," said Herbie, and his head sank a little lower.

In nine cases out of ten, Uncle Sandy would have been right in thinking that movies were a greater loss than dancing class. How could he know that the art of dancing was like a steep wall between Herbie and his beloved Lucille, a wall that the boy was panting to level once for all? It never occurred to him to take the lad's plea seriously.

So Herbie Bookbinder didn't learn to dance. And that small circumstance was to be the cause of great trouble.

16

The Triumph of Lennie

THE FIRST WEEK of August brought the great annual combat with Camp Penobscot.

Camp Penobscot was an institution much like Manitou, situated on another semi-lake eight miles away. Each year one camp piled its best athletes and a small group of boys with loud voices, known as a cheering section, into wheezing country busses, and sent them off to the grounds of the other to do battle. A game of baseball in the morning, and one of basketball in the afternoon, was the rule.

The rivalry, built up over many years, was bitter, and both sides in the past had resorted to tricks such as using waiters and young counselors on their teams. In 1926, two years before the time of our story, this had resulted in a nasty crisis. Uncle Sandy, in the middle of a basketball game which Manitou was losing badly, had suddenly blown his whistle, stalked onto the court, pointed at the star Penobscot player (who was six feet tall), and declared that he would call off the game unless this "adult" were removed at once. A hellish clamor had ensued, ending in a fist fight between the Penobscot star, who really was a counselor, and the best player of the Manitou side, who also was one. Since then an uneasy truce had been maintained, on the mutually pledged honor of Mr. Gauss and Mr. Papay, the owner of Penobscot, that only paying campers would compete.

Two days before the contest a disaster befell Manitou. The huge Super-senior Yishy Gabelson had been led by his love for wild blackberries into a patch of poison ivy, and was a puffed-up, bandaged, itching, helpless giant. Mr. Gauss had at once telephoned Penobscot to ask for a postponement. But he foolishly told Mr. Papay the reason; whereupon Mr. Papay swore that the busses had been hired, the teams trained, the camp routine set, and diminished rations ordered for the remaining campers. In short, postponement was impossible. Gloom swept Manitou, and Yishy, who had been the revered leader of the camp until now, was cursed and despised for being so hoggish about blackberries.

One hope remained. A hard rain would force postponement, and once that happened Mr. Gauss could put off the games for as long as it took a bad case of poison ivy to clear away. The boys of Manitou prayed for rain like savages in a drought. Mr. Gauss himself would have given perhaps twenty-five dollars to a really reputable rain maker. Even Herbie, even Ted, spent hours on the night before the event, guessing the possible water content of the clouds which here and there obscured the stars. Little as they loved Uncle Gussie and his camp, it was their own land, for better or worse, when invasion loomed. Uncle Sandy had no cause to complain of the lack of camp spirit during the days before the Penobscot games.

The bugle on the fated morning woke the boys to a sparkling day. Not a wisp of white moisture trimmed the blue. With a community groan, the campers prepared to meet the onslaught. Bunks were cleaned for inspection like Army barracks; everybody's best uniform was hauled out of the trunk; and the entire Intermediate and Junior divisions were marched across the grounds in a single, slowly moving line, to pick up stray papers. The ordinarily seedy camp never came closer to smartness than it did on the day of the Penobscot visit. (Exactly the same was true of Camp Penobscot's appearance each time Manitou came.)

A few forlorn inquiries were made about Yishy Gabelson's condition, but the word soon spread that he had spent a sleepless night, itching devilishly and reading through three whole Tarzan books. Succor from that quarter was hopeless.

Promptly at ten the bugle blew. The boys of Manitou lined up stiffly in front of their bunks, and the Penobscot horde came marching down Company Street, dressed in the hated green and gray uniforms, carrying many banners, and singing with gusto a lively marching song that began with the words, "Over hill, over dale, as we hit the dusty trail, as Penobscot goes rolling along." They halted at the foot of Company Street and finished their song. A blast from Uncle Sandy's whistle, and the array of Manitou burst into their own marching air, which went:

> *Bulldog, bulldog, bow-wow-wow,*
> *Man-i-tou.*
> *We always will come through,*
> *Bulldog, bulldog, bow-wow-wow,*

and so on. This anthem was a relic of the first head counselor, Uncle Yale, a graduate of Old Eli, of course, and now a drudging lawyer far from the Berkshires. When Herbie first heard the song he had been puzzled by the numerous references to bulldogs, but everybody else seemed to think it made sense, so he refrained from showing his ignorance. Soon he, like the others, took the words for granted, and formed a sentimental liking for them.

But he had never heard "Bulldog" sung before as it was

this day. Thrill chased thrill down his back as he shouted the tune with all his might. He glanced sidelong at Ted, and saw that the cynical old Gauss-hater was singing his soul out, too, his skinny face lit with fervor, his big mouth working, his eyes wet and glistening. Poor Ted! The love in a boy's heart must go out to familiar things. What had he had to love, for six long summers, but Camp Manitou?

Out to the best baseball diamond, which had been newly clipped, trimmed, and marked with whitewash, marched the Penobscots, followed by the whole Gaussian crew from the Midgets to the Super-seniors. Soon the enemy were seated along the first-base line, while the Manitou spectators ranged along the path to third base. Now in the distance sweet voices were heard chanting "Over hill, over dale," and the girls' camp hove into sight, dressed as prettily as for services and singing the Penobscot tune with roguish glances at the strangers. It was considered a handsome gesture by everybody except the Manitou boys, who looked sullen. A whisper spread through their ranks that Aunt Tillie was "sweet" on the head counselor of Penobscot, Uncle Husky, a tall, long-jawed man with blond hair and a heavy tan. Indeed, Aunt Tillie did look almost slim for once in a gleaming white dress, and her freckles were mysteriously not in evidence. The boys, ignorant through they were of the arts of cosmetics and corsetry, nevertheless were suspicious of the striking change. And when Aunt Tillie, smiling happily, shook hands with this Uncle Husky, she stood condemned as a weak-minded traitress, and scattered jeers were heard from the vicinity of third base.

The girls' camp was placed beside the Penobscots. Herbie could not see his sister, but luckily both he and Lucille were in front ranks. It was not easy to send passionate glances across the breadth of a baseball diamond, but Herbie did his best, and though the features of his loved one were indistinct, he could see her returning his look and smiling. The boy decided that it might be a pleasant day after all.

The Manitou team took the field, to a vigorous "Oink-

oink, bow-wow" led by Uncle Irish. All the players were
Seniors or Super-seniors, except for the shortstop, Lennie
Krieger. Though Lennie was large for his age, he was
puny in this company; nor would he have been in the
game, except for the ivy poisoning of Yishy Gabelson. He
had taken the place of the Senior shortstop, Boy Kaiser,
who had been shifted to Yishy's pitching duty. Misgivings
about Lennie were rife when he trotted to his post, a
grammar-school boy among youths of fifteen, but in the
few moments of warming up before play he showed that
he was not overmatched. The speed and accuracy of his
throws, the deftness of his running catches, were good to
see. A wave of sympathy for him spread among the
spectators. The Penobscot cheering section astonished and
pleased their hosts by rendering their camp cry, "Bang
chugga bang," in honor of Lennie. The girls' camp, led by
Aunt Tillie herself, immediately took up the idea with:

> *Strawberry shortcake, huckleberry pie,*
> *V-I-C-T-O-R-Y,*
> *Are we in it? Well, I guess.*
> *Lennie! Lennie! Yes, yes, yes!*

After this there was nothing left for the boys to do but to
honor Lennie with an "Oink-oink, bow-wow" all for himself. Lennie acknowledged these unusual tributes with
modest nods, and continued to practice coolly. Cast for
once in the role of underdog, Lennie had never been a
more sympathetic figure. Herbie felt he could forgive him
the injuries of all the years if only he would help to win
the game.

But, faultlessly as the Intermediate performed, it soon
became evident that Yishy Gabelson's passion for blackberries was going to cost Manitou dear. Boy Kaiser
seemed to be serving up his pitches to the Penobscot
athletes for batting practice. They hit, and hit, and hit,
and were only retired when the outfielders were lucky
enough to catch long flies. At the end of the fourth inning
the score was 17 to 2 in favor of the Penobscot side.
Silence hung over the sunlit field, broken only by the

excited squeaks of the little cluster of enemy cheerers. Boy Kaiser was replaced by the first baseman, Gooch Lefko, who had never pitched before, and the girls and boys of Manitou counted the game lost.

Then lo, hope sprang up. Gooch struck out two carelessly confident Penobscot batters, and the third went out on a fly. Manitou came to bat, and, urged on by an anguished "Oink-oink, bow-wow," let loose a thunderstorm of hits. With the bases full, undersize Lennie hit the ball clear into the tennis courts for a home run. From the shrieking demonstration that ensued it was obvious that he could have married any female of Manitou, camper or counselor, at that moment, with the possible exception of Aunt Tillie. The tumultuous inning ended with the score at 17-11. As Lennie trotted out to his position at short-stop, Herbie, quite beside himself, danced up to third base and yelled, "Come on, Lennie, you can win this game yourself! For good old Homer Avenue!" And Lennie waved at him and grinned, and Herbie was as proud as if he had received a letter from the President.

But this flurry was the last. The Penobscot boys blasted Gooch Lefko out of the pitcher's box, and a dismal parade of substitutes failed to stem them. The home team lost heart. Soon it became a matter of hoping for a quick finish. Unlike more primitive struggles like war and boxing, which can end when one side is hopelessly done for, the rules of baseball require the ceremony of nine innings no matter what happens. With the score at the unbelievable figure of 41 to 11, and the game stretching into the lunch time, the Penobscots finally brought the debacle to its close by the humiliating stunt of sending their cheering section to bat. Even so, the crushed Manitou team permitted two more runs; and so the game went down in history, an everlasting stain on the escutcheon of the cohorts of Gauss, 43 to 12.

But the ghastly blow was neutralized at once in an unexpected way.

It had been the custom in previous years for the teams and spectators to march from the baseball field to the dining halls, led by the Manitou head counselor on horseback. Technical difficulties had arisen this year in connection with using Clever Sam. Uncle Sandy, having had a couple of duels with the horse, flatly informed Mr. Gauss that he would not ride him. It was not his own feelings, he admitted under pressure, but the sentiments of the horse, that were decisive. But the camp owner was anxious to avoid giving Penobscot the impression that Manitou was having a horseless year. It was decided that Cliff should ride the horse to the baseball diamond and back again, if Clever Sam proved to have no objections to the traditional green and gray blanket which read, "Welcome, Penobscot." As it turned out, he was philosophically indifferent to it.

When the game ended, Cliff, who had been lurking behind a far-off tree with the animal, came cantering into the field, the blanket flapping its faded message to the breeze. He stopped for a moment before the Penobscots, who forthwith rendered a "Bang chugga bang" for Clever Sam. After this Cliff brought his steed alongside Uncle Sandy at third base. It happened that the Penobscot leader, Uncle Husky, was conferring with Sandy at that moment. Aunt Tillie had edged herself into the talk, too, and it was noticed glumly by the boys that she and the fellow called Husky were in rare spirits, while Sandy, like a true man of Manitou, was downcast.

"Well, Sandy," said Uncle Husky with a laugh, as Clever Sam came up, panting, "are we going to have the riding exhibition now?"

"No," said Sandy sulkily.

Husky looked carefully at Clever Sam. "New horse, eh? Moth-eaten beast."

"Maybe, but he's too much for me," said Sandy. "He's a devil. That kid is the only one in camp who can ride him."

Aunt Tillie spoke up. Her voice was a loud one, and all the boys could hear her. "It's a shame to spoil the parade. Husky, why don't you ride him?"

The handsome stranger smiled.

"Nonsense, Tillie," put in Uncle Sandy. "You know perfectly well the animal is unmanageable."

"For you, maybe, but not for Husky," shrilled Aunt Tillie, with a superior smile. "He's a magnificent horseman. He's won cups."

Hate radiated at her from the entire boys' camp. But under certain conditions women develop leaden hides.

"I don't mind trying him," said the Penobscot carelessly, "if Sandy doesn't object."

The head counselor hesitated. All the boys were listening.

"Go ahead, Uncle Sandy!" shouted Herbie suddenly from the ranks. "*Let* him try."

Uncle Sandy's vexed look slowly faded, and was replaced, equally slowly, almost with the sound of cogs grinding, by an expression of the most Satanic cunning.

"Why, of course," he said, grinning and squinting. "By all means, Husky. Let him have the horse, Cliff."

The boy dismounted, handed the reins to Uncle Husky, and backed off hurriedly. For a moment the Penobscot leader and Clever Sam looked each other in the eye. Uncle Husky seemed to flinch slightly at what he saw. He said, "Tillie, I'd better mount him away from the kids," and led the willing horse out to the center of the field.

Penobscot's chief counselor swung himself into the saddle with grace; and as soon as his thighs settled against the leather, Clever Sam's head dropped to the ground as though released by a spring and he began eating grass. The tall, powerful rider looked astounded, and snickers were heard in the ranks of Manitou. The next moment Clever Sam's head was yanked into the air by a pull that all but tore it off his neck.

"None of your nonsense!" cried Husky. He gave the animal a potent kick in the ribs. "Let's go, horse."

Clever Sam turned and studied his rider briefly. Then he seized the man's right sneaker in his teeth, tore it off, and dropped it on the ground.

All Manitou cheered.

Aunt Tillie screamed, "Husky, be careful! The beast is vicious!"

Husky threw her a contemptuous look, gave his mount a slap on the flank that resounded among the hills like a pistol shot, and jerked the horse's head back as far as it could go three times. "Get going, horse!" he commanded.

Clever Sam got going, in his fashion. He began to do a decidedly original waltzing step, backward, and backed and backed. With his rider cursing, sawing the reins, and pummeling him with fists and heels, he backed around in a circle twice, then backed into the ragged wire netting behind home plate. Here he tried to rub his rider off against the posts, but Husky hung on, at the cost of a nasty scratching from the wire. The boys and girls of Manitou were rolling on the grass, half dead with laughter. The Penobscots were still. Aunt Tillie, in tears, was pleading for someone to go to the rider's aid, but nobody paid any attention to her, or noticed that her freckles were reappearing here and there in streaks along her face.

Clever Sam finally stopped trying to rub his rider off. He pranced sideways to the center of the field, and assumed a pose that can only be described as standing on his head, and issued several hoarse, grating noises. The third time he kicked up his hind legs to renew this position Uncle Husky gave up and thumped to the ground almost on the spot where he had mounted. Clever Sam at once ceased his ridiculous antics, and resumed his consumption of grass. Husky rose to his feet, dusted himself off angrily, and returned to his group, ignoring Aunt Tillie's anxious call, "Husky, Husky, are you all right?"

With one accord, without benefit of cheer leader, the boys of Manitou gave Clever Sam the loudest "Oink-oink, bow-bow" of all time.

Cliff trotted out to the horse, mounted him, and rode him off the field toward the dining halls, to great hosannas. The Penobscots had beaten Manitou in one contest, but had just as certainly been trounced in another. The score for the day stood at one victory apiece.

A sumptuous lunch followed. The noonday meal at Manitou, except on weekends (when most parents came to visit) was usually an affair of vague stew or creamed, chipped beef or Spanish omelet—wholesome, perhaps,

but conceived in a spirit of compromise between bankbook
and cookbook rather than in the intent to delight. Today,
however, there was turkey, with fresh corn and watermelon. Penobscot's meals took a similar turn for the better
when the games were on their grounds. The camp owners
probably hoped to do some polite recruiting in this way,
but they reckoned without the emotions the rivalry
aroused. The boys were, in general, fooled into believing
their enemies were better fed, but it only made them more
bitter, both about the other camp and about their own.
Manitou campers frequently went elsewhere after a summer under Gauss, but never to Penobscot, and there were
no ex-Penobscots in the Gauss domain. This banquet was
perhaps the only useless expenditure that the camp owner
made, and he hopefully went on making it year after
year.

An hour was set aside after lunch for sleeping, during
which nobody slept. All thoughts were on the coming
basketball game. The Penobscots lay about under trees,
glorying over the baseball massacre and anticipating new
conquest. Among the Manitous the mood was bleak. Mr.
Gauss visited Yishy Gabelson in the infirmary to see if
there were the slightest chance of allowing him to play. A
thrill of hope raced through the camp when he was seen
to enter the sick ward. As is usual in such situations, hope
quickly gave birth to rumor. Defying the rest-hour rules, a
lone Junior came capering along the deserted Company
Street, shouting, "Yishy's all better! Yishy's gonna
play!"

Everybody believed him. The campers leaped off their
beds and danced out of their bunks into Company Street,
yelling. Uncle Sandy charged from his tent and dispersed
the carnival with a blast of his whistle. But the boys
simply retreated into the bunks and kept up the wild
merriment, jumping from bed to bed, swinging on rafters,
and hugging each other. Mr. Gauss hurried out of the
infirmary and exchanged words with the head counselor,
who stood glaring in the middle of the empty street. Once
again he blew his whistle, and shouted through the
megaphone, "An announcement!" The noise stopped as

though shut off by a switch. Boys stood on one foot or hung from rafters in rigid listening attitudes.

"The disgraceful exhibition that has just taken place gets its proper reward. Mr. Gauss informs me that Yishy can't possibly play and won't play. Now return to your cots and keep quiet! This is rest hour."

The order to keep quiet was superfluous. Crushed, the boys dropped heavily on their beds, and moped away the rest of the hour. Herbie, who had danced and cheered as hard as anybody, lay with his face in his pillow. The honor of Camp Manitou, this flimsy, rundown device of poor Mr. Gauss, existing only to eke out his small salary as a schoolmaster, had become as important to Herbie Bookbinder as his own destiny.

The basketball game, surprisingly enough, began as a tight, vicious fight, in which Lennie Krieger outshone everybody on the court. He played in a frenzy of courage. Darting in and out among opponents a head taller than himself, twisting, scrambling, pouncing on the ball like a wild animal and tearing it out of the hands of opposing players, he kept the score even almost single-handed through three thrilling quarters. Victory began to seem likely, only because of him. His performance raised howl upon howl.

The best that was in Lennie came out in this game. He was a boy who, usually to his misfortune, saw reality in terms of ball games. Nothing but athletic prowess was vital to him, and this was why he could not study school subjects. This was also why he was a ruffian—caring for only one thing in life makes for crude manners; and this was why he was a bully—judging other boys by the yardstick of his own skill, he was left with a rough contempt for nearly all of them. But in the present instance he was challenged to his heart, and he met the challenge. An ancient sage said, "Despise no thing and no man—for there is no man that has not his hour, and no thing that has not its place." This basketball game was Lennie Krieger's hour, and it was fine and grand.

At the very start of the fourth quarter, wrestling for the ball with the captain of the Penobscots, Lennie pulled his heavy opponent to the ground on top of him in a tangle of arms and legs, and rose with his right arm hanging queerly. He could not move it, and was obviously in pain, though he made no outcry. The game was halted. The doctor examined him, gave a verdict of dislocation and possible fracture, and ordered him to leave the court. A great moan came from the spectators, and even the Penobscots sympathized. "Please, please, I can play with my left hand," Lennie begged the doctor, and reached wildly for the sweat-soaked basketball on the dusty ground to prove it. But the doctor held him back. Not until Uncle Sandy came and put his arm around the boy's shoulders did he wilt and permit himself to be led off the field, red-faced and weeping with pain and frustration. For whatever consolation it could give him, he received a cheer almost as loud as Clever Sam had had in the morning, as he dwindled away with the doctor toward the infirmary.

Penobscot proceeded to win the game, 45 to 35, and rode off cheering and singing in their busses, gorged with triumph. They left behind them a funereal atmosphere.

That night was movie night. When the show was an old cowboy picture, as was usually the case, it was run off on separate evenings for the boys and the girls. But now and then Mr. Gauss would pay the larger fee for a new film. In that case the camps were both assembled in the social hall at once, so that the owner could save money by keeping the print only one night. When Yishy had come down with poison ivy, Mr. Gauss, foreseeing the gloomy outcome, had hired a stirring new Douglas Fairbanks picture to lighten the misery of his campers. It was a humane notion. Merely assembling with the opposite sex on a week night gave the children a sense of festivity, and the thought of seeing a picture of later vintage than 1925 was gay, too. Trooping into the social hall, they found their grief diminishing.

Uncle Sid was playing "Bulldog, Bulldog" on the old piano with spirit, as the lines of boys and girls marched through the door side by side. The first thing the children noticed, besides the familiar white sheet and bulky movie projector, was the impressive figure of Lennie, seated alone in the first row, his right arm in a fresh white sling. Around his neck hung a placard announcing his election to the Royal Order of Gooferdusters. The sight of the wounded hero, thus singled out for distinction, lifted their hearts yet more. They took their seats in a state approaching comfort.

Uncle Nig, the movie operator, slipped the first reel into the projector. The usual hush was over the audience. He signaled for the turning out of the lights—and at that moment Mr. Gauss rose dramatically, exclaimed, "One moment, please," and walked to the front of the hall. Here he stood, his back to the blank canvas sheet, and faced the puzzled children with a smile.

17

The Victory Speech of Mr. Gauss

"BOYS AND GIRLS," said the camp owner, "before we see this wonderful, exciting picture, *The Black Pirate,* I want to tell you just one thing about the events of this day."

He looked around at the silent faces. Herbie, buried in one of the rear rows, wondered what he could possibly have to say. Wasn't it best to forget the Penobscot horror as quickly as possible?

"I want to tell you, boys and girls," went on Mr. Gauss, "that today Camp Manitou was *not defeated*."

There was a stunned stillness for a moment, then a tumult of yells and clapping. Mr. Gauss permitted the noise for perhaps thirty seconds, then quieted it with a raised hand.

"I saw those games," he declaimed. "I know how the

scores read. And still I say to you campers of Manitou we did not lose today. *We won.*"

More cheers. Herbie, not quite knowing what Mr. Gauss meant, but sensing a vague, wonderful meaning in his words, cheered too.

"Boys and girls, there are victories in the scoreboard sense, and there are victories in the moral sense. George Washington at Valley Forge won a victory in the moral sense. General Custer in his last stand won a victory in the moral sense. Moses, standing on the mountains of Moab, seeing the Land of Promise which he could not enter, won a victory in the moral sense. If Washington was truly defeated, if Custer was truly defeated, if Moses was truly defeated, then today Camp Manitou was defeated. But if those great heroes of history each won a great victory—*and you know that they did*—then today Camp Manitou won a great victory!"

(Vigorous applause. Sniffles among the girls.)

"What kind of showing would the French have made in their great wars without Napoleon? What kind of showing would the British have made at Waterloo without Wellington? Think of this for a moment. And then ask yourselves, boys and girls, did our boys not make the most splendid showing in all Manitou history—without Yishy Gabelson?"

(Cries of "Yes, yes!"

Cry from Ted: "Let's throw Yishy in the lake.")

"Somebody has suggested that we throw Yishy in the lake. (Laughter.) No, we will not throw Yishy in the lake. First of all, it would raise a high tide. (Yells of laughter.) Second of all, from what I have seen of his condition it would contaminate the lake, and we still want to do some swimming."

(Laughter and applause. Remark of Herbie Bookbinder to an unidentified neighbor: "You know, Mr. Gauss ain't such a bad guy, really." Reply of neighbor: "Doggone right.")

"No, boys and girls, we don't have to do that to Yishy. We can simply let him drown in the misery of knowing that due to his uncontrollable urge for blackberries (laughter), he has been completely overshadowed by a boy half his size—and you all know who I mean."

(Cheers. Cries of "We want Lennie! Stand up, Lennie." Slight blush in the hero's impassive face.)

"Yes, boys and girls, King George the Third met his Washington, Caesar met his Brutus, Goliath met his David, and Camp Penobscot met Lennie Krieger! (Cheers) Stand up, Lennie. (Lennie obviously reluctant.) Come on, my boy. We know that heroes are always modest."

(Laughter and clapping. Lennie rises. Uncle Sid plays "Bulldog, Bulldog." Indescribable sensation. Herbie Bookbinder, eyes wet with pride, says to neighbor, "He's my pal. He lives on my block. His father and my father are partners." Neighbor's reply: "Boy, yer lucky. Wisht I was you." Mr. Gauss again restores order with upraised hand.)

"Perhaps you think, boys and girls, that I have singled this young man out for praise at this time solely because of his great display of camp spirit this afternoon. That is not the case. I have had my eye on Leonard Krieger for many years. I have watched him at school and in camp. And I will say here and now that never in all my experience have I observed in a boy more of the sterling qualities that go into that mysterious and all-important thing known as Character. If I would say one thing about Lennie Krieger, I would say he has Character. What is Character? Modesty, cheerfulness, intelligence, good nature, obedience, co-operation, respect of elders, truthfulness, hard work, gentleness—all these things are part of Character, and part of Lennie Krieger. But still that is no definition. I will sum it all up for you. Character *is* Lennie Krieger! (Applause.)

"Lennie, give me your hand to shake. Yes, I know, my lad, only your left hand is free. But let me tell you this. I would rather shake the *left* hand of Lennie Krieger than the *right* hand of anybody, counselor or boy, in all of Camp Penobscot!"

With this master stroke of eloquence, Mr. Gauss pumped Lennie's left hand. Handclapping, stamping, and shouting shook the hall. This is not a figure of speech, for the hall was cheaply built and shook easily. Mr. Gauss waited for the enthusiasm to spend itself, and then went on, still holding Lennie's hand:

"But in praising the character of this perfect camper, let me not appear to minimize his glorious deeds on the field today. You all know what they were, and I shall not expand on them. Suffice it to say that they will stand forever in the annals of Manitou as a symbol of true camp spirit. And there is none of us here who will not wish to thank Lennie from a full heart—with the exception, perhaps—I say perhaps"—and here Mr. Gauss's face creaked painfully into a mischievous expression—"with the exception, perhaps, of our dear good Aunt Tillie."

This joke was the high point of Mr. Gauss's long career of oratory. The shrieks, squeals, and whoops of boyish and girlish laughter which followed, the sliding of doubled-over bodies helplessly to the floor, the streaming eyes of the counselors, made an effect he never again equaled.

Aunt Tillie blushed lobster-red, tried to smile and failed dismally, threw furious glances at Mr. Gauss, and finally, as the screaming mirth continued, got up and walked from the hall. It was a delicious moment for the whole camp. Mr. Gauss, by throwing Aunt Tillie to the lions, gained a real, if temporary, popularity. So Roman rulers used martyrs in their day.

"Seriously, boys and girls," he said at last, "I am happier over the events of this day than I would have been had we defeated Penobscot in both games by a hundred to one. What have we lost? Nothing. Mere numbers on a scoreboard. What have we gained? Everything. We have gained a true appreciation of Character. So all hail, campers of Manitou—all hail, with a real 'Oink-oink, bow-wow' to the young man who embodies Character, who *is* Character—the young man, moreover, who, whatever the scoreboard says, today gave Camp Penobscot the worst beating of their lives—Leonard Krieger!"

And Uncle Irish leaped up to cue, and one more animated tribute was paid to the sterling Character of Lennie; after which the hall went dark and the movie began.

This historic victory speech of Mr. Gauss may serve as a model for the generations to come. In every contest there must be a losing side, and on every losing side a Lennie can usually be found in the dazzle of whose exploits the unpleasant fact of defeat can be obscured by a Mr. Gauss who talks long enough and loud enough. In war and in politics, as well as in children's games, there are Gaussian victories. And it is well that it should be so. Life is full of struggles, and it is not given to everyone to gain a real triumph; but nearly all of us can manage a Gaussian one.

Strangely enough, the speech of the owner of Camp Penobscot, welcoming his returning teams that night, was very much shorter, and the rival camp was full of buoyant hilarity for days after the contest, all unaware that they had undergone such a Gaussian trouncing. That is the unique charm of a Gaussian victory. It elates the "winning" side, and does not in the least depress the other.

The Black Pirate was a happy dream of sailing, fighting, and lovemaking in "natural color." It lasted an hour and a half, and then the lights were switched on, the reeled-up dream was dropped into a tin can, and the blinking children found themselves in the dingy wooden social hall of Camp Manitou once more.

It seemed less cheerful than ever to Herbie this evening. The naked electric bulbs dangling overhead on black cords, the unpainted rough boards of the walls and rafters, the threadbare brown curtain of the stage, the rows of boys and girls, dressed alike, rubbing their eyes and yawning—how dreary, how dreary! He became aware of the rhythmic song of the crickets that filled the night outside the open windows, and realized with a little shock that he had become so used to the sound that he no longer heard it except at moments like this. And yet it was a very loud noise. A wave of homesickness came over him, and he longed for the hot, humid night of Homer Avenue under the brilliant street lamps, the boys and girls in city clothes, eating ice-cream cones and chaffing in front of Borowsky's candy store, the parked automobiles, the trolley cars clanging and rumbling around the corner on

Westchester Avenue, the vacant lots where a cricket was
a rare, fascinating thing, and, most of all, the climb up the
stone steps to Apartment 3A, and his mother and father
sitting in the kitchen, eating fruit from the basket made of
the shell of an armadillo, talking about the Place. These
things seemed bathed in a rich amber light as he saw
them in his mind's eye. What was he doing among
strangers in this barn on the shore of a nameless swamp, a
hundred miles from home?

But Mr. Gauss was on his feet before the empty white
sheet, speaking again.

"—celebrate our boys' splendid showing tomorrow
night," he was saying, "by a dance for the boys and girls
who want to dance, and a wiener roast on the beach for
the rest of the camp!"

Evidently Herbie was not the only camper caught in
depression. The announcement of a wiener roast or a
dance would ordinarily have touched off a jubilee, but the
response was only mild applause. Celebrating the Gaussian victory seemed to have drained the children of enthusiasm for the night.

"And now," said the camp owner, beaming benevolent-
ly, "we shall have ten minutes of—ah—shall we say,
socializing among the boys and girls, before we all retire
for a well-earned rest."

This boon brought the dull assembly to life. Jumping
up from their benches, the ranks of boys and girls quickly
melted into one jumble in the aisle, chattering, laughing,
pushing and waving. Herbie, who had been unable to
note Lucille's place in the benches, began threading
through the crowd. It struck him again how unattractive
girls were as a species. In camp clothing they looked
worse than otherwise. Once or twice it had appeared to
him that the radiance of Lucille herself flickered when he
beheld her in loose white blouse and flopping blue
bloomers.

A pair of soft hands suddenly came from behind him
and covered his eyes. Overjoyed, he peeled them off and
turned to discover Felicia. His joy subsided.

"Hello, my darling brother. Bet you thought I was someone else."

"I sure did. See you later, Fleece." He started to move on. She caught his hand.

"Gosh, won't you talk to me for a minute even? We hardly ever see each other. I may not be Lucille, but I'm your sister."

Herbert was startled by the tone of appeal in which she said this. He looked more carefully at Felicia. In an indefinable way she was prettier and older. He became aware, with a touch of shame, that he never thought of her.

"Sure, Fleece. I didn't know you felt like talking to me."

"Well, I do."

"Well, I'd like to talk to you, too."

Thereupon they both became tongue-tied, and looked at each other sheepishly for half a minute.

Said the sister at last, "You having a good time, Herbie?"

"Sure," said Herbie in an injured way, as though she had accused him of some obscure offense. "Aren't you?"

"Well, of course. Aunt Dora is just wonderful."

"Uncle Sid is a big ol' dope, but my bunk is O.K."

"How is it living with Lennie? Does he pick on you?"

The aura of Character was strong around his tormentor in Herbie's mind. "Who, Lennie? Naw! He's all different now. He's been swell."

Felicia looked happy at this. "He's the big hero now, isn't he?"

"Yeah. Camp is great for a guy like him."

"And he's great for the camp," said the girl.

"You bet."

After a pause during which Felicia studied her brother's face, she said, "Herbie, I'm surprised you like camp. There's so much ball playing."

"Aw, I get to read a lot," said Herbie.

"Just like you did at home."

"Yeah, only under a tree."

"Same old bookworm."

The brother and sister exchanged a smile of unusual warmth. Herbie felt that perhaps he should talk to his sister more often. Then he remembered Lucille, and began to glance around impatiently.

"Oh, go ahead and find her," snapped Felicia, seeing his eyes stray. "Honest, the way you go after that red-headed little thing someone would think you were fifteen years old."

Herbie, rather flattered at being thus described as a mature lover, said, "I'll be back in a minute, Fleece," and plunged in among the milling children. He came upon Lucille almost at once, in no very pleasing circumstance. She was one of a cluster of perhaps eleven girls around Lennie. Only the hero's face was visible, the rest of him being obscured by the girls' heads, white blouses, and blue bloomers. Herbie hovered near the circle, trying to catch Lucille's eye. It was a couple minutes before he succeeded. When she saw him she smiled very brightly and came to him.

"H'lo, I was searching all over for you," said she. Herbie hadn't detected any symptoms of search while he was watching her, but her smile erased the inconsistency.

"Swell movie, wasn't it?" he said.

"Uh-huh."

"Come on over by the window a minute."

"Well, I have to go back to my counselor right away." But she followed him. They leaned on the sill and looked out at trees, lake and stars.

"Listen to them crickets," Herbie was inspired to remark, after a while.

"I don't like them. I wish they would all go away."

"Yeah, so do I. Say, that wienie roast is gonna be fun. Ted says the boys and girls get to sit around two by two and build their own little fires. Won't that be swell?"

The girl said cautiously, "Wouldn't you rather go to the dance?"

"Heck no. Dancing is for dopes."

"Well, I love it."

"Well, I think it's dopey."

"Go on. You know it's fun."

"Yeah. For lunatics."

Herbie was making the mistake of ridiculing something beyond his power to do. Few errors make one appear more foolish. Lucille gave him a cool, appraising look which caused him much discomfort. At the age of eleven a girl is not likely to be deceived in these matters by a boy of eleven and a half.

"*Can* you dance?" she said.

"Naw, and I ain't never gonna learn, neither. Jumpin' around like an ape."

"All the counselors dance."

"Sure, they're all apes."

One remark more feeble than the rest: this was the course Herbie was sliding down, having taken his false position. He thrashed around for a straw to arrest his tumble.

"Boy, do I love wienies! I really love 'em. Wienies! Yum!"

"I like marshmallows better," replied Lucille.

"Not me. Shucks, I'd rather eat one roasted wienie than dance for a million years. And fires an' everything. I can't hardly wait for tomorrow night."

"Fires!" said the girl scornfully. "Fires are for babies."

Now, the word "baby" among adults is a pleasant, even an endearing term. But in the present company it was the ultimate printable insult. Herbie found nothing more to say.

"Well," said the little red-headed beauty after a graceless silence, "I gotta go back to my counselor. G'by."

"See you at the wienie roast?" said Herbie as she turned away.

Lucille halted, and stood fingering the starched hem of her blouse.

"I told you, Herbie, I just don't like wienies. I'd rather stay in bed than go to a rotten old wienie roast. So I guess I'll go to the dance. 'By."

"Yeah," jeered Herbie at her retreating back, "just 'cause Lennie Krieger'll be there."

Lucille turned on him swiftly.

"That's right, smarty, 'cause Lennie'll be there. What did you do that was so wonderful today, that you have the right to make fun of Lennie? If you wanna know something, he *asked* me to go, with ten other girls standing around—some of them Seniors. An' I didn't even say I would, 'cause I was waiting to see if you were going. But as long as you're being such a baby I *will* go. There now. And I hope you eat so many wienies that you bust."

And off she flounced, or came as near flouncing as anyone can in blue bloomers.

There was a mournful hush in Bunk Thirteen that night after taps, in place of the usual pleasant whispering. Lennie's bed was empty; the young man of Character was spending the night in the infirmary. Herbie had ample cause for misery, but he wondered a little at the silence of his bunkmates. At last Ted said hoarsely, "Hey, guys, ain't ol' Gauss a real bag o' hot air?"

"You bet! An' how! What a stinker!" came a husky chorus in reply.

"All that boloney about a victory," said Ted. "We got skunked. Who was he kiddin'?"

"Them Penobscots murdered us," said one boy in the darkness.

"I'd like to murder Yishy Gabelson," said another.

"Character!" hissed Ted. "Lennie played swell ball today, but he's still the guy that don't make his bed and picks on guys smaller'n him."

"Aw, Lennie's O.K.," said Herbie.

"That movie stunk, too," observed Eddie Bromberg irrelevantly.

Silence again, except for thunderous music from the crickets. The duty counselor crunched by on the gravel outside, flashed a beam of light through the screen door, said, "Why is this camp so blasted quiet tonight, anyhow?" and could be heard walking away.

"You know what, guys?" whispered Eddie. "I'm sick of camp. I wish to heck the summer was over."

"Who doesn't?" said Ted. "If I had a home, I'd wish I was home. But even boardin' school's better'n this."

Herbie said, "I got a home, an' by God I wish I was there."

And on this note the evening's conversation ended, and the lads tossed and fidgeted until one by one they dropped asleep. Poor boys! The trouble with a Gaussian victory is that its aftertaste is so miserable. Honest defeat honestly swallowed is a bitter dose, but a clean brief one. Why will adults never understand that, bad as castor oil may be, castor oil diluted with orange juice is twice as horrible?

18

The Dance

HERBIE SAID HE had a headache next evening, and asked to be excused from the festivities. Uncle Sid was alarmed. He did not imagine that any ailment short of apoplexy could keep a boy from a feast of frankfurters. With some difficulty, Herbie convinced the counselor that he was not mortally ill, and received permission to go to bed early.

The sun was still sending pallid rays across the lake when Herbie undressed and climbed into his cot, while his bunkmates clad themselves in holiday whites. All of them were going to the dance to try out their newly learned art, except Ted. He roundly declared that he had yet to meet the girl who could give him as much pleasure as a frankfurter. The other boys hooted at him.

"I can dance as good as any of you," he retorted to the jeers. "All I know is, you eat a wienie and you've ate a wienie. You dance with a girl and how are you better off?"

Time went merrily until the bugle sent the disputants scurrying out to assembly. The bedridden invalid heard Uncle Sandy bellow through a megaphone the standard warnings about conduct in the presence of girls. Then came the spirited tread of feet marching off to revelry. Herbie remained the lone living creature on Company Street, excepting, of course, those with six or more legs, who were present in their usual multitudes.

Now, there was a certain young miser in Bunk Eleven who owned a precious thing, a bright red copy of the newest Tarzan book, *Tarzan and the Men from Mars*. Herbie had palpitated for weeks to read this epic, but its owner had obstinately declined to lend it to anybody or even to permit the applicants to read snatches of it in his bungalow. He was a skinny, unhappy little rich boy called Daisy, an embittered failure in athletics and in day-to-day life with his fellows, who, finding he had something at last that was wanted, revenged himself on the world by denying it to everyone.

As soon as the sound of the march died away, Herbie leaped from his bed, dressed, took a flashlight, and went to Bunk Eleven. Daisy's treasure was there, on a shelf above his cot. He took the book, caressed its bright binding, and settled down to read it on Daisy's trunk, leaning his back against the foot of the bed. He felt no scruples. Had Daisy written the tale, that he had the right to withhold it from anyone? The fat boy would never have pilfered the book itself, but instinct told him that the rule of property stopped short in the domain of literature. All who had eyes had the right to read. The author of *Tarzan* probably would have supported Daisy's view in the matter, preferring that every boy buy a new copy of the book. But authors are a hungry, surly lot, anyway.

Whether conscience was gnawing away at Herbie's unconscious mind, or whether a procession of astral frankfurters was dancing across the pages, the boy soon discovered that he was not enjoying the book very much. Tarzan was brawny and heroic as ever, and the men from Mars proved to be fine, gruesome fellows with immense heads, luminous skins, eight spidery arms, and transparent bodies; but despite these literary charms, Herbie's attention kept wandering.

He had planned this evening's activity as a defiance of the temptations of the flesh. Wienies and Lucille alike were going to be proven matters of indifference to Herbie Bookbinder, the ascetic scholar. But this was more easily resolved upon than executed. Jealousy mocked him with images of Lucille floating daintily on Lennie's good arm. Hunger, after a while, caused him to smell the odor of roasting frankfurters as plainly as if the campfire were next door, though in fact Herbie was a quarter of a mile from the scene of the grilling, and upwind. Meantime, Tarzan was slaying the Martians with fine fury as they swarmed from their rocket ship; they fell beneath his knife oozing a horrid yellow blood; but Herbie followed these great exploits only listlessly.

A pleasant fancy intruded itself on his imagination, causing Tarzan to fade away in mid-combat. It occurred to him that his bunkmates would tell Lucille of his illness. She would be smitten with remorse. She would realize that his health was breaking under her neglect. Surely when she understood the depths of such devotion she would sneak away from the dance, visit him in his fallen state, and beg his forgiveness with sweet words and tears. As he dwelled on this attractive picture it came to seem such a strong likelihood that he put the book on its shelf, went back to his bunk, and actually undressed, and lay in his cot, waiting for his beloved to appear.

The sunset faded, the darkness deepened, and presently it was black outside, for there was no moon. It soon became more and more evident that there would be no Lucille, either. Herbie's mood shifted slowly from expectancy to impatience, then to exasperation, then to rage—mostly at himself for his sheep-headed folly. He perceived after a while that his imagination had tricked him again—conjured up a mirage out of his own wishes, and made him believe in it. Strains of Uncle Sid's clodhopping jazz piano came down the night breeze. Lucille was there at the social hall hugely enjoying herself, and was no more likely to stumble out into the dark, against all rules, to visit him on the boys' grounds, than she was apt to flap her arms and fly to him. He rose and dressed again, struggling with his clothes in the gloom and grumbling various uncomplimentary remarks at himself such as, "Hurry up, stupid," and "Why don't you just go out and drown yourself?" and "Any girl'd hafta be loony to like a dope like you." In this low frame of mind he stole to the social hall, and peeked in through a window.

Strange, how the aspect of a building could change in twenty-four hours. Last night the social hall had seemed to Herbie an ugly barn; tonight it was a place of splendor. Nothing was different—there were not even any decorations—and the same Uncle Sid banged at the same piano in the same corner. But tonight Herbie was outside, looking in at a dance. Not many events on this earth appear more heavenly than a dance seen through a window by someone who cannot join it. We can go to a hundred dances and know them for the hot, shoving, boisterous, and banal affairs that they are. Then we pass by a place where there are twirling couples and music, and we press our noses to the glass and seem to be looking in on Paradise. This feeling struck Herbie all the more strongly because it was new to him, and because his girl was one of the dancers. Small wonder that magic invested the social hall! And who is to say on which night he was more nearly correct? His viewpoint had changed. Viewpoint is everything.

Quite as Herbie had imagined, Lucille was dancing with Lennie. The hero's right arm was out of its sling though still bandaged, and sufficiently healed to enable him to hug his smiling partner. The sight hurt Herbie. His throat swelled, his stomach knotted, and all appetite and good will passed from him. He could not have eaten the most succulent roasted wienie in the world; no, nor even a frap. It was the day of Mortimer Gorkin all over again, and greatly more painful, for this time he had lost his love not to a stranger but to his old enemy.

Herbie was so plunged in misery that he heard the sound of feminine sniffling near by for several seconds before it struck him as a thing requiring investigation. The noise was coming from around the corner of the social hall. He walked cautiously along the wall to the end of the building and peered past the edge. Sitting on the rickety steps that came down from the locked stage door was the dim form of a girl, her head bowed, her hair falling over her face. Before he thought, he said, "Hello, what's the matter?" The girl looked up. It was his sister Felicia.

"Herbie! I thought you were in bed!"

"I sneaked out. I feel O.K. now. Why you cryin', Fleece?"

"I'm not crying. Don't be silly. I just came out for some fresh air."

"I heard you cry."

"You didn't hear anything. Oh, yes, I guess I was blowing my nose." Hereupon she drew out a fresh handkerchief and made a noise into it, not in the least resembling the sounds Herbie had just heard. "I caught a little cold today swimming."

Herbie was too dejected by his own trouble to hound down the lie. Felicia might have been sniffling for any one of a hundred silly girls' reasons. What did it matter, after all?

"You havin' fun at the dance, Fleece?"

"Fun!" said the girl bitterly. "It's the rottenest dance that ever was. Nothing but babies, babies, babies, crowding all over the floor. Why didn't they have a separate dance for Seniors? I wish I could go back to my bunk and go to bed."

"I just been doin' that," said Herbie. "That's even worse."

Brother and sister became silent, each communing with private grief. The picture of Lennie dancing with Lucille haunted Herbie in bright colors. It brought along a vague idea about his sister's distress.

"Hey, you danced with Lennie yet, Fleece?"

"I wouldn't dance with that stuck-up baby," burst out the girl, "if he begged me on his knees. *On his knees!* Only babies dance with babies."

This made it plain to Herbie that his guess was correct.

He had always suspected that Felicia, for all her superior airs, admired Lennie. It was beneath her to admit it, because she was half a year older. Now he saw that she was suffering over the model of Character even as he was over the faithless redhead.

He felt only moderately sorry for her, for he knew the depth of her pain could not equal his. Furthermore, she had the consolation of the epithet "baby."

Differences in age serve much the same useful function among children that differences in income do among adults. They offer a permanent, simple scale of snobbery. The scorn of age thirteen for age eleven is equaled only by the disdain of a hundred dollars a week for fifty dollars a week. In both cases superiority rests on the unshakable basis of numbers which everybody can grasp and nobody can deny. Unluckily for Herbie, Lennie was older than he and Lucille was practically the same age; otherwise he would certainly have taken solace, as Felicia did, in an arithmetical sneer.

The girl did not like the knowing look Herbie gave her and said shortly, "Why aren't you at the dance, if you feel all right?"

"I dunno how to dance."

"Go on. They had a class for all the Intermediates."

"Yeah, but I couldn't go."

Herbie sat beside his sister on the wooden steps. The gloom, the sweet smells of the night air, inspired intimacy. He told her the adventure of the blank letters. Finding her a sympathetic listener, he broke open his heart and recounted his quarrel with Lucille. This tale threw Felicia into an astonishing fury.

"Why that snippy child, that good-for-nothing, spoiled, conceited, lazy little infant!" she raged. Never had Herbie seen Felicia so wholeheartedly on his side. "How dare she snub you! Why, she's the joke of the camp. She won't do any work, she can't play any games, and she spends all her time in front of a mirror. Imagine, a babe-in-arms eleven years old in front of a mirror! And she uses powder to cover up her freckles, I know she does."

Felicia jumped up and walked to and fro, fuming.

"My brother isn't good enough for her 'cause he can't dance, eh? *We'll* show her. Come on, Herbie." She tugged him to his feet. "You're gonna learn how to dance right this minute. And then you're gonna go in there and dance with every girl in the social hall—*except her*. And she can go right on dancing with that left-back 7B dumbbell until they both drop."

"Aw, Fleece, forget it," said Herbie, taken aback at her crusading fervor. But he was dealing with a mighty force of which he knew little.

"You shut up! Come on, how much did you learn before you got docked out of dancing class?"

It developed that Herbie had acquired the rudiments of the box step, and mainly lacked confidence. The long and the short of it was that Felicia box-stepped around with him on the grass for fifteen minutes and then announced that he was as skillful as the best Senior in the hall, and "ten times as good as that big dope Lennie."

"Come on, in we go," said the sister, dragging him toward the entrance with eagerness.

Herbie hung back, protesting, and at last dug his heels into the ground. "Holy smoke, Fleece, look at me. I'm dressed in khakis. They're all in whites."

"Oh, who'll notice?"

"Everybody'll notice, that's who. They'll die laughing at me."

Felicia weighed the objection briefly. "All right, I'll give you five minutes to put on whites. And if you don't come back I'll go after you and murder you."

Herbie was quite cowed at this point by his sister's stormy energy. He galloped back to his bunk, fished a set of whites out of his trunk, and put them on, thinking the while that he seemed to be spending most of this night undressing and dressing again.

"How do I look?" he said diffidently as he reported back to Felicia, who was pacing up and down in the darkness near the door of the social hall.

"Wonderful," she answered, seizing his hand and ignoring the rest of him. "Let's go."

And before Herbie could draw another breath he was

in the social hall, squinting at the bright light. He half expected that everyone present would turn and stare at him, but they all went on dancing and chattering as though the great event—his First Coming to a dance— had not occurred. Uncle Sid's piano was near the doorway.

"Hello there, boy," called the counselor, not interrupting his methodical assassination of "The Darktown Strutters' Ball." "Feel better, do you? That's fine."

Felicia was hauling him out into the middle of the floor.

"Hey, wait a second, Fleece," whispered Herbie, frightened, "can't we start off in a corner somewhere? I forgot everything."

"You forgot nothing," said his sister sternly. She planted herself facing him, pulled his arm around her waist, clamped a steely grip on his shoulder, and said, "All right. Now dance."

And Herbie obeyed. With painful concentration he ticked off one—two—three—four, one—two—three— four with his feet in time to the music, and found himself revolving stiffly among the dancers, for all the world like one of them. After a minute of this he felt a surge of triumph. Why, as quickly as in a dream he had leaped the Great Wall that divided the world into sheep and goats. He was dancing. *Dancing!*

Felicia hissed at him, "Stop counting one, two, three, four out loud, you imbecile."

Herbie heard himself doing it and pressed his lips together with vexation.

"And quit looking at your feet. They won't fall off."

Herbie raised his eyes from the floor to which they had been fixed. He danced on in silence, maneuvered firmly here and there by his sister to avoid collisions. She smiled at him.

"You're doing swell. I told you you could dance. You'll show her!"

The music ended in a groan of jumping discords, Uncle Sid's notion of a jazzy climax. Felicia unclamped her hold on the boy and applauded politely. Herbie relaxed his body, which he had been holding rigid as a post, and glanced around. He found himself looking Lennie square- ly in the eye. The athlete was holding Lucille's hand. Herbie's heart pounded.

"Hi, General," said Lennie with good-natured con- tempt. "Say, Fleece, can't you find nobody better to dance with than him?"

Felicia tossed her head. "I don't see anybody better. The only people I see are two years older'n him and a year under him in school."

"This ain't school, this is real life," said Lennie with a grin. The music began again. Lennie caught Felicia's hand. "C'mon, stuck-up, let's see if you can still dance. S'long, Lucille, see you later." Felicia crimsoned and pro- tested, but allowed herself to be whirled away with some- thing remarkably like a happy expression on her face. The estranged lovers were left together.

"So!" said Lucille, with an arch glance at Herbie. "You *can* dance. Why did you lie to me?"

Herbie was so surprised to find himself in the wrong at this point that he was speechless.

"You just care more for wienies than for me, you fat pig." But the insult was accompanied with a soft smile. The past vanished, the world was new, and Lucille had never been anything to Herbie but an adorable, faithful sweetheart.

"I'll show you who's a fat pig," said Herbie gaily. "Come on, let's dance." He seized his beloved's hand, and swept into an enthusiastic one—two—three—four. He felt indestructibly confident as they twirled around.

"Gee, you're good," said Lucille, sending his happiness pressure up to the danger point.

"Heck, I still say it's for apes, but if I gotta do it I do it."

"Can you dip?"

The boy was suddenly sobered and began moving more stiffly again.

"Whaddyamean, dip?" he said, trying to sound offhand.

"Why, dip. Everyone knows what dip is. There, what Felix and Sylvia just did."

Felix and Sylvia, a foot away from them, had gracefully executed a "dip." This consisted of the boy leaning backward on one leg and bending the knee, while the girl leaned forward and bent the corresponding knee. It took but a moment to do and looked pretty, but to Herbie it seemed a complicated, dangerous maneuver.

"Oh sure, *that,*" he said. "Anybody can do that. But I never do it. It looks dumb."

"I like it. Let's dip."

"No."

"Yes."

"No, I say."

"Oh, come on, you're mean."

"Dipping," said Herbie desperately, "is only for babies."

"Babies? You're crazy. Look, Uncle Nig and Aunt Bernice just dipped."

"Well, let 'em. I ain't gonna."

"Herbie Bookbinder, you're such a liar. You know you can't dip."

"Oh I can't, can't I? All right, then, here goes." Blindly, like a horse ridden over a cliff to its doom, Herbie dipped. He leaned back much too far, tried to straighten up again, failed, grabbed both Lucille's shoulders in panic, and fell flat on his back, pulling the girl on top of him. The thud shook the floor. A ring of couples formed around them, giggling. The music stopped. Lucille jumped to her feet, tears of shame and rage in her eyes. Herbert sat up stupidly, his head ringing from the concussion. With perhaps two dozen boys and girls listening for his words, he had the hard luck to say, "I *told* you I didn't like to dip."

There was a shout of laughter, of course. Lucille glared around and ran out through the door. Herbie picked himself up and followed her. Uncle Sid, seeing that no great harm had been done, resumed his music, and the couples promptly forgot the incident and returned pair by pair to their own pursuit of happiness.

"Go away," snarled Lucille at Herbie as he drew near her with hanging head in the half-gloom outside the door.

"I—I'm sorry, Lucille," stammered the boy.

She looked at him with the narrowed eyes of contempt. "Go eat wienies."

Herbie caught her hand. "Lucille, remember what you said in the museum? You said you'd be my girl at camp."

"That was then." She pulled her hand away.

As long as the world lasts, there will be no other reply to the plaint of the discarded lover than the words: "That was then." They will always seem a sufficient answer to the person who says them, and a meaningless one to the person who hears them. And so it will go, on and on, the piteous question and the short answer, until the sun will dim, the earth will freeze, and lovers' quarrels will die away—probably the last human sounds to be heard on the icy wind.

"Gosh, Lucille, just 'cause I slipped and fell down once—"

"Oh, will you go away? You make me tired—General Garbage!"

It was the first time he had heard the epithet from those pretty lips. By all the rules he should have collected what was left of his dignity and stalked off. But instead he wavered for a moment and then whined, "Aw, please, let's go back and dance some more. We were having fun."

The girl turned away, nose in the air. "I'm going back in by myself. And don't you dare follow me. I'm here with Lennie." And she was gone.

Not knowing or caring what he was doing, Herbie stumbled off into the blackness, in the direction of the lake. The emotional ups and downs of the evening had exhausted his young spirit and left him as numb as a gray old man, and as hopeless about the future. As he trudged senselessly through dewy weeds and bushes toward the glow of the campfire, he weighed himself in the balance. He was a clown, a small fat boy, superfluous in baseball,

incapable of dipping, habituated to telling lies transparent
as glass which always shattered and lacerated him, and
aged a paltry eleven and a half years. None of these
conditions seemed likely to improve, not even his age. He
felt he would be eleven and a half for ever.

He had come to the beach. Peering through the last
fringe of bushes he saw that the wienie roast was over.
The boys and girls stood around the dying fire in a huge
circle, their arms raised over their heads. Mr. Gauss stood
by the embers, wearing an Indian feathered headdress,
his arms stretched heavenward. It was the moment of the
final Indian prayer that closed each campfire. Mr. Gauss
began lowering his arms stiffly before him. The children
followed his movements, and chanted in a weird tune:

> *"Wakoo dow dowse doo*
> *Weepee dad—oh tone hee."*

They repeated the mournful chant three times, raising and
lowering their arms each time. It had been taught to them
as meaning: "Great Spirit, a humble Indian asks your
blessing, I am he." Herbie could hear most of the boys
singing the traditional villainous parody which almost, but
not quite, blended with the chant:

> *"What could old Gauss do*
> *If he had no money?"*

This was one of the most happy jests of Manitou life, but
tonight it brought no mirth to him. He turned heavily
away from the picturesque scene and plodded back up the
embankment, along Company Street and into Bunk Thirteen. Soon his whites, damp with dew and dirty in the
seat and shoulders where he had made contact with the
dance floor, were piled on the foot of his bed, and the boy
was huddled under the coarse brown blankets. He sank
into sleep at once. So ended a truly grim evening for
Herbie Bookbinder.

Two days later, on Friday, Mr. and Mrs. Bookbinder

visited Camp Manitou. They stayed at the guest house, with its attractive view of the girls' lawn. They ate an excellent dinner, and were enchanted by the spectacle of the boys and girls in white rows on the lawn at sunset services. During visiting hours next day they toured the bungalows and playing fields, which were still natty from their polishing for the Penobscot invasion. That night they attended the dramatic show, and were proud and happy to see their son raising much laughter with a comic performance as a fat old lady. Sunday morning they watched a baseball game for the championships between the Lucky Strikes and the Marlboros, and marveled at the intensity of excitement among the children on the sidelines. Their pleasure was completed when Herbie made an appearance for the Lucky Strikes in right field, a novelty which bewildered the boy and the team (it was diplomatically arranged between Uncle Sandy and the Lucky Strike mentor, Uncle Peewee). Before the parents left on Sunday afternoon they spent an hour with Felicia and Herbie on the cool veranda of the guest house. Ice cream was always served Sunday afternoon on the veranda.

In short, the parents chugged off in their old automobile to return to the city that evening, persuaded that their offspring were enviably privileged creatures.

"I'll say one thing," said Jacob Bookbinder, as the car swung out through the ramshackle wooden gate of the camp, "they both look wonderful. Sunburned, well fed—"

"I should say so," said his wife. "It was lovely to see them that way."

They drove down the dirt road for a while, turning over in their minds the pleasant pictures they had seen.

"Did you notice," said the father, "that they both somehow seemed quieter than before? Herbie, especially."

"Of course. Their manners have improved beautifully. I think it's lovely."

Jacob Bookbinder was ninety-eight per cent satisfied with this explanation of his son's subdued air, the one odd fact he had observed. Wishing to believe the best, he soon decided to let it pass for one hundred per cent, and forgot about it. Nor was he far wrong. There was nothing really the matter with Herbie.

A broken spirit is merely a state of mind.

19

Herbie's Ride—I

HERBIE EVENTUALLY RECOVERED, but his way out of humiliation had an important drawback. It led him into crime.

Boys enter upon this planet as free wild animals, and have to be tamed. Respect for the law comes, but slowly. The sweetest mollycoddle will swipe an apple from a fruit stand—if only once; the saintliest choir boy will "borrow" a quarter from his mother's purse—if only once. What makes them all behave at last is partly upbringing, partly what Mr. Gauss calls Character, and partly the invisible barbed wire of Law, which sooner or later gives nearly every boy a nasty raking—if only once.

It was the last week of camp, and everyone was in the doldrums. Uncle Sandy's schedule was exhausted. Pepsodents, Oldsmobiles, Lucky Strikes, and John Barrymores had enjoyed their brief triumph and had been dissolved. The giant struggle between the Yellows and the Reds, with one half of the camp pitted against the other for three racking days, had also passed into history, a Yellow victory.

This "color war," as it was called, had been fought in the early years of Manitou during the last three days of the season, but the arrangement developed weaknesses which caused Mr. Gauss to change it. First of all, it sent half the camp home in a mood of embitterment which no amount of talk about a Gaussian victory could heal (the defeated team always won a tremendous Gaussian victory, according to the camp owner). Second, it returned victors and losers alike to their homes worn out, nervous, and often battered. Mr. Gauss had therefore issued another of his unpopular decrees, advancing the date of the color war a week and leaving seven days for the recuperation and fattening of his campers. The price was heavy: a week of anti-climax and boredom. But Mr. Gauss, caught in the old dilemma of expediency versus the children's desires, had gone his usual way.

To assuage the postwar dullness he invented a couple of holidays: Manitou Mardi Gras, which was held two days before the season ended, and Campers' Day, which followed it. The boy who was judged to have invented the best diversion of the Mardi Gras—whether it was a costume, an act, or a display—was acclaimed "Skipper for a Day." He ruled the camp, appointed boys to supplant all the counselors (the counselors became those boys), and all in all won an enviable amount of glory. Uncle Sandy and Mr. Gauss usually managed to give the award to one of the more sober Super-seniors, who could be counted on to keep Campers' Day from becoming an orgy of hazing of the counselors.

It was a good idea. The boys consumed several mornings and afternoons preparing for the Mardi Gras, which usually became a gay sort of carnival. Campers' Day gave them a chance to release the grudges of a whole season in horseplay. The climax of the festivity was always the throwing of Uncle Sandy into the lake by the Seniors, in the presence of the whole camp. This happy event in itself reconciled large numbers of the boys to life at Manitou, and made them look forward to next year when they could see it done again. Every summer there were elaborate conspiracies to throw Mr. Gauss into the water, too, but the plots had never come off. He always seemed to vanish at the critical time.

"What th' heck does Mardigrass mean, anyhow?" said Lennie, addressing a circle of boys sitting on the grass around him. Bunks Twelve and Thirteen were having a period of horseback riding again, which meant, as usual, that Cliff gave Clever Sam a workout for an hour while the others lolled and gossiped.

"Hey, Lennie, is it Mardigrass or Mardigrah?" said one of the boys. "Uncle Gussie keeps sayin' 'Mardigrah.' "

"Shucks, dincha see the big sign they got stretched across Company Street?" said Lennie. "It says 'Mardigrass Saturday,' don't it? Mardigrass with a *s*."

"Uncle Gussie says it's French."

"Maybe, but I ain't no Frenchman."

This caused a burst of laughter. Lennie had solidified his position as a hero during the color war by winning a couple of crucial games for the Yellows. Everything about a hero is magnified, and a joke uttered by him is much funnier than if it comes from ordinary flesh and blood. Encouraged by the laugh, Lennie added, "Maybe Uncle Gussie is French. He always sounds like he's been eatin' frogs."

This was considered pricelessly humorous, and several of the boys rolled on the grass in merriment.

"That still don't answer what it means, though," said Lennie.

The boys sobered, and tried to think of an explanation.

"Maybe," said Ted, "it has somethin' to do with grass. This is grass-cuttin' time, for makin' hay, ain't it? O.K., maybe in French Mar-di-grass means 'Cut the grass.' "

The circle all looked to Lennie for his opinion. The hero wrinkled his brow judiciously and said, "Sounds right. I bet that's it."

Everyone else nodded now, except Herbie, and one boy said, "Pretty smart, Ted, figuring it out like that."

"Er—I looked it up in the dictionary," Herbie put in diffidently. "It means 'Fat Tuesday.' "

"What!" Lennie's tone hovered between amazement and scorn.

Herbie was at low ebb in his own esteem and everyone else's. He had been of no use at all to the Reds in the color war. His usual good spirits had been lacking since the night of the fateful dance, and Lucille had avoided his presence and even his glance since that time.

"Well, I know it sounds funny," he faltered. "But—but Fat Tuesday is what it says."

Murmurs of resentment were heard.

"General Garbage, the only thing you can do good is lie," said Lennie. "If we'd of had a lying contest, the Reds would of won the color war."

"Haw! Haw! Haw!" from the chorus.

Then a rapid fire of wit:

"How could they have a Fat Tuesday on a Saturday?"

"You sure it wasn't Skinny Wednesday?"

"Or Pot-Bellied Friday?"

"Or Bowlegged Sunday?"

"Haw! Haw! Haw! Fat Tuesday!"

"I know what he means, guys," exclaimed Lennie. "He means *he's* fat Tuesday and every other day."

The hilarity which followed this epigram was so prolonged that Uncle Sid broke away from a conversation with Elmer Bean and inquired what the joke was.

"Herbie says," Lennie gasped between guffaws, "that Mardigrass means 'Fat Tuesday.' "

"You pronounce it 'Mardigrah,' and it does mean 'Fat Tuesday.' It's the name of an ancient religious holiday," answered the counselor, and walked away.

After a short silence conversation was resumed on other topics. No more jokes were made about Fat Tuesday. Herbie was noticeably shouldered out of the talk. He had committed that breach of manners, unforgivable among adults as well as among boys: he had known more than the leader.

When the group started down the hill for the swimming period, Herbie got permission to remain behind with Cliff and Elmer Bean while they unsaddled Clever Sam.

Elmer Bean was regarded by Herbie as an oracle on camp matters. The rough handy man gave straight answers, uncolored by contempt or satire, and he seemed to have a fuller understanding of the ways of Mr. Gauss than anybody. Also, unlike a counselor, he did not stand in opposition to boys in the nature of his duty.

"Say, Elmer," said Herbie, as he watched Cliff and the handy man fussing with the horse's girths, "has a Intermediate got a chance to become Skipper-for-a-Day?"

Elmer paused in his work, and regarded Herbie with a twinkling eye. "Why? You figger on bein' it?"

"Well, no," said Herbie, " 'course not. But still a guy likes to know if he got a chance."

"Nobody but a Super-senior ain't got it yet, Herb. Mr. Gauss likes to make sure, see, that the thing don't get to be all hog-wild."

"O.K. That's all I wanted to know."

Cliff swung the saddle off Clever Sam's back and stood holding it. "Why, Herbie?" he said. "You got a good idea for the Mardigrass?"

"Pretty fair, I thought. But it don't make no difference."

"What's the idea?" said Elmer Bean.

"Aw, just a ride."

"What kind of ride?"

"It's—it's hard to explain. Anyway, I might as well forget it."

Elmer took the horse's bridle and led him toward the barn. "Come on, talk up, Herb," he said. "What's yer big idea? Maybe you might be the first Intermediate to make Skipper."

"Well," Herbie began, following Elmer, "I figure this Mardigrass is kind of like Coney Island, ain't it? Well, my pop took me to Coney Island once. The most fun I had was on a thing they called the Devil's Slide. It was a big boat that slid down into a tank of water. Boy, oh boy, when that thing hit the water—zowie!"

Cliff said, "I been on that. You ain't figuring to build no Devil's Slide out here, are you, Herbie? Heck, that would take a year."

"It's all built, Cliff!" Herbie answered excitedly. "Don't you see? The doggone girls' lawn slants right down to the lake, don't it? All right. All you gotta do it put a rowboat on wheels, see, an' bang! You got the Devil's Slide!"

"How," said Elmer dryly, "do you steer this rowboat on wheels an' keep it from runnin' into a bench or Aunt Tillie?"

Herbie's face fell. "I never thought of that."

Cliff said, "Heck, you could steer it with ropes or somethin'."

"A heavy rowboat fulla people barrelin' down a hill? Son, you need wire cables and Samson pullin' 'em to steer that."

They were in the tumbledown stable now, redolent faintly of straw and strongly of Clever Sam. Elmer backed the horse into his stall and closed the door. Clever Sam leaned against the wall and closed his eyes with a peaceful sigh.

"I tell you what," said Herbie. "What's the matter with layin' a couple of rails down the hill just like they had it in Coney? The boat could slide down the rails. All you need's a few boards."

"You mean greased boards," said Elmer.

"Of course greased boards," replied Herbie, although it hadn't occurred to him that the boards would have to be greased.

"Hm. Four hundred feet of two-by-fours and twenty gallons of axle grease wouldn't hardly begin to do it."

"O.K.," said Herbie dejectedly. "I said forget about it."

"An' after the boat gets down in the water once, how do you git it back up the hill?"

"O.K., O.K., Elmer."

"An' anyway, what keeps the boat from flyin' clean off the greased boards halfway down the hill an' roostin' up in a tree?"

"Heck, Elmer, do you have to poke fun at me? It was a crazy idea, that's all. I'll go to the lousy Mardigrass dressed like a old lady or somethin'. You said I couldn't win, anyhow." He sat on a perilous old chair with one leg missing, tilted it against the horse's stall, and slouched.

"For that matter," Cliff remarked slowly, as though talking to himself, "Clever Sam could pull the boat back up the hill easy."

"For cryin' out loud, forget the thing, Cliff," said Herbie.

"Why are you so red hot fer gettin' to be Skipper?" asked Elmer, squatting opposite Herbie and stuffing a grimy pipe from a tobacco pouch.

"Because I'm the camp joke, that's why!" burst out Herbie. "The little fat baby that can't run, can't play ball, can't fight, can't do nothin'! That's me an' everyone knows it. An' they're right. That's just what I am."

"Why, hold on, Herb. A guy shouldn't think that bad of hisself. You're a good kid, an' you got brains. You'll have the laugh on 'em all someday. You know you ain't that terrible."

"Lennie stole his girl," observed Cliff, looking out at the sunny green fields.

"Hm." Elmer smiled for an instant, but when Herbie glanced at him suspiciously his face was serious. "Why, Herb, any girl who likes Lennie I say oughta be welcome to him, an' good riddance to both of 'em."

"An' why does the boat have to fly off the rails, now I think of it?" said Herbie. "Heck, you nail a couple boards under the rowboat, see, so's they fit just inside the rails, an' how's that rotten boat gonna slip off them rotten rails?"

Elmer smiled, and lit his pipe with a thick wooden match. Cliff looked at his cousin admiringly. "Hey, Herb, that's good. I told you"—he turned to Elmer—"he's got a head."

"Say, Herb, which girl is it?" asked the handy man, still grinning.

"Aw, Cliff's crazy."

"I think maybe he ain't."

"O.K., I don't care if you know. It's Lucille, the red-headed one."

"Oh. That one." Elmer nodded with great comprehension. "Yeah. Many's the snake I've known like that one. Bigger, but the same idea."

"Snake!" said Herbie, aghast.

Cliff explained, with a little pride of inside knowledge, "That's what they call girls in the Navy."

"You been in the Navy, Elmer?"

"He had four years," said Cliff.

Herbie looked at the handy man with new admiration.

"Herb, she ain't worth feelin' low about," said Elmer. The boy dropped his eyes. "But I reckon my sayin' so don't make it so."

"She said she was my girl. An' then just 'cause I couldn't dance good—" Herbie choked.

"Where you gonna get fifty dollars?" Elmer asked.

Herbie was startled. "What for?"

"Why, with fifty dollars fer lumber and grease and a little help from me I think maybe you could rig up yer doggone ride at that."

Hope gleamed in the boy's eye. He sputtered, "Why Mr. Gauss—Uncle Sandy—anybody'll give it to me. Shucks, you charge a quarter a ride, an' with everybody takin' a couple rides an' the parents an' the visitors from the village an' all, you'd make easy a hundred an' fifty dollars. I figured all that out."

Elmer shook his head. "I guess possibly you would, but them guys won't lend you no fifty dollars. The whole idea sounds crazy. Maybe it could work, but you ain't gonna get them convinced. Would yer ma er pa give it to you?"

Herbie thought of wrangles with his mother over quarters, and the frequent earnest discussions between his parents over the narrowness of the family income. He shrugged. "I could try, but Mom is pretty tough. An' whenever I want somethin' my pop just says what my mom says."

Cliff remarked, "I got five dollars."

They all fell silent. Some happy horseflies buzzed back and forth between the sunshine outside and the fragrant shade of the stable. Clever Sam pawed the floor and heaved another long sigh in his sleep.

"It wouldn't be fair anyhow," Herbie spoke up, "if you helped me build it. They'd disqualify me."

Elmer blew a vast cloud of blue smoke, which wreathed in the still air. "Wouldn't nobody get to be

Skipper if that was how it worked. I build the whole Mardigrass, more or less. Last year they give Skipper to Yishy Gabelson fer the House of Hell. Shucks, all he did was say 'Elmer, less make Bunk Sixteen into a House of Hell.' I thought up th' traps an' all that, an' built 'em, what's more."

"I'd help build it," said Cliff. "I ain't got no idea of my own. This sounds like fun."

"Well, I think I know where I can get the fifty dollars," Herbie said, slowly and reluctantly.

The handy man's eyes opened wide. "Yeah? Where?"

"Never mind. I can get it."

Elmer stood and knocked gray ash and red embers out of his pipe against the heel of his boot. "You git it an' I'll build it," he said. "That's to say, I'll help you build it. You kids'll have to work like stevedores. I have a heap o' other things to build, too." He slipped the pipe into his shirt pocket and walked out.

Cliff whispered excitedly, "Hey Herb, where in the—" and broke off as he saw the handy man's head poke around the doorway again.

"Herb, I still say she ain't worth it. There ain't no snake worth all that work," he said. His head disappeared and the boys heard him shuffling placidly away.

"Cliff," whispered Herbie, though there was no reason to whisper, "remember the time we sneaked in the Place on a Sunday?"

"Yeah."

"An' that safe in the office, and my pop saying the combination was my birthday?"

Cliff's jaw fell open, and he stared at his cousin.

"I'm gonna get the fifty dollars outta that safe!" Herbie said defiantly.

"Herb, you—you gonna *steal?*"

"Steal your Aunt Sadie! I'm gonna *borrow* fifty bucks. You heard Elmer say we'd make a hundred fifty easy. All right, I get that money tonight, we build the ride, I earn a hundred fifty Saturday night. Sunday I mail fifty bucks back to the Place—no, seventy-five bucks," he said in a burst of virtuous inspiration, "twenty-five bucks interest. Is that fair or ain't it?"

"Yeah, but Herbie—opening yer own father's safe—"

"I'll stick a note in the safe, see? It'll *say* that the money ain't stole, only borrowed." Herbie was warming up to the project. "If *they* know I ain't stole it, and *I* know I ain't stole it; then who says it's stealing?"

"I say so," answered Cliff.

"Why?"

" 'Cause it is."

Herbie considered this a very vexing answer, the more so since it had a ring of truth. But he felt logic all on his side.

"Look, Cliff. Suppose I were to take Clever Sam outta here now, see? An' ride him away, an' never bring him back, but instead bring back a fine race horse and stick him in the stall. Would that be stealing?"

"Takin' Clever Sam sure would be."

"The heck it would! How about the race horse?"

"Where would you get the race horse?"

"What difference does that make? I'd swap Clever Sam for him."

"Oh! Then you wouldn't have the race horse to start with?"

" 'Course not, stupid. If I had the race horse, I wouldn't need Clever Sam."

"Guess not."

"All right, then. You see my point."

"Yeah. If you had fifty bucks, you wouldn't hafta steal it."

Herbie grew red in the face and shouted, "All right, all right, all right! Then it's stealing! You'll die before you admit a plain fact. I don't care what you call it, I'm gonna do it!"

"How you gonna get to New York?"

"Hitch-hike."

"How you gonna get outta camp?"

"Sneak out after taps."

"You gonna go to New York an' back in one night an' get back before reveille?"

"Yeah."

"Herbie, it's three miles to the main highway. There ain't no cars go by here after sunset, you know that."

"I'll walk to the main highway." Herbie's answers were getting weaker and more sullen.

"An' back in the morning?"

"An' back in the morning."

"O.K. Taps is at ten o'clock, reveille at seven. That's nine hours. You got two hours of walkin', seven hours of drivin'—that's sayin' you get hitches right away, no waits —an' at least an hour gettin' the money. Ten hours' work to do in nine hours."

Herbie saw his plan in all its outrageous foolishness. He walked up and down the stable and kicked disconsolately at stones and straws. "You win. I go to the Mardigrass as an old lady. I wasn't so anxious to steal from my pop's safe, anyway. What are you gonna do?"

"I dunno. I can't ever think of them kinda things."

"Whyncha go as Tarzan? We could fake up a leopard skin—"

"I know how you could save pretty near an hour gettin' to the highway," interrupted Cliff.

Herbie looked at his cousin doubtfully. Cliff seemed serious.

"Well, how?"

"Clever Sam."

"Are you nuts? I can't ride him."

"No. But both of us can, I think."

"Cliff, you wanna get mixed up in this? I thought you said it was bad business."

"I said it was stealin'. I dunno if it's bad or not. If you think it ain't bad, I guess it ain't. Maybe sometime a guy's gotta steal."

Had Herbie been a philosopher he would surely have taken this as his cue to expound the popular modern doctrine "The end justifies the means." But he was only a boy trying to recapture a lost love, so he said, "Would Clever Sam stand for it?"

"We can find out easy enough."

Cliff opened the door of the stall and punched Clever

Sam in the ribs. The horse opened his eyes and looked around murderously, until he saw who was disturbing him. Then he groaned, yawned, heaved himself away from the wall, and suffered himself to be led out of his stall. Cliff leaped up on his bare back.

"We don't have to saddle him. Get up on this bench here and climb aboard."

Herbie obeyed, not without some trembling. Seated astride the beast in front of Cliff he felt himself seventeen feet in the air and very insecure. The horse's long backbone seemed to sag slightly at the double weight, and he looked around at his burden and snorted indignantly.

"Yeah, I know, Sam," said Cliff, "but this is an emergency. If you don't like it, we won't do it. Gee-up."

Clever Sam shuffled, backed, pawed the floor, and moaned. Then, at a few coaxing tugs of the reins, he walked out of the stable. Cliff made him trot twenty yards and turned him back. The animal was obedient, but the short trot was enough to jar the bones loose in Herbie's skeleton, or so he felt. Back in the stable he climbed shakily off Clever Sam and sensed a new sweetness in the feeling of a floor under his feet.

"He'll do it," said Cliff, returning the horse to his stall.

"I'm beginning to think that it's just a crazy notion," said Herbie, running his tongue over extremely dry lips.

But Cliff, whose ignition point was higher than Herbie's, was at last taking fire from the flame of adventure. "No, no, Herb. Honest, I think you could get away with it."

"But it *is* stealing. You were right."

"Yeah, sure, but if you give 'em back seventy-five, there ain't anything really wrong with it, is there?"

"Aw, it's impossible. Hitching all the way to the city, alone at night—I musta been outta my head. The heck with Lennie. The heck with Lucille. Who cares about her? That snake!"

"Herbie—*I'll go with you to the city!*"

Herbie was dumbfounded.

"I mean it. That'll make it a cinch. I tie up Clever Sam

in the woods by the highway, see? He'll just eat grass or sleep till we get back. You know you can't climb in the window of the Place, anyway. You need a boost from me."

Herbie had forgotten this little detail, which would have been enough to wreck his whole enterprise. He wondered frantically what other pitfalls there were, even as he felt tempted. Until now the project had merely been one of the dreams which his imagination produced so easily. But he had made the mistake of sharing this dream with Cliff, so that he could no longer let it die away when it ceased to amuse him. It had become half-substantial in the act of speaking it aloud.

"Gosh, Cliff, suppose we get caught! Why should you take any risks? We could get put in jail!"

"Heck, Herbie, if you wanna do the thing, I wanna help you, that's all. Do you wanna do it or doncha?"

"Why, I—sure, I wanna do it. Why d'you suppose I thought it all up?"

"O.K. When do we go?"

And just as daydreams sometimes seemed as vivid as reality to Herbie, this reality now began to seem to him as far off and tenuous as a dream. Still not quite believing it was all happening, he heard himself say with the coolness of a general, "First off we gotta get our city clothes outta the camphor locker. They'd pick us up sure, wanderin' around at night in camp clothes."

"I never thought of that."

"Wait after taps until your whole bunk's asleep, see, then sneak on down to the camphor locker an' meet me there. The duty counselor won't give us no trouble. It's Uncle Sid tonight, an' all he does is sit in the social hall an' write letters."

"I gotcha. Hey, this'll be good."

"The heck it will." Herbie felt a tightening around his heart. "It's a crazy scheme. An' I still think I oughta do it alone, Cliff."

"Well, never mind about that. I'll see you at the camphor locker."

"Now, we don't say nothin' to nobody."

" 'Course. Let's go. It's lunch time."

The boys left the stable and went down the hill arm in arm.

Herbie ate little lunch. He sat dreamily at the table, composing in his mind the letter to be left in the safe, explaining that the money was only being borrowed. Immediately after the meal he rushed to the empty office of the camp newspaper and wrote out the note on the rheumatic typewriter, hitting each key painfully with one finger.

All day he turned the midnight sortie over and over in his mind, and like a snowball it seemed to pick up perils and terrors with each turning. The ultimate object, the building of the ride for the Mardi Gras, seemed centuries away. He half hoped that Cliff would beg off—and he half hoped that he wouldn't, and that it would all prove a glorious adventure with fame and triumph as the prize. In this irresolute state he counted the hours as they dragged toward sunset, and he did some remarkably absent-minded things during the day, such as putting a pair of trousers on backward after his afternoon swim, and eating a whole plateful of the odious creamed mackerel known as "Gussie's Goo" for dinner, while his bunkmates regarded him incredulously. Herbie hunted up Cliff in the evening during letter-writing period and threw out veiled "feelers" about the difficulty and danger of the excursion, but Cliff persisted in talking calmly of other things. If he had had a change of heart, he was concealing it.

Night came. The bugle blew taps, and the camp was darkened. Herbie, curled tensely in his cot, glanced at the phosphorescent numerals of his wrist watch, a handsome two-dollar birthday gift that he had never expected to put to such suspenseful use. It read ten minutes after ten. From now on every moment counted; already he had been cheated of ten precious minutes out of the nine allotted hours by a laggard bugler.

And now a new aggravation cropped up. His bunk-mates were wakeful and talkative. While Herbie wriggled and fretted under his blanket, getting hotter and more impatient every minute, they held a long, thorough inquiry on the question whether Uncle Sid was or was not the worst counselor in the camp (the affirmative won). Then they thrashed out the historic problem, was Jesus Christ a Jew or a Christian (no decision); then they carefully reviewed all the Intermediate girls one by one from the physical, mental, and moral standpoints; and, just when they seemed to be dropping off, Uncle Sid came by with a flashlight and bawled at them for talking after taps, bringing them all wide awake again and starting a fresh discussion of his failings. Luckily this topic had been well worked over once. When the talk finally died away and Herbie cautiously slipped out of the bunk, his watch read ten minutes to eleven.

Cliff, a shadowy figure already dressed in city clothes, was pacing in front of the camphor locker when Herbie arrived.

"Holy cats, I thought you'd given up," said Cliff.

"Not me." By the light of Cliff's flash, Herbie groped into the locker and donned his city clothes, choking over the camphor fumes.

"Howdja get the lock open, Cliff?"

"The wood's rotten. Pried it loose with a stone."

"We gotta hammer it up again."

"Yeah, in the morning when we get back."

" 'Ja bring money?"

"Five dollars. 'Ja bring the note to stick in the safe?"

"Yeah. Got it in my back pants pocket. Don't lemme forget it."

"You bet I won't."

Skulking from shadow to shadow, the two boys went up the hill to the stable. At the top of the rise Herbie paused and looked back at the sleeping camp, two rows of black little boxes by the moonlit lake. The cold night wind stirred his hair. A sense of the enormity of lawbreaking on which they were embarked overwhelmed him.

"Cliff, fer the last time—lemme go this alone. You ain't gonna get nothin' out of it but trouble."

"Come on, we got no time to talk," answered his cousin.

They avoided the light that streamed from the windows

of the guest house and reached the gloomy stable. The door opened at a push with a startling creak. Clever Sam neighed and stamped.

"Hey, take it easy, Sam, it's us," whispered Cliff. Nimbly he led the horse out of his stall and saddled him.

"Come on, Herbie, climb on the bench and get on behind me," he said, and jumped into the saddle. Herbie felt as though he were being carried away on a powerful black tide, against which it was useless to struggle. He ascended via the bench to his risky perch in back of Cliff. His cousin walked the horse outside, closed the stable with a shove of one strong arm, and turned the animal's head toward the gate.

"Gee-up," he said, "we got a long way to go."

Clever Sam pranced to one side and to the other, then broke into a quiet trot. With no further antics he carried his double burden out through the gate and, at a click of Cliff's tongue, quickened his pace and set off toward the highway.

Clip-clop, clip-clop, jounce, jounce, jounce, jounce, down the deserted dirt road in the moonlight went the two boys on their aged, ramshackle steed. Clever Sam's gait was stiff and bumpy. Cliff rode to it well, but his cousin did not. Herbie clutched Cliff's middle and tried not to think about the pounding at his posteriors. The insides of his legs began to feel warm. Then they grew hot. Then they became fiery. Then they were raw steaks broiling on either side of a red-hot grill sliding up and down, up and down between them—

"Cliff," faintly, "this is murder."

"Oh, sorry, Herbie. Can't you post?"

"Wha—" (bounce) "what's post?"

"Every time the horse goes up, *you* go up. Every time he comes down, *you* come down. See, like me."

Herbie flung himself up and down in time with his cousin a few moments, lost the rhythm, came down when Clever Sam was going up, struck hard, and tumbled off the horse into the road. Cliff and the animal vanished into the night.

Herbie stood up, brushed the dirt off his back, rubbed his sore head, and groaned, "Oh, Lord, whose idea was this?"

His cousin came trotting back to him and held out his hand.

"Here, stick your foot in the stirrup. I'll pull you up."

Herbie obeyed. With a wrench of his arm in its socket that made a dull horrid noise, he was back in his place behind Cliff. His clothes were damp inside with sweat; the night air chilled him.

"I guess trotting is tough on you, Herbie. I'll see if I can get him to single-foot."

They started off again. But Clever Sam, for all his rich background, had evidently never heard of single-footing. Cliff's efforts to lead him into the gait resulted in an even rougher and more ungainly trot. Herbie felt as though he were being punished for all the sins he had ever committed. From the waist down he seemed to be in flames.

"Ohhhh, Cliff!"

"Hm. I'm afraid to gallop. Well, I *know* he can lope. Hey, Sam—ck, ck."

The horse faltered and subsided into an easy rocking motion that was balm to Herbie.

"That's wonderful, Cliff. That's great. Whew!"

And so they loped out to the highway. When Cliff spied the broad ribbon of concrete, he pulled Clever Sam up. The boys jumped to the ground. While Herbie staggered here and there, trying to restore his legs to their normal functioning, his cousin led the horse off the road and went out of sight among thick shrubs and trees. After two minutes he reappeared.

"Whadja do with him, Cliff?"

"Tied him up good an' told him to stay put. He'll be O.K. Nobody won't find him."

Two cars flashed by in succession along the highway.

"Come on," said Cliff. "One o' them mighta taken us."

The boys ran to the main road and stood waiting. Soon a pair of headlights gleamed in the distance. They waved their hands eagerly as the car bore toward them, but it roared past. Then all was silence and cloudy moonlight.

"Not so good," said Herbie.

"What time is it?"

"Five to twelve."

"Boy. It's gonna be close."

Another pair of headlights appeared, far off.

"I got a feeling," said Herbie. "This is it."

It was. The car slowed at their summons and stopped a few feet past them. The cousins scampered toward the door held open for them.

"Hop in, fellows," shouted a husky voice.

The next instant Herbie felt himself yanked by the arm into the bushes. His cousin, Cliff, held his upper arm in a pincers grip, and was dragging him further into the gloom of the woods.

"Hey, what's goin' on?"

"Sh-sh." Cliff pulled the fat boy with him into the middle of some thick bushes, unmindful of scratched skin and ripping clothes, and crouched. "Dincha see the car when we got up close? The guy's a state trooper!"

20

Herbie's Ride—II

HERBIE'S BREATH FAILED him for a moment. Then he gasped, "Whew! Thanks, Cliff. I never noticed. It's lucky—"

"Sh-sh! For cryin' out loud!"

The boys heard the car door closing. Then came the steps of the trooper, crunching on twigs and leaves. A flashlight beam poked here and there between the shadowy trees.

"All right, kids! You needn't be afraid of me. Come on out." The trooper's raised voice was coming from some distance. The boys did not speak or stir. "All I want to know is what you're doing out on the road so late at night. If you're in trouble, I'll help you."

More cracking of twigs under heavy boots. The flashlight beam hit the bushes in which the boys were hiding, but only a thin gleam filtered through to them. It moved and left them in blackness.

"Come on, now. I can find you easily enough if I want to."

Pause. Stamping, cracking, beating of bushes, and gyration of flashlight beam. Then:

"O.K. Spend the night in the woods if you prefer. I have a whole highway to patrol. I'm offering you a lift, but have it your own way. I'm leaving."

The steps moved off. The car door opened and slammed, and the motor roared up and faded away. Cliff began groping out of the bushes. His cousin seized him by the slack of the jacket.

"Are you nuts? Bet he's pullin' a trick. Stay right here."

They waited ten minutes by the glowing dial of Herbie's wristwatch. Peculiar noises from the trees—cracks, groans, sighs, hoots—startled them now and again. Crickets were making music with full orchestra. After a while ants began to dispute the terrain with them.

"Hey," said Cliff, scratching and slapping himself, "do we lay here all night, or what?"

"All right, let's peek now," whispered Herbie.

The boys made their way to the road. Their two heads poked out of the brush, and suddenly drew in again like a pair of snail's horns.

"He—he's still watchin' for us," Herbie murmured. "We'll be stuck here forever."

The boys had seen a car parked by the roadside, its headlights agleam, not fifty feet from them.

"I dunno. It didn't look exactly like the same car."

Cliff slowly poked his head out again. "Nope. It ain't the same." He stepped boldly into the light. "It's a Buick. There's a fat guy in it. Come on!"

The boys approached the automobile. The inside light was burning, and they could see plainly a stout, grizzled man in a creased green suit, with a pallid face and stubbly jaws, slouched at the wheel, his eyes closed. Half a cigar, ashy and no longer burning, protruded from his mouth. One hand in his lap held a flat brown bottle.

"Asleep," said Cliff.

"Maybe he's sick or somethin'," said Herbie, and rapped on the driver's window. The fat man started and opened his eyes. He rolled the window down.

"Whaddya want?" he said hoarsely and sleepily.

"If you're goin' to New York, mister, could we have a hitch?" said Herbie.

The fat man squeezed his eyes, shook his head, and rubbed both hands over his face. "Sure, sure, hop in," he said, and threw open the back door. "Glad you woke me. I pretty near fell asleep three times at the wheel. Hadda stop for a doze for a minute. Like to have company to talk to on these long runs. Keeps me awake."

The cousins gratefully nestled in the back seat amid boxes, books, and luggage. They noticed a powerful smell in the car, but said nothing. The driver started up the car, shifted gears, and suddenly snapped the motor off and turned on the boys with narrowed bloodshot eyes.

"Hey! What are a coupla kids like you doing out on the road at midnight, anyhow?"

Cliff and Herbie looked at each other helplessly.

"Well, talk, boys. Where are you from?"

"Camp Manitou," Herbie managed to say.

"What's that?"

"Boys' camp near here."

"Where you going?"

"New York, like we said."

"Why?" said the man, with a squint of drunken cunning.

"My brother's dying."

The driver's suspicious look altered. He spoke more softly.

"Oh. Well, now. Who's this other boy?"

"He's my brother."

Herbie could feel Cliff jump slightly.

"What? He don't look like he's dying."

"He ain't. He's O.K. He's my brother Cliff. My brother Lennie is dying."

"What from?"

"He got run over. My pa sent us a telegram to come home right away."

"Why aren't you on a train?"

"Ain't no train till morning. We figured we could hitch and maybe get there sooner in case Lennie dies. Mr. Gauss gave us permission. He even drove us out to the highway."

"Who's Mr. Gauss?"

"He owns the camp. You can call him up an' ask him, only please, mister, hurry."

The driver said to Cliff, "Is all this true?"

"Why should Herbie lie?" said Cliff.

The driver pondered a moment. He picked up the brown bottle, twisted off the metal cap, and took a drink. Herbie pulled out a handkerchief and sniffled. Luckily he had been required to weep in the last camp show. His imitation was polished.

"Gosh, mister, call up my father an' reverse the charges if you wanna. His name's Jacob Bookbinder, we live in the Bronx, an' the number's Dayton 6174. Or let us outta the car an' we'll get another hitch. We gotta get goin'. How do we know Lennie won't be dead when we get there?" His grief became louder.

"Well, hold on, boy. I'll take you where you're going. I just don't want to be mixed up in trouble, see? I got enough of my own. Heck, I'll drive you right to the door. I go through the Bronx. Sit way back in that seat and relax."

He started up the car and they went rocketing into the night. Herbie tried to continue the sniffling, but it was hard work. His fiction had conjured up the vivid picture of Lennie Krieger on a bed of pain, which was rather pleasant than otherwise. He soon left off, seeing that the fat man was convinced.

During the next hour and a half they learned that the driver was a Mr. Butcher, of Albany. That by profession he was a seller of dolls, wholesale. That the doll business was terrible. That he intended someday to get into a "line" which didn't require a weekly trip to New York. That his wife was a sour old crab, and thought all he did in New York was have gay times with girls, which was a lie. That there was a new doll in his "line," the latest thing, which not only cried and closed its eyes but drank water and did astonishing things thereafter. That this doll, "Weepy Willie," was at present the bread and butter of Mr. Butcher. The boys received this information in an unceasing narrative poured into their ears, punctuated by wheezes, gasps for breath, and occasional sputtering. They gleaned additional facts by observation, such as that Mr. Butcher liked to drive his Buick at seventy-five miles an hour, not slowing for curves; that he was very thirsty, for he kept swallowing drinks from the brown bottle; and that he was still sleepy, for now and then his head would slump on his chest, the automobile would careen, and Mr. Butcher would wake up and snatch the wheel just in time to keep his Buick from climbing a tree. The boys did not at all share Mr. Butcher's sleepiness—they had never, in fact, been more wide awake. After they rounded one sharp curve on two screaming wheels Cliff suggested in pantomime to Herbie that they open the door and jump from the car. Herbie's whitish face turned a shade whiter, and he shook his head emphatically. His lack of color might have been due to the closeness of the air in the car. All the windows were shut, and a musty mixture of the aromas of old cigars, strong drink, and what can only be described as Mr. Butcher himself, saturated the atmosphere. Once or twice as they sped through the darkness Herbie had the feeling that he was in a nightmare, and that Mr. Butcher would melt away at the sound of a bugle. The next moment a near-collision shaking him to his innermost parts would convince him that it was all excessively real.

But it was not written that Herbie and Cliff should perish that night on the Bronx River Parkway. After a dozen narrow escapes from tragedy, Mr. Butcher and his chariot came whistling into the city streets at a speed that made the boys' hair stand on end. The fat man turned around casually to ask where Homer Avenue was, while his car raced between the "El" pillars of White Plains Road. "Look *out!*" yelled Cliff, and Mr. Butcher looked out, and swerved the car away from a pillar which was about to fold car and occupants to its bosom.

But after all these horrors he kept his word, depositing the boys at Herbie's very doorstep. By this time he was mellow, and swore that if he had had a couple of sons like Cliff and Herbie instead of one sour-faced daughter, the image of her mother, his whole life might have been different. He bade the boys a loving farewell, pressed a "Weepy Willie" doll on them, and drove off to an unknown destiny. Perhaps he is motoring back and forth wildly between New York and Albany to this day. You will be passed by many a car on that highway that could easily have Mr. Butcher at the wheel. But alas, it is all too likely that his lucky charm ran out, and that he now sleeps under flowers.

Herbie looked at his watch and gasped, "Cliff, look!" and extended his arm. It was a quarter to two. Their benefactor had come nearly a hundred miles in an hour and a half. The wonder of gasoline, that gives wheezy fat men the swiftness of eagles!

"We're lucky we got here alive," said Cliff, still breathing hard.

Herbie looked at the dark apartment house where his mother and father were sleeping. Set down suddenly at dead of night in his old haunts, he felt more than ever that he was in a dream. It was unbelievable that he could mount a flight of steps, ring a bell, and embrace his mother amid the old furniture. In his mind she and the apartment were still a hundred miles away. He shook his head to clear away these dizzying ideas, dropped "Weepy

Willie" in the gutter, and said, "Let's go, Cliff. We got a good chance to make it now."

The boys scampered through the electric-lit silent streets to the Place.

"Will there be anyone there?" said Cliff.

"Just one engineer tendin' the machines," replied Herbie between gasps. "They make ice all night. But he'll be down the other end from the office. Once we get past him he won't hear us."

"Maybe we better jump him and tie him up."

"If it's Irving we better not. Irving is twice as big as Uncle Sandy."

Cliff got a vivid impression of an Irving twelve feet high, and abandoned the notion of binding and gagging him.

"Hey, what's this?" A block from the Place Herbie stopped short, and pointed at the building in dismay.

"Whatsamatter?"

"The office. It's lit up. Somebody's there!"

Cliff saw that the little high window of the office, facing the street, was a square of bright yellow.

"Maybe it's the engineer, Herbie."

"Engineers ain't allowed in the office. Who could be there two o'clock in the morning?"

"Might as well find out," said Cliff. He sprinted for the Place, followed by his laboring cousin. Standing beneath the office window, he placed both hands on the sill, jumped up, peered inside for a moment, and dropped back to the ground.

"Who is it?" panted Herbie as he came up.

"Mr. Krieger," said Cliff, "an' that guy Powers. They're foolin' around with some big books."

"We're skunked," said Herbie. "How can we get to the safe with them there?"

"I dunno." Cliff went to the wooden door beside the window and pressed his ear against it. "Hey, you can hear 'em."

Herbie followed his example. The voices of the two men came through the partition, muffled but understandable. Powers sounded very angry.

"—all right. You should have had those figures in a file for me when I came to your house."

"Not much longer. Soon go cup coffee. Not sure what figures Burlingame wanted. Could be this, could be that—"

"Any businessman knows what a potential buyer wants! Profit and loss statements, depreciation figures, inventories, book value—good grief, man, what would *you* want to know before buying an ice plant?"

"Not so fast buying. Burlingame say blue paper maybe good. I sit right there next to you when he say, and—"

"Never mind the blasted blue paper. Burlingame will give us a cash offer conditional on Bookbinder agreeing to sell. When Bookbinder hears the cash figure he'll sell, blue paper or no. It's going to be plenty high."

"You not know Jake. Jake not sell no million years. Jake want better poor but own boss. Here, all inventory figures."

"Good. How about profit and loss for the past ten years?"

"Take five more minutes—"

"Confound it, Krieger, this is ridiculous. Where's the file of annual statements? That's all I need."

"Jake got. Accountant got, too. Not in office. Just books. Simple arrangement."

"Why, man, haven't you enough interest in your own firm to keep a file of the annual statements in your home? Dragging me down here in the middle of the night—"

"Please. All very last minute. I say this way, peaceable. You telephone me suddenly want all kind figures. One—two—three. Got to have eight o'clock tomorrow morning. Who got all figures in head? Little by little we got all nearly now, just take a few—"

"I'm sorry. I'm tired and nervous. Is there a place around here where we can get coffee right now? Then we can come back and clean this up."

"Why not?"

Herbie, straining his ear against the door though not comprehending the conversation, heard Mr. Krieger shout, "Irving! Me and Mr. Powers go cup coffee. Back ten minutes." He heard a faint "O.K." from the interior of the building. The doorknob started to turn, an inch from Herbie's nose. Like cats the boys darted around the corner of the building, and watched the men come out of the office, cross the avenue, and walk out of sight down a side street.

"What now?" whispered Cliff.

"We got ten minutes. You still game?"

"Come on."

"Good. You boost me through."

But as they emerged from the alley Herbie had another idea. "Wait a second," he said, and cautiously tried the office door. It opened.

He and Cliff slipped inside and closed the door as softly as against velvet cushions. They could hear Irving walking around on the brine tank, and the hissing suction of the pipe taking impure water from the cores of the ice cakes. The safe, the object of their fantastic journey, stood squat and ugly before them.

"O.K., you keep watch," whispered Herbie. "Here goes."

Cliff shuttled between the door leading to the interior of the Place and the window on the street, while Herbie carefully turned the dial. On his first try the safe failed to open.

"Must of done it wrong," he muttered, and ran through the numbers of his birthday again; three spins to the right, two to the left, and one to the right. The safe did not yield. Herbie was distraught.

"Hey, Cliff, it don't work."

"You sure you done the combination right?"

"Well, see, I dunno. All I know is the numbers. I tried three turns, two turns, an' one turn—hey, wait, I got it. I bet you have to start by turnin' the dial to the *left*. I been startin' to the right."

"Make it fast, whatever you do."

More frantic twisting. Then: "Cliff, it still don't open."

"Holy smoke, Herbie, I thought you knew the combination."

"Well, I do know the numbers, but jiminy, I dunno

which goes how. I figured sure it would be three turns, two turns, an' one turn, like the locker in gym."

"Herbie, them guys'll be back in a coupla minutes."

"I'll try startin' with four turns." Despairingly he whirled the dial, pressed the handle, and tugged at the door. It swung open so easily he fell to the floor.

"Attaboy, Herbie. Hurry!"

The cash box was behind the other tin box labeled "J.B." Herbie pulled the latter off the shelf and laid it on the seat of the chair. He took out the cash box, placed it on the desk, and opened it. It was full of five, ten, and twenty dollar bills.

"Cliff, there's hundreds!"

"How much you gonna take?"

"Exactly what I gotta borrow. Fifty. Not a penny more," said Herbert primly, and selected two twenties and a ten.

"Herbie! Herbie! Here come them two guys!" Cliff's whisper was strident. "I didn't see 'em comin' till just now. They're on top of us! We can't make it out the door!"

"Follow me, Cliff!"

Herbie plunged through a thick door opposite the street entrance with Cliff at his heels. The boys came into a long, high, terribly chilly room filled with gleaming blue piles of ice cakes. Huge bare electric bulbs were placed here and there in the ceiling. Beside the door, right over the boys' heads, hung the stiff frozen body of a calf head down, its tongue hanging out, its dead eyes staring at them.

"There's another door outta this icebox," whispered Herbie. "Irving's down by it now. In a minute we'll be able to get out."

"It's freezing in here."

"Yeah, sure is. Gimme a boost, Cliff."

He stepped on Cliff's clasped hands and looked warily into the office through a tiny pane of glass set high in the wall. He saw Krieger and Powers come into the office and register amazement at the sight of the open safe and cash box.

"Irving! Irving! Irving!" shouted Krieger. An immense bald man in ragged blue overalls, his face streaked with black grease, came pounding into the office.

"Look what happened while we gone!" Krieger exclaimed, pointing at the safe. "Didn't you see or hear anything?" (Mr. Krieger reversed the case of almost all other human beings. Under great stress he spoke more clearly than usual.)

"No, sir, Mr. Krieger," said the giant, his eyes popping with surprise. "I been busy suckin' the cores on number eight. You know that makes a lotta noise. I didn't hear a thing."

"I told you keep an eye on the office. Run quickly, call a policeman."

"Yes, sir." Irving lumbered out through the street door.

"Hey, Herbie, I'm gettin' tired holdin' you up," said Cliff softly. His cousin's heel was digging painfully into his interlaced fingers. The damp cold of the storehouse was making his arms ache. "Can't we sneak out the other door now?"

"They'll be listenin' for every sound now. Wait a second," whispered Herbie.

He heard Powers exclaim, "Look! They took Bookbinder's box!" The young man ran his hand along the empty shelf.

"Don't understand something. Why they don't take all the money?" said Krieger, counting the cash hurriedly. "Only got fifty, and leave behind—"

"What does that matter? Listen to me! Does Bookbinder have photostats of that blue paper?"

"No photostats. One paper always right here in safe, better so—"

"Then, by God," said Powers, "the memorandum is gone, and Bookbinder is through." He shook his head. "Tough luck for Bookbinder—I hate to see it happen this way—"

"Mr. Powers look please."

Krieger pointed to the box labeled "J.B." lying on the chair. Both men stared at it. Then they looked each other in the eye. Then both lunged for the box. Krieger got his hands on it first and hugged it.

"What you think? Honest man. Thirty years in the ice business. Never funny business. Jake Bookbinder my partner—"

In the ice room Cliff was staggering under his burden and shivering. His numb fingers were giving way. "Herbie, I gotta let go for a minute."

"One second more, Cliff!"

"Listen to me, Krieger," said Powers, speaking quickly and earnestly, "the best favor you can do Bookbinder—"

Crash! Herbie thudded to the floor as Cliff's fingers refused to obey him any longer.

"*Now* we're in it. Come on!" Herbie picked himself up and charged down a narrow corridor between blue walls of ice. He turned sharply to the right as they came to a break in the pile of cakes, and rushed through another foot-thick refrigerator door, followed by the other boy. The warm air of the engine space smote their faces. They were at one end of the brine tank, at the point where the crane dumped finished ice. The crane stood ten feet away over number eight row, loaded with dripping, yard-long rectangular cans.

"Stay right by this door, Cliff. I'll be back in a second!"

Herbie ran over the loose boards covering the tank to the crane, making a wild clatter, and yanked a chain that hung down between the two middle cans. The crane began to move ponderously toward Cliff, with clanking and groaning. Krieger could be heard shouting, "I hear them! Out by the tank!" and there was a running of feet. Herbie came back to Cliff, barely ahead of the moving crane, and gasped, "Now's our chance. Come on!" He pulled his cousin back through the refrigerator door and raced between the ice piles to the other door that opened to the office. Behind them they heard the crane crash into the end of its framework, and the excited voices of Krieger and Powers echoing through the tank room.

"Pray to God," whispered Herbie, and opened the door. The office was empty. The boys were out in the street and around in the darkness of the alley in an instant. From the building they could still hear faintly the shouts of the two men. Herbie peered around the corner of the building for a moment and saw Irving with a policeman a block away, running toward the Place down the middle of the street.

"Here comes the cop," he said, and added disdainfully, "He ain't half as big as Irving."

"Boy, Herbie, I thought we were cooked."

The boys slipped down the alley, crossed a vacant lot filled with rubbish behind the Place, and turned left into a shorter alley between two store buildings. They emerged on a street of small shops, a block away from the ice plant. There was an elevated subway station at one end of the street.

"Herb, how about the subway?"

"They might see us goin' up the steps, but we better try it. They'll have more cops around here in a minute."

Winded and leg-weary, the cousins ran up the steep staircase of the elevated at a rate that threatened to burst Herbie's heart in his chest. Luck was with them. They had scarcely staggered through the turnstiles when a Pelham Bay local train, all but empty, lurched into the station. They boarded it. The doors closed, and the train carried them off to safety with squeals and screams.

The boys sat in a stupor of fatigue and relief while the train passed two stations. Then Cliff said dully, "What time is it anyhow? Five o'clock?"

Herbie looked at his wrist watch and silently held it out toward his cousin. It read five minutes past two.

"What? You sure it ain't stopped?"

Herbie held the timepiece to his ear and heard a healthy, regular ticking. "That's all it is, five after two."

"Gosh, twenty minutes, just twenty minutes since Mr. Butcher dropped us off!"

The boys silently marveled at the strange ways of time. Twenty crowded minutes of adventure and peril had seemed longer to them than many hours.

"Hey, you know what?" said Cliff slowly, his mind

emerging from the fog of danger. "We still got a chance to make it back to camp."

"Yeah, a good chance!" said Herbie, with a lift of surprise and pleasure. "I sure never thought we would. Come, we'll get off next station."

The boys jumped up from their straw seats and stood with noses pressed impatiently against the glass of the car door. As soon as the train stopped they were out of it and trampling headlong down the staircase with a great noise. For a while the focus of their minds had narrowed to the single urgent problem of not getting caught. Now it broadened again to include the purpose of their trip, which began to seem miraculously close to accomplishment. They had more than four hours to get back to Manitou.

The train thundered away over their heads, and they stood on a quiet, empty, gloomy boulevard. Two blocks away a patrolman was strolling with his back toward them, swinging his night stick. So silent was the sleeping city that the boys could hear the metallic click and scrape of his heels on the sidewalk. Across the street a Negro in a gray shirt and brown cap dozed at the wheel of a dilapidated taxicab. The vehicle had been hand-painted bright blue, in an unsuccessful attempt to hide the fact that it had first seen the light around 1921.

"That's what we want," said Herbie, "if it runs."

They crossed the street and woke the driver by climbing into the back of the taxi and slamming the door.

"Uh-huh, where to?" said the driver, sitting erect with a jerk.

"We wanna go where the Bronx River Parkway starts," said Herbie.

"Huh?" The colored man looked around at his passengers, with big eyes that grew bigger as he saw two lads in kneepants. "What you boys want in my cab?"

"I told you, mister, we wanna go to the Bronx River Parkway."

"Why, boy, that cost you three dollars."

"Show him the money, Cliff."

Cliff briefly waved a five-dollar bill before the driver's eyes, and returned it to his pocket.

"Say, what you boys up to this time o' night? You runnin' away from home?"

"Yeah. We got a stepfather beats up our mother. We're runnin' away to our uncle in Albany. His name is—is Butcher."

The Negro laughed. "Name's Butcher. I see. You lie pretty good, boy. You jest make it up?"

Herbie regarded the driver uncertainly, then joined the laugh and said, "Just made it up."

"Boy, I don't care why you wanna go to Bronx River Parkway. I got a cab, and you got d'money, an' I'm open for business. We off."

It turned out that the sky-blue wreck could travel fast enough, though not without horrible jolting and grinding. The Negro let them out at the foot of the Parkway in little less than half an hour. Cliff handed him the five-dollar bill, and the boys waited in some trepidation for their change. Not another car or human being was in sight near the brilliantly lit highway entrance. The driver saw their troubled expressions and chuckled.

"You hear lotta bad talk 'bout cullud people, don't you, boys?" He held two single bills out to Cliff, who clasped them gratefully. "Jes' 'member, now, a cullud man done you a favor once an' didn't ask no questions." He waved, and the blue relic rattled away.

Herbie's watch read fifteen minutes before three. There remained four and a quarter hours to reveille.

"Cliff, we're gonna come through easy," he said. The cousins began walking confidently, almost cockily, along the highway.

It is not advisable to tempt fate with such remarks. Five, ten, fifteen minutes wore away. Only two cars had passed, and the drivers had ignored the boys.

"Someone better pick us up soon," said Cliff.

"Shucks, we got hours yet," bravely answered his cousin.

The boys trudged on. They spoke little about the thrilling passages of the night. In the anticlimax to the tension

of their escape both began to feel shaky and scared as
they moved slowly along the margin of the broad vacant
highway. The road was filling up with fog, and becoming
increasingly murky between the pools of light around the
widely spaced lamps. It was, in truth, a lonely place for
two foot-sore, sleepy boys.

Another half hour passed, with every minute a dragging torment, and still they were walking.

"Cliff—Cliff, I gotta sit down."

Herbie sank to the side of the roadway and rested his
damp head on his knees. His cousin remained standing
beside him. "Sure. Take it easy, Herbie."

"We ain't gonna make it. Why did I ever get you into
this? You'll get kicked out of camp an' everything on
accounta me—"

"Wait a second. Here comes another car."

"He won't pick us up. No one won't pick us up. We'll
have to walk all the way to Manitou. It serves me right,
but you—"

Fate, however, chose to joke with Herbie again. The
car stopped, and the boys gratefully scrambled in.

The driver was as different from their first benefactor,
Mr. Butcher, as he could have been without being of
another species than the human; in fact, had he been a
full-grown hog the difference might arguably have been
less wide. He was emaciated, his body was bowed over
the wheel like a half hoop, and he had a small, round,
smooth pink face like a baby's, except for a few strands of
gray hair creeping down from under his hat, a long pointed nose, and steel-rimmed glasses such as seldom decorate
a baby. His suit was a gray affair that hung shapelessly on
him, with here and there a ridge or corner of bone showing
under the cloth.

"Where to, fellows?" He spoke in a high, weak voice.

"We're goin' just outside Panksville, but as far as you're
goin'll be swell, mister."

"Going right past there. Expect to be in Hudson by
seven," said the apparition, and shifted gears with a skinny hand that seemed likely to snap in the process. It did
not, however; and the car, a bulky old Pierce Arrow,

inhaled a deep draught of gasoline and snorted away into the fog.

The driver spoke no more, nor did he look at his passengers after taking them into the vehicle. He drove with desperate concentration. Steering the big auto required the leverage of his whole body. He would fly up in the air when the car passed over a bump, and would clutch the wheel like a jockey hanging to the reins of a stallion. Herbie watched this strange struggle, fascinated. It was the first time he had ever realized that an automobile was a thing mightier than its driver. The wise men who build these terrors in Detroit have bridled them with gears and reined them with levers and throttled them with pinhole breathing to a point where they seem harmless to an ordinary man. Herbie's new chauffeur, however, was so far below average human weight and strength that the monster, shackled as it was, could still give him a fight— and it did fight, with the senseless bitterness of metal and grease come to life. But Herbie's fund of fear, indeed of all emotions, was almost spent. He observed the battle with waning interest when it grew clear to him that the driver, by however thin a margin, maintained the upper hand. He felt Cliff's head on his shoulder; his cousin had dropped asleep. He resolved to keep his own eyes open, not trusting the silent skeleton at the wheel. But he had been awake now for twenty hours, and had performed more violent exercise in that time than in twenty previous months. . . .

The car stopped with a jolt that shook both boys awake. Opening their eyes, they were amazed to see a bright pink sky and clear daylight.

"Panksville, boys," piped the driver. The car stood at the crossroads of the dusty village, in front of Scudder's General Store.

"Gee, thanks a lot, mister. We were sleepin'," said Herbie, stretching. "We can get off here, but we're going about a mile further down this road."

"Oh, yes? I'll be happy to take you there." The car started again.

Herbie looked at his watch and showed it to his yawning cousin. Five minutes past six.

"We make it," he whispered.

"Did you boys have a good nap?" said the driver in his creaky voice.

"Yeah, swell," said Herbie.

"Sorry I didn't talk to you, but driving is hard for me. I can't see well, and this car's hard to handle. You must be going to one of these camps out here."

Herbie felt a prickling of his skin, and said, "Uh-yeah, that's right."

"Penobscot?"

The boys exchanged wary glances.

"No," said Herbie.

"Must be Manitou, then. Charming gentleman, Mr. Gauss. Very pleasant to deal with, always. You boys are fortunate to be at such a splendid—"

The car went whooping around a curve and tried to take charge and dive into a ditch. No helmsman in a hurricane ever fought harder with a wheel than this featherweight driver did, and he was panting when he brought the engine back under control.

"You see—huff—what I mean, boys? Huff. I really should use the train, but in my work I just can't. Well! Here's your road."

Herbie wanted to find out what sort of work this reedy creature did, but he wanted much more strongly to vacate the vicinity of anybody who knew Mr. Gauss. The boys jumped from the car. "Thanks, mister."

"Quite welcome, boys," answered the frail man, and drove away.

Herbie imagined he had seen the last of him. He was mistaken; but neither men nor boys can see into the future much beyond the bend of the next forty-eight hours.

Cliff ran into the woods and came out leading a very stiff-legged and balky Clever Sam. The animal was obviously outraged at having been tied up in dew and darkness all night. He grunted, neighed, pulled his head this way and that, and bucked.

"This ain't gonna be good," said Herbie.

"No, it ain't," agreed his cousin, and mounted to the saddle. Clever Sam looked around at him, then walked to a thick old oak tree and, leaning against it at a sharp angle, rubbed the boy off his back. Cliff dropped harmlessly to the ground and stood up at once. Clever Sam began cropping goldenrod with sullen glances from under his knobby brows at his ex-rider.

"Cliff, it's twenty after. The bugler gets up at ten of."

Cliff approached the horse again cautiously. "I think maybe he'll be O.K. now. I don't blame him. Hey, Sam, I'm sorry. I wouldn't of done it if I didn't have to. We gotta get back to camp fast. Be a good guy."

He got back into the saddle. The horse raised his head and stood quietly, until Herbie drew near. Then he flattened his ears, whinnied, and stamped his hoofs.

"He's got it in for you, too, Herbie."

"What'll he do to me?" said Herbie fearfully.

"You'll just have to climb aboard an' find out."

Assisted by his cousin, Herbie managed to heave himself up on the horse's back. He grasped Cliff around the waist and awaited the worst. The worst turned out to be fairly bad. Clever Sam set forth toward camp at a ragged, violent trot, with an amazing amount of up-and-down movement. His flanks bobbed like buoys in a storm, and the worst of the bobbing took place between Herbie's chubby thighs. Cliff tried in vain to induce Clever Sam to lope, to gallop, and finally, when Herbie began to groan like a dying man, even to walk. The horse maintained exactly the same excruciating pace from the highway to the stable. The slapping, scraping, pounding, and burning that Herbie endured is beyond the power of words to tell. But if purging by fire is truly the penalty for sin, then Clever Sam ransomed Herbie from retribution in hell for anything he had done that night.

Herbie's watch read twenty minutes to seven, and Cliff was just backing Clever Sam into his stall, when Elmer Bean walked into the stable. The handy man staggered with astonishment when he saw the two haggard, dirty boys in their city clothes, but when Herbie handed him the fifty dollars he was constrained to sit, trembling a little, on the bench.

"I said I'd get it, and I got it," said Herbie.

"Where the blazes you guys been?"

"What difference does that make? We can build the ride now, can't we?"

"I guess so, but—where'd you git it, Herb? Know somebody in another camp?"

"What's the difference? See you later, Elmer. We gotta get back into our bunks before reveille. Come on, Cliff!"

"You didn't—you didn't steal it, fellers?"

"Heck, no!" said Herbie over his shoulder with immense righteous indignation. "We borrowed it."

The boys ran down the hill. The camp was as still as a row of pyramids. In fifteen minutes it would be swarming with life. Keeping to the bushes to evade possible early risers, Cliff and Herbie made their way to the camphor locker, doffed their clothes, and pressed the spring lock back into place loosely.

"We better come back an' hammer it later. We'll wake 'em up," said Cliff, pushing at the nails with his fist. He glanced at his cousin for approval, and saw Herbie standing with a horror-stricken look on his face.

"Cliff," he said hollowly. "You know what? I forgot to leave the note in the safe saying we borrowed the money. So we stole it after all. We stole the money, Cliff!"

"Aw, they'll get it back with interest, won't they?"

"Yeah, but meantime—meantime we're just plain crooks."

"For cryin' out loud, let's worry about that later. We gotta get into our bunks."

Clad in brief white drawers, the two boys crept up behind the bungalows, avoiding Company Street, and each tiptoed into his own bunk. As Herbie slid into his cot it squeaked, and he heard Uncle Sid make the familiar snores and snuffles that preceded his waking. The boy closed his eyes and pretended unconsciousness. In a minute the make believe was a reality; he was fast asleep. When the squalling bugle, ten minutes later, brought all his bunkmates tumbling out of bed, it failed to awake him. He lay like one dead.

"All right, boys," said Uncle Sid. "Flophouse reveille for Herbie Bookbinder."

"A pleasure," exclaimed Lennie. He and Eddie Bromberg sprang to the ends of Herbie's cot and upset it sideways. The sleeper sprawled to the floor and opened red, bleary eyes.

"Top o' the morning, General Garbage!" said Lennie.

"Get a move on," said Uncle Sid. "You'd think you hadn't slept at all."

Herbie groaned, picked his bruised, partly skinned, dog-tired body off the floor, and stumbled out with the other boys to greet the new day—with fifteen minutes of setting-up exercises.

21

Herbie's Ride—III

MR. GAUSS CAME shuffling absently across the girls' lawn later that same morning, moodily weighing the advantages and disadvantages of using only three busses instead of four to carry the children to the railway station the following week. He had just about decided that the saving of money was worth the bitterness that would be caused by the overcrowding when a surprising sight drove the matter from his mind. Two parallel lines of fresh white lumber stretched from the top of the hill a quarter of the way down. There was a great pile of boards and cans where the lines began, and his handy man and three boys were working like ants around the pile. As he watched, two of the boys, Herbie and Ted, left the pile carrying four boards together by the ends. They walked down the hill, laid the boards so as to lengthen the lines, and scampered uphill again.

"Here, here!" exclaimed the camp owner, approaching and waving a reproachful forefinger before him, his usual battle emblem. "What on earth is the meaning of all this?"

Herbie, Ted, and Cliff dropped their work and clustered around Elmer, as though for protection.

"It's for the Mardigrass, Mr. Gauss—er, Skipper," said Herbie eagerly.

"Boy's got an idea for some kind of ride," said Elmer Bean. "I think it'll be O.K."

"Yes, but—who gave anyone permission to build this thing? And where did all this material come from? Why, it looks like a hundred dollars' worth. Who's paying for all this, I want to know?"

Herbie looked appealingly at the handy man, who said, "Well, sir, it's like this. I know Tom Nostrand down to the Panksville Lumber Yard, see, an' I tole him about this idea this boy had. He's a pretty good guy, an' he gave me this stuff. See, he has no kids hisself, and he's pretty soft where kids are concerned."

This was not a complete lie; Elmer Bean was hardly as facile a fictionizer as Herbie. It had turned out that fifty dollars was not much more than half of what was needed to buy the materials from the lumber yard. Elmer had wheedled the stuff at a short price from Tom Nostrand in the manner just described. In recounting the tale to Mr. Gauss he simply took the precaution of omitting the detail of the mysterious cash the boys had given him.

Mr. Gauss was partly placated by the answer, to the extent that he knew he was not out of pocket. But he grumbled, "What sort of silly ride is it?"

Herbie started to describe his project with hot enthusiasm, but before the Skipper's fishy stare and pursed lips his force waned quickly, and he ended by stammering, apologizing, and not making much sense.

"Anyway, Uncle Sandy said," Herbie concluded lamely, "we could try anything we wanted. Can't we?"

"I never heard worse foolishness," said Mr. Gauss. "And to think of wasting all this fine material on such a harebrained scheme! Elmer, I'm disappointed in you. You shouldn't encourage them. These boards will do nicely to repair the canoe dock. Better haul them down there right away. The grease can go in the garage. You needn't do the repairs, of course, till after the season."

"You mean," exclaimed Herbie in dismay, "we don't get to build our ride, after everything we done?"

"Not done, did—past tense," said Mr. Gauss. "Of course not, Herbie. I'm sorry, but it'll never work. You should thank me for preventing you from wasting your time."

Herbie's stiff, exhausted body failed him. He fell to the ground and cried.

"Now, now, none of that," said Mr. Gauss, a little flustered. "Be a man, Herbie. Get up."

The boy stifled his sobs in an elbow, but did not stir.

"Why, look, Mr. Gauss," said the handy man, "I don't guess I can do what you said."

"What's this?" The camp owner glared at the mutineer.

"Well, see, I got that stuff offa Tom Nostrand fer the kids. Now, if we jest use it fer camp repairs, why, we gotta pay fer it, if we're honest. So if I do what you said, I'll have to tell Tom an' you'll get a bill fer the stuff tomorrow. A hunnerd dollars. Er do you want me to be dishonest an' not tell him 'bout it?"

With three children listening, the question was an embarrassing one for Mr. Gauss. "That's got nothing to do with it. I simply thought, as long as the stuff is here—of course I don't want to pay for it. The canoe dock doesn't need repairs that badly."

"Why, sir, we can use it to repair the dock all right," said Elmer, "*after* the Mardigrass. See, the wood'll still be here. It won't be new, but it'll be good. Tom Nostrand won't have no use for it, see, *once we build Herbie's ride.*"

This presentation of the case licked the camp owner. As the price of getting a hundred dollars' worth of lumber for nothing, he probably would have permitted the boys to build an altar to Baal.

"Well, I've never been one to interfere with the children's pleasures," he said, "so long as they're not hurtful. Go ahead, boys, waste your time, so long as you're having fun. That's what camp is for. You have my permission to build your ride." He swept a happy smile over the group, like a water hose washing away any possible ill feeling, and his rotund back parts swayed rhythmically as he ascended to the camp office.

The beaver is the handy comparison when hard work is to be described, but has a beaver ever equaled what Herbie did that day? The fat boy had hardly slept for thirty-six hours and his body was one great ache, yet in that condition he did the longest, hardest day's work of his life. Cliff was in a bad case, too, but he was stronger than his cousin, and he had not taken the battering from Clever Sam that still throbbed in Herbie's muscles and bones. As Herbie toiled and sweated, carrying out Elmer Bean's directions, a red mist swam before his eyes. His feet and hands blistered. Often it seemed to him that his arms would refuse to come away from his sides when he willed them to. Yet somehow, stumbling and slipping, he did whatever he was told.

Ted was an early recruit to the labor. He came with Lennie to jeer, and remained without the model of Character to work. Later in the morning, Felicia, hearing the spreading news of her brother's project, came and joined the labor gang. By lunch time both camps were gratefully gnawing this bone of novelty, and Herbie had acquired a quick notoriety, not exactly favorable. A few boys and girls appreciated the daring of the scheme and predicted it would work, but the popular reaction was one of ridicule. Some fine jokes were passed about "General Garbage's ride." Herbie, Cliff, and Ted came late into the dining hall, having received permission to be absent from the regular marching lines, and a spontaneous cheer arose from the seated campers:

> *"Here comes boloney*
> *Riding on a pony.*
> *Hooray, General Garbage!"*

But Herbie was too tired to care. He fell into his seat, happier for the rest than for the food, and dozed through most of the meal.

Strangely enough, he revived in the afternoon. His joints grew limber, his eyes cleared, and he made merry remarks to cheer on his fellow workers. The handy man left him in charge while he went to do other chores, and was surprised at his return two hours later to find the rails laid to the edge of the water. Then came the tedious task of securing the boards to each other and to the ground, a drudgery in which the children were still engaged when they heard the call for the evening meal. Herbie went to his bunk to change his clothes, still feeling spry, but he sat on his bed to take off his socks, and instantly toppled over and fell asleep. His "second wind," that occult burst of energy which nature gives us in desperate straits when normal strength is burnt out, was gone. His bunkmates could hardly jar him into opening his eyes. Uncle Sid, with unusual wisdom, decided to let him be. Herbie lay as he was until midnight, when he awoke ragingly hungry and thirsty. He crept up to the dining hall by the light of the moon, and foraged in the dark kitchen until he came upon one of the long loaves of bread that served an entire bunk at a meal. He ate the whole loaf, washing it down with six glasses of water from the dishwasher's faucet, and decided that the most delicious food in the world was bread and water. Then he returned to his bunk, undressed, and slept like a brass idol until reveille.

He woke to a new day, refreshed and easier in his limbs, but low spirited. The weather was sultry. Felicia retired from the gang early in the morning, made faint by the heat. The handy man and the three boys labored on at the Ride with streaming brows, wet bodies, and slippery palms. Herbie had not in his life done such honest work. He discovered gratefully that work was the River of

Forgetfulness of the storybooks, a plunge into which caused the past to disappear, if only for a while.

Deep in his heart was the guilty knowledge that his gigantic enterprise was built upon a theft. Herbie had excused the deed to himself with the device of the note; but he had failed to leave the note. The same boyish logic which had persuaded him that stealing explained by a note really wasn't stealing now prodded him with a spiky warning of evil consequences. He tried to reassure himself that once he returned the money he would be cleared, but meantime he felt himself a sinner. Would not the wrath come down on him before the Ride was finished? Would he ever have his chance to pay the money back? These painful thoughts came to him when he opened his eyes in the morning, and stayed with him until he joined Elmer on the hill. They vanished in the hammering, the dragging, the sawing, and the greasing.

Later that afternoon the Ride was ready for its first trial. The rowboat, secured by a slipknot to a stake in the ground, rested at the top of the greased rails. Clever Sam, harnessed for towing, stood by in the custody of Cliff. A distinguished group, including Mr. Gauss, both head counselors, Yishy Gabelson, Uncle Sid, and all of Herbie's bunk, as well as a number of girls, were looking curiously at the contraption and at the four sweat-streaked, grease-covered figures who had created it. The watchers talked in low tones, and sometimes they laughed, as Elmer Bean and his assistants puttered.

At last the handy man brushed the hair from his eyes, rose from his kneeling position beside the boat, and said, "She's ready. Who rides down in 'er first?"

"Me," said Herbie jealously and loudly, expecting a chorus of other volunteers, and surprised to hear his voice ring out alone.

"Why does anyone have to take a chance?" demanded Mr. Gauss. "Let it go and see what happens."

"Lot easier," said the handy man, "if someone's in 'er to paddle 'er back to shore. Wouldn' mind goin' myself. Oughta be fun."

"It's my idea, ain't it?" said Herbie. "I wanna go. Please, Mr. Gauss."

Uncle Sandy said with a slight smile, "I really don't believe it's dangerous, Skipper."

"All right, Sandy, on your say-so. But the life of that boy is my responsibility, you know. People don't think of those things."

Herbie climbed into the boat, his pulse thumping, and established himself on a front seat, clutching a long yellow paddle.

"Sit in the bottom, Herb," said Elmer. "You might fly out that way."

The boy obeyed.

"And put aside that paddle. Might knock out a few teeth if she bumps."

Herbie dropped the paddle as though it were hot.

"All set, Herb? She's gonna rip when I yank this line." The handy man's hand was on the running end of the slipknot.

"All"—Herbie swallowed to clear an unexpected dryness—"all set."

"Here you go!" Elmer pulled the slipknot free.

The boat did not move at all.

A few snickers were heard. The handy man said, "That's nothin'. She's sot down in the grease," and pushed the boat with his foot. It slid a few inches and came to a halt with a slushy noise. Herbie looked around at the handy man. His expression was piteous—but we are a cruel species. When the spectators saw his face, there was a roar of laughter.

"Hey, Robert Fulton, give up!"

"Oh, boy, what a great idea!"

"Water's kinda dry, ain't it, Herbie?"

"Don't that speed make you dizzy?"

"Go back to your garbage, General!" (This last gem contributed by Lennie.)

"Well, Yishy, guess you have nothing to worry about," one of the bigger girls giggled. It was known that Yishy was contriving an elaborate freak show, and except for this crazy undertaking of Herbie's his claim for the prize seemed without much competition. The stout Super-senior, six feet tall and with the shadow of a mustache on his swarthy upper lip, smiled quietly. He felt sorry for the small boy who had sought to challenge him so desperately and foolishly.

"What's the matter, Elmer?" Herbie cried.

The handy man was scratching his head. "Dunno, Herbie, I swear," he said. "That boat oughta be barrelin' down the hill. Unless—I tell you what, the grease is so fresh and thick, maybe it ain't slicked down good yet. Y'know, like fresh snow. Hey, Ted, Cliff! Give us a hand."

Elmer and the two boys began shoving the boat down the incline. They had only pushed it a few steps when it acquired its own momentum and ran away from under their hands.

"There she goes now, Herb!" cried the handy man.

There she went without a doubt. Accelerating at every yard, the rowboat was soon speeding. Herbie's dark head could barely be seen above the gunwale, looking straight ahead as the boat slid downward. Faster and faster the strange vehicle rattled along the slippery rails. In a few moments it whizzed over the bank, and struck the water with a towering splash. The spectators sent up a real cheer this time, for it was a thrilling thing, after all, to see a boy's wild dream come true. But the cheer died when the splash subsided. Herbie and the yellow paddle remained floating on the water. The rowboat had disappeared.

Mr. Gauss became violently agitated. "Someone save that boy! I knew this was sheer folly! Don't let that paddle drift away! Dismantle this thing immediately! Find the rowboat!" he shouted, waving his arms in many directions and running two full circles around the stupefied handy man. While he was engaged in this useful activity, Uncle Sandy, Ted, and Cliff trampled down the hill, and Clever Sam loped after Cliff, trailing his towing harness. When this strange rescue cavalcade reached the shore, it became evident that lifesaving would not be part of its duties. Herbie floundered to shallow water and began wading sadly ashore, dragging the paddle. Behind his back the rowboat rose to the surface with bloated laziness and rolled over, its greased bottom, adorned with two parallel rails, rocking gently just above the water. The whole scene was a study in the ludicrous, worthy to be sketched by a good-natured painter and titled "Failure."

The feelings of the drenched boy as he stumbled ashore under the eyes of most of the girls' camp, which had gathered at the news of the mishap, cannot in charity be examined. But Ted and Cliff heard him muttering fiercely, "I deserve it! Deserve it! Deserve worse than that," over and over, as he doggedly sloshed up the hill, declining assistance.

"Don't take it too hard, Herb," said Uncle Sandy, striding beside him. "All of us have ideas that don't come off. It was a swell try."

Herbie did not answer.

"What happened, Herb?" said Elmer Bean, coming down to meet him.

"Elmer, the doggone boat just hit the water an' kept goin' straight down." Herbie leaned on the handy man's arm for a moment, pulled off a shoe, and poured a stream of muddy water out of it. He did the same with the other shoe, and padded along the grass in his water-logged stockings, holding the shoes in one hand. "Somethin's wrong with the whole business, Elmer. There's a curse on me. It ain't never gonna work."

"Don' give up that easy, Herb."

"I ain't givin' up easy. But you can't fight a curse. I got all this comin'."

They were at the top of the slide now, and the large semicircle of spectators stared silently at the boy. He was brought too low to be an object of jokes. Felicia pushed to the front of the crowd and cried, "Herbie, are you all right?"

"Sure I'm all right. Water don't hurt nobody," the sopping boy answered shortly, and turned away from her.

Mr. Gauss's arms were still waving, but more slowly

and in fewer directions as he drew near. "Splendid camp spirit, Herbie. You're taking defeat like a man. Not injured a bit, are you? You look just fine. No need to notify your parents, I'm sure. Why upset them? All you need is dry clothes and a nice hot supper. Yes, yes, Herbie, you deserve honorable mention for your idea. It is not a failure, my boy. Look on it as a success, a moral success in which you learned many lessons."

Few things could have been less palatable to Herbie at this point than a dose of Gaussian victory.

"Guess I'll go change my clothes," he mumbled. As he turned to the narrow path to Company Street, he saw Lucille Glass standing close behind Mr. Gauss, peeping at him with round, sympathetic eyes. She gave him her most winning smile and nodded encouragement. But suddenly she seemed only a gawky little girl in white blouse and blue bloomers, with carroty hair. She had a great many freckles, and when she smiled her upper row of teeth showed crooked, one on each side being set far back in the gum. The thought that for this creature's favor he had undergone all his vain giant labors was preposterous to Herbie. He could not summon up an answering smile. He trudged away, stooped and dripping. The last thing he heard was the camp owner's order, "Start the dismantling right after supper, Elmer. I want this lawn clear by morning," and Elmer's reply, a morose "Um."

Mr. Gauss sat on the veranda of the guest house that evening, listening with pleasure to the sawing, ripping, and banging in the darkness on the hill. To the uninitiated it was harsh noise, but to him it was a sweet song of lumber acquired free of charge. He mused a while on the amazing burst of energy of young Herbie Bookbinder, which had brought into being the useless structure now being demolished. Boys were powder kegs, he concluded, veritable powder kegs. The quietest of them could go off with a great bang when properly ignited. What had enabled the small fat boy to work so hard and even to infect the comatose Elmer Bean with his fanaticism? Why would boys never show such fine spirit in the little tasks he set them? Mr. Gauss sighed, and slapped a mosquito into the hereafter. Another hummed up to take vengeance. Mr. Gauss was in no mood for the nightly duel with the fauna of Manitou. He rose and retreated to his room, where he fell asleep with the sound of hammer and crowbar still in his ears, and a vision of a neat pile of boards in his mind's eye.

In the morning he was awakened by a hail outside his window: "Mr. Gauss! Hey, Mr. Gauss!" Rolling his reluctant body out of bed, he noticed with blinking surprise that the battered one-legged tin clock on his dresser read only ten minutes after seven. Nobody ever disturbed him until eight.

"Take a look out here, Mr. Gauss!"

The voice was the handy man's. Mr. Gauss shuffled to the window, looked out at the lawn, and came wide awake with astonishment and anger. Herbie's Ride stretched down to the water exactly as before. The rowboat was fastened with a slipknot again at the top of the slide, with Clever Sam happily cropping grass nearby. Ted, Cliff, and Herbie sat on the seats of the boat. Elmer stood up in it, with the running end of the knot in his hand. As soon as the handy man saw Mr. Gauss's head he shouted, "She's O.K. now, Mr. Gauss. Watch us go!"

"Elmer, I forbid you!" yelled Mr. Gauss, but even as he uttered the words the handy man pulled the line free and dropped to a seat. The rowboat began sliding. A quarter of the way down the hill it picked up speed, and raced. Just as it came to the water's edge it seemed to jump upward. The boys raised canvas flaps on either side of the gunwales to protect themselves from the splash. The boat flew off shore, hit the water as gracefully as a gull, with a small burst of spray, and coasted to a halt. As soon as the splattering was over the boys dropped the flaps, took up paddles, and waved them gleefully at Mr. Gauss.

The camp owner, trembling with mingled relief and annoyance, dressed and hurried out to the slide. When he arrived the rowboat was already back at the top, and Cliff was releasing Clever Sam from the tow.

"Next ride fer you, Skipper!" said the handy man, saluting him gaily.

"Elmer, my orders were distinctly—"

"Shucks, Mr. Gauss, I knew fer sure you din' wanna make them kids unhappy after all that work, not if we could help it. There's four o' them, see, an' we want 'em to come back next year, don't we? Well, there wasn't nuthin' wrong with the old slide, 'cept I fergot to put in the old ski-jump tilt to the bottom, see? Boat was headin' straight down when it hit water 'stead o' comin' in belly up like a bird. We fixed it easy last night. Jest a little scaffoldin' an' a short ramp."

"Please, Mr. Gauss," said Herbie, looking at him with dog's eyes, "take a ride. We tried it eight times already. It's great. You'll be our first real passenger."

"Very well, Herbie." Mr. Gauss smiled broadly and patted his head. "You have real camp spirit. My hat is off to you." He stepped majestically into the boat and sat. Elmer released the rope and Mr. Gauss had the luxury of a fine thrilling ride, and not a drop of water splashed on him, either. Ted in the bow, and Herbie in the stern, swiftly paddled the boat to the pebbly beach, and helped the camp owner alight. Mr. Gauss watched admiringly as the boys pulled the boat into place on a greased ramp, fastened the towing harness of Clever Sam to a mooring ring in the stern, and guided it up into place on the up-tilted rails at the foot of the Ride. The horse began dragging the boat up the hill smoothly and easily.

There is no arguing with success, and Mr. Gauss knew it. "Herbie, I congratulate you," he said, walking up behind the lad. "You have performed a wonder, my boy."

"I ain't the one. Elmer an' Cliff an' Ted—mostly Elmer—they done it. I can't even do half as much work as Ted. I'm just no good at it."

"But you, my boy, you had the vision. The vision and the enterprise. Did I build Camp Manitou, my boy? Why, I did not nail one stick to another. Yet it is my camp. And this is your ride. Herbie's Ride."

Herbie would have thanked Mr. Gauss to compare his

ride to something better than Camp Manitou, but he realized that the camp owner was exerting himself to be pleasant. So he said, "Sure glad you enjoyed it, Mr. Gauss—er, Skipper," and hurried away up the hill.

22

The Triumph of Herbie

AND SO IT was that Herbie's Ride came into being after all. Four days ago it had been a cloudy notion in a small boy's mind, a ridiculous dream of a rowboat on wheels coasting downhill. Now, real and working, the slide dominated the landscape of the girls' camp. Elmer added a handsome frill: an archway at the top, bearing the words "HERBIE'S RIDE" cut out of a semicircular frame of cardboard in letters a foot high, with bright red electric lights behind it. Delighted with his handiwork, he drove hastily into town and returned with an electric interrupter switch which he attached to the lights. When dusk fell and the boys and girls turned out in gay costumes for the Mardi Gras, this sign, flashing on and off, on and off, was a striking sight. It was the first thing visitors saw, driving into the camp or crossing from the boys' grounds to the girls' lawn. There was nothing as splendid anywhere else in Manitou. When the other booths, games, rides, and entertainments had hardly been visited, a line of twenty children and adults already stretched before the Ride.

Directly under the archway stood Herbie in Elmer's sailor cap and blouse. The cap tended to drop down over his ears, and the blouse was loose enough to have held Cliff inside it, too, but the nautical effect was fine nevertheless. At first Herbie made a few efforts in the way of a cry: "Step right up, folks, best ride you ever been on! Slip down the slide on the slippery slope for only a quarter, twenty-five cents, the fourth part of a dollar," and so forth. But within a few minutes, with two dozen paid passengers waiting their turns, more coming each moment, and a large crowd watching the Ride and exclaiming in admiration, the cry seemed unnecessary, and he gave it up.

Thereafter the night was one of swimming pleasure for him. Money and congratulations poured in. Many passengers came up the hill from their first ride and walked into line for another. The Ride went smooth as oil. Ted and Felicia stayed in the rowboat, paddling it back to shore. Cliff and Clever Sam accomplished recovery with more and more ease as the evening wore on. Herbie collected fares and stored them in a cigar box, and tied up and released the boat with a slipknot, as Elmer had taught him. All four children felt the luxurious pride of participation in a great success, and even Clever Sam was in mellow good humor, and accepted much petting and light thwacks from the onlookers with friendly rolls of the eyes.

In this hour of exalted happiness Herbie's conscience packed up and departed. He amassed fifty dollars in less than two hours. The "borrowing" episode would be erased from the Book of Sins in the morning. The curse was forgotten. All was well. "Boy, you win Skipper sure!" was said to him perhaps a hundred times. Vision and enterprise had carried the day. Heaven had decided mercifully that stealing wasn't really stealing sometimes, and had suspended the Eighth Commandment for Herbie Bookbinder's benefit. What a wonderful old world it was, to be sure!

Yes, and even Lucille came around. Herbie's triumph had been in swing for three hours, and he was quite drunk with praise and profits, when he felt a timid tug at his oversize sleeve.

"Congratulations, Herbie," said a caroling voice.

The boy looked round at a beautiful little red-headed pirate dressed in a ragged gold shirt, a crimson sash, and short black trousers carefully torn at the bottom. She carried a little dagger and wore a black silk patch over one eye, but the other eye shone with enough admiration and love for two. Herbie, who had thought yesterday he was cured of his romantic affliction, suddenly wondered if he really was. Lucille, the radiant Lucille, was humbling herself to him, and it was a sweet sensation.

" 'Lo, Lucille. 'Scuse me a minute."

He made change for a batch of eight passengers as they boarded the boat, and flourished the cigar box so that Lucille had a long look at its overflowing green and silver contents. Then he pulled the rope with careless ease, and the boat thundered away down the slope.

"Gosh, Herbie." The girl's voice was awed, crushed. "However did you think up such a thing? You're wonderful!"

"Aw, Elmer Bean an' Cliff done it all. I ain't so hot," said Herbie. He paused, glanced at her and, as it were, took aim. Then he slowly added, *"I can't even dip."*

The pirate's cheeks all at once became the color of her sash. She pulled the patch off her face, evidently judging she needed both eyes for the work at hand, and said softly, looking at him with innocent appeal, "Herbie, I'm sorry I been so bad to you. You know what, I haven't even talked to Lennie all night. Except once he wanted to take me on your ride, an' I said I wanted to go alone."

Herbie's congealed affections were melting in the warmth of her voice, low, musical, almost whispering. But he called up the memory of his injuries and said indifferently, "Wanna ride now?"

"Yes, Herbie."

"O.K. You kin go free. An' you don't hafta wait on line."

The flashing sign showed surprise, darkness, disappointment, darkness, then a winsome smile that remained on the girl's face through several flashes. "Won't you come with me?"

"Heck, no, Lucille. See, I gotta take care o' the finances."

"Oh. Maybe after a while you'll come to the dancing at the social hall. I'd like to dance with you."

"Maybe."

Lucille fell silent, and watched Clever Sam towing the rowboat back to the top. Herbie made a great show of counting the money—there was a hundred seven dollars now—and wished Lucille would grovel a little more; but she didn't. So he said at last, "How's the rest of the Mardigrass, Lucille? I ain't had a chance to see it."

"Terrible. Everybody says your ride is the only good thing."

"How's Yishy's freak show?"

The girl sniffed contemptuously in answer.

"What's Lennie doing?"

"Oh, he's got a baseball suit on with 'New York Yankees' on it, an' a pillow in his stomach, an' goes around saying he's Babe Ruth. What a dumb idea!"

Herbie silently compared this inspiration with his own, and concluded that there were rare moments when brawn did not automatically rule the world. It did not occur to him that Lennie, at least, had not stolen the baseball suit.

The rowboat came creaking to the top of the slide. Herbie lashed it to the stake as Cliff freed Clever Sam. Then he gallantly handed Lucille into the boat, while several boys and girls waiting in line squealed a protest. Felicia, sitting in the bow, looked around, and said, "Humph! Starting all over again." She threw down her paddle and stepped out of the boat.

"Hey, Fleece, where you goin'?" said Herbie.

"As long as we're getting romantic again," snapped his sister as she stalked away, "I'm going to dance for a while at the social hall."

"Never mind, Herbie." Ted spoke up from the stern. "I can handle it myself."

"Thank you for the ride, Herbie. I hope I'll see you later," said Lucille demurely. Now the other passengers piled in, thrusting money at the boy. Lucille all the while gazed up at him worshipfully. Herbie felt foolish and happy and warm, and at the pinnacle of life and time. It was with reluctance that he tripped the rope and sent the boat rumbling downhill with its lovely burden.

Not long afterward three prolonged blasts of Uncle Sandy's whistle echoed through the camp, signaling the end of the Mardi Gras. Grumbling, a line of about a dozen passengers disbanded, all of them campers awaiting a second or third ride, except for a stout lady from the village with a dismal white-headed child. Herbie counted the receipts again while Ted beached the boat and Cliff returned the horse to the stable. Felicia came up from the dance in a glowing, happy mood. When all the colleagues were gathered again under the flashing sign, Herbie announced gaily the income from their labors: a hundred thirteen dollars and fifty cents.

"Holy smoke, we're rich," said Ted.

"How do we divvy it?" said Felicia.

"First of all I owe seventy-five bucks for materials," said Herbie. The others nodded. "That still leaves almost forty bucks, or ten bucks apiece."

Mr. Gauss appeared out of the darkness, smiling broadly. He was carrying half a dozen cigar boxes similar to the one in Herbie's hands.

"Well, well, the gold mine," he said cheerfully. "Let me have your box, Herbie. I'll keep it in the safe overnight for you. I'm doing the same for all the boys that made any real money."

"Gee, thanks, Mr. Gauss," said Herbie, huddling the box protectingly against his side, "but I can take care of it O.K."

"Nonsense, my boy. We don't want to tempt sneak thieves, you know." He grasped the box firmly and pried it out of Herbie's arms. "The safe is the only place for so much money as you made. I'll send for you first thing in the morning and return it to you. Congratulations, all of you!" He walked off toward the guest house.

"Good-by, hundred thirteen bucks," croaked Ted, loud enough for the camp owner to hear him, but Mr. Gauss padded obliviously away.

"G'wan," said Herbie. "He wouldn't take that money for himself."

"He couldn't!" said Felicia.

Cliff said, "Even Mr. Gauss ain't that low. He'll give us some back, anyway."

"O.K., O.K.," said Ted. "I been at this camp a long time. If we see a nickel o' that dough again, it'll be a miracle."

"He's *gotta* gimme back the seventy-five bucks for material!" said Herbie. "I owe it."

"Don't be silly," exclaimed Felicia fretfully. "What are you boys talking about? He's got to give us back *all* of it. You talk as though there was a question about it. Is he a robber? It's our money, not his. How can he possibly keep a penny of it?"

Ted looked sidelong at her out of one eye, like a rooster. "This is my sixth year at Manitou," he said. "Inside that box is money, an' outside that box is Mr. Gauss. All there is between 'em is a lid. It ain't enough. . . . Well, it was fun anyhow." He shrugged. "More fun than I ever had in this hellhole. Thanks for lettin' me in on it, Herb."

"Aw, yer crazy, Ted," Herbie began, but the bugle sounded retreat, and on this foreboding note of Ted's they were compelled to part.

A few minutes later the boys of Bunk Thirteen sat around on their cots in pajamas, awaiting Uncle Sandy's announcement of the Skipper-for-a-Day.

"Who you gonna appoint for Uncle Sandy, Herb?" said Lennie deferentially.

"Heck, Lennie, I ain't won yet."

"You won. Nobody else can possibly win."

The other boys voiced a chorus of assents to this. They were proud of Herbie now. Boys from other bunks were shouting congratulations through the screen.

"Well, let's wait till he announces it, anyhow," said Herbie.

Uncle Sid said, "I'm proud of you, Herbie, I really am. What you did was remarkable. You have a great future." He puffed anxiously at a forbidden cigarette held in the hollow of his hand. Poor Uncle Sid was actually tense and nervous on Herbie's behalf. It is a strange thing that happens to these harassed adults and near-adults called

counselors. Submerged in a children's world for the sake
of a few dollars and a summer in the country, they come
to take the events of that world with unsmiling earnest-
ness. After all, the matters which people regard seriously
in adult life are seldom less trivial, or indeed very different in kind, from the concerns of the boys at Manitou—
the quest for success, the rivalries of cliques, the pursuit
of pleasure, the evasion of irksome rules; where are the
grownups whose years are not spent in those ways?

A preliminary blast of Uncle Sandy's unmistakable
whistle came from outer darkness, and cut dead all conversation. His voice boomed out of a megaphone.

"Now the announcement you've all been waiting for.
The judges—Aunt Tillie, the Skipper, and myself—had a
tough time deciding among the many excellent entries,
two in particular that you all know about.

"The Skipper of the Day is"—a long, agonizing pause;
then hurriedly—"Yishy Gabelson for his freak show, with
special honorable mention to Herbie Bookbinder for his
excellent ride. That's all."

But that was not all. Cries from every bungalow along
Company Street tore the night.

"Boo!"

"Gyps!"

"Robbers!"

"General Garbage won!"

"Crooks!"

The whistle blew furiously several times and quieted
the din.

"Now, cut that out!" roared the head counselor.
"You're not at home yet, you're still in camp. It isn't what
you want, it's what we decide that goes here!"

This was a provocative announcement that Uncle Sandy might have spared himself. But he was angry, and
feeling guilty, too, to tell the truth, so he acted with poor
judgment.

"Yah!"

"Boo!"

"Ssss!"

"You bet it ain't what we want!"

"It ain't *never* what we want!"

"Let's hang Uncle Gussie to a sour-apple tree!"

These and forty other insolent cries were flung through the screens. Confused and at a loss, Uncle Sandy stepped back into his tent. Meantime, Ted in Bunk Thirteen jumped from his bed and seized a tin pan and spoon from his hiking pack.

"Don't worry, General," he grated to the dumbfounded, pallid Herbie. "This is one time Uncle Gussie don't get away with it."

"Ted! You come back here!" exclaimed Uncle Sid, but Ted was already outside and marching up Company Street alone, beating the tin pan rhythmically and shouting, "We want Herbie! We want Herbie!" This was all the spark that was needed. In a twinkling twenty boys were in the street banging resounding objects—a glass, a drum, a tin canteen, and even a washtub were among them—and chanting, "We want Herbie!" The counselors were powerless to stop the irruption, and none of them particularly wanted to stop it. By the time the howling crowd of boys in pajamas had reached Uncle Sandy's tent their number included almost the whole camp. They milled under the large white electric light that hung on a pole at the end of the street, and chanted and yelled in a way to frighten the cloud of bugs that danced overhead.

Inside the hot yellow tent sat Mr. Gauss and the two head counselors, with sullen expressions.

"I say again, Sandy," spoke out the camp owner, "are you going to do nothing about this breakdown of discipline?"

"Skipper, I'm just one man. The counselors should have stopped it before it got started. Evidently they feel the same way I do, and I—"

The bulky form of Yishy Gabelson catapulted into the tent, crowding it uncomfortably.

"Uncle Sandy, Mr. Gauss, you can't do it to me. Them guys out there are ready to jump me. You know that kid won!" stammered the Super-senior, in a sweat.

"Now, Yishy, don't be childish," said Mr. Gauss. "Your freak show was admirable. And anyway, you know it's impossible to let an Intermediate be Skipper. It's too risky."

"You shoulda thought of that when you made up the contest!" shouted Yishy. "You shoulda said no Intermediates allowed to compete. It's too late to go makin' up rules now, Mr. Gauss. That kid won and you know it. You can do what you like, but I ain't gonna be your Skipper. I'm no crook!"

He bolted from the tent and the three judges heard him yell above the din that greeted him, "I *tole* 'em! I tole 'em I wouldn't take it!" Thereupon the jeers changed to shouts of approval, and merged into a tremendous chant: "We want Herbie! We want Herbie!"

"It seems to me, Mr. Gauss," said Uncle Sandy, wiping his thick glasses with a handkerchief and laying emphasis on the camp owner's last name, "that we have a choice of calling off Campers' Day, or giving Skipper to Herbie Bookbinder."

"Nonsense. They'll forget all about it after a night's sleep. We'll give them ice cream for lunch," said Mr. Gauss.

"So far as I'm concerned," said Aunt Tillie sourly, "the boy obviously did win. I simply went along with the Skipper's insistence that we needed an older boy to run the camp."

"You haven't got the older boy any more," observed Uncle Sandy.

"We want Herbie! We want Herbie!" came with undiminished gusto from outside, accompanied by bangs, rattles, clanks, and stamping.

Mr. Gauss looked from one head counselor to another. He saw two decidedly hostile faces.

"In view of the fact that I have no support from you, who should give it to me," he said, "I seem compelled to abandon the only sensible policy. Do as you please, Uncle Sandy, on your own responsibility. I have no more to say."

"Do we call off the Campers' Day, sir, or give Skipper to the boy?"

"I have no more to say."

Uncle Sandy stepped out of the tent. The mob of boys sensed news, and the chant died. The head counselor squinted around at the strange sight of his campers herded together in night clothes, in complete disorder. In the center of the crowd Herbie Bookbinder loomed high, naked except for white drawers, perched on the shoulders of Yishy and three other Seniors. When Sandy saw the fat boy thus glorified, he burst out laughing. "Come down, Herbie, you win. You're Skipper!" he shouted, and continued his good-natured guffawing.

Great yells of triumph went up. Though the boys knew nothing of what had passed in the tent, they gathered from Uncle Sandy's manner that the change was as welcome to him as to them, and they pressed around him to shake his hand and pound him lovingly with their fists. The four Seniors who were holding Herbie up commenced dancing, and nearly dropped the hero of the evening several times. Cries of congratulations, good wishes, and admiration came up to the erstwhile General Garbage from every side, and they were all addressed to "Herbie."

Under no circumstances but these could he have received such an ovation, which exceeded anything that Lennie or Yishy had ever received for athletic prowess. He had become the symbol of resistance to Mr. Gauss, and in his victory every boy felt the throwing off of the yoke from his own shoulders. It was a brief temporary success, to be sure—tomorrow the heavy Gauss rules and edicts would be in force as always—but once, at least once, Uncle Gussie had been forced to give ground. "Hooray for Herbie! Hooray for Herbie!" cheered the boys, with all their hearts and lungs.

And Herbie, bouncing and swaying on his perilous perch under the glare of the lamp amid the darting insects, surrounded by a host of friendly, admiring, upturned faces, his ears ringing with cheers and praise, felt warm tears of joy and wonder trickling down his face. None of his many daydreams of triumph had ever been as sweet as this. "There is no man that has not his hour, and no thing that has not its place." General Garbage, the fat, the unathletic, the despised, had come into his hour at last.

23

Disaster

HERBIE WOKE BEFORE reveille next day from a most horrible dream. The morning was misty gray outside the dripping screens. His bunkmates lay sleeping all around him. Uncle Sid snored in a fitful, choking way. The crickets were silent. Streamers of mist floated through the screens and hung inside the bungalow, thick to the eye and clammy when they brushed the skin. Herbie shuddered as the events of the dream came back to him, hanging in his memory like the streamers of mist.

He had murdered a man and buried him in the vacant lot behind the Place. Who the man was, he could not remember, but the murder had been done and covered up long ago and he had almost forgotten it. Then for some reason his father had decided to dig a hole behind the Place, and had selected the very spot where the body lay buried. His father, Mr. Krieger, and Mr. Powers had begun digging vigorously, and soon had a deep brown hole which grew deeper every moment. With increasing panic, Herbie, watching them excavate, had realized that the corpse must soon be found. And suddenly, with a ghastly shock of terror that was so powerful it woke him up, he remembered he had left a clue on the body that would instantly identify him as the murderer. As Herbie sat up in bed, still horrified, he strained to recall what the clue had been, and finally caught the fading image of it, though it made no sense. It was the cigar box in which he had kept the fares collected at the Ride.

So vivid had the nightmare been that the drowsy boy actually began reviewing all the events of the night of his trip to the city to see if he had really killed someone, and it was with some relief that he came wider awake and dismissed the absurd fancy. The thought of the cigar box now grew stronger in his mind. He spent some time in imaginary arguments with Mr. Gauss; the camp owner tried to keep the money on various pretexts which Herbie scornfully exploded one by one. Then he dwelled on the glories of the previous night, and pictured some of the pleasures of his forthcoming day as lord of the camp. Little by little his mood of guilty foreboding caused by the dream faded, as the morning mist dissipated before the rising sun. When the bugle blew after what seemed a very long time, he was as cheery as the newly awakened ones, and jumped from bed faster than any of them.

"Hey, Herbie, whaddayou gettin' up for? You're Uncle Gussie," said Lennie, yawning.

"He is not," Uncle Sid put in promptly, rubbing a blue bristling jowl with the back of his hand. "Campers' Day doesn't start until ten o'clock."

"Sure, otherwise the counselors would hafta stand inspection," sneered Ted as he stepped into ragged, dirty slippers. "Mr. Gauss made up that rule after the first year—leave it to Uncle Gussie. Boy, that was fun when the counselors hadda sweep the floor an' all. Campers' Day ain't no good now."

"Shut up and get out to drill, all of you," said Uncle Sid, and fell back on his cot with closed eyes as the boys trooped out the door.

An hour later during breakfast the head counselor walked by the table of Bunk Thirteen and said casually, "Herbie, come to my tent after breakfast. Uncle Sid, have one of the other boys make Herbie's bed."

"Yes, sir," said Uncle Sid.

Herbie looked modestly into his plate while his bunkmates regarded him respectfully and enviously.

"Hey, Herb, who ya gonna make head counselor?" said Lennie, ladling a generous portion of scrambled eggs into the fat boy's plate. "Don't forget your old pals. We been old pals for years, Herbie, you know we have."

"You?" said Ted, wrinkling his thin beak at Lennie in disgust. "After the way you haunted him all summer, how can you have the nerve to wanna be Uncle Sandy? 'Bout all he should appoint you is Clever Sam."

The other boys chortled.

"That's well said," remarked Uncle Sid. "As a matter of fact, Lennie, I appoint you to make Herbie's bed. And if it's Frenched or tricked up in any way, you'll spend Camper's Day on your cot."

"Why would I French it? I'm glad to make Herbie's bed," said Lennie, with a rather frightening simulation of gladness on his face. "We're old pals, Herbie an' me. Ain't we, Herbie? Remember old Mrs. Gorkin's class, huh, Herbie? That was fun, wasn't it? Hey, I wonder what our fathers are doing now, down at the Place."

Herbie, choking a little at the mention of the Place, pretended to have a mouthful of eggs, and answered Lennie with a meaningless grunt. The other boy continued his demonstrations of friendship throughout the meal, and left his eggs untasted in his eagerness to remind Herbie of their many sentimental ties. Herbie tried his best to say nothing in reply.

"Boy, Herb, with you as Skipper an' me as Sandy, what stunts we couldn't work up, huh? We could really put this camp on its ear. We'll give 'em the old Homer Avenue treatment!"

Herbie stood. " 'Scuse me, Uncle Sid, could I leave the table early? I think maybe Uncle Sandy'll want to see me as soon as possible."

"Of course, go right ahead—Skipper!" said Uncle Sid, smiling.

"Don't forget, Herbie," called Lennie after him. "You an' me'll stick together, huh? Old Herbie an' Lennie! A coupla regular guys from Homer Avenue!"

Lennie's new-found affection somehow depressed Herbie. As he made his way through the dining room he was the target of dozens of friendly hails; but he did not enjoy the homage quite as much as he might have. It all reminded him too forcibly of an incident he had observed a week ago. Daisy, the miserable, abhorred Daisy, had enjoyed a brief reign of dazzling popularity when the mail brought him a package containing four salamis. From the respect and cordiality lavished on him one might have thought Daisy had suddenly grown two feet taller. His head turned by the intoxication of being loved, poor Daisy had seized a knife and forthwith sliced up and given away all four salamis piece by piece to a swarm of outstretched hands. The last slice gone, he had just as suddenly shrunk to normal size, and Herbie recalled vividly the picture of the thin bespectacled boy, sitting alone on his expensive brass-bound trunk, the greasy knife still in his hand, peering around at the empty bungalow. What was so different, Herbie wondered, between Daisy with his salamis and General Garbage as Skipper? These were sad ideas for a boy of eleven at the height of good luck to be thinking and, like all cynicism, only partly true. Daisy's glory had been so brief because it was all salami and no achievement. But the fact is, in this summer Herbie had come far in knowledge of certain ways of the world. He was to come farther before another sun set.

He knocked diffidently on the pole at the entrance to Uncle Sandy's tent. A hearty voice summoned him inside.

"Hi, Herb. Sit down." Uncle Sandy pointed with a smoking pipe to a three-legged stool beside his narrow desk. The desk was a piece of beaverboard supported by four planks. "First of all, congratulations. You're a remarkable little kid."

"If not for Elmer Bean an' my cousin Cliff, I wouldn't be nothin'. I had good luck," said Herbie as he sat.

"I know that. The fact that you know it, too, is good. But nobody ever makes a success without luck and help. You deserve your reward."

"Thanks, Uncle Sandy."

"Now, let's move fast." The head counselor thrust a typewritten list and a pencil into his hand. "I've always run Campers' Day on the level, Herb, as much as—hm—

as much as I was allowed to. That's why it's been a success. You go through that list and tick off the boy you want to be the counselor in each bunk."

"Yes, sir." Herbie studied the sheet and made slow, careful marks.

"By the way, who's going to be me?"

Herbie answered at once, "Cliff."

Uncle Sandy grinned. "Well, this is the one day Uncle Sandy'll be able to ride Clever Sam. I think Cliff'll be fine." He glanced over Herbie's shoulder, nodding. "Good. Good choices. Ted for Uncle Sid, eh? Fine. Poor Ted hasn't been a counselor in all his years." He returned to writing at his desk. In a few minutes Herbie handed the sheet to him. The head counselor examined it and gave it back. "You haven't filled in names for the doctor and nurse."

"Nurse?" Herbie scratched his head and stared.

"We always do that for laughs. Put down anybody who'll look funny in a nurse's uniform. Yishy would be fine, but you've got him as Uncle Peewee."

Herbie thought a moment; then he scrawled on the paper and passed it to the head counselor, who looked at it and laughed aloud. The writing read:

Doctor—Daisy Gloster
Nurse—Lennie Krieger

Uncle Sandy glanced at the large cheap watch hanging on a nail over his bedside. "Nine twenty-five. Mr. Gauss wants to see you at nine-thirty, Herbie. Better run on up the hill. Come back here when you're through."

"What's he want to see you about?"

The head counselor kept his eyes on his desk. "Can't say. About the money from the Ride, possibly. Hurry, boy."

There was in Uncle Sandy's manner a sudden aloof cautiousness that Herbie didn't like. He left the tent and trotted up the hill, feeling the gloom of his dream stealing upon him again. He came to the steps of the guest house panting and red-faced, and as he paused for breath he was surprised to see Yishy Gabelson issue from the doorway of the camp office, shaking his head and grinding his teeth.

"Oh, that ——! Oh, that fat old ——!" muttered the Super-senior, using two epithets from the very bottom of the barrel of bad language. "Oh, that ——!" he added, using one even worse, and actually strange to Herbie's ears.

"Hey, Yishy, what's the matter?" cried Herbie anxiously, as the other strode past him unseeing. Yishy glanced around at him, startled.

"What are you still doing here? You know what's happened."

"No, I don't," quavered Herbie.

"WHAT? You mean he hasn't spoken to you about the money yet?"

Herbie's stomach contracted into a stony lump. "No, Yishy, honest."

"Oh, that old liar!" Yishy staggered, put his hand to his forehead, and groaned. "Oh, that ——! That ——!" He repeated one old epithet and a brand-new one. Then he stumbled off down the hill, blaspheming and shaking his fists in the air. Herbie looked after this wild sight in wonder, and trudged unhappily up the steps and into the office.

An even greater surprise awaited him. Mr. Gauss was smiling as usual behind his desk, and seated near him on a dirty old plush chair—Herbie almost fainted as he beheld the man—was the emaciated driver, skinny and queer as ever, who had given him and Cliff the hitch from New York to Panksville!

"Ah, good morning, Herbie," Mr. Gauss beamed. "And let me introduce you to Mr. Drabkind. Mr. Drabkind, this is one of our finest, cleverest, most outstanding campers. Herbie Bookbinder—I'm proud to say, also a pupil at my school."

Mr. Drabkind extended a bluish hand to Herbie. The boy grasped the cold finger tips, pumping them once, and dropped them. The thin man peered at him through glasses thick as the bottoms of bottles.

"I don't see too well," he apologized in his unforgettable reedy voice, "but it seems I've met you, Master Bookbinder, rather recently."

Herbie shrugged, and tried to still the quivering of his knees. "I don't see how that's possible," said Mr. Gauss, looking hard at Herbie. "Do you, Herbert?"

Herbie shook his head, unable to utter a sound.

"You must be mistaken, Mr. Drabkind," said the camp owner. "This is your first visit here this summer. Unless," he added archly, "Herbie has been out traveling, unbeknownst to me."

Was it a cat-and-mouse game, Herbie wondered through the fog of fear that enveloped his mind? He waited for the blow, if one was to fall.

"Well, I see so many boys—so many boys," sighed Mr. Drabkind. He sat in the chair again, his frame curved like a wilting flower. "Though I don't somehow remember him as being in a crowd."

"No, you wouldn't. Our Herbert stands out very much from the crowd," said Mr. Gauss, and both men giggled politely and, Herbie thought, somewhat eerily. There was a short silence.

"Well, Mr. Gauss, we may as well come to the point," piped the frail man. "I can't stay long, you know."

"Herbie, you don't know who Mr. Drabkind is, do you?" said Mr. Gauss, looking down at his finger tips clasped before him.

As emphatically as he could, Herbie shook his head again.

"Of course he wouldn't," said Mr. Drabkind. He took a card from a black wallet and handed it to Herbie. The boy read:

HENRY JUNIUS DRABKIND

Field Representative
Berkshire Free Camp Fund

"Mr. Drabkind represents one of the worthiest causes I know of, Herbert," said Mr. Gauss. "The Berkshire Free Camp gives several hundred poor city boys just the same kind of wonderful vacation you're having—well, of course, not as fine as we can give you in Manitou, but for a charity camp, as I say, a wonderful vacation."

"Thanks in good part to men like you, Mr. Gauss—and to boys like Master Bookbinder," interposed the wispy Mr. Drabkind.

Mr. Gauss directed a mechanical nod and smile at the visitor.

"Now, Herbie, if you had been here in previous years you'd know that we take a collection every summer for the Free Camp. We who are fortunate enough to have parents who can pay to give us a wonderful vacation at Manitou ought to help the boys who are not so lucky— don't you agree?"

Though not understanding the camp owner's drift, Herbie sensed that it would be better for him not to agree. But there seemed no help for it. He nodded.

"Fine. You see, you don't have to work very hard, Mr. Drabkind, to make a boy of the mental caliber of Herbert Bookbinder understand a simple matter. . . . Then I take it, Herbie, you approve of what I have done in writing this check."

He held toward the boy a green slip. Herbie did not take it, but read the writing. The check was made out to the Berkshire Free Camp Fund, in the sum of two hundred dollars. He looked questioningly at Mr. Gauss.

"That sum of two hundred dollars, Herbie, represents the total earnings of your Ride, Yishy Gabelson's Freak Show, Gooch Lefko's House of Mirrors, and—ah—thirty-five dollars and fifty cents out of my own pocket. There were other little booths that took in some money, but they were not important enough, I feel, to be invited to share in this privilege. . . . Were you about to say something, Herbie?"

The boy had indeed opened his mouth to protest. But he glanced fearfully at Mr. Drabkind, shut it again without a word, and shook his head.

"Ah, then to go on. You understand, Herbie, that the money you earned at the Ride came out of the campers' pockets to begin with. You had the glory of—shall I say—assembling it. And I want to know, will you join Yishy, Gooch, and myself in contributing your collection to Mr. Drabkind's poor boys?"

Torn between anguish at the thought of losing the seventy-five dollars he must have to wipe out the theft, and fear that Mr. Drabkind would recognize his voice and betray him, Herbie was the most miserable boy in those mountains. How could he risk having Mr. Gauss, and thereafter his parents, learn that he had been picked up hitchhiking on Bronx River Parkway on the night of the robbery at the Place? His head buzzed with rage, frustration, and dread.

"Well, Herbie, shall I assume you approve, and hand Mr. Drabkind this check?" said Mr. Gauss, waving the fatal document in the direction of the thin man. "Yishy and Gooch have already gladly, I may say enthusiastically, contributed their entire earnings. It's all up to you now."

Herbie thought of Yishy's actions, which had been enthusiasm of a sort, but hardly a glad enthusiasm. It was clear to him that Mr. Gauss must have told Yishy that he, Herbie, had already contributed his hundred and thirteen dollars.

What had actually happened was that Yishy, backed into the same corner that Herbie was in now, but not having his situation complicated by terror of Mr. Drabkind, had ventured an objection: "Shucks. I dunno. You mean to say Herbie Bookbinder's gonna give every nickel he made?" To this Mr. Gauss had replied, "I certainly would not ask you to do so if that were not the situation." Yishy had surrendered with a surly "O.K., then," and rushed from the office, to encounter Herbie in the way we have seen. Now, to be strict, Mr. Gauss had perhaps lied to Yishy. But he had phrased his answer carefully, and if caught in the apparent discrepancy, would have at once explained that his reply meant that he intended to *ask* Herbie to give all his money, just as he was asking Yishy.

The gray world of half truth, in which our gray Mr. Gausses spend their gray hours, fumbling for little gray advantages! Mr. Gauss's purpose in this complicated maneuver was simply to save himself about fifteen dollars, and at the same time gain a little prestige. The collection for the Free Camp in previous years had always netted about the same amount—fifty dollars—to which Mr. Gauss added fifty out of the camp treasury to make the round sum of a hundred. This equaled the regular contribution of Penobscot and other institutions of the size of Manitou. When Mr. Gauss had collected the cigar boxes the previous evening, he had fully intended to return the money to the boys. But next morning the Tempter brought Mr. Drabkind. It occurred to the camp owner, upon a rapid mental calculation, that he could double the Manitou contribution and lessen the usual cost to himself by the simple device of inviting the three most successful Mardi Gras enterprises to donate their earnings. He justified the act to himself and to Uncle Sandy by pointing out that the money was not "really" Herbie's, Yishy's, or Gooch's, but had come out of the payments of the campers. In any case (he declared in explaining the scheme to the head counselor) the boys would be given a free choice of contributing or declining to do so, therefore no objection could possibly be made. Uncle Sandy, a weary workhorse who knew his master well, bent a little lower under the burden of the summer and said nothing. He was counting the hours to his release. Only forty-eight remained.

And so Herbie was offered the free choice of contributing or not. With the check written out and hovering a few inches from the charity collector's hand, with two grown men cajoling him and prodding him, he had the choice of consenting to something practically done, or of trying to reverse events at the last instant, thus bringing on himself the odium of being uncharitable. There was the added pressure, though Mr. Gauss cannot be blamed therefor, of possible recognition by Mr. Drabkind at any moment.

Wonderful to relate, the boy in these circumstances still managed to produce an ounce of resistance. He tried to disguise his voice by pitching it very high, and almost neighed, "Do I have to give all of it?"

"Pardon me?" said Mr. Gauss.

Herbie repeated, "Do I have to give all of it?" still sounding more like Clever Sam than himself. Mr. Drabkind looked amazed at the sound, but there was no light of remembrance in his expression, which was all that mattered to the boy.

"Why, no, Herbert, of course you don't," said Mr. Gauss, also puzzled by the queer tones, but attributing them to nervousness. "Let me be perfectly clear on that point. You don't have to give one single solitary penny, Herbert. I know you received your materials for nothing through Elmer Bean's friend, otherwise I would of course suggest deducting about seventy-five dollars for expenses. But you may have all your money back if you wish." He held the check pinched between thumbs and forefingers as though to tear it down the middle. "Say the word, and I'll send Mr. Drabkind away without this check. Say the word, and I'll give Gooch and Yishy their money back, too, and simply say, 'Herbie Bookbinder has different ideas about charity than the rest of us.' Say the word, Herbie, and the Free Camp gets not one cent of yours. It's all up to you, as I have said before. Shall I tear the check up or shall I hand it to Mr. Drabkind?"

Herbie, loaded down with his own lies, weakened by his fears of the gaunt man who had come back from his buried night of crime to haunt him, pressed without mercy by Mr. Gauss, caved in. He shrugged and nodded his head. At once the camp owner put the check in the hand of the charity collector.

"Thank you, Herbert!" he exclaimed. "You're the sort of young man I've always thought you were."

"And let me thank you, Master Bookbinder," shrilled Mr. Drabkind, folding the check carefully into his black wallet, "in the name of two hundred poor boys who will benefit by your—"

But Herbie was tottering out through the doorway. He

bore a face of such utter tragedy that the camp owner felt an unfamiliar momentary sensation in his heart: doubt of his own rectitude.

"Herbie, come back here!" he called. "You shouldn't go like that." The boy tramped down the steps and did not turn back.

"Well, thank you once more, Mr. Gauss, for an extraordinarily generous contribution, and good-by," said Mr. Drabkind hurriedly. "Admirable boy, that Master Bookbinder. Admirable camp you run, indeed, Mr. Gauss. No, please don't trouble to see me out; my car's only a few feet from the house. Good-by, good-by." In his haste, jamming his hat on his head and putting his wallet in his pocket, the willowy charity collector omitted to shake the camp owner's hand and took a quick departure.

When Herbie arrived back at Uncle Sandy's tent, it was five minutes to ten. Cliff was already there, dressed in the head counselor's famous old blue sweater and gray baseball cap, holding his megaphone and wearing the whistle, emblem of boys' camp sovereignty, on a thong around his neck. Sandy was earnestly giving him a multitude of last-minute suggestions as he struggled into a gray and green jersey of Cliff's that was laughably small on him. Herbie stood around feeling dull and useless.

"How 'bout me, Uncle Sandy?" he said at last.

"Why, you really have nothing to do, Herb, except be boss—just like the Skipper. Cliff does all the work," said the head counselor with a grin at his own wit. He took a pair of large green sun glasses and Mr. Gauss's feather headdress from the shelf. "Put these on. Then just walk around, looking important. All right, Cliff, it's ten o'clock. Take over."

The head counselor and his successor went outside. Herbie threw aside his costume and lay on the cot face upward. The sun fell in a flecked orange square on the canvas above his eyes. The air was hot in the tent. He heard the familiar three blasts of the whistle that summoned the bunks into two lines along Company Street, the running of feet on gravel, the slamming of many doors, and a thousand squeals and yelps of mirth as the campers saw the counselors in their silly boys' clothes. The entire joke seemed flat and stale to the Skipper-for-a-Day. He put his hand to his eyes and involuntarily moaned. He was a wretch who had stolen money from his own father, and could never pay it back.

"All right, fellows!" he heard Cliff shout. "Now I want you to show some real camp spirit when you greet Uncle Gus—I mean the Skipper. Here he comes now—our own dear Skipper."

Herbie rose heavily and dashed the tears from his face. He donned the glasses and the feather headdress as he walked to the entrance of the tent. He contorted his body so that he jutted to a remarkable extent before and behind. Then he stepped out into the sunshine, and waddled majestically down Company Street, holding up the corners of his mouth in a fixed smile with two forefingers, and pointing his feet outward like a duck's.

The campers screamed and danced and so did the counselors. Several of them fell to the ground and rolled around, giggling. Uncle Sandy, standing among the boys of Bunk Thirteen, maintained a straight face for perhaps ten seconds, then burst out in helpless bellow after bellow which touched off a perfect riot of hilarity. Herbie waggled his behind impassively as he strolled between the lines, nodding his head here and there. When he reached the end of the street he vanished in the direction of the lake, leaving the camp still in disorderly convulsions of mirth.

He was not seen again that merry morning, for he spent it lying on a flat rock near the shore, hidden by underbrush. A lonesome, quiet situation, you might say, yet he had plenty of company. Misery sat at the fat boy's right hand, and Shame at the left; and they made the morning mighty lively for Herbie between them.

24

Lennie and Mr. Gauss Take Falls

So THE DAY of Herbie's greatest success turned into the bitterest of his young life, because the fruit of triumph had a rotten core. Probably he should have hardened his heart and enjoyed himself, but he could not. Remorse ate him. To a better judge of crime—let us say, a policeman—this remorse might have seemed some days late in setting about its gnawing, but to Herbie his offense had been no offense until Mr. Gauss deprived him of the means to repay with interest the "borrowed" money.

Now, here the boy showed himself of pretty good mettle, for he wasted little breath blaming the camp owner, but took the disaster on his own conscience. A thousand weaklings, of either sex and all ages, will commit a misdeed which they plan to make up for later. Then if someone happens to prevent them from covering, they will throw all the blame for the original offense on that someone, and hold themselves virtuous. If you have not seen this happen yet, watch the feeble ones around you today and tomorrow. Herbie digested the thought of his own wickedness all during Campers' Day, and had a colicky time of it, and never sought the relief of saying "It's really Gauss's fault."

Herbie and Cliff were eating lunch in grandeur at the head counselor's table. They still wore their costumes. Herbie's many-colored feather headdress provided a gay touch to the bleak dining hall.

"What are we gonna do during rest hour?" said Herbie to his cousin.

"Don't we have to stay in our bunks, same as always?" said Cliff.

"What, and us the bosses of the camp? Cliff, you don't use your head sometimes."

The boys both gloated over the prospect of not being compelled to spend the hour after lunch on their cots in silence with shoes and stockings off.

"Hey, know what, Herb?" Cliff suddenly smiled. "Let's go up the hill an' say good-by to Elmer Bean an' Clever Sam. We won't hardly get to see 'em tomorrow, everything'll be so rushed goin' to the train."

"Good," said Herbie. "Why don't we go right now? I ain't hungry."

A tumult of whistles, jeers, and flirtatious calls distracted them. Lennie, his face red, was sidling into the dining room in his white nurse's cap and gown. Baseball sneakers and stockings completed his costume and added to its foolishness. He was looking here and there, trying to smile and flinging an occasional answer to the jibes.

Herbie said, "Where the heck has he been, comin' in so late?"

"Aw, the poor guy's been hidin'. He probably didn't even hear the bugle," said Cliff.

Lennie sat at the table of Bunk Thirteen, and the din ebbed. In his case the exchange of identity was incomplete. The camp nurse was not required to become a boy. But dressing up a well-known athlete in feminine garb was too rich a comic idea to be sacrificed for a point of logic, and the mock nurse was always a feature of the day. Lennie was an angry, slow-witted butt, therefore an exceptionally good one. After being heavily badgered for an hour he had disappeared, not to be seen until lunch time.

Herbie and Cliff quitted their table of honor and walked through the huge bare wooden hall to the door—and behold, there was no commotion, nobody cracked jokes, and scarcely any campers turned away from the important business of stuffing Spanish omelet into their mouths. Herbie had wisely ceased his waddling after the first great hit; by now it would have been a wearisome jest. Cliff, as Uncle Sandy, had at no time caused much amusement. Lennie had made a sensation where the cousins went unnoticed, for the reason that impersonation is only entertaining when someone is degraded by it.

The boys were halfway up the hill when they met Elmer Bean rattling down with three enormous coarse cloth bags piled in a wheelbarrow. Cliff greeted him with, "Hi, Elmer! Last laundry, huh?"

"Last everythin', fellers. This time tomorrer yer free men. This time a week from now I am." The handy man braced himself, brought the plunging wheelbarrow to a stop, and leaned against one of the bags. "You guys are the big shots o' the camp, huh?"

"Thanks to you," said Herbie.

"Herb, there's somethin' I wish you'd do fer me on yer twenty-first birthday."

"What, Elmer?"

"Write an' tell me where you guys got that fifty bucks."

Herbie looked sick all at once. Cliff quickly said, "Clever Sam up in the stable, Elmer?"

"He was when I last saw him. Gonna kiss 'im goodby?"

Cliff smiled bashfully.

"Hey, Elmer," said Herbie, "how 'bout us guys writin' to you? Will you write back?"

The handy man laughed. He looked around at the panorama of lake and bungalows, at the trees with creepers along their trunks already flaming in premature autumn colors, and at the two grotesquely dressed boys. The feathers of Herbie's headdress wagged in a breeze that had turned chilly. Elmer felt an impulse of pity for the small fat boy, whom he was sure he would never see after tomorrow, and whom he regarded as such an odd, self-tormenting mixture of good and bad.

"I tell yer, Herb," I said, "I been shipmates with guys that I swore I'd write to regular when I got transferred, see? My first coupla years I did write, too, maybe one or two times, but it wasn't no good. You think a letter's gonna be somethin', see, but it ain't nothin'. You were shipmates once, and now yer on other ships an' it's all different. I dunno why."

"I just thought maybe a letter just once in a long while," persisted the boy. "You know, after all we done on the Ride together an' all—"

"Why, sure, Herb, write if you feel like it." The handy man hesitated a moment, then blurted, "Don't be surprised if you git an answer that looks like you wrote it yourself in the fifth grade. I don't write such a hell of a lot, Herb."

"I'll write, too, Elmer," said Cliff.

Both boys looked intensely unhappy.

"Look, fellers," said the handy man, "don't let old Gauss work on yer feelin's next year, see? You know— remember good old Elmer, remember good old this, good old that? I sure would like to see you again, an' I'll be here too, like as not, 'cause I ain't good fer much else, but don't come back, fellers. What's better than bein' free? Yer free when you git outta school, free fer a whole summer, see, and old Gauss gets you marchin' an' workin' again. And you sing them songs, an' you git choked up an' you think you love camp. I know all about them songs. In the Navy we called 'em shippin'-over music. They played 'em whenever the recruitin' officer come to sign us up fer another hitch. I got all the orders an' salutin' an' bugles I ever want in the Navy. And git this straight, I'm *proud* I was a sailor—but they paid me, see, and what's more important I was doin' somethin'. I was on a ship to defend the country. I wasn't fattenin' up no old turkey like Gauss. Don't come back, guys. I like you both swell. Cliff, yer O.K., yer a real guy." He took the boy's hand and shook it. "Herb—I dunno what to tell you, Herb. You might be a very big guy someday, an' then again I dunno. Herb, is yer father alive?"

Herbie nodded. The question touched off a storm of emotion, and he dared not speak.

"Listen, feller, do what yer father tells you, see? In a coupla years yer gonna start thinkin' he's all wet about everything. Maybe you do now. Well, I'm tellin' you,

Herb, do whatever yer father says. A guy like you needs his pa."

The handy man patted Herbie's shoulder. Then he bent and picked up the handles of the wheelbarrow.

"We had fun, didn't we, guys? There ain't never been nothin' like Herbie's Ride in this camp, and there ain't never gonna be again. It took the three of us, see, an' Herbie bein' jealous over Lucille, an' all. Them things only happen once." He started to wheel away his burden, and said over his shoulder, "Sure, write to me here at Panksville. Only like I say, don't mind none about the way I spell an' write. I ain't nothin' but a country boy."

He went off down the hill, leaning backward to keep the wheelbarrow from running away, his yellow hair flying.

The boys walked to the stable in silence. As they came to the door Cliff said, "Clever Sam must be asleep. Can't hear him movin' at all." The boys went inside and, to their astonishment, found the stall empty.

"Maybe he's outside eatin' grass," Herbie suggested.

"Elmer said he was in here," Cliff said anxiously, but he went outside and looked in the practice ring. The horse was not there, nor anywhere in sight.

"Hey, Herbie, whaddya suppose has happened to him?"

"I dunno. Maybe he wandered off down the road."

"Clever Sam don't wander. He likes the barn better'n any place. Listen, there's somethin' wrong. Let's go down and tell Elmer."

The boys descended the hill at a run. With each step they bounded twice as far as they would have on level ground, and felt fleet as stags. Pounding around the corner of a bungalow into Company Street they came to a quick halt, for there was Clever Sam in the middle of the gravel path, surrounded by laughing, chattering boys. He was walking slowly, his head hanging in a woebegone way, the reins dragging from his bridle, and on his side there was white-washed in crude letters, "HERBIE THE SISSY."

"Come on, Herb," exclaimed Cliff. He plunged into the

crowd, followed by his cousin, and elbowed his way to the horse. He put his arm around Clever Sam's neck, saying, "Whoa, boy. What're they doin' to you? O.K., boy."

Hearing Cliff's voice, the animal raised his head, neighed, and nuzzled against him. Herbie, coming up to Clever Sam, saw that his skin had been whitewashed on his other side too, with the words, "SKIPPER GARBAGE."

The laughter and jokes subsided. A few boys sneaked away from the fringe of the group into bungalows. Curious noses pressed against screens up and down the street.

"O.K.," said Cliff to the crowd. "Who done it?"

"Not me." "I don't know." "I just got here." "The horse just come walkin' along." These and answers like them came in a chorus. But the boys looked at each other with knowing smiles. Uncle Sandy appeared in the doorway of Bunk Twelve, still dressed as Cliff. He observed the scene and said nothing. Cliff glanced hesitantly at the head counselor, then at the crowd.

"First I'm gonna take care o' this poor horse, then I'll come back an' find out who done it."

He was leading the horse to the road up the hill, and was just passing Bunk Thirteen. Lennie stepped out of the doorway, picked up the edges of his white nurse's skirt, and made a clumsy curtsy.

"Why, Mr. Head Counselor, is there somethin' the matter?" he said in effeminate tones.

Herbie, walking beside his cousin, whispered, "Lookit his left arm, Cliff."

Cliff saw a streak of whitewash running from the wrist to the elbow. Lennie noticed where his eyes were directed and rubbed his right hand along the streak, smiling insolently at the other boy.

"O.K., Lennie, you done it, huh?" said Cliff.

"Who's Lennie? I'm Nurse Geiger, dearie," Lennie twittered. "That little fat Skipper next to you appointed me, dincha, Skipper Garbage?"

Cliff took his arm from Clever Sam's neck and walked close to Lennie. The watching boys became quiet. Several counselors were on the outskirts of the group now, but none interfered.

"All right, Lennie. You're gonna come with me and clean off that horse."

"Why, Uncle Sandy," said Lennie in falsetto, "I'm a nurse. I treat human beings, not horses."

Cliff sprang at Lennie, wrapping his arms around him, and toppled him to the ground, falling on top of him. In a moment he was seated astride Lennie, pinning his arms with his knees.

"You gonna clean that horse?"

Lennie, astounded at being on his back, but not at all cowed, said, "Dear me, Uncle Sandy, how rough you play!"

A ringing slap across his face followed. Cliff's expression was peculiarly solemn, except at the instant of the slap, when he bared his teeth.

"Now you gonna clean that horse?"

Lennie heaved his body upward and threw Cliff off him. Both boys sprang to their feet. Lennie raised his fists in fighting position and danced angrily.

"Jump a guy when he ain't lookin' for it, huh?" he growled. "O.K., Cousin Garbage, come an' get murdered!"

One of the counselors shouted, "Uncle Sandy, shall I stop it?"

Uncle Sandy, still leaning in the doorway of Bunk Twelve only a few feet away, said, "If you mean me, my name is Cliff until five o'clock. Looks like Uncle Sandy's trying to maintain discipline in this camp by force. He'd better make it stick."

Lennie punched Cliff lightly in the chest. Cliff put up his hands awkwardly and stood with legs spread wide apart. Three times more Lennie hit him, none very hard blows, and at last Cliff countered with a long swing that missed Lennie by a foot. The pugilist in the nurse's uniform laughed aloud and punched Cliff's head with all his might. Cliff staggered, and then jumped on Lennie and bore him to the dirt exactly as he had done before. Seated on top of him he began cuffing the athlete's face with echoing slaps that could have been heard in the near-by hills.

"Will you clean that horse? Will you clean that horse? *Will* you clean that horse?"

Lennie struggled and squirmed, but could not unseat his foe. Cliff's eyes were bloodshot and he made the same painful face each time he hit Lennie, as though an aching tooth were giving him twinges. Slap! Slap! Slap! Slap! Lennie made two supreme efforts to throw off his tormentor, arching his back and twisting, but Cliff clung to his seat. Slap! Slap! Lennie flattened to the ground.

"I'll clean him!" came a muffled shout from the model of Character.

At once Cliff stood, helped Lennie to his feet, and put out his hand to him.

"Friends, Lennie?" he said.

The athlete's gown was more black than white, and crumpled and torn. His hair hung in his eyes, and his cheeks showed fiery marks from the persuasion he had undergone. He glanced at Cliff from under contracted brows, looked around at the spectators, then touched Cliff's hand with his own and ran into his bungalow.

"I'm bringin' the horse to the stable," Cliff called after him. "Come on up with me."

"I'll come when I'm good and ready," a surly voice answered from the bungalow.

Cliff pointed at one of the counselors in boys' clothes. "You, Peanuts Wishnik. If he ain't at the stable in ten minutes, you bring him up, please."

"Sure, Uncle Sandy," came the grinning reply.

But Lennie arrived at the stable under his own power only a minute or two after the cousins and the dispirited horse. Cliff had already began to scrub Clever Sam with a large brush and a bucket of soapy warm water. He passed these implements to Lennie without a word, and while the athlete glumly set about erasing his mischief, Cliff walked to the head of the horse and embraced him.

"You'll be O.K. now, Clever Sam," he said. "Well, so

long. Good luck." He patted the animal's nose and walked out of the stable.

Herbie hurried after him, exclaiming, "Holy cats, ain't you gonna say no more good-by to the horse than that?"

Cliff regarded his cousin with dulled eyes. "What else should I say?"

"Well, I thought you liked the horse."

"Well, I do."

"Shucks, tell him you're sorry you're leavin' him, an' you'll miss him, an' all that. Hey, didn't you ever read that poem, 'An Arab's Farewell to His Steed'? I bet it's fifteen stanzas long. That guy really says good-by to the horse."

Cliff said, "Yeah, we read it in 6B. That's just a poem." He looked at the ground for a few moments. Then he added, "Herb, do me a favor, huh? Go down an' tell Uncle Sandy that I wanna be excused. You can give the orders from now on. There's only a coupla more hours, anyhow."

He turned on his heel and walked back to the stable. Herbie stood irresolutely for a while, but curiosity overcame him. He went to the door and peeped in. Lennie was drying his hands on some old newspapers and walking toward the door with a surprised smile. And Cliff, with a much happier smile, was lovingly, silently washing Clever Sam.

It has been said already that Mr. Gauss was in the habit of vanishing for the duration of Campers' Day. The explanation he gave to himself and the counselors was that much as he regretted missing the fun, it was inconsistent with his "symbolic prestige" to join in horseplay.

Mr. Gauss made a great thing of his symbolic prestige. In his speech to the counselors at the start of each season he always trotted out the phrase and delivered a painstaking exposition of it. The gist of his annual remarks was that in his position of director he was not merely Mr. Gauss the man but a symbol of Camp Manitou, and as such he had to behave, and had to ask the counselors to behave, in ways that would constantly maintain his symbolic prestige. In coarse English this meant that the counselors were to show respect for him even if they didn't feel it. It was a sound administrative rule, and may be met with in all walks of life. Now, the truth is that Mr. Gauss's disappearance on Campers' Day was not entirely a matter of symbolic prestige. He could not swim and had a strong natural fear of the water, consequently he dreaded a ducking. This fact, however, was not mentioned.

The camp owner was lounging on his bed in the guest house, propped up with pillows, clad only in the inevitable khaki shorts, peacefully sipping iced coffee, and leafing through a four-week-old Sunday book-review section of the New York *Times*. Mr. Gauss was fond of book-review sections. In his weary pursuit of small monetary gains he found no time for reading, yet as an educator he was obliged to have some knowledge of current literature. The reviews gave him an acquaintance with titles and authors that served to work the necessary grace into his conversation. He was impressing his memory with the plot of a now-forgotten novel, which the reviewer compared favorably to the works of Dickens and Fielding, when there came a knock at the door. He glanced at his clock. It lacked an hour of five, when Campers' Day would end and it would be safe for him to sally forth.

"Who is it? he called crossly.

The voice of the handy man said, "Mrs. Gloster just drove in with her chauffeur. He's parkin' the car an' she's sittin' on the veranda. Thought you'd like to know."

Mr. Gauss leaped off the bed exclaiming, "Thanks, Elmer. Tell her I'll be right down, will you?"

"Um," said the voice.

Mrs. Gloster was the mother of the unfortunate Daisy, and also of four girls, all of whom were campers. She was the richest of all the Manitou parents, and her patronage had brought in its wake perhaps a dozen children. This may explain why Mr. Gauss began dressing with a comical haste that would seriously have injured his symbolic prestige, had there been any onlookers. He flung on his best white flannel trousers, and a snowy short-sleeved shirt, and white socks, and freshly chalked white shoes that he had been saving for the homeward journey. He hastily combed his few strands of hair, crouching to see his image in the tilted mirror of the cheap dresser, and ran out of the room, snatching his green sun glasses from a shelf as he passed through the door.

Mrs. Gloster, a thin, small, bright-eyed lady wearing a smart gray traveling suit, sat in a wicker armchair on the veranda, smoking a cigarette and tapping her foot. Each year it was her practice to drive up to camp and take her children home by automobile to save them from the dirty, stuffy train ride which all the other children endured. She dropped the cigarette and crushed it with her toe as the camp owner approached.

"My dear Mrs. Gloster, how do you manage to keep so young? I declare you look more like one of my counselors than the mother of five wonderful children."

Mrs. Gloster beamed. Her husband, immersed in the textile trade, paid her a huge allowance but no compliments.

"You look splendid yourself, Mr. Gauss. I can't understand how the responsibility for so many children agrees with you, but evidently it does. May I see Raymond now?" (Raymond was Daisy's name in the outside world.)

Mr. Gauss peeked apprehensively through a window of the veranda. The wall clock in the camp office read four-twenty.

"Ah—wouldn't you like to see the girls first? They're right here, you know. Then a little later—perhaps after dinner—a visit to the boys' camp?"

The wealthy lady made no objection. Mr. Gauss summoned a passing girl counselor and sent her flying to call the Gloster girls. Four squealing, giggling children came tumbling up the veranda steps a few minutes later. Unluckily for Mr. Gauss, all they could talk about was Raymond's comic appearance as the camp doctor. Poor Daisy had thrown heart and soul into the impersonation, which gave him something to do at last, and had caused a near riot of hilarity in the girls' camp by bursting in on the lunch hour brandishing a stethoscope and a hypodermic needle, and trying to inoculate everyone against "Gauss-itis." This description of her son in such fettle doubled Mrs. Gloster's anxiety to see him at once.

"Oh, it must be a perfect scream. Do let's go down the hill now, Mr. Gauss," she said.

Mr. Gauss looked through the window again. Twenty minutes to five.

"I'll be delighted, of course, to escort you down to the boys' camp. Just let's have a nice refreshing cup of tea first. You've been through a long, hot drive—"

"Better hurry, Ma," broke in one of the girls. "Campers' Day is over five o'clock."

The mother said, "Why, Mr. Gauss, let's just skip the tea," but Mr. Gauss was already dancing backward through the entrance.

"It won't take a minute, not a minute," he insisted archly, wagging a finger at her as he disappeared. Nevertheless, he hoped it would take twenty. He told the cook, a weary, gray-haired woman in a white smock, to serve tea for two on the veranda, and came outside again, confident of the usual delay of a quarter of an hour. But it happened that the cook was brewing some for herself, and, impatient at the interruption, hurried to bring out the tea so as to be able to drink her own at leisure. Mr. Gauss was flabbergasted to see a tray, tea service for two, and the cook emerge from the door some forty seconds after himself. The mother gulped her tea in a few moments and set down her cup and saucer with a meaningful clink. Mr. Gauss dawdled. Mrs. Gloster curtly sent her daughters scrampering off to their bungalows. She stood, straightened her skirt, pulled in her belt, and walked to the steps of the veranda. Still Mr. Gauss sipped and sipped. And well he might. It lacked twelve minutes to five.

"You know," he sighed, "I wonder sometimes whether lovely ladies of social position like yourself, Mrs. Gloster, don't miss some of the quiet pleasures of life as you dash through the mad whirl. Now, a cup of tea, with me, is a ritual."

"Mr. Gauss, you may teach manners to my children,

but I'm a little old for correction. Your ritual is taking an awfully long time."

The camp owner perceived that he had blundered. He clattered the cup and saucer to the table and rose. "My dear Mrs. Gloster, by all means let us go. I had no idea—really, you quite misunderstood me. I wish all our parents had one-tenth the polish and gracefulness of yourself. If I made an unfortunate choice of language I regret it, but what I meant—" He smoothed the path down the hill with many apologies and blandishments.

The camp was empty of boys, and silent. The slant afternoon sun cast parallel rays between the walls of the bungalows across the deserted gravel street.

"Why, Mr. Gauss, where can the boys be?"

"Ah—down at the waterfront, I believe."

Said the mother with a delighted cry, "Oh, they're ducking Uncle Sandy!" (The girls had told her about it.) "Come, come, we must see that!"

She took the camp owner's arm and dragged him along the path. When they came to the shore, they saw a group of Seniors and Super-seniors marching up the dock, carrying the horizontal limp form of Uncle Sandy high in the air, and chanting,

> *"In the water he must go,*
> *He must go,*
> *He must go.*
> *In the water he must go,*
> *My fair Sandy."*

The rest of the campers lined the beach in disorder, cheering and laughing. Herbie Bookbinder, in green glasses and feather headdress, stood at the end of the dock with folded arms. The Seniors brought Uncle Sandy before him. Yishy cried, "What'll we do with him, Skipper?"

Herbie proclaimed, "Cliff Block, you have appeared on Company Street in clothes too small for you. In the water you must go!"

At once the Seniors grasped the unresisting head counselor by the arms and legs, swung him back and forth twice, then pitched him in. The splash wet them all. The spectators cheered.

Mrs. Gloster clapped her hands. "What fun! I don't see Raymond. I hope he's here." She lifted her voice and called, "Ray-*mond!* Where are you?" This served to turn everybody's eyes on her—and on Mr. Gauss. Raymond answered thinly, from far down the beach, "Here I am, Mother!"

But his cry was ignored. Herbie came striding down the dock shouting, "There's Herbie Bookbinder, men, wearing white flannels before sundown. Grab him!"

The thought of seizing Mr. Gauss was so audacious that the whole camp gasped. But the Seniors, with whoops and howls, came trampling after the fat boy, their steps drumming on the hollow wooden dock. The camp owner quailed, but stood his ground. A few feet from him the boys stopped short, and began fidgeting and murmuring.

"Now, lads," said Mr. Gauss, smiling with all his might, "you know an old Manitou tradition excludes the real Skipper from Campers' Day. I wish I could join the fun, but as you see I'm here with a lady, and I'm afraid I can't join you."

Mrs. Gloster exclaimed quickly, "Oh, please don't let *me* interfere," and fell away from his side several paces, leaving him quite alone, and raising an uneasy laugh among the boys.

"Grab him, I say!" shouted Herbie. But no one moved toward the camp owner.

"Now, Herbie," said Mr. Gauss, "you've had your fun and you've done very well, I understand. And it's five o'clock, so let's have no more of this foolery. Hand me that headdress. You're just Herbie Bookbinder again."

Herbie glanced at his watch, and brandished it for all the larger boys to see.

"It's *three minutes to five,*" he bawled, "and I'm still Mr. Gauss by Mr. Gauss's own rules. And I say throw Herbie Bookbinder in the lake!"

The close-pressed ranks of the Seniors divided as a

smaller figure thrust to the front. It was Ted, his long beak quivering, his birdlike eyes glaring. "Didn't you big lugs hear the Skipper's orders?" he roared. "Come on, let's get him!" He dived for Mr. Gauss's legs.

And Mr. Gauss, in his panicky fear of the water, made a dreadful mistake. He turned and ran.

Instantly he had twenty pursuers. The yellowest hound will chase anything that flees. With yaps and hoots, the Seniors ran after him and laid violent hands on him before he had gone ten yards. In a moment he was struggling in the air, held aloft by a dozen pairs of strong arms.

> *"In the water he must go,*
> *My fair Gussie!"*

chanted his captors.

Alas for symbolic prestige!

Mr. Gauss did not react well in this adversity. As the boys bore him toward the water he squirmed, bucked, and yelled, "Sandy! Sandy! Blow your whistle! Stop them! Put me down, you foolish boys! SAN-DEE!"

To the boys his behavior seemed queer, for they knew nothing of his terror of the water. But in becoming a wriggling victim Mr. Gauss lost any chance he might have had of rescuing himself, and became a simple figure of fun. Uncle Sandy was in a poor position to come to his aid. He was himself clambering up the ladder out of the lake. It is true that he was nearly up on the dock when the bearers of Mr. Gauss were still far from the edge. He might perhaps have jumped forward, dripping as he was, and saved his master by shouting and charging at the group. But strange to tell, as soon as his nearsighted eyes took in what was happening he lost his footing on the ladder—through sheer surprise, he swore a hundred times in after years—and fell back into the water helplessly.

Mr. Gauss entered the most forceful objections to the very last—objections in the form of kicks, punches, shrieks, threats, and an amount of writhing that was re- markable in a man of his years and weight. A few feet from the edge of the dock the boys actually lost their hold on the legs of the white-clad, struggling figure. Mr. Gauss gained temporary footing on the wooden dock and balked like a maddened elephant. But immediately a cluster of boys' arms whisked his feet into the air once more. And with no further ado, omitting the ceremony of swinging, his captors rushed him to the edge and dumped him in.

The camp owner struck the water stomach first with a horrid *splat,* and sank out of sight. He bobbed up again in a few seconds, gurgling, and flailing so furiously that he seemed to have ten arms and legs.

"It's five o'clock, guys! Campers' Day is over!" yelled Herbie, dashing his feather headdress to the dock. "Run like hell!"

All the boys stampeded up the path away from the lake. So quickly did they evacuate that by the time Uncle Sandy hauled his bedraggled, shuddering, choking employer up the ladder, the camp owner had but one spectator of his misery—Mrs. Gloster, who was leaning against a tree, holding her sides in an agony of giggling. Mr. Gauss mechanically picked up the feather headdress from the dock and put it on his head.

"Ye gods, Skipper, what are you doing?" exclaimed Uncle Sandy.

The camp owner looked at him foggily, then snatched the headdress off. He became aware of Mrs. Gloster's laughter, echoing across the water. He smiled and walked down the dock, his shirt clinging, his white flannel trousers making slushy noises with each step. "You see, Mrs. Gloster," he said as he approached the lady, with a gay laugh that was rather horrible to hear, "we do inculcate the democratic spirit at Manitou."

On Company Street there was light, and gladness, and joy, and honor. Herbie Bookbinder and Cliff Block were marched up and down by a select committee of eminent athletes—not including Lennie—with placards around their necks proclaiming that they had received the sublime and ultimate glory of Manitou: in the last hours of the summer, they had been initiated into the Royal Order of Gooferdusters.

25

Going Home

THE GLASS OF the train window was cold against Herbie's forehead as he took his last long look at the hills among which Camp Manitou was hidden. Not only regret kept his eyes fastened on the pleasant scenes he was leaving, but embarrassment, for tears were running down his cheeks. He had quite broken down on the railway platform when Uncle Irish had led both camps in the singing of "Bulldog, Bulldog," as the train appeared around a bend in the distance and came puffing toward them, growing bigger with each puff. The pathos had overwhelmed him, but he had managed to repress the water in his eyes until he could scramble into a seat in the railroad car and turn his face to the window. Now he was giving way freely.

Cliff, who knew his cousin's weakness well enough after years of hearing him snivel in the darkness of movie houses, sat beside him as a screen. Cliff was not moved by the departure. The one thing he regretted in all of Manitou was Clever Sam, and in washing the horse he had expressed his emotion fully. His common sense told him that Clever Sam could find no place in the city; and since the separation was not to be avoided, he saw no sense in crying over it.

The curious part of it was that Herbie had not even the horse to regret. He was thoroughly, unreservedly happy at quitting Mr. Gauss's camp. But that was not the point. This was a parting, and there had been nostalgic music and a puffing train, and Herbie could not deprive himself of the luxury of sentiment. So he sat with his face pressed to the dirty pane, mourning, and enjoying the mourning all the more because he had nothing whatever to mourn for.

This is thought to be a feminine trait but you will find it among boys and men, too, disguised as good-natured brusqueness in those less volatile than Herbie. All it requires is an active imagination which can wring out of any farewell the sense that it is a little bit of death, and can overlook, for the moment, the fact that some parts of life are much better dead and done with. You will see prep-school lads misty-eyed at leaving institutions where they have been wretched, and a clerk sniffling to write his last entry in the ledger of an office where he has been hardly more than a dog. It is folly, but a private, pleasant little folly. There is this much harm in it, however: it creates delusions. Herbie was persuaded now that he had always loved Manitou, and that he couldn't wait to return. There were many children on the train succumbing to the same foolishness. The matter-of-fact ones like Cliff were a minority. Do you know, a few seats away poor Ted also had his face to the window? There will always be summer camps, so long as the owners have the sagacity to make the children sing the camp song as the homebound train comes into the station.

Herbie was enjoying his grief so much that he was disappointed when it started to wane like the glow from an ice-cream soda, after only a few minutes. He began using devices to work it up and keep it alive, such as humming "Bulldog, Bulldog" and taps dismally to himself, and reviewing every detail of his final hours at camp. It will be remembered that he did no such thing when he was overcome upon leaving his parents two months ago, but was glad to be distracted from his emotion as soon as possible. True sorrow is painful. Sham sorrow compares to it as riding down a roller coaster does to falling off a roof. The thrill is there, but not the cost. Just as a child will yell in terror as the roller coaster dives, and then beg another ride, so sentimentalists like Herbie do their best to keep on weeping when the sadness is synthetic. They do not, of course, know what they are doing. Herbie would have taken his oath that he was in terrible misery.

The pictures he recalled were pathetic enough to keep the waterworks pumping for a while.

After the revenge on Mr. Gauss and the inconceivable grandeur of becoming a Gooferduster, he had wandered down to the deserted lake front to enjoy the last sunset and to think melancholy thoughts. Mindful of a last-minute comparison of sunburns in the bunk before dinner, when he had turned out several shades paler than the others, Herbie sat on a rock by the still water, took off his shirt, and bared his chest to the yellow rays of the descending sun. A year of exposure to such feeble light would not have tanned him one atom, but he felt like a brawny outdoors man in doing it, and economical, too. While others were frittering away these precious last seconds of sunlight, he was using them.

As he sat gazing at the lake and trying to screw his mood up to a sublime level, he perceived something strange. Felicia and Lucille were in a canoe together, paddling slowly around the promontory that hid the girls' dock from view. Canoeing at sunset was a delight usually reserved for counselors off duty, but evidently Aunt Tillie had decided to bestow it on the girls this last evening in order to seal the book of summer with a pleasant memory, for here came several other canoes behind the first, fanning out on the lake this way and that.

"Hi, Fleece! Hi, Lucille!" Herbie called, waving his arms. His voice carried easily over the water. The girls saw him and began paddling vigorously toward him.

The boy was at a loss to understand this new companionship between his sister and his love, for in the tug of war over Lennie they had come to despise each other with feminine vigor. Neither of them had ever admitted that there had been a contest, but it had been a real, bitter struggle all the same. As the canoe drew near he could hear them chatting amiably. The mystery was partly cleared when the canoe grated to a stop on the shore a few feet from him, and Yishy Gabelson stepped out of the bushes to haul the canoe high out of the water and graciously help Felicia alight.

The fact is that a last-minute romance had kindled between his sister and Yishy at the Mardi Gras dance, and it burned the more brightly for the shortness of time left to enjoy it. Felicia's hankering for the younger Lennie, engendered mostly by pique at seeing him drift out of his normal attitude of adoration, had been a degrading, dog-in-the-manger sort of feeling. Yishy was almost three years older than she, perhaps not so handsome as Lennie, but in every other way more suited to her. She had arranged this rendezvous with her new cavalier by an exchange of notes, and had selected Lucille to share her secret. She sensed that the red-haired girl really wanted to shift her affections back to the aggrandized Herbie, and therefore was likely to be discreet. This was a correct guess. The conversation in the canoe consisted of a hundred eloquent ways of expressing loathing for Lennie, and alternate praises of Herbie and the hulking Super-senior. The girls almost loved each other by the time the canoe grounded.

Buttoning on his shirt, Herbie ran to the canoe and took the hand that Lucille shyly extended to him. Yishy and Felicia were already strolling down the beach, holding hands and murmuring.

"Won't they catch you?" said Herbie. "You can't come to the boys' beach."

"It's your sister's idea. What difference does it make now, anyway?"

Herbie remembered with a lifting of the heart that at this time tomorrow all the laws of Gauss would be as dead as the codes of Egypt.

"Well, I'm sure glad I was sittin' here."

"So am I."

He led Lucille to his favorite rock, and they sat side by side. His hand rested over hers. It felt cool and small. The sun was going down in immense splashes of red and gold over the whole sky.

"Herbie, I've been very bad to you."

"Aw, it's O.K."

"I like you a thousand times better'n Lennie."

"I like you a million times better'n anybody—'cept my father an' mother."

These declarations might have seemed to a cold onlooker to be deficient in poetry, but they were musically sweet and thrilling to both sweethearts. A delicious silence ensued, and Herbie, forgetting the guilt and misery of his recent money transactions, felt that the world was an almost unbearably lovely and happy place.

The train, bouncing suddenly as it rounded a curve, cracked Herbie's nose against the window with much force, bringing sincere tears to his eyes to reinforce the pumped-up ones. The lake scene disappeared under the impact of pain and would not come back into his imagination. He tried to recapture the solemn awe of the passing of time which he had felt as he lay on his cot in the darkness listening to the wailing bugle notes of the last taps, but this effort was a failure, too. He was all cried out. Regretfully he passed a handkerchief over his eyes and turned his face back to the crowded, noisy car.

"Say, Herb," said Cliff promptly—he had been waiting for his cousin to pull himself together—"what are you gonna do about the money?"

This was the reality that Herbie had been avoiding with his eyes turned to the romantic past. An ill, ugly feeling came over him. The train was carrying him to face his father. Only a few hours intervened before that dreaded meeting.

"What can I do?"

"Gonna tell your father?"

Herbie slouched and mumbled, "Dunno."

"You shouldn't of let Gauss talk you outta that money."

"I know I shouldn't of."

"Rotten ol' Gauss."

"Aw, why blame him? I shouldn't of stole it, that's all."

"Well, heck, you didn't think it was stealing."

"I was crazy."

The train was speeding through forests and fields, but

the city seemed close to Herbie. He could almost smell asphalt, auto fumes, and the acrid electric air of the subway. He fished a cardboard box out of his pocket and opened it. A little rose-colored lizard looked out at the boys with bulging, steady eyes. The pouch under its throat palpitated.

"He's cursin' you," said Cliff.

"He's cursin' because he's goin' to the city."

"I like the city."

"Why?"

"Oh, I dunno. I just like it. You can play ball when you feel like it, not when some counselor says so, and there's good movies and everythin'."

"Yeah—and school."

"Well, school is pretty awful," Cliff admitted.

The lizard reached up one claw and made a half-hearted attempt to get out of the box. Herbie pushed it back, shut the lid, and returned the box to his pocket.

"He'll be dead when you get home, Herbie."

"Naw, he'll be O.K. I'll put him in a goldfish bowl. I want somethin' to remind me of the country."

Uncle Sandy's whistle blew, loud and out of place in the narrow car.

"All Gooferdusters report to the lounge!"

The cousins rose, self-conscious in the extreme newness of their distinction, and walked down the aisle and through the dusty green curtains into the lounging room. The black leather seats were already filled with Manitou nobility. A few boys were perched on the edge of the metal washbasins. Uncle Sandy leaned against a mirror on the wall, smoking his pipe.

The Gooferdusters consisted of a few of the younger counselors who had once been eminent campers, also all the leading athletes like Yishy, Gooch Lefko, and Lennie, and a few boys like Herbie and Cliff who had won unusual attention in one way or another. For example there was Willie Sutro, who was an Intermediate of the most ordinary sort, except that he came from Toledo, Ohio. Since everybody else in camp was from New York,

Willie enjoyed a sort of geographical glamour that had won him speedy election to the Gooferdusters.

It is impossible to describe how wonderful it was considered at Manitou to be a Gooferduster, and luckily it is not necessary. There is no community, no walk of life, no age group without its Gooferdusters, and every reader knows exactly how fine it is to be in the elect circle, and how sad it is to be out. No matter what they are called—circles, clubs, societies, sororities, or what you please—they are all Gooferdusters, and their virtue lies in this, that they enable a few people to come together and agree solemnly among themselves that they are better than other people. Such is the power of positive assertion, this verdict is usually accepted by the unlucky outsiders. At the last judgment all this shall pass away, and we shall every one of us become Gooferdusters.

Uncle Sandy put away his pipe, drew himself up, and raised his right hand with the two middle fingers bent under the thumb, and the index and little fingers standing up like horns.

"*Sinai,* Gooferdusters," he intoned.

"*Sinai,* Goofermaster," responded the others, imitating his salute.

The head counselor dropped his hand, and with it his priestly attitude, and became casual.

"Now, fellows, you know it's the ancient Gooferduster custom to meet for the last time on the train. The old members tell the new members who were elected this year the great secret—the real meaning of the password 'Sinai.' I suppose you neophytes all think it means the same as Mount Sinai, in the Bible." Uncle Sandy grinned knowingly.

The new members looked abashed, and the old members exchanged glances of superior wisdom.

"Well, it doesn't. It's spelled S-Y-N-Y. Sinai, S-Y-N-Y. . . . And now the Gooferdusters will whisper the real meaning to the neophytes."

Gooch Lefko pulled Herbie toward him by an arm, bent, and enunciated hoarsely in his ear, "S-Y-N-Y. *See You Next Year.* Syny!"

"Syny!" Herbie whispered in return, feeling that this was expected of him. But his heart wasn't in the ritual, and the disclosure of the awful mystery gave him no thrill. Cliff's unpleasant reminder of the stolen money was haunting him.

"O.K., fellows," said Uncle Sandy. "Now, remember, this is a secret that will never be mentioned again until the train ride home next year, on your honor, now. Well, boys, you're the cream of Manitou and it's been a great season, hasn't it? It sure has. So thanks again for your swell co-operation and—SYNY!" He gave the horned salute once more, and all the Gooferdusters responded with the gesture and the password.

Herbie looked around at the cream of Manitou. A week ago he had had no more thought of being included in this high caste than of becoming President. These superior beings who ran, jumped, swam, and threw balls so well were the giants of the earth, and he was of the stunted herd. Now, in their city clothes, crowded into this lounge, they looked very much like a group of trolley-car riders after school hours. Once off the grounds of Manitou, the glitter of the Gooferdusters was fading remarkably.

Uncle Sandy paused in stepping through the curtains and said, "You Gooferdusters have exclusive use of the lounge for the next quarter hour. Then break it up." He went out. One of the counselors offered cigarettes around; two of the Super-seniors accepted them and puffed awkwardly. The athletes began talking about the Senior girls in sniggering tones. Somebody twitted Yishy about Felicia. He made a sullen answer, and Herbie felt his face grow hot.

"Let's get outta here, Cliff."

The cousins were the first to leave the aristocratic meeting. As they walked down the swaying aisle to their seats, friendly jokes and greetings were thrown at them, for their exploits were fresh in the campers' minds. But Herbie found little pleasure in the popularity. The campers were beginning to look different. He was used to seeing these faces on brown, half-naked bodies. Overdressed, muffled

in voluminous city clothes, choked up with clean collars
and dangling ties, they wore a new aspect. Herbie was not
the only one to sense the change. Throughout the car
conversation had lost the free, bantering tone of summer
days and had become uneasy, bashful, or too loud. The
common fate which had bound the boys was dissolving.
Transition from comradeship to strangeness was taking
place rapidly. Abuse of Mr. Gauss was the last subject
that could bring warmth into the chatter, and even that
once infinite resource was running low, because freedom
was so near.

"I wish to heck this ride was over," said Herbie, dropping into the seat heavily.

"So do I," said Cliff. "Gee, it was such fun comin' out,
too."

Herbie leaned back on the head cushion and dozed. It
was not a refreshing nap, but a sickly half-sleeping, half-
waking condition wherein he dreamed a dozen times of
the stern face of his father listening to his confession.

"Lunch, Herbie."

The boy opened his eyes and saw Uncle Sid standing in
the aisle, holding a wrapped sandwich and a container of
milk toward him. Cliff was already removing the paper
from his sandwich. Herbie took the food and thanked the
counselor. Looking out of the window, he saw by the
landscape that they were much nearer the city. There was
no wilderness any more. Highways with well-tended
shrubbery and groups of houses or entire villages, neat
and civilized, were moving quickly across the view. A
clutching fear killed his appetite. He bit the sandwich
once and laid it aside. He managed to sip most of the
milk, but each swallow was an effort.

Oddly enough, there was nothing for him to fear. Jacob
Bookbinder did not know of his deed, and would surely
give him an affectionate welcome. But Herbie felt the
strongest possible aversion to the prospect of looking his
father in the face. Jumping up from his seat, he walked to
the rear platform of the car and paced back and forth in
the roaring, drafty space, ransacking his brain for a way
out of the trap which was closing on him.

Mingled with the frantic search for an escape was
wonderment at his own criminal foolishness for running
into this dead end. The midnight trip to the city, the
robbery, the triumph of the Ride, all seemed more fantastic, less substantial now than many dreams he could
remember. Could it all have happened? Could he, Herbie
Bookbinder, Class 8B-3, have done these things? He had
nothing to show for them. All had vanished, leaving a
tortured conscience and the certainty that, after all, fifty
dollars had been taken from the safe of the Place—taken
by him. He turned hither and yon like a scared mouse,
alone there on the platform, and beat his forehead with
his fists.

A half hour passed and he returned to his seat, pallid
and gloomy.

"Know what, Cliff?" he said.

"What?" said Cliff, looking up from a tattered copy of
Weird Tales, in which he was happily perusing a narrative
entitled, "Blood-Drinkers of the Sepulcher."

"I figured out what I'm gonna do about the money."

"Oh, what?" said Cliff, laying the magazine aside and
looking at his cousin with interest.

"I'm gonna pay it back," said Herbie dramatically.

"Yeah, but how?"

"I know what yer gonna say. I ain't got the money.
Well, I'm gonna save it. I figure I get about a quarter a
week for candy an' sodas. Well, I don't have to eat 'em,
do I? A quarter a week is thirteen dollars a year. In four
years I'll have fifty-two dollars. Then I'll walk up to my
pop and give him the money an' tell him everything that
happened."

Cliff said at once, "You mean you ain't gonna tell your
father for four years?"

"I just explained to you," said Herbie in exasperation,
"that I wanna punish myself an' pay back the money.
Maybe I can go without movies, too, an' save it up in
three an' a half years. But I wanna pay it back, see? It
don't do no good to tell without payin' it back, does it?"

Cliff was silent.

"Well, whaddya think?" said Herbie, after waiting half a minute.

"Well, it's an easy way out," said his cousin.

Herbie grew very angry. "What's so easy about it?" he snapped. "Goin' without candy or a soda for four years! You call that easy?"

"Yeah, but meantime you don't have to tell your father," said Cliff. "That's what you want, ain't it?"

"O.K., smart guy. Tell me this. What would *you* do if you was me?"

Cliff considered the question. "I dunno. I think maybe I'd just forget the whole thing."

"Aha!" said Herbie with vast sarcasm. "I suppose that ain't an easy way out!"

"Sure. It's a lot easier'n your way. If I was too scared to tell, why should I fool around with skippin' candy an' sodas? That don't make it right."

"But I *am* gonna tell—after four years," said Herbie, almost in a frenzy at Cliff's stupidity.

"O.K., Herbie. If you think yer doin' right, maybe you are. I don't know nothin'. Me, I'd either tell or shut up, that's all."

"Honest, Cliff, if you can't understand that what I'm doin' is right you're dumb. Just plain, thick dumb. Dumb!"

"I never said I was as smart as you," Cliff answered without rancor.

"You make me sore. 'Scuse me, I'm gonna sit somewheres else."

Herbie rose, stalked to a narrow empty half seat in the back of the car, pushed a tennis racket off it, and sat, fuming at the denseness of his cousin. The scheme he had evolved seemed to him to have every conceivable merit. It was noble. It was self-sacrificing. It required four years of spectacular saintliness. And it spared him the distressing necessity of confessing the robbery an hour from now. If Cliff had said aloud what both boys knew in their hearts—that Herbie would gradually forget about the four-year plan once the first meeting with his father was safely passed—Herbie could have shouted him down. As it was Cliff had spoiled the charm of the scheme, leaving Herbie to wrestle with the question and arrive at no conclusion. At this hour Herbie almost hated his cousin. He did not speak to him during the rest of the ride.

The scenery changed to small, scattered suburbs, then to large, closely settled ones. Apartment houses, those brick hives that indicate the presence of city dwellers as surely as wigwams indicate Indians, began to fly past in increasing numbers. Herbie's spirits sank lower and lower. Soon he was gazing at a succession of Bronx back yards. The scenery began to appear familiar indeed, and he realized something he had overlooked on the journey outward, being then distracted by Uncle Sandy's speech— this train ran along the "creek," along the very track he and Cliff had crossed on the day they had encountered the two ragged creek gangsters with their bottles of minnows. He looked sharp, and caught a glimpse of the Place, with the faded red and white sign painted across the top of its long side, "Bronx River Ice Company." Then the train dived into the tunnel to go under the East River, the same tunnel out of which the freight cars had emerged on that memorable day to cut off the cousins' retreat from the brigands.

It was exceedingly strange to have the two worlds of Manitou and the Bronx collide. Vivid memories revived of his eavesdropping on the business meeting, and his discovery of the combination of the safe. Uncle Sandy began shouting orders about leaving the train, but Herbie heard them vaguely through a swarm of memories and regrets. The scene of the eavesdropping arose in his mind as though it were happening outside the black window before his eyes. He could see his father turning the dial of the safe, hear him saying with sarcastic bitterness, "You'll be interested to know, Mr. Powers, that the combination is my son Herbie's birthday, 1-14-17. I gave him that little honor because with his small hands he smeared the plaster for the cornerstone when he was three years old. . . ."

The train slowed. Campers began tumbling over each other, reaching for parcels, putting on coats, shaking

hands, exchanging last-minute gifts and jokes, retrieving
books, rackets, bats, banners, crudely carved wooden
canes and dishes, strips of white birch bark, footballs,
basketballs, volley balls, baseballs, tennis balls, and all
the other debris of summer. Uncle Irish started up "Bulldog, Bulldog," but it went mighty dismally, a few discord-
ant voices chiming in with his dogged bellowing while the
others were raised in impudent chatter or in more impudent jeers. Uncle Sandy blew his whistle and started to
yell a last order, but at the same moment the train came
into the lighted platform with jerks, crashes, and hisses,
and nobody heard what he said. The cars were still moving slightly when a couple of the more daring boys opened
the doors and leaped out with hurrahs. Uncle Sandy
galloped after them. The train stopped. Boys came froth-
ing out of one car and girls out of another. A cordon of
counselors hurriedly lined up and shunted the rejoicing
mob through the gate into a roped-off area of the huge
Terminal concourse, where the sign

MANITOU

hung again as it had hung two eternal months ago. Eager-
eyed parents crowded against the ropes, and greetings and
cries tore the air as the children appeared.

There was one boy who neither rejoiced nor was eager
as he was carried along in the tumultuous rush from the
train. Herbie scanned the ranks of parents and could find
neither of the familiar faces he longed, yet dreaded to
see. One event he noticed which startled him. It was Mr.
Gauss being embraced directly under the banner by a big
blond-haired, black-browed woman of middle age, who
wore a silver-fox cape around her shoulders, though the
weather was warm, with a purple orchid pinned to the
fur. She hugged Mr. Gauss, who was half a head shorter
than she, with one hand. With the other she held a tall,
pale girl of about thirteen by the elbow. Herbie had heard
legends about Mrs. Gauss from Ted. She had stayed at
Manitou during the first two summers, and caused mass

resignations of the girl counselors during both seasons; and since that time had gone to California each summer to visit her parents, taking her daughter Flora with her. There were legends about Flora, too; legends not unlike those that have sprung up around the shadowy figure of Judas Iscariot. Nevertheless, it was clear to see that both mother and daughter were human beings. It seemed most odd to Herbie that Mr. Gauss should possess such natural ties. The camp owner had a monolithic grandeur in the eyes of the boy. He had become one of the seven wonders of the world, a colossus of evil, and it detracted much from his stature that he had a real wife and child. Nevertheless, there were the females. Herbie never felt the same way about Mr. Gauss after this moment. He was only a man, after all. Looking at the brawny, flamboyant Mrs. Gauss and the pale, nervous daughter, Herbie dimly sensed that it was even possible that Mr. Gauss, like all the boys who hated him, could suffer.

"Herbie! Herbie! Here we are, over here!" It was his mother's voice, cutting through the noise of fourscore other reunions. Herbie turned and spied a lady's dowdy brown hat which he knew at the back of the crowd, and a hand waving in a familiar way above the hat. He plunged toward these symbols of home. Then came a jumble of kissing, hugging, and excited greetings with both his parents, and in the turmoil he hugged and kissed Felicia, too, though he had seen her on the platform a few minutes ago. To repeated inquiries of the mother the children protested that they felt swell and had had a swell time and everything was swell. The family walked out of the Terminal to the automobile, Mrs. Bookbinder plying Herbie with questions at every step about his great last-minute glory at camp. She listened to his account with greedy happiness. As he spoke Herbie often glanced sideways at his father. Jacob Bookbinder looked older and more tired than Herbie remembered him, and after the first greetings he paid little attention to the children, walking beside them in a silent study.

When they reached the car and his father unlocked the door, Herbie could resist no longer. He broke off his narrative to his mother and said, "How's everything at the Place, Pop?"

Mr. Bookbinder paused with his hand on the lock. He looked at the boy, compressed his lips, and smiled wryly over his son's head at the mother. Then he opened the door and climbed into the automobile.

Herbie turned to his mother in wonderment. She patted him on the back and said with a forced grin, "Come, come, get into the car."

Silently the children and Mrs. Bookbinder entered the automobile, and silently the father started up the motor and began driving through the thick traffic.

"But what about the Place?" said Herbie, in a sudden chill of fear that ran to his fingers and toes.

"Papa has sold the Place," said Mrs. Bookbinder.

26

The Truth Will Out

AFTER THIS SHOCKING announcement, the drive to the Bronx was grim. Mr. and Mrs. Bookbinder did not speak. Felicia, after a flutter of astonishment, looked dreamily out of the window at the traffic, the stony streets, and the high dirty buildings, and bethought her of the manly figure of Yishy Gabelson. Herbie's thoughts were in turmoil; he longed to know more, but dreaded to ask.

"Why is Papa selling the Place, Mama?" the boy inquired after a long silence, trying to sound very young and innocent.

"Well, Herbie, there was a robbery at the Place."

"Oh," said Herbie with wide eyes, "and did the robbers steal all the money and that's why we have to sell it?"

Mrs. Bookbinder shook her head gently at her son's childishness. "No, my boy, they didn't take much money. But they took certain very important papers, and without them—well, Papa knows what he's doing. It'll all be for the best."

Herbie immediately recalled the wrangle of Krieger and Powers, on the night of his expedition, over the box marked "J.B." containing the blue memorandum.

"When—when did Papa sell the Place?"

"It was decided yesterday. Thursday the men are coming to our house to sign all the contracts."

Mr. Bookbinder broke his silence to observe with rough sarcasm, "Tell the boy the terms of the settlement, and what my salary will be, and everything else. Why must you talk to the children about it at all?"

"Herbie is our boy. Naturally he's interested," retorted the mother, with unusual spirit. "I think it's fine that he shows an intelligent interest."

"Papa," said Herbie timidly, "what'll happen to the crooks if they catch them?"

"They should be burned or hanged!" shouted his father, honking his horn furiously at a truck that suddenly lurched out of a side street in front of them. "But the least they'll get is ten years in prison, I hope."

"What if they were kids?"

His father threw a swift keen glance at the boy on the seat behind him, and turned his eyes back to the street. "Kids? Kids rob the Place? What kids?"

"Well, you know about—about the creek gang," Herbie stammered. "They got pistols an' knives an' I bet burglar tools—an' they hang around near the Place—"

"Grandma stories!" said his father.

"But if it was kids," Herbie persisted, with a feeling that he was stretching his luck to pursue the topic, "would they go to jail for ten years, too?"

"If they were young kids they'd go to reform school. That's the same as prison. But this robbery wasn't done by kids," said Jacob Bookbinder curtly.

"You know, Jake, maybe Herbie has hit on something," said the mother. "That would explain a silly thing

like taking the box with the blue paper and leaving most
of the cash. Who but kids would—"

"What are you now, a policewoman? The police say
definitely it was done by two men. What would kids be
doing there three o'clock in the morning? How could kids
break into a safe?"

Felicia said, "It could have been young fellows fifteen
or sixteen. I know one who could easily stay up all
night—and strong enough to break open a safe with his
bare hands, almost."

"I suppose you mean Yishy Gabelson," said Herbie.

"Never mind who I mean," Felicia answered, redden-
ing with pleasure at hearing the ineffable name spoken
aloud.

"Do me a favor, all of you, and stop talking about the
robbery and the Place," said the father.

Conversation languished. Mrs. Bookbinder tried to start
the topic of camp life once more, but both her children
gave short, absent-minded answers to her questions. She
desisted after a while. The family finished the ride in
somber quiet.

As soon as they came home, Herbie rushed to the
telephone in the kitchen while the rest of the family went
to the bedrooms. He spoke in a near-whisper.

"Intervale 6465. . . . Hello, Cliff? This is Herbie. Hey,
I'm sorry I got sore on the train. . . . Well, O.K., thanks,
Cliff. . . . Listen, how about doing me a favor? Can you
meet me over in front of Lennie's house in fifteen minutes? . . . Yeah. It's important, Cliff." He lowered his
voice so that he just breathed the next words. "It's about
the money. . . . O.K. So long."

Herbie tiptoed out of the kitchen and softly opened the
front door.

"Where do you think you're going?"

The classic challenge of mothers rang out clear. Herbie
did not have one foot outside, which would have justified
a quick escape on the pretense of not having heard the
question. He was fairly halted. His mother stood in the
hallway, regarding him mistrustfully.

"I'm just goin' over to Lennie's for a minute."

"To Lennie's? You're home two minutes and you're ready to run out! Aren't you glad to be home?"

"Sure. It's great to be home. It's swell, Mom. Only Lennie has something of mine I wanna get. I'll be right back." He risked a dive through the doorway and got away successfully.

Lennie lived on Homer Avenue two blocks further away from the school, in an apartment house of the same size, shape, age, and dinginess as the Bookbinder abode. Herbie ran the two blocks and arrived perspiring and blowing. Cliff was not there. The fat boy paced back and forth before the entrance. Two minutes later Cliff came in sight around the corner, and Herbie scampered to meet him.

"Holy smoke, what took you so long? Listen—" Herbie breathlessly summarized the news about the Place. Cliff was thunderstruck.

"Gosh, Herb, it's all our fault. On accounta us your father's gonna sell the Place!"

"I know," said Herbie despairingly. "Come on, now!" He pulled his cousin by the hand into the building and skipped up the stairs.

"What do we do here?" Cliff panted as he followed him.

"First let's see who's home."

They trampled up to the third landing and Herbie rang a bell. In a moment the door was opened by Lennie. The athlete scowled when he saw who his visitors were.

"Whadda you guys want?"

"Aw, we're lonesome for camp," said Herbie. "We were walkin' by and figured we'd come up an' talk about good old Manitou."

Lennie's expression became much pleasanter and he made way for the cousins to enter.

"Boy, you're lonesome, too, are you?" he said. "I'm about ready to bust out an' cry. Go on into the parlor." He followed the others, adding, "When I think I gotta live a whole winter in this dump! Boy, remember them ball fields an' that lake? I wish camp was all year round."

"Me, too," said Herbie. He looked around inquisitively

at the Krieger home, where he was an infrequent visitor. It much resembled his own in dimensions and furnishings, except that clothing, magazines, and newspapers were scattered about, and dust lay in films on tables and chair arms. (Mrs. Bookbinder never tolerated such details, and never failed to refer to them scornfully when the Krieger establishment was mentioned.)

"Your folks home, Lennie?" said Cliff.

"Naw. My mother brought me home an' went right out shoppin'. Herb, you know about the robbery an' about the Place being sold?"

"Yeah, ain't that terrible?" said Herbie.

"I dunno. My mother says the robbers only got fifty bucks. An' she says we're gettin' a terrific lot o' money for the Place, an' it's a good thing we're sellin' it. Hey, whaddya think we're gettin'? Five million dollars?"

"Nearer ten million," said Herbie. "That's a mighty big place."

"It sure is. Say, we'll be rich, Herb. When our fathers die we can own speedboats an' live in Florida, an' all that stuff. Boy, that's what I want, a speedboat."

"That's a heck of a thing to say," put in Cliff. "You want your father to die?"

"Don't be a sap," Lennie said angrily. "But nobody don't live forever, do they? Yer just sore 'cause you ain't in on this dough like Herb an' me."

"All right, don't you guys start fightin' again," said Herbie. He added craftily, "Unless you wanna do an Indian leg wrestle or somethin'. Bet Cliff can take you, Lennie."

"Bet he can't!"

Lennie still resented the beating he had received from Cliff. He knew that his opponent had won with the abnormal strength of fury, and believed that in an unemotional state Cliff was no match for him. "Come on, Cliff, lay down," he urged. "Two out of three, Indian leg wrestle."

Cliff threw a questioning look at his cousin and understood that this was what Herbie wanted. "Well, O.K.," he said, reclining in the middle of the floor. "But no bets,

Herbie. This guy was the best Indian leg wrestler in camp, pretty near."

"Hey, Lennie, I'm gonna get a glass of water." Herbie rose from his chair as Lennie eagerly dropped to the floor beside his erstwhile conqueror.

"Sure, go ahead," said the athlete. As Herbie left the room the wrestlers were raising and dropping opposed legs in the traditional manner and counting, "One, two . . ."

Herbie prowled through the apartment, looking under beds, and in closets, ransacking drawers, and climbing up to examine shelves. From the parlor came the noises and grunts of combat. He searched for perhaps five minutes, then all at once discontinued his quest and returned to the parlor. The two boys stood toe to toe, flushed and breathing hard, locked in a hand wrestle. As Herbie entered, Lennie pulled Cliff sharply to one side and threw him to the floor. He laughed triumphantly and said to Herbie, "How about that? Three outta three leg wrestle, an' three outta three hand wrestle!"

"I ain't no good at that stuff, I guess," said Cliff goodnaturedly, picking himself up.

"You're really great, Lennie," said Herbie. "Hey, come on, Cliff, we better get goin'."

"What's your hurry?" said Lennie, feeling extremely pleased with life. "Stick around. There's some jello in the icebox. We can have some fun."

"Naw, thanks, they're waitin' for me at home," said Herbie. "We were just passin' by."

He took Cliff by the arm and walked out of the room. Lennie went with them to the door.

"Well, come around again. It's pretty dead here after camp."

"We sure will, Lennie," said Herbie. As the cousins walked down the stairs, Lennie shouted after them, "So long, Herb the millionaire!"

"So long, Speedboat Lennie!" Herbie called back. They heard the athlete laugh and close the door.

"Well, whadja find, Herbie?" exclaimed Cliff.

"*It's there, Cliff*. That box marked 'J.B.' is there in a closet."

Cliff whistled. The boys went out to the street and walked in the direction of Herbie's home. The fat boy's face was pale and his brows knitted.

"Cliff, my father said if kids done the robbery they go to reform school for ten years. Reform school is a prison for kids."

"Yeah, but if we *confess* we done it, do we still go to reform school?" said Cliff, looking as worried as his cousin.

"Why not? The police are lookin' for us, Cliff. They think we were two big guys. I dunno, maybe if we tell we only get five years."

"Herb, I'll do whatever you say."

They were approaching Mr. Borowsky's candy store. Herbie fished two dimes out of his pocket.

"I don't figure they got fraps in reform school," he observed, with a laugh of theatrical bravado. "Wanna join me in a last frap?"

Cliff gasped, "You gonna tell?"

"I ain't gonna tell about you. All you done was help me, anyhow. I'm gonna say I done it myself."

"O.K., Herb. That's swell of you."

Herbie was slightly disappointed in Cliff's answer. He had expected some sort of argument, a heroic insistence on sharing the punishment, but none was forthcoming. Cliff believed that Herbie should own up, and also felt that the robbery was entirely his cousin's responsibility. So he approved gratefully of Herbie's decision.

The boys ate their fraps without a word. Herbie assumed an expression of magnificent mournfulness, in imitation of Robin Hood just prior to his hanging, as played by Douglas Fairbanks. Now that the resolve was taken he felt a martyr. He even looked forward to reform school with a little curiosity and excitement. A vision of vast barred steel gates closing on him, not to be opened for five years, came into his mind, pathetic and thrilling. It was a fall, but a tremendous, showy fall. He would write constantly to his family and to Lucille. She would wait for him. He would emerge in five years and proceed to become a great man: a general or a Senator. He would show the world how Herbie Bookbinder could rise above reform school!

"Ain't no use scrapin' that dish any more, Herb," said Cliff. "It's dry."

Herbie realized that his spoon had been rasping futilely in the shallow tin dish while he had been lost in dreams.

"O.K. Here we go." He stood up and walked out of the candy store. His steps were not sprightly.

"Want me to come with you?" said Cliff.

"It don't matter," said the self-condemned boy. He felt the same sense of unreality creeping over him that he had experienced on the moonlit night when he and Cliff had mounted rickety old Clever Sam to start their journey to New York.

"Well, I won't come then," said Cliff.

"Guess I'd rather be alone, at that," Herbie remarked absently.

Cliff held out his hand. "Good luck, Herbie," he said. "Maybe it'll all come out O.K."

The fat boy clasped his cousin's palm. This was the first time the boys had shaken hands in the memory of either; they were too close for such a gesture, ordinarily. It made them both self-conscious.

"So long, pal," said Herbie. "I ain't afraid. Whatever happens, I'll face it. Don't you worry about old Herbie. I can take my medicine. Thanks for helpin' me an' everything. So long, pal."

He wanted to say "pard," which seemed to belong with the rest of this speech, but he felt the word would sound odd amid the stones and bricks of Homer Avenue, so he compromised on "pal." Cliff was not at all as good as Herbie at improvising dramatic dialogue. He answered, "Yeah. Well, g'bye," dropped his cousin's hand, and walked down the avenue, hastening a little in embarrassment.

Aflame with virtue and determination, Herbie scampered up the stairs to the Bookbinder apartment. He came upon his father and mother in the parlor, deep in a financial discussion, with ledgers, notebooks, yellow bank

statements, and impressive engraved certificates spread
around them on the floor and furniture. His father was
writing in a notebook propped on his knees. As the boy
entered he looked up.

"Well?" he said. "We're busy."

One glance at his parent's deep-lined, gray, unhappy
face, and Herbie's resolution burned blue and flickered
out. "Uh, sorry, Pa," he said. "I was gonna bang around
on the piano. 'Scuse me." He sneaked from the room.

That night Cliff telephoned him to ascertain whether he
was on his way to reform school. Herbie said with some
shame that he "hadn't had a chance yet" to make his
confession. The next night, and the next after that, he was
forced to give the same report to his wondering cousin. It
was not true, of course; he had dozens of chances. But the
grim aspect of his father scared him off each time he
nerved himself to approach.

Thursday came, and Thursday afternoon, and Herbie
had not yet taken his medicine, and Jacob Bookbinder
was still in the dark. The father, dressed in his best
clothes, was pacing back and forth in the parlor, pausing
now and again to thump miserable discords on the piano.
His son stood in the dining room, contemplating a table
spread for tea and laden with pastries and layer cakes. He
was not hungry. His gaze was far away. He was, in fact,
trying to persuade himself that perhaps it would be a good
thing if the Place were sold for five million dollars, after
all; that perhaps it would be wrong of him to interfere at
this late hour. He was very nearly convinced, too.

His mother came in. She wore a big green apron over
the black silk dress reserved for occasions of great pomp.
Her face looked much less faded than usual, and the
double string of amber beads, unmistakable sign of stirring events, dangled over the apron.

"All right, you can forget about helping yourself. We're
having important company in a minute. Go on downstairs
and play for an hour."

"Ma, is the company comin' about buyin' the
Place?"

A bark from Mr. Bookbinder in the parlor. "Tell that

boy to get out of the house!" And a crash of a fist's breadth of notes on the piano.

Mrs. Bookbinder looked anxiously at Herbie. "You heard Papa. Run along."

"Where's Felicia?" With the fateful moment at hand, Herbie suddenly wanted to spar for a few more seconds.

"She's at Emily's. Go, I say. This is no time for you to be in the house."

Herbie slowly walked down the hallway to the outside door. He put his hand on the knob. Then he turned and just as slowly walked into the parlor.

"Pa."

His father was looking out of the window. He whirled at the sound of Herbie's voice.

"Will you go downstairs, boy?"

"Pa, are you looking for a green tin box marked 'J.B.'?"

The father stared at him in stupefaction. Then he ran at the boy and gripped his shoulders brutally.

"What are you talking about? Yes, I'm looking for such a box. It was stolen."

Herbie's shoulders were full of pain. He was more frightened than he had ever been in his life. But he caught his breath and said, "I saw it Monday in Mr. Krieger's house. In a bedroom closet. Under a pile of old shoes. I figured it would be there because I myself—"

"Are you crazy, boy? Do you know what you're saying?"

The doorbell rang. Father and son heard the door opened at once, and the voice of Mrs. Bookbinder in words of welcome, and several men's voices. The father seized Herbie's right hand and dragged him into the dining room. Mrs. Bookbinder came in with Powers, Krieger, and the lawyer Glass. There was also a tall, broad-shouldered, bald stranger. He had pouchy little eyes, and wore stiff dark clothes. Mr. Glass, who was holding a thick brief case under one arm, said as they entered, "Mr. Burlingame, I'd like you to meet Mr. Bookbinder, the manager of Bronx River."

The stranger put out his hand and said with a cold smile, "Delighted. You have a reputation in the industry."

Bookbinder took the extended hand and shook it. His eyes were on his partner. Krieger avoided the glance.

"If you gentlemen will excuse me for a moment, I'd like to have a word alone in the next room with Mr. Krieger."

Powers, whose face was strained and lined, quickly said, "Mr. Bookbinder, I hope there's nothing to be said now that can't be said in front of all of us. We've made a deal with Mr. Burlingame, and it's impossible to go back on it. The present occasion is a formality. For all intents and purposes Bronx River is now the property of Mr. Burlingame, you know."

"All right," said Jacob Bookbinder calmly. But Herbie knew he was not calm, for he was crushing the boy's hand, and trembling a little.

"Krieger, have you got the box with the blue paper?"

Krieger looked at him agape. No words issued from the open mouth.

"What on earth do you mean by such a question?" Powers said hurriedly. "You know perfectly well the box was stolen."

"My boy Herbie here says he saw the box in a closet in Krieger's home."

There was a confusion of exclamations by everyone in the room.

MR. POWERS:	*"He's crazy. Let's get on with our business."*
MRS. BOOKBINDER:	*"Herbie, I told you to go downstairs."*
MR. KRIEGER:	*"Haybie mistake. I got a box, nothing like blue paper box."*
LAWYER GLASS:	*"What does this boy know about the whole business, anyway?"*
HERBIE:	*"That's right. I did see it."*

The above remarks came all at once in loud tones, and nobody understood anybody else.

Mr. Burlingame's voice emerged, deep and irritated, from the babble. "See here, gentlemen, I had the clear assurance of all of you yesterday that the matter of the so-called blue paper had been amicably settled, and that all of you wanted to sell. If there is still a shadow of doubt on this transaction, why, I—"

"There's no doubt whatever," said Powers. "Mr. Glass, let's get on with the contracts, shall we? The blue paper is stolen and gone."

"It ain't stolen," Herbie insisted loudly.

All the adults stared at him now.

"How do you know so much, young man?" said the lawyer impatiently.

"*Because I stole the fifty dollars from the Place myself. And I didn't take no box!*"

Now the fat was in the fire. In the hubbub of questions and cries, Mrs. Bookbinder ran to the boy's side and put her arm around him.

Haltingly at first, and then with a freer flow as the grownups grew silent with amazement, Herbie told the story of his midnight adventure. He confessed to the eavesdropping that had given him the idea. He explained his motive of getting money to build the Ride. He emphasized that he had intended to return the money, describing the note he had written but failed to leave, and he narrated the treachery of Mr. Gauss, without trying to excuse himself on that account. He omitted the parts played by Cliff and Clever Sam, and he did not mention the scene between Krieger and Powers which he had witnessed from the refrigeration vault. It took him many minutes to unburden himself. Midway, his father dropped his perspiring hand and leaned with both elbows behind him on the buffet, regarding his son with a mixture of perplexity and anger which did not increase the boy's ease. The others listened in various attitudes of astonishment, now and then stopping the boy with brief questions. Lawyer Glass did most of the questioning. At last Herbie carried his confession to the end, concluding breathlessly, "So that's how I done it, an' I'm glad I told, even if I do hafta go to reform school now. *But I didn't take no box."*

Mrs. Bookbinder, eyes wet and face flushed, pulled him close against her side and said, "You won't have to go to reform school."

The men looked at each other wonderingly.

Powers spoke first. "I think the boy has imagined the whole thing. He supposes he's being a hero. It's an utterly incredible story."

Jacob Bookbinder had not taken his eyes off his son. Now he said in a hoarse, harsh voice, "Herbie, you have been the laziest boy in the Bronx all your life. If you did all those crazy things, what did you do them for?"

Herbie glanced at the lawyer, blushed, and transferred his gaze to the floor.

"Come, come, boy," said Mr. Glass, "nobody will hurt you if you speak the truth—speak the truth. Why did you do all this?"

Still no answer.

"Tell us, Herbie, please," said his mother softly. "You must tell us."

Herbie saw no way out. Scarlet-faced, he blurted, "All right. I wanted to make a hit with Lucille Glass."

All the grownups except Powers burst out laughing. It may seem surprising that they did so at such a grim time, but that is how people are. Anyone who has attended a funeral knows of the boisterous laughter in the coaches coming from a cemetery. It is a safety-valve action. The hilarity faded quickly, and Jacob Bookbinder said, "Now, if he didn't take the box, the next question is, where is it?"

"When I was hidin' in the ice room," said Herbie, "I seen Mr. Krieger an' Mr. Powers standin' in front o' the open safe, arguin' over it. Mr. Krieger was holdin' the box—"

Krieger interrupted, his voice shrill. "All right, wait, all honest men. I know facts, explain better. Yes, sure I keep box. Protect you, Jake, only protect you. Powers like iron, say burn up paper one two three. Blue paper safe now because I protect—"

"Krieger, you're a damned liar!" shouted Powers, pounding the dining-room table so that the dishes rattled and two éclairs rolled to the floor. Mrs. Bookbinder instinctively dived for the éclairs, exclaiming, "Please, gentlemen, the child, the child!"

"Herbie, go to your room and get undressed," said his father. It was bright and early in the afternoon, and the order boded ill. Herbie started to slink from the room.

Mr. Burlingame ran a flat palm once over his naked pate and picked up his hat from a chair. "Mr. Bookbinder, you have a remarkable son, remarkable. Will you please understand, gentlemen, that Interborough withdraws completely from this negotiation? We don't want to buy Bronx River on any terms. The best of luck to all of you."

Powers jumped in front of him, barring his exit from the dining room, and also preventing the boy from leaving. Herbie fell back into a corner and tried to look invisible.

"Mr. Burlingame, that memorandum of my father's is meaningless. Glass says so, and Sullivan of Guarantee Building and Loan says so. I can prove it in court. This business of the robbery is a silly misunderstanding. You can't withdraw from a closed deal, sir, because of the wild talk of an eleven-year-old boy."

Mr. Burlingame donned his hat and pulled it down firmly. "Bob, the Bronx River property is not wanted without the good will and continued management of Bookbinder, as I told you. And Interborough doesn't buy a property with the slightest question as to title. I knew your father, Bob. He wouldn't have been pleased with this day's work. Kindly excuse me."

Powers stepped aside. Mr. Burlingame went out. The young man's handsome face became greenish-pale. He dropped into a chair, and covered his eyes with one hand, pressing his thumb and finger into the corners.

"Oh, come, Bob," said Mr. Glass, stepping quickly to his side and putting a hand on his shoulder, as the outer door was heard closing. "It's nothing that serious—nothing that serious."

Powers looked up at the rotund lawyer. His shoulders

drooped. Tears stood in his eyes. Herbie had never before seen a man show visible grief. He stared at the scene from his corner between the bureau and the wall.

"Property is property," added the attorney, patting Powers' shoulder. "Property is property. Your interest in Bronx River is still worth fifty thousand, easily."

"Find me a buyer for thirty," said Powers in a choked voice. "Why do you suppose I've been pushing this thing, Louis? I've got to have thirty thousand dollars cash. Oh, God, what a mess!"

The lawyer nodded gravely. He said in tones that Herbie could barely hear, "Bob, is it that Montauk business I advised you against?"

Powers answered with a short nod. Mr. Glass pulled down the corners of his mouth, and looked at Bookbinder.

"What's done is done. How about it?" he said. "Here's your chance to corner all the equity cheaply—all the equity cheaply. Will you buy Bob out for thirty?"

Herbie's father turned his palms outward in the eternal gesture which means "No weapons" among savages and "No funds" among civilized men. The lawyer glanced toward Mr. Krieger, but the partner was looking steadily out of the window, keeping his face hidden from the others.

"Herbie!" said Jacob Bookbinder all at once, as his eyes chanced on his son. The fat boy jumped, and ran for the door. "I told you ten minutes ago to go to your room and get undressed. Now do as I say or—"

But Herbie heard no more. His scuttling little legs had already carried him out of the dining room and into the bedroom, where he closed the door after him.

27

The Truth Often Hurts

A FEW MINUTES later Mrs. Bookbinder came into Herbie's room. She found her son in crisp fresh yellow pajamas, lying face downward on his bed. She sat beside him softly and caressed his shoulder, saying, "What's the matter, Herbie?"

The boy turned over and sat up. He was dry eyed, but his look was despairing.

"Matter? Holy smoke, Mom, that's a heck of a question."

"You won't go to reform school, my boy. Mr. Glass is a big man. He'll go to the police and explain the whole thing. Nothing will happen to you."

"Yeah. Maybe not." Herbie appeared not at all reassured as he drew up his knees, rested his elbows on them, and placed his chin in his hands. "But I stole, didn't I?"

"Herbie, what happened to the note?"

"What note?"

"The note you said you were going to leave in the safe, promising to return the money. Did you really write one, or was that a lie?"

"Sure I wrote it," said Herbie indignantly. "I'd of left it, too, if Mr. Krieger an' Mr. Powers hadn't come back so soon that night. They drunk their coffee awful fast, that's all I gotta say."

"Well, where is it now?"

"I dunno. I had it in my suit in one o' the pockets. I guess maybe it's still there."

Mrs. Bookbinder rose and searched the pockets of his jacket.

"What's this?" she said, pulling out the cardboard box.

"Gosh! I bet he's dead!" Herbie jumped up, took the box, and opened it. The lizard was stirring. He picked up the little pink reptile by its tail and set it on the bed. Frightened by the sudden change, the lizard stood still, its chin-pouch palpitating. Herbie lay beside the creature and studied it. Mrs. Bookbinder, muttering about the things boys brought into the house, went through the pockets of Herbie's trousers. From a back pocket she extracted a crumpled sheet of yellow paper.

"That's it," said Herbie, looking up as he heard the paper crackle. Mrs. Bookbinder unfolded the paper, smoothed it, and read:

WE ARE THECREEK ~~ØET~~ GANG AND 1 OF OUR

GANG NEEDS AN <u>OPERATION</u> THAT COSTS ~~($%)~~ $50

SO WE ARE <u>BORROWING</u> NOT STEALING ~~($%)~~

~~($%)~~ $50 FROM YOUR SAFE.YOU'LL GET THE

$50 BACK BY MAIL NEXT WEEK WITHOUT FAIL SO

DON'T CALL THE POLICE ORNOTHING BECUASE

YOU'LL GET THE ~~(%$)~~ $50 <u>BACK</u>___.WITH

INTEREST MAKING IT ~~$1%~~ $75.

                    the creek gang.'

When the mother had absorbed the contents of this interesting document, she ran to Herbie and interrupted his study of natural history to hug and kiss him.

"God bless you, my boy. You meant well."

"Yeah," said Herbie, enduring the affection without response.

"Why did you sign it the Creek Gang?"

"What was I gonna do?" said Herbie, talking as best he could with his head muffled against his mother's bosom. "Sign my own name? I just wanted Pop to know he was gonna get paid back."

"That's right, of course. It was all that rotten Mr. Gauss's fault. I'll never send you back to that terrible camp."

Herbie broke from her arms just in time to save the lizard from diving over the edge of the bed. He placed the creature carefully in the middle of the bedspread.

"Where's Pop?" he inquired uneasily.

"Still busy with the men." The mother sat on the bed once more.

"Ma, hasn't Pa got thirty thousand dollars to buy out that rotten Mr. Powers?"

"Hush, what business is that of yours? What do you know about money? It'll be healthier for you to keep your nose out of Papa's affairs from now on. . . . You listen to me, I want to talk to you about—"

"But is Mr. Powers still here? What's happening, Ma? Gosh, I wanna know—"

"Mr. Glass is on the telephone in the kitchen, talking to I don't know who. That's none of your affair. What I want to know, Herbie, is—are you really— I don't know what to say. Interested in this Lucille Glass?"

Herbie barely nodded. He stroked the lizard's back with one finger.

"Don't you think you're a little young to be—interested —in girls?"

Another nod, even barer.

"Mind you, I have nothing against Lucille. She's a nice little girl, although she's very spoiled. And I must say I don't see that she's pretty. But I suppose you think she is."

A slight motion of the head, which might be a nod or the bobbing occasioned by a deep breath.

"Well, there's no harm in it. Just so long as you understand that it doesn't mean anything at all, and that you'll both forget all about it in a couple of weeks."

Herbie and the reptile in equal states of immobility.

"You do understand that, don't you?"

Herbie found himself wishing his mother would go to the market, or to the movies, or on any other mission that would require her immediate removal from the room.

"I'm telling you this just for your own good, my boy. Lucille is much too old for you, first of all. When you're sixteen and a half, she'll be sixteen. A boy that age is still a baby. A girl of sixteen can get married. I married Papa when I was seventeen."

Herbie picked up the lizard in his palm and gave him an intense inspection.

"Well, what have you got to say, Herbie?"

The boy said "Mmmm" in a dry tone that conveyed no meaning at all.

"Good," said the mother quickly. "I'm glad you agree with me. You're a sensible boy."

She fell to patting Herbie's hair. He ignored the caresses and concentrated on the lizard. Restored to air and light, the animal had become more lively. It scuttled around in the boy's palm and tried to climb up his curving fingers. Herbie felt sorry for the rosy, gold-spotted creature, which seemed so out of place in the narrow Bronx bedroom. The lizard brought back visions of the bright broad skies of Manitou, and the fields, and the lake, and the mossy rocks along the shore where the boy had captured his living souvenir. How cramped and small the apartment seemed to Herbie, and the street outside the window, too! Everything in the city seemed to have shrunk to half its size during the summer.

"Guess I'll turn you loose in the lots," Herbie said to the lizard. "I shouldn't of brought you here."

The door of the bedroom was thrown open. Mr. Bookbinder stood in the doorway. At once the mother rose and placed herself between him and the boy.

"Where are the men?" she said.

"They've gone. Glass bought out Powers. We have a new partner."

Mrs. Bookbinder was staggered by the development. "Glass!" she ejaculated.

"He was on the telephone fifteen minutes with his wife, explaining the proposition to her. Don't worry, he's a clever man. Thirty thousand for Powers' share! Leave it to a lawyer to smell a bargain."

"And—and the blue paper?"

"Glass accepts it. He's going to draw it up in legal form. He's a gentleman, always was. Powers is out—finished."

The mother pulled herself together and seized on the amazing news as a means to her end. "Well, so it all comes out fine! Congratulations, Jake! What are we waiting for? Let's all go out and celebrate!"

The father's expression changed. "This boy, too?" he said, in a tone that caused Herbie to cower.

"Why not? Look at this letter. He meant well, Papa, all the time. Hasn't he been punished enough, worrying himself sick?"

She held out the Creek Gang note to him. Mr. Bookbinder read it, crumpled it, and threw it into a corner.

"Leave me alone with him."

"Papa, don't hit him too hard! He meant no harm."

"Leave me alone with him."

Herbie quavered from the bed, "Go ahead, leave us alone, Mom."

"Papa, remember he's just a small boy. Remember!"

Reluctantly the mother left the room. Mr. Bookbinder closed the door and proceeded to give Herbie a tolerably warm licking. Starting with miscellaneous cuffs and clouts, he soon organized the task, sat on the bed, turned the boy over his knees, and drubbed his rear resoundingly and long. He said nothing during the operation. Herbie had resolved to "take it like a man," but his resolution waned halfway through the spanking and he ended by taking it like a boy, with wall-shaking howls. Despite the mother's description of him as a small boy, he was pretty big for this sort of thing, and made a cumbersome figure, draped over his father's knees. Mr. Bookbinder managed well enough, however. Mrs. Bookbinder stood outside the door, trembling from head to foot and wincing each time she heard the whack that signaled another contact between palm and posterior. After perhaps two minutes she could bear no more. She burst into the room, wailing, "All right, all right! Must you murder him?"

"Nobody was ever spanked to death yet," panted the father, but he brought the punishment to a close with a crescendo of thwacks. He rolled the yelling boy back on the bed with surprising gentleness, and walked out, saying, "He can get dressed now, if he wants."

Herbie availed himself of this permission immediately. His mother slowed the dressing process by fussing with his clothes, trying to soften the effect of the licking, until the boy said impatiently, "Gosh, Mom, I ain't been crippled. I can still dress myself." Then she was wounded by the ingratitude, and left him alone. She did not understand that her son was rather glad of the beating than otherwise. The guilt feeling had been dusted out of him. Without reasoning closely, he sensed that the reform-school threat was gone. He feared his father's sternness, but he had faith in his justice, and he knew that if prison had loomed Jacob Bookbinder would not have added a whaling to it. The smarting here and there on his anatomy was unpleasant, but it was a welcome substitute for five years behind bars. He cheered up quickly as he dressed.

He was sliding a brilliant yellow and red tie under his collar when he heard his father say in the next room, "Mom, let's eat at Golden's tonight."

"But, Papa, I have a roast."

"You said yourself we ought to celebrate. I think you're right."

A slight pause. Then his mother's voice, somewhat hesitant. "Herbie, too?"

"Of course Herbie, too. We're not going to treat him like a criminal until he's twenty-one, are we?"

Herbie did a caper before the mirror, and sobered instantly as his father came into the room.

"What's taking you so long to dress?"

"I'm done now, Pa." Herbie knotted his tie with blinding speed.

"Let's go for a walk."

"Yes, Pa." Herbie glanced around the room, and picked the lizard off the floor. "Can I drop this guy in the lots? It ain't right to keep him in no apartment."

The father nodded. As his son followed him to the front door Mr. Bookbinder called, "Mom! Get Felicia and meet us at Golden's at six."

"Fine, fine, fine!" Sounds of drawers sliding and closets opening punctuated each "Fine," as Mrs. Bookbinder hurried to reorganize her costume for dinner in public.

Father and son walked a block in silence along Homer Avenue toward the lots.

"Well," said Jacob Bookbinder, as they crossed Cervantes Street, "what did you think of the licking?"

"I deserved it," said Herbie humbly.

"Why?"

" 'Cause I stole."

"But you were going to leave that note that Mom showed me. Didn't that make it all right?"

"I thought it did, but it didn't."

"Why not?"

They began to climb the steep, rough rocks of the lot. Herbie was still struggling with the question when they reached the top. The lot was full of dusty weeds that reached almost to his waist, with scattered patches of hardy autumn wildflowers, blue, yellow, and white. Rocks jutted above the vegetation. The boy gratefully sniffed the strong, sweetish smell of this familiar Bronx greenery. It was not as pretty as a field in the Berkshires, but it was home.

"I dunno, Pa. But the note didn't make it right."

The lizard began wriggling in his palm, as though sensing the nearness of freedom. Herbie stooped and allowed it to run off his hand among the weeds. It was gone immediately.

"So long, Camp Manitou," said Herbie.

"You probably have plenty of fun in these lots, Herbie," said his father.

"Yeah. More fun than anyplace."

The father took his hand and led him to a rock, where they both sat.

"In the old country I spent all my time in the fields when I was a boy. I loved them."

Herbie tried to picture his father as a boy, but it was impossible. Jacob Bookbinder was as fixed in his present appearance, to the boy's mind, as George Washington in the Stuart portrait that hung in the classrooms at school.

The city noises swam up to them in this solitude, softened by distance.

"Tell me what was wrong with that letter, Herbie."

"Well—I was doin' somethin' bad when I stole, see?"

"Yes."

"And I was only *promisin'* to do somethin' good later to make up for it."

The father looked at him as though he were about to smile. It was the first time Herbie had seen a pleasant light in his parent's eye since the arrival from camp. Thus encouraged, he stammered on, "An'—an' the big catch in that was, how did I know *for sure* I was gonna get a chance to do good? Look what happened. Mr. Gauss skunked me."

Jacob Bookbinder nodded. Many lines faded from his worn face as he smiled. "So what emerges, Herbie?"

Herbie had been through these dialogue lessons with his father before. He knew that a pithy summary was expected of him. He wrestled with words a moment, and said, "I guess—I guess it ain't never right to do bad now and figure to do good later on."

His father put his arm around the boy's shoulder, briefly squeezed him, and stood. It was a small gesture, but Herbie felt as though he had been set free.

"Let's go to Golden's," was all his father said.

Indeed, for an eleven-year-old boy, Herbie had not badly stated his lesson. "The end does not justify the means." Considering that the whole world has been trying to learn that lesson since history began, and is now standing in the corner wearing a flaming dunce cap for its failure to do so, perhaps we may say the boy earned some leniency by understanding his error.

The Bookbinder men went on to the rendezvous with their women folk at Golden's. Felicia, brilliant in a new purple dress, silk stockings, pumps, and rouge, took no part in the lively conversation at dinner. For in the afternoon mail she had received a letter composed on the train by Yishy Gabelson, and she remained in an amorous trance. This epistle was guarded from the eyes of her family, of course, but she did condescend to whisper to Herbie that it contained an original poem. The reader will probably be satisfied by the first couplet, and will ask for no more of the composition:

> *Beautiful Felicia,*
> *It was sure swell to meetcha. . . .*

As for Herbie, he had learned more lessons than one in the course of his adventures. He ordered one of Golden's steaks instead of boiled haddock. And he was careful to eat only four pastries.

28

The Reward

ROUND AND ROUND a spiral staircase, up and up in a queer greenish twilight, went a boy, a girl, and another boy, all in Sunday best. Above and below them on the winding staircase the trampling of hundreds of feet sounded. The three familiar faces in this climbing procession were Cliff, Lucille, and Herbie, mounting to the top of the Statue of Liberty by the stairway inside the image. Cliff sprang lightly up the steps, pausing now and again to allow his companions to catch up. Lucille plodded steadily, and Herbie wheezed and sweated behind her, grimly maintaining his self-respect by not allowing the gap between himself and the girl to widen. Just when Herbie's heart, lungs, and legs were advising him in strong terms of their intention to quit this nonsense at once even if he wouldn't, a little diffused daylight appeared overhead, and in a last burst of gladness the three children reached the top of the stairway, on the inside of Liberty's head.

At once they ran to the windows. A handsome spectacle rewarded their toil. The great towers of downtown New York, the endless acres of apartment houses crisscrossed with streets, the green parks, the sparkling, twisting rivers with their webby bridges and fringes of wharfs, all lay spread out before them. The children were awed. Never had they been able to see more than a block or two of the city in any direction. New York is a mammoth cave without a roof, and the walkers in the labyrinths seldom have a notion of its true look.

"Boy, I can see Homer Avenue plain as anything!" Herbie cried.

"Where?" said Cliff.

"Right out there! See, near the river. Good old Homer Avenue!"

"That's Brooklyn."

"How do you know?" said Herbie belligerently.

"This map here by the window. It says what every place is."

The children spent a delightful quarter hour picking out the city's landmarks with the help of the map.

"Gosh," said Herbie at last, staring out at the far bluish hills beyond the streets and buildings, "I bet if we had a telescope we could even see good old Camp Manitou."

"Who wants to?" said Cliff.

"Not me," giggled Lucille. "I hope I never see it again. That place was a jail."

"Aw, I kinda liked camp," said Herbie.

"You couldn't get me to go back to any camp," said Cliff. "I'm cured."

"Bet we're all back there next year," said Herbie.

They became quiet, each child reviewing favored memories. Cliff, after a while, could almost see a ghostly Clever Sam, rusty and bony as ever, cropping phantom grass in the blue air above New York harbor. He felt a peculiar choking sensation. Being unsentimental, he merely wished it would go away, and it did in a moment, together with the vision. Cliff glanced at Herbie and Lucille. They were holding hands.

"I'm kinda tired," he observed quietly. "Guess I'll sit down a while." He withdrew to a bench near by. Neither his cousin nor the girl heeded his going. Lucille looked shyly out of the window. Herbie looked shyly at Lucille.

Finally Herbie said, "Wanna hear somethin' crazy?"

"What?" The girl still regarded the scenery.

"My mother says you're too old for me."

Lucille turned eyes round as silver dollars at him. "But I'm younger'n you."

"Yeah, but she says when you're sixteen you'll be ready to get married, and me, I'll still be a—hm!—a young feller." (The word "baby" caught in his throat.)

"That *is* crazy. I don't wanna get married when I'm sixteen."

"When do you figure on gettin' married?"

"Well, when do you?"

"Aw, not forever, almost."

"Me neither," said Lucille.

"My mom is all wrong, ain't she?"

"Aw, Herbie, you know how mothers are."

"Yeah, but anyway," Herbie persisted despondently, "with you living in Mosholu Parkway an' goin' to a new school I bet we won't see each other any more after a while."

"Oh, Herbie, how can you say that? We'll see each other lots an' lots of times, for always."

An extremely dapper boy with blond wavy hair, dressed in a gray suit and carrying a dark green pork-pie hat with a jaunty feather in the band, came lounging past them.

"Why, hello, Lucille," he said with elaborate wonder, and stopped on the other side of her.

"Hello, Davey. Gee, what are you doing here?"

"Oh, I haven't been here for a few years. Just thought I'd like to see the old statue again."

Herbie examined Davey and found him repulsively good-looking and tall.

"Well, what a surprise," said Lucille. "This here is Herbie Bookbinder, an old friend of mine from my old school, P.S. 50. Herbie, this is Davey Carmichael. He lives on my block."

The boys nodded at each other, Herbie sullenly, Davey with the pure joyous insolence that only exists in childhood by virtue of the advantage of an inch or two or a year or two.

"Where do you live, Herbie?" said the other boy, with a condescending emphasis on "Herbie" that the fat lad resented. Not being able to think of a crushing reply, he muttered, "Homer Avenue."

"Oh," said Davey with raised eyebrows. "The *East* Bronx. Hmm.—Well, see you later, Lucille." He lounged away.

"Did you tell that big sap," Herbie whispered fiercely to Lucille, "that you were coming here today?"

"Sure," said the girl with tinkling innocence, "but I know he didn't come here 'cause of me."

"How do you know?"

"Oh, he's way too old. Why, he's in Junior High School."

The words were so many knives in Herbie's heart. All his claim to prowess lay in his dizzy scholastic height of 8B. The blond boy, whom he hated with red fury on the basis of a thirty-second conversation, had the advantage of him there, as in all the more obvious ways.

"O.K.," he said bitterly. "Why dontcha go home with him? He lives right on your block. Cliff an' me'll have more fun without a girl taggin' along, anyway."

"Herbie, why are you so crazy? I hardly ever spoke to Davey. I don't even know which is his house. Are you going to spoil all our fun again?"

The previous occasions implied by the word "again" were not specified. But Herbie was placed in the class of a surly brute with the simple word, and was silenced. These are devices that a little girl is incapable of learning or inventing. She knows them as a wasp knows how to build a nest.

Lucille, gazing dreamily out at the panorama, said, "Know what? I don't want to live in the Bronx when I'm big. I wanna live in Manhattan."

"Where in Manhattan?"

"There."

The girl pointed a finger which in imagination clove downward through several miles of empty air and rested on the western bank of the bristling island.

"Riverside Drive, huh?" said Herbie.

"Yeah. Wouldn't that be swell?"

"Sure would. You could see the river all the time an' everything."

Lucille bent a mischievous glance at him and said, "All right, then. It's settled. When we get married we live on Riverside Drive."

Herbie looked wonderingly at her. Was she making fun of him? No, her eyes were soft and kind. She twined her fingers in his, and they stood side by side, gazing down at the city of their birth.

"Anything you say, Lucille," Herbie answered. "We'll live on Riverside Drive." He tried to match her joking tone, but the words came with difficulty. The blond lad from the West Bronx was leaning against the wall a few feet away, watching them. Herbie was uncomfortably aware of his presence.

And then, with a sting of despair, the fat boy noticed that Lucille's glance shifted briefly, it seemed flirtatiously, to his new rival, and back out the window again. It was the merest flicker. It could have been a mistake. It *was* a mistake, he desperately decided. She couldn't prove faithless again—not so soon! His vast toils and sufferings could not come to this miserable finish, a jilting even before school resumed. The world was simply not constructed so cruelly.

"Boy, oh boy, Lucille," he said with brave gaiety, "won't we have fun this year! Don't worry, I'll come to see you once a week, at least. Maybe even twice a week!"

Cliff, from his bench, observed the whole scene. He shook his head. "Poor Herb!" he said sadly to himself. "It was all for nothin'. Elmer was right."

But Herbie knew better, of course. His jealousy of the blond boy was a ridiculous error. There! Wasn't Lucille pressing his hand?